He couldn't forget her eyes.

The way she'd looked at him that morning, as if he were the first man she'd ever seen and she found him completely fascinating. And the fantasies he'd tried all day to ward off became impossible to resist.

In that solitary moment, he denied himself nothing. In his mind, he saw her body naked on cool white sheets, saw her melting with acceptance. His blood heated and began to pound. He could almost feel his flesh meet hers as he came down to lie with her and took her in his arms. His blood pounded harder as he imagined her breasts crush against his chest, her belly press against his loins....

Drenched in sweat, his breathing ragged, Connor knew this was trouble.

Dear Reader,

Welcome to Silhouette **Special Edition** . . . welcome to romance. Each month, Silhouette **Special Edition** publishes six novels with you in mind—stories of love and life, tales that you can identify with—romance with that little ''something special'' added in.

And may this December bring you all the warmth and joy of the holiday season. The holidays in Chicago form the perfect backdrop for Patricia McLinn's *Prelude to a Wedding,* the first book in her new duo, WEDDING DUET. Don't miss the festivities!

Rounding out December are more stories by some of your favorite authors: Victoria Pade, Gina Ferris, Mary Kirk and Sherryl Woods—who has written Joshua's story— *Joshua and the Cowgirl,* a spinoff from *My Dearest Cal* (SE #669).

As an extraspecial surprise, don't miss *Luring a Lady* by Nora Roberts. This warm, tender tale introduces us to Mikhail—a character you met in *Taming Natasha* (SE #583). Yes, Natasha's brother is here to win your heart—as well as the heart of the lovely Sydney Hayward!

In each Silhouette **Special Edition** novel, we're dedicated to bringing you the romances that you dream about—the types of stories that delight as well as bring a tear to the eye. And that's what Silhouette **Special Edition** is all about—special books by special authors for special readers!

I hope you enjoy this book and all of the stories to come.

Sincerely,

Tara Gavin
Senior Editor

MARY
KIRK
Embers

Silhouette Special Edition

Published by Silhouette Books New York

America's Publisher of Contemporary Romance

To my family for their unfailing support. To Ruth, Diane,
Connie, Mary Jo, Pat and Lydia for their endurance. To
Tara for her patience. And to Leslie, who knows why.
A special thanks to Joseph Frederick, Tred Avon expert,
who also draws a great boat, and my brother Dr. Michael
Kilchenstein, who graciously provided psychiatric
consultations on my fictional characters.

SILHOUETTE BOOKS
300 East 42nd St., New York, N.Y. 10017

EMBERS

Books by Mary Kirk

Silhouette Desire

In Your Wildest Dreams #387

Silhouette Special Edition

Promises #462
Phoenix Rising #524
Miracles #628
Embers #714

*co-authored as Mary Alice Kirk

MARY KIRK

was born and raised in Baltimore, Maryland, where she currently resides with her husband and two sons. She has studied music extensively and holds a degree in American Studies and history; however, it was when she began penning fiction that her creative energies found their focus.

Mary says she writes novels that reflect her "profound respect for the capacity of the human spirit to survive and flourish. I feel very much a part of the ongoing dialogue among women who are questioning what it is they want in life and love. As a writer, I strive to present the most hopeful visions this dialogue has to offer." Her last Silhouette Special Edition novel, *Miracles,* won the *Romantic Times* Reviewer's Choice Award for Best Series Romance of 1990.

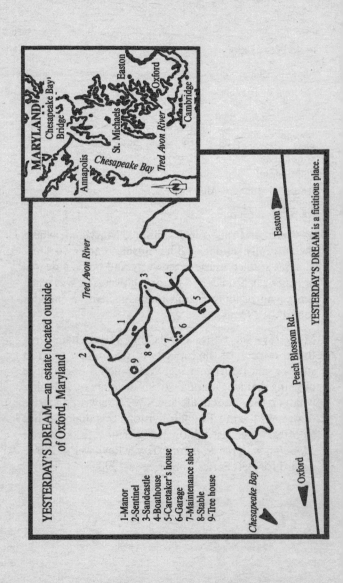

YESTERDAY'S DREAM—an estate located outside
of Oxford, Maryland

1-Manor
2-Sentinel
3-Sandcastle
4-Boathouse
5-Caretaker's house
6-Garage
7-Maintenance shed
8-Stable
9-Tree house

Tred Avon River

Peach Blossom Rd.

Oxford

Easton

Chesapeake Bay

YESTERDAY'S DREAM is a fictitious place.

MARYLAND

Chesapeake Bay
Bridge

Annapolis

Chesapeake Bay

St. Michaels

Easton

Oxford

Tred Avon River

Cambridge

Prologue

He smelled smoke. The acrid odor drifted through the open windows of Connor's pickup as he drove between the entrance posts of the Marquel estate and started up the half-mile stretch of gravel road, toward the river.

At first, he didn't believe it. Who would be fool enough to light a fire on a night like this? But he sniffed at the heavy, humid air, anyway. He smelled honeysuckle, wild roses, salt water. And smoke. His nostrils flared when the odor grew stronger.

Connor straightened in his seat, shutting off the radio, tuning his senses to the surrounding woods. The caretaker's house, where his mother lived, came up on the left, and he slowed to scan the outside of it. Victorian clapboard—in a fire, it would go up like a matchbox. All appeared dark and quiet, but he was about to stop to double-check, when, in the distance, he heard a dog's insistent, repeated bark. Rogue. What was he doing out roaming around this time of night?

The sound acted like a summons, and Connor drove on. Faster now, listening, his eyes searching for signs of a blaze and for Rogue's black form.

The estate didn't belong to him—he was a McLeod, not a Marquel—but he'd lived on the property for twenty-two years, and for the past sixteen its well-being had been his responsibility. He knew every inch of ground. He knew the river, too, the Tred Avon, that flowed past on its way to the Chesapeake Bay. The place had become his prison. But it was his job to take care of it, and a fire in these woods when there'd been no rain for a month could mean disaster.

But it wasn't the woods that was burning. Connor took the bend in the road that gave him an unobstructed view of the manor, and he saw it. Amber flames crackling inside the windows of the kitchen wing. And, racing back and forth in front of the windows, as if he could hold the flames at bay, was Rogue.

"Oh, God . . ." Connor jerked the steering wheel and hit the accelerator, and the truck tires tore into the lawn, heading for the front entrance. The plumes of smoke billowing into the starlit sky brought him to the edge of panic. But as the truck skidded to a halt and he bolted for the door, a flicker of relief touched his awareness: The house was empty. He didn't have to rescue anyone. He only had to get to a phone.

At twelve-thirty Wednesday morning, ten minutes after the phone had awakened her, Anne Marquel sat on the edge of her bed, staring at the spot of moonlight on her closet door. For several minutes she remained motionless, too dazed even to think. Unable to believe what she'd agreed to do.

Finally, with a ragged sigh, she raised her hands to her face, rubbing away the effects of sleep, trying, also, to order her thoughts. Bad news in the middle of the night delivered by a voice from the past. Fire. The manor ablaze. Police and fire fighters everywhere, with Aaron in Europe for a month and no way to reach him—so Mrs. McLeod had told her in frantic tones.

She couldn't expect the McLeods to cope with this on their own. She'd have to go. No, she couldn't simply fall back to sleep and forget the phone had rung.

Shuddering, as if she could shake off the ominous feeling that chilled her skin, Anne turned on the bedside lamp. Then, in the brighter atmosphere, she forced herself to face the facts. Her father's death the year before had made half of the estate hers; however little she might care about it, in Aaron's absence, she was the responsible party. The thought of returning to the home she'd fled twelve years ago made her blood run cold. But, really, under the circumstances, it *ought* to be all right.

In the quiet comfort of her Baltimore apartment, surrounded by reminders of the happy, productive life she led, Anne asked herself what could possibly happen. Nothing she couldn't handle, surely. And at least one thing might make all the unpleasant aspects of the trip worthwhile. She would see Connor again.

That thought brought Anne's sleepy brain fully awake, and, slowly, she smiled. She'd given up hope long ago of ever seeing him again, but suddenly she could think of nothing else. Her gaze flashed across the room to her bureau, and she hopped up to open the bottom drawer. Digging beneath a pile of sweaters, she found her photo album and carried it back to bed, sitting cross-legged on the flowered sheets to open it across her lap.

The picture she wanted occupied the first plasticized page: a slightly fuzzy image of a dark-haired youth, dressed in cutoff jeans, perched astride a limb of the old beech tree he'd taught her to climb. With his hair cropped close for the summer, his ribs and shoulder bones sticking out, and the railroad-track braces plainly displayed in his wide grin, he appeared every inch the gregarious, warmhearted fifteen-year-old she remembered as he posed indulgently for her camera.

He'd been happy to indulge her in those days. It hadn't been until he was nineteen or so that he'd grown tired of her childish demands on his attention. Yet Anne knew the six-year difference in their ages had made it inevitable that they'd grow apart. Connor wasn't to blame any more than she for the deterioration of their friendship, and it had never occurred to her to hold it against him.

Staring at the photograph, remembering the day she'd taken it, Anne's vision blurred, and, as if it were yesterday, she heard two young voices floating down out of the leaves of the big old tree. . . .

"When will it be finished, Con?"

"As soon as I get the railing up on this last side."

"Does it have to have a railing *all* the way around?"

"Darn right it does. If you fall out of this tree, your father and my mother will both have my hide."

"Daddy won't. Besides, they don't know you're building it for me. And I'm not going to tell them."

"Do me a favor and don't tell Maureen or Nancy, either. Okay?"

"I won't. They're too little to be climbing this high up."

"That's right."

"But nine is old enough."

"Annie, you know I'm counting on you to be careful."

"Don't worry. I promise, I will be."

"That's my girl."

"And I'll never let Aaron know you built this tree house for me. I bet he'd chop holes in it or something.... But do you think he'll find out?"

"Mmm, I doubt it. The leaves hide it in summer, he's away at school fall through spring—mostly—and he doesn't wander around the grounds much, anyway. If you watch that he doesn't follow you when you come here, he'll probably never see it."

"Good. Because it's going to be my secret hideout. The only people that can know about it are me and you."

"I can pretend I don't know it's here, too, if you want."

"Con, that's silly. You built it. But even if you didn't—like if it was already here and I found it—you know I'd still tell you. I'd never keep a secret from you...."

Except, in the end, she had kept secrets from him. Terrible ones. And Anne knew deep inside that it was those secrets, more than anything else, that had driven them apart.

But the secrets were part of the past, over and done and, most of the time, forgotten. The present filled her mind, and there was nothing about it she felt compelled to hide.

Upon further reflection, Anne felt a tentative excitement creep through her. She'd never tried to salvage anything from the wreckage of her childhood, having thought anything worth having irrevocably lost. But perhaps she was wrong. While it would be foolish to expect to be bosom pals with Connor again, she couldn't think of a reason they shouldn't at least be able to share a good memory or two. Which might mean that, when this disagreeable trip was over, she'd have something besides a faded photograph to remind her that the first sixteen years of her life hadn't been a total loss.

* * *

It was 4:00 a.m. when the last fire truck left. Connor watched from the porch of the caretaker's house as it drove past. He'd been at the scene all night but had come to check on his mother, whom he'd found at midnight standing on the manor lawn, watching the disaster take place. He'd sent her home, telling her to keep Rogue out of the way—and to call Anne.

Leaning against the porch railing, he looked down at the piece of paper clutched in his hand. The sultry night was quiet. Not a breeze stirred. Not even the frogs and crickets made a sound. Rogue lay beside him asleep. His mother was asleep, too, but he'd found this note by her kitchen phone: *Anne arriving late today.*

He'd figured the phone call would be a waste of time. Hadn't expected Anne to come, much less so quickly. What shocked him most, though, was the pleasure he felt at the prospect of seeing her again.

He didn't want to feel pleased. Didn't want to feel anything. He knew nothing about her anymore—where she lived, what she was doing—and he didn't want to know. They'd been friends, once, and, as the saying went, it was good while it lasted. But his friendship with Anne Marquel had been over for years, and he'd learned to do without it.

It wouldn't have been his choice. He'd seen the bridges of their friendship crumbling and had tried to shore them up. But Anne had burned the final bridge the day she'd left without bothering to say goodbye. He'd gotten the message, loud and clear: She was a Marquel, and he was a McLeod. She was an heiress, and he was the son of her housekeeper. The line that childhood had blurred sharpened as adulthood approached, and when their friendship became an embarrassment for her, she'd ended it. His mistake had been in thinking it might ever be otherwise.

Crumpling the note, Connor stuffed it into his pocket and started down the steps toward his truck, motioning to Rogue to stay put when the dog jumped up to follow. What did he care if Anne came home? He was her employee, nothing more. After all this time, they'd be strangers. He had too many other things on his mind to be letting her get under his skin again. Nor was he fool enough to try to stir up the ashes of a friendship that had long since grown cold.

Chapter One

Yesterday's Dream, indeed. More like yesterday's nightmare. Windows shattered, red brick blackened with soot, shutters hanging crookedly on only half their hinges, the old Georgian manor looked like a victim of Sherman's march to the sea. It had survived, but casualties of the conflict lay strewn all over the well-groomed lawn and two-hundred-year-old boxwood. Singed rugs, water-soaked furniture, other unrecognizable charred remains: the vanquished awaiting burial.

Standing beside her car back along the drive, where she'd stopped to view the results of last night's blaze, Anne had but one thought: She wished it had burned to the ground. Maybe then she'd have been rid of the shackles Yesterday's Dream had put on her soul. Exorcism. That's what it would have been. Purification by fire. Burn the place where the evil forces dwelled, and she'd be purged.

Oh, and wouldn't it be wonderful if it were that easy? She might have tried burning it down long ago. At times she'd been that desperate.

Swallowing against the tightness in her throat, Anne let her eyes wander over her childhood home. A charming three-story manor with matching pairs of end chimneys, a graceful hipped roof, and a small two-story wing on the west side that softened the Georgian symmetry. Nothing forbidding about it. Nothing sinister. Yet the sight of it was almost more than she could tolerate. For, scarred as it was, the manor was a cruel reminder of her own scars and inadequacies.

Anne called herself a fool, remembering her quick confidence of the previous night that being here wouldn't distress her. How could it not? She'd lived in this house for sixteen years and hadn't a single good memory to show for it. Nothing but a few vague images of her mother, gathered during those innocent years before death became real. All she truly remembered was the loneliness. And the terror. Especially that. It had colored her view of the world and of herself. It had ruined her youth and could still, under certain circumstances, rule her.

She wanted to leave. She wanted to go home to Baltimore, to her apartment and her friends and the classroom of bright-eyed kindergartners she'd be getting in September. The part of her that wasn't, and perhaps never would be, rational about this place feared for the life she'd fought to build, feared that it would be contaminated if she stayed even a moment longer.

But she couldn't leave. Not until she'd put Yesterday's Dream on the road to recovery. Never mind that she'd rather hire a demolition team to finish the job the fire had started.

Anne's bitter musings ended abruptly and her stomach took an excited flip when a man, dark-haired and shirtless, appeared around the corner of the manor, carrying a stack of cut plywood sheets above his head. Intent upon his work, he didn't see her standing in the shade of the big catalpa tree at the curve of the drive. She recognized him, though, and her first impulse was to call out, arms waving, as she ran to meet him.

Instead, she hesitated, concerned that such an overt greeting might only reinforce his memories of the child in pigtails who'd dogged his heels throughout his adolescence. Suddenly shy, she watched him carry the wood to the aluminum extension ladder set near the columned porch. Stopping beside the white hydrangea that grew by the parlor window, he swung the plywood to the ground, and as he straightened, her eyes skimmed over his bare shoulders and back. She'd forgotten how darkly he tanned; his skin was the color of coffee with a hint of cream, and even from a distance it glistened with the sweat of labor under the sweltering midsummer sun.

Pausing to remove one work glove, he swiped at his forehead with the back of his hand. Then, replacing the glove, he hefted a piece of wood onto his shoulder, took hold of the ladder and climbed up to the first-floor window. There he fitted the wood over the shattered panes. A hammer and a fistful of nails appeared out of a tool pouch hanging against his right hip, and he began nailing the board into place.

How many times had she watched him work like this? Countless numbers, she supposed. Given what he'd once told her of his plans, he shouldn't still be here. By all rights, he never should have been. But at that moment she was too pleased by the sight of him—the way the picture of him working matched the one in her memory—to question her good fortune.

Anne's heart was beating rapidly as she left the protection of the catalpa and started across the lawn. Lifting a hand to shade her eyes against the dazzling sun, she still had to squint to keep her quarry in sight. The pounding of his hammer and the carpet of grass drowned out any sounds of her approach, and five feet from the ladder she stopped, a hand resting on one of the porch columns and her lips curved in a tentative smile. She waited until he'd pounded the last nail and climbed down far enough to put one foot on the ground. Then she spoke, on a slightly shaky note.

"Connor?"

His head jerked around, and his eyes—as blue as ever—met hers. A flicker of surprise crossed his features, and for an instant she thought he seemed pleased. Then his face went blank.

Turning slowly to face her, he nodded. "Anne."

No smile. No open arms. Not even a step toward her. His voice was deep and sonorous, the way she remembered it, but it held no warmth.

Her smile wavered. "I hope I didn't startle you."

"No." His gaze took in her fashionably permed chestnut curls, skimmed over the print skirt and yellow blouse clinging damply to her slender figure, then returned to examine her small, refined features. "You look like your mother," he said. "Like the painting in your father's study."

Nothing he might have said could have pleased Anne more, for her mother had been quite beautiful. And there'd been a time when she'd have turned Connor's simple statement into a fantasy of growing up, him falling in love with her, and the two of them living happily ever after. But such fantasies had been spun by a lonely little girl with a crush on an adolescent boy who'd been kind to her, and the lonely girl had become a disillusioned woman who rarely fantasized at all.

Besides, the coolness in Connor's tone didn't allow for daydreams. Rather, it forced her to deal with the present, which consisted of blazing heat, the burned ruins of Yesterday's Dream, and uneasy proximity to a bare-chested male.

"You haven't changed much," she said, clinging to the belief that he was the same. Although, as her nervous glances cataloged his appearance, it began to sink in that he wasn't.

Thick black hair. A face made up of sharp, clean lines. A wide, expressive mouth and those heavily lashed eyes of sapphire blue. His features were familiar, as were the dark Irish good looks that governed them. But there the familiar gave way to the changes twelve years had wrought.

His face was older, at once more settled and more intense. His hair was much longer, a rumpled mop of sweat-dampened silk that clung to his forehead and, in the back, curled as it touched his shoulders. He was still several inches under six feet, but he was bigger, heavier, than she remembered, for muscle had thickened his neck, rounded out his shoulders, and ridged his stomach. His arms, even relaxed at his sides, were full of bulges and sinewy lines of strength.

Not knowing what she'd expected, Ann was shocked to realize that this wasn't the cute adolescent of her memories. Nor was it the lean and hungry-looking young man she'd last seen. This was a man fully grown whose face and body had matured to the kind of blatant virility that could take a woman's breath away. Even a woman proven time and again to be immune to such things.

"The fire marshal wanted to talk to you when you got here."

Anne's gaze snapped up to Connor's. "Oh. Well, I'll call him this afternoon."

She was about to ask how he had been when he turned, hooked an arm through the ladder, then leaned to grasp another piece of plywood. The ladder clattered as he hauled it around a trellised pyracantha to the next window.

"You can go inside if you want," he said. "The fire department roped off the places it's dangerous to walk. The fire started in Mom's workroom and went right through the wing. Burned out everything except the outer walls and chimneys, including the roof."

Settling the ladder by the second parlor window, he climbed up, braced himself sideways, and lifted the wood into place. He went on working as if seeing her was an everyday occurrence, and as she stood under the broiling sun, watching him, the joy Anne had felt when he first appeared drained away.

Connor snagged the hammer and nails out of his work pouch and began pounding. "As far as the main house goes, the dining room and parlor are gone. They saved the hall, but it's not great. The stairs are okay, but be careful—the railing's shot."

"I will, but, Con, can't we—" She stopped short, and he paused between nails to glance down at her. The distant expression in his eyes made the words stick in her throat, and her gaze flickered away. "Never mind."

He turned back to his work, continuing in that same controlled, civil tone. "Upstairs, the floor in the master bedroom is bad. The rest is intact. But everything, attic to cellar, is full of soot, including the insides of every closet and drawer—and a lot of it's wet from the hoses." For good measure, he added, "The place is a holy mess. You're looking at years of work, and nobody's going to be living in it for months."

The pounding of Connor's hammer resounded in Anne's ears as she stared at his sweat-slick back. Grim as the news was, it didn't depress her nearly as much as the manner in which he'd delivered it. His flat tone, his disregard of her presence—his indifference—told her that his memories of her were nowhere near as fond as hers were of him. That, coupled with the enormity of the task facing her, made it almost impossible not to say, "Forget it. I'm leaving."

But it wasn't that simple. She was twenty-eight, not sixteen. She had a responsibility to the estate, and even more, to herself, and it demanded that she ignore her childish desire to flee from the ghosts and demons of her past, with or without the support of Connor McLeod's friendship.

Surveying the wreckage lying about the lawn, Anne muttered, "How on earth do you clean up something like this?"

"You don't." Connor clattered down the ladder. "You hire somebody to do it for you. Mom was making a list this morning."

"A list?"

"Of cleaning and salvage companies."

He yanked the ladder back a couple of feet, away from the foundation, then glanced at the window directly above. Gauging the distance, he began hauling on the rope that extended the ladder, his voice rising to compete with the scraping metallic noise. "The insurance company will probably want to look things over first, before anything else gets done."

Only half-interested, Anne asked, "If Aaron's not home, how did it start?"

Connor didn't answer right away, and she watched him whack the metal brackets holding the extension aloft to hook them in place. His heavy boots and jeans were smudged with soot. So were his arms and chest. When he pulled out the hand towel stuck in his back pocket and used it to mop the sweat off his face and neck, her eyes skated over him, taking in details that both fascinated and alarmed her. The play of muscles in his back. The patch of black hair revealed beneath his arm when he raised it, the light dusting of it across his broad chest, the silky line that ran down his abdomen to his navel . . . and beyond.

Bewildered and stunned by the unfamiliar quivering inside her, Anne felt beads of moisture trickling down her own back beneath her cotton blouse, although the hands she tucked into her skirt pockets were cold.

Focusing her eyes on the manor, it hit her suddenly that Connor hadn't answered her question, then her gaze snapped back to him. He was standing with one foot on the bottom rung of the ladder, looking up at the second-floor window, his lips drawn into a thin line. All at once it flashed through her mind that maybe she hadn't yet heard the entire story. Maybe Mrs. McLeod hadn't wanted to deliver the news over the phone. Maybe Aaron hadn't been away. Maybe . . .

"Con, he *wasn't* here . . . was he?"

His gaze shot to hers, taking in the strange mix of emotions warring on her features. "Good God, don't you think Mom or I would have told you if—" He gave his head a quick shake. "He left three days ago. Said he'd be gone a month, but he didn't leave numbers where he could be reached. He never does."

Anne had to wait for her heart to slow down before she could speak. "So, how did the fire start?"

Connor answered tonelessly. "A basket of laundry got set next to a space heater in the workroom."

"A space heater? But—"

"You might as well know right now, it looks like it was Mom's fault." Letting go of the ladder, he turned to face her. "The heater cord was next to the cord for the iron, but it was the heater that was plugged in."

"I see," Anne murmured.

He went on as if she hadn't spoken. "Mom did a load of laundry yesterday morning, but she says she left it on top of the dryer—not on the floor by the heater. She wasn't going to iron, so she doesn't see how she could have accidentally plugged in the heater. But there's no question the heater caused the fire, and nobody else has been in the house since Aaron left." Pausing, he finished, "I'd like to know what you're planning to do."

Anne hesitated, confused, casting her gaze over the blackened brick. "To be perfectly honest, I haven't the vaguest idea where to start. I suppose I'll—"

"I meant what you're planning to do to Mom."

Her lips parted, her green eyes widening in amazement as he continued on an increasingly aggressive note.

"She had a spell of heart trouble last year, and I don't want her upset any more than she already is. She feels guilty as sin. So if you're going to turn this into a—"

"Con!" Anne cut in. "You can't think I'd take it out on her!"

But his wary scowl made it clear he *could* think it.

Who was this man? Did she know him? The icy look in his eyes said he didn't know her—and didn't want to. They were strangers. No, worse than that. For she suddenly realized that under the surface of Connor's seeming indifference lay some deeper, more potent emotion—anger, suspicion . . .

Anne couldn't define it, but she felt threatened by it. And her instinctive reaction to that threat was both immediate and extreme. Her back stiffened, her features froze into an expressionless mask, and every muscle in her body grew taut. She felt the familiar defense seize control of her and tried to prevent it. But standing on Yesterday's Dream, where she'd been forced to learn the art of emotional self-protection, she was powerless to keep the shroud from wrapping her in its brittle folds.

When Anne spoke it was with studied calm. "Frankly, it's hard to imagine your mother making such a mistake, unless she's changed dramatically."

"She's as sharp as ever," Connor insisted.

"Couldn't Aaron have plugged the heater in before he left?"

His mouth twisted in mockery of the idea. "Aaron never goes into the workroom. And if he had, it wouldn't have been to plug in a space heater in August, much less to iron. Besides, those clothes wouldn't have taken two days to catch fire."

"So we have to believe she did it." Anne accepted the conclusion with reluctance. Then, meeting his gaze, she said, "I assure you, Con, I have no intention of holding the one mistake your mother has made in twenty-two years against her."

Her words, stilted as they were, had little effect. He stopped scowling, but he looked as unapproachable as ever.

Turning abruptly, Anne motioned toward her car, parked under the tree at the curve of the drive. "I suppose I'd better think about where I'm going to stay."

"Mom opened Sandcastle for you," Connor said.

"Oh. Well, yes. That didn't occur to me." Sandcastle was the smaller of two guest cottages at Yesterday's Dream, Sentinel being the other. She didn't want to stay in either and had planned to get a room at the Robert Morris Inn in Oxford. But this didn't seem like a good time to say so.

"You'll need the key." Connor reached for the chain clipped to his belt and pulled a set of keys from his pocket. Flipping through the assortment until he found the one he wanted, he twisted it off the ring and held it out to her. Anne reached toward him, and their outstretched arms just spanned the gap; neither moved an inch closer to the other. He dropped the key into her palm without touching her, she murmured a stiff "Thank you," and they both lowered their arms to their sides.

When he turned away to pick up another piece of plywood, she said, "I'll see your mother before I go to Sandcastle. And I suppose I'll ... see you later."

He acknowledged her words with a nod, and Anne started to leave. Then, on impulse, she turned back to ask, "Connor, is something wrong? Something besides the fire?"

With one hand on the ladder, the other supporting the plywood on his shoulder, he spared her a glance. "Like what?"

"I don't know." She waved a hand in a small, searching gesture. "Something I've done to ... upset you?"

He was silent a moment, then said evenly, "How could you have done anything to me? You haven't seen or talked to me in twelve years." Then he planted a foot on the ladder and started up to the second floor.

Confused and ready to cry, Anne watched him climb. She didn't need this. She didn't need Connor McLeod destroying the only part of her childhood she'd hoped to save. She didn't need his flagrantly masculine presence taunting her, reminding her of the problems her last three years at Yesterday's Dream had created. And she didn't need to have the only man she'd ever looked up to, the only one who'd ever come close to fulfilling her girlish fantasies of a knight in shining armor, prove to her once and for all that there were no heroes. Not then, not now. Not ever.

Not for her.

Chapter Two

"Anne! My goodness!" Mary McLeod opened the screen door, motioning Anne off the side porch and into her kitchen. "I didn't expect to see you this soon."

Anne hesitated. "Am I coming at a bad time?"

"No, please, come in. I can't promise air-conditioning, but I've got enough fans running to blow this miserable air around a bit. And don't mind Rogue. He's harmless."

The dog at Mrs. McLeod's side—a Gordon Setter, identical to the Irish variety but for being black—wagged his feathered tail, and Anne stepped into the spacious kitchen extending a hand for his inspection. Watching as he gave her fingers an approving lick, she hid her reaction to the silver in Mrs. McLeod's dark hair and the lines marring her complexion. Her eyes remained the same brilliant blue as her son's, but there was a fragility about her petite form that spoke of recent illness.

"He belongs to Con," Mrs. McLeod said, though Anne had already guessed as much. Connor had always had at least one dog, and invariably they were well-mannered, affectionate creatures.

"He's beautiful," she said, giving the setter a final pat, then watching as he padded over to flop down under the broad, whirling blades of the overhead fan. "And smart," she added, meeting Mrs. McLeod's smile with one of her own.

The older woman chuckled. "He's a sharp one, all right. Why last night he—" Hesitating briefly, she rushed to explain, "Con said he found Rogue at the manor. He'd ... smelled the smoke." Pausing again, she gave Anne an anxious look. "Have you seen it?"

Anne grimaced. "I'm afraid so."

Mrs. McLeod closed her eyes and shuddered. "Isn't it dreadful? The fire marshal insists it began with the space heater in my workroom, and I suppose I must believe him, but—"

"Con told me."

She caught her breath, looking, Anne thought, as if she were certain the axe was about to fall.

"I met him up at the manor," Anne continued. "He explained about the iron and heater cord mix-up."

"Anne, I swear, I don't see how I could have—"

"I don't see how, either, but—"

"You don't know how bad I feel. All those paintings and antiques and—and your grandmother's china and—"

"We aren't going to waste time worrying about them."

"I don't know what I'll ever do to—"

"Mrs. McLeod, stop, please." Noting the older woman's agitated state and remembering Connor's mention of heart trouble, Anne said gently, "What's done is done."

Mrs. McLeod looked close to tears, and Anne was shocked. She had never seen the woman less than poised and confident. Pleasant and kind, yes, but never overtly emotional or affectionate, never crossing the strict line of propriety to reach out to her employer's child. Which made Anne feel as if she were breaching an invisible wall when she laid a comforting hand on Mrs. McLeod's arm and said, "Please, don't worry anymore."

Mrs. McLeod's chin trembled. "But, Anne, if it's truly my fault, I should—"

"No." Anne shook her head. "Listen to me. We both know what you put up with from my father, never knowing from one day to the next whether you'd have to endure his maudlin ramblings or his rages, or if he'd be too drunk even to talk."

Mrs. McLeod's look became grave. "He was a sad man."

That was putting it politely. Kenneth Marquel's emotional stability had never been certain, but Anne knew her mother's death had broken him. She frowned, remembering how he'd lock himself in his study for days without eating, simply sitting behind his desk, drinking, staring out the window at the river—or at his dead wife's portrait above the fireplace.

Focusing once more on Mrs. McLeod, she insisted, "He was a terror to work for. You and I between us probably couldn't count how many cooks and maids he scared off, and you were a saint to put up with him."

Seeing the older woman's cheeks grow pink, Anne knew very well that she'd had little choice but to put up with Kenneth Marquel; still, few people, no matter how pressured, would have been as tolerant of him as Mary McLeod had been.

"That's very kind of you, Anne," Mrs. McLeod said.

"It was very kind of *you*. No one could criticize the way you've taken care of Yesterday's Dream, so we're not going to discuss whose fault this fire was. As far as I'm concerned, it just happened." Her fingers tightened a little on Mrs. McLeod's arm. "We're going to concentrate on what to do about it."

She could see Mary McLeod assessing her, meeting her for the first time as one adult to another, and she knew the moment the older woman decided she liked what she saw. The smile that curved her lips lit her eyes with the kind of warmth Anne had wanted to see in Connor's but hadn't.

"Of course," Mrs. McLeod said. "We've quite a job ahead of us, and the sooner we get started, the better. I did a little research this morning, and after lunch we can go over the lists I made." Glancing at the clock above the refrigerator, she added, "Con will be in to eat soon, and I was just finishing—"

"Please—" Anne gestured toward the counter where meal preparations were in progress. "Don't let me interrupt you. Why don't I come back later when you're not—"

"Nonsense. Do sit down and have some lunch." Her composure restored, Mrs. McLeod went back to slicing cold chicken breast off the bone. "I've already eaten, but there's plenty here, and you're welcome to stay."

Anne shifted nervously. The idea of sharing a meal with Connor after their miserable encounter made her stomach knot. "Thank you," she replied, "but, honestly, I'm not hungry. Besides, Connor said you opened Sandcastle for me, which I appreciate, and I should get settled in."

A slight frown crossed Mrs. McLeod's brow. "I hope you'll be comfortable there, with that tiny kitchen."

The size of Sandcastle's kitchen was the least of her worries. Still, she couldn't think of an excuse as to why she would prefer staying at the Inn, especially after Mrs. McLeod had gone to the trouble of readying the cottage.

"I'm sure it will be fine," she said. Then, curious, she inquired, "Is something wrong with Sentinel? I wouldn't ask you to open it, but since it is bigger, I wondered why—" Anne stopped short when Mrs. McLeod shot her a concerned look.

"You don't know about Sentinel?" the older woman asked.

Anne grimaced. "Don't tell me a storm finally washed away the point and that old stone relic along with it."

"No, nothing like that. But Con's been living there . . . Let's see—he made the arrangements with your father two years before the girls left for college, so I guess it's been eight years." At Anne's amazed look, Mrs. McLeod became flustered. "Aaron hasn't objected, but we assumed you knew and—"

"I don't have any objections," Anne put in. "I was just interested when you mentioned Nancy and Maureen. They both went away to college?"

Her expression clearing, Mrs. McLeod smiled. "They graduated spring of last year from the University of Maryland. Maureen with a degree in commercial art and Nancy with one in library science." Pausing, she added, "Con put them through."

Anne's eyes widened. Connor had paid his sisters' college expenses? But how?

Mrs. McLeod satisfied her curiosity without her having to think of a tactful way to ask. "His tree service business has been quite successful. He finally had to hire a full-time crew to handle all the work. Which pleases me, because it means he spends less time himself in trees. He's broken his left arm twice, and I've lost count of how many times he's broken his collarbone and ribs. It's very dangerous work, you know."

"Yes," Anne murmured, hiding her shock. She knew why Connor had postponed college, remembered how he'd agonized over the decision to turn down the scholarships he'd been offered in order to become caretaker for Yesterday's Dream. And she remembered when he'd started taking outside landscaping jobs to supplement his income. Yet as intellectually motivated as he was, it was hard to believe he'd given up on his education. Then again, it was hard to believe the man she'd met that morning was the same person who, twenty-two years ago, had talked in impassioned terms of his high-minded plans for the future.

Lost in thought, Anne glanced up to find Mrs. McLeod studying her.

"Forgive me for staring," the housekeeper apologized, turning back to the task of spreading mayonnaise on a slice of bread. "It's quite a surprise to see you. You've changed so."

Anne laughed softly. "Thank heavens for that. I was afraid I'd always be able to pass for a skinny twelve-year-old boy."

"No, no." Mrs. McLeod shook her head. "You were a darling girl. But you've become a truly beautiful woman. The very image of your mother, judging by the painting in your father's study. I'm sure she'd have been proud of you."

Anne lowered her gaze, murmuring a polite thank-you and thinking that, although her mother had loved her in her mercurial fashion, it was likely she'd have found her daughter peculiar and rather disappointing. For she suspected Evelyn Marquel never would have understood a woman who was shy, indifferent to horses, and seemingly uninterested in men.

"Anne—" Mrs. McLeod turned to face her "—please, sit down. At least let me get you a glass of iced tea."

Torn between her desire to put off going to Sandcastle and her trepidations about seeing Connor again, Anne made motions toward the door. "I really should go unpack."

Mrs. McLeod looked at her in reproach. "Won't you feel more like it with something cold to drink first? Besides, it's been such a long time. And soon we'll be caught up in dealing with the fire damage. Please, stay and visit for a bit."

Anne couldn't have refused even if she'd wanted to. But as she moved toward the round oak table, saying, "Yes, thank you, I'd like that, too," she cast a nervous glance through the screen door to see if Connor was in sight.

Mrs. McLeod put a glass of iced tea on the table in front of her, and Anne sipped at it, alternately watching the door, Rogue sleeping under the fan, and Mrs. McLeod washing lettuce.

"Tell me more about Maureen and Nancy," she said, ashamed of the tension in her voice.

Mrs. McLeod didn't appear to notice her uneasiness. "Maureen works for an advertising firm in Washington, and Nancy's a librarian at an elementary school in Easton." With a quick smile, she added, "Nancy was married last fall to an accountant named Jonathan Bennett. They're expecting in February.''

"That's wonderful," Anne remarked, genuinely pleased. Although they'd been too much younger to be her girlfriends, she'd liked Connor's sisters. At six, she'd found the two-year-old identical twins an interesting enigma, and for several years she'd occasionally enjoyed playing with them. But as she'd grown into adolescence, the age gap had widened. At thirteen, she'd had little in common with nine-year-old Nancy and Maureen. At fifteen…well, she'd had nothing in common with them. Or, for that matter, with any other girl she'd known. At fifteen, she'd lived in a world totally isolated from everyone.

Knowing such musings would lead her down paths she didn't want to travel, Anne dragged herself back to the present, speaking as Mrs. McLeod set Connor's lunch on the table. "How are you doing, with all your children gone?"

The older woman offered a polite response. "Quite well, thank you. It's awfully quiet at times, but I keep busy."

"Connor told me you've had some trouble with your heart."

Mrs. McLeod made an exasperated sound. "Oh, you know Con. He worries too much. It was nothing, really—some minor chest pain." Looking as energetic as ever, she went about straightening up the counter. It seemed an afterthought when she said, "Of course, Con badgers me constantly about retiring."

Anne considered the matter briefly. "Why don't you?"

"Heavens, I'd go insane, not knowing what to do with myself." Mrs. McLeod's laugh sounded lighthearted, but her tone had an underlying note of seriousness as she added, "And, really, it's not that simple."

Anne frowned, realizing she had no idea what provisions had been made for Mary McLeod's retirement—if any. Surely her father would have planned for his housekeeper's pension. Then again, perhaps not. And if he hadn't Mrs. McLeod might be dependent upon her children to support her when she could no longer work. Which probably meant being dependent upon Connor.

Connor, who'd ended his education to help support his family. Connor, who'd put his sisters through college and who was worried about his mother's health. Connor, who once had vowed to vindicate his father's name and work toward reclaiming his family's place in society but who, instead, was cutting down trees and hammering boards over *her* broken windows.

"Gracious! Listen to me talking about retirement!" Mrs. McLeod's exclamation captured Anne's attention. "I don't know how I could even have mentioned the word with the manor in such deplorable shape. When I think about the cleaning—"

"*Don't* think about it."

The screen door banged shut, and Anne jumped in her chair when Connor tromped into the kitchen. Rogue sprinted over to greet him as if he hadn't seen him in a year, and Connor paused to give the dog's head a scratch. He gave no more acknowledgment of her presence than he had earlier—a glance and a nod—as he passed her on his way to the sink.

Anne's gaze followed him, her nostrils flaring at the sharp scent of sweat and sunshine he'd brought inside. Was this the man she'd been thinking about in such lucid and sympathetic terms only moments ago? All rational thought had suddenly vanished, dispelled by his forbidding attitude and his overwhelmingly male presence—though she couldn't have said which affected her more. Regardless, in mere seconds he had every nerve in her body tingling with a crazy mixture of excitement and alarm.

What alarmed her most was her defensive response to him. The cloak of rigidity came over her instantly; she looked down to find her hands folded precisely on the table in front of her, and she knew, if she looked in a mirror, her face would be devoid of emotion. It was as if someone else had taken over her thoughts and her body. Which was exactly true. And it both frightened and angered her that, after all this time, she had only to set foot on Yesterday's Dream and she had no more power to prevent it from happening than she'd had when she'd left.

Turning on the cold-water tap full blast, Connor reached for a glass out of the cupboard as he told his mother, "You aren't going to clean up that mess, and that's final."

Mrs. McLeod pursed her lips at his dictatorial tone.

"Con's right," Anne said. "The manor and everything in it is insured. I see no reason not to let the insurance pay for whatever I can hire someone else to do."

"But I can't just sit and do nothing!"

"I'm certain there will be things I can't let outsiders do—sorting through clothing, making decorating decisions. Your help is too valuable to me to be wasted on a mop and a bucket."

"You hear that?" Connor drained his glass in one long swallow, then cupped his hand under the gushing faucet to splash water over his face. "She's the boss lady. You listen to her."

The tendons in Anne's neck stood out as she clenched her teeth. She'd intended to support his cause. But the sarcasm in his tone—the way he'd called her "the boss lady"—made her flinch. Unfortunately, she was afraid that was, indeed, the way she sounded.

"Well, all right," Mrs. McLeod said, then grumbled at Connor, "but you don't have to be such a bear about it."

Connor shut off the tap, and, leaning over, rested his forearms on the edge of the sink and let his head drop forward. "I'm sorry," he muttered. "It's hot."

"And you've been up all night," his mother added. "Why don't you take a nap after lunch?"

Connor shook his head without straightening. "I want to get those windows covered before it rains or some kid climbs in to snoop around and winds up getting hurt."

Anne cleared her throat. "Perhaps I could find someone else to do it."

"You want to wait a week?" he growled.

"But surely if they knew it was an emergency—"

"It's my job."

"But—"

"And I want it finished this afternoon."

"Save your breath, Anne," Mrs. McLeod put in. "When it's a matter of *duty,* you're arguing with a brick wall. He hasn't changed a bit as far as that goes. . . . Just like his father."

Connor mumbled something unintelligible, then, slowly, he straightened, and turned to lean against the counter, folding his arms over his chest and crossing his booted feet at the ankles. The casual pose brought his pectorals and biceps into high relief and made the worn denim of his jeans gather disturbingly around the bulge that declared his sex.

Shivering despite the heat, Anne tore her gaze away to stare at her half-empty glass of iced tea. How could he frighten her at the same time he made her senses spin? The fear she recognized and understood—a familiar tight knot in her stomach.

But this rare, quivering warmth she didn't understand at all, and it added immeasurably to her confusion that it was being caused by a man who clearly wanted nothing to do with her.

Connor's mother was neither confused about nor appreciative of his appearance. Looking him over with a critical eye, she said, "Your lunch is on the table, but it will wait if you want to shower."

He shook his head. "I'll just wash up."

"Your laundry's done. I'll get you a clean shirt."

He headed for the hallway with Rogue at his heels. Mrs. McLeod followed but returned a few moments later to sit at the table, across from Anne, and let out a frustrated sound.

"I must apologize," she said. "You know Con isn't normally so... abrupt."

Read that *rude,* Anne thought. "I understand," she said. "It's almost a hundred degrees out there, and he's obviously exhausted." She wished she believed those were the only reasons both Connor and she were behaving so badly. Sighing, she added, "Frankly, I'm grateful he's able to set priorities. One look at that manor was enough to immobilize me."

Mrs. McLeod grimaced. "Did you go inside?"

"I didn't have the nerve."

"My dear, I'm afraid you're in for quite a shock. Of course, there wouldn't be anything left at all if Con's class hadn't been canceled."

"I beg your pardon?"

"He didn't tell you how he discovered the fire?" When Anne shook her head, Mrs. McLeod explained. "He's taking an evening course at Chesapeake Community College—something to do with computers—and he isn't usually home until after eleven. But the class was canceled, so he came home early."

And if he hadn't, Anne realized, her unspeakable wish would have come true: The manor would have burned to the ground.

Mrs. McLeod went on with a description of the previous evening's events—how Connor had found all the entrances to the manor impassable and had finally broken in through the study window to call the fire department—but Anne only half listened. She was more interested in knowing how a man who'd been offered scholarships to a host of Ivy League schools, and who'd talked of pursuing a law degree, had ended up taking night courses in computers at a local community college.

When Mrs. McLeod waved a hand, saying, "That's enough unpleasant talk. Tell me what you've been doing," Anne smiled, grateful for something positive on which to focus.

"I'm teaching kindergarten," she said, her smile widening at Mrs. McLeod's obvious surprise.

"Kindergarten!" the older woman exclaimed. "That's lovely. But I had no idea you were inclined toward teaching—and such little ones, too!"

"I wouldn't have thought so, either. But I'll be starting my sixth year this fall, and I love it." Wrinkling her nose a little, Anne admitted, "Besides, teaching gives me an excuse to do things I never did as a child. Like last Saturday, when I took four of my students from last year to Hershey Park." At Mrs. McLeod's puzzled look, she explained, "An amusement park in Pennsylvania."

Mrs. McLeod smiled. "It's nice you're comfortable enough with the children to socialize with them. Nancy tells me so many teachers in her school feel they have to be distant to maintain discipline."

Anne laughed. "If I *weren't* comfortable, they'd run all over me." Then, with mock seriousness, she added, "But, of course, these outings aren't billed as 'social' occasions. They're rewards. The four kids I took to Hershey are learning disabled, and I told them if they memorized their alphabet by June, I'd take them. And they did, so—"

"Is this the latest teaching method? 'Let's make a deal'?"

Anne stiffened in reaction to Connor's bottom-of-the-ocean baritone as he passed behind her, and she breathed only slightly easier when she saw he'd put on a T-shirt. As he pulled out his chair and straddled it, motioning Rogue to lie down at his feet, she raised an eyebrow in his direction and stated primly, "I don't 'make deals.' I offer incentives."

Connor paused, sandwich in hand, to arch an eyebrow back at her. "I see."

Blushing, Anne clamped her mouth shut to avoid voicing some even more self-righteous retort.

Mrs. McLeod cast a displeased glance at her son, then turned to her. "I suppose, under the circumstances, it's fortunate your work leaves your summers free. I hated bothering you, but, as I said, Aaron can't be reached."

"It's not a bother," Anne murmured.

"I don't know what sort of decisions he would make, but—"

"He's not here. He'll have to live with whatever I decide."

Connor's laugh was harsh. "Not for long. He'll be gone before the ink dries on the contract selling this place."

Startled, Anne shot him a glance. "What are you talking about? No one's selling Yesterday's Dream."

Exchanging a look with his mother, he drawled, "That's funny. Aaron sure thinks it's being sold. He's had three or four developers out here, passing their greedy little eyes over all the lots they expect to carve out of the place."

"Well, they won't carve *any*," Anne said firmly. "It's true, Aaron's had Howard Stone pass along several offers to buy out my part of the estate, but I've turned them down. I have no intention of selling."

Connor's expression was inscrutable as he studied her; then, with a careless shrug, he returned to his sandwich.

"Aaron hasn't said so," his mother continued, "but we've understood that after he and Blaine Thorpe are married, he'll be moving to—"

"He's engaged?" Anne spoke impulsively, then just as quickly regretted it.

"Well . . . yes." Mrs. McLeod paused. "You didn't know?"

She shook her head. Then, because she knew the truth would soon become obvious, she added, "Frankly, Mrs. McLeod, I haven't seen or talked to Aaron since I left home. I haven't any idea what he's doing."

Mrs. McLeod's shock was apparent. She felt Connor's surprise, too, as he stopped with his iced-tea glass halfway to his mouth. No doubt both of them already thought the worst of her because she hadn't come home for her father's funeral. Would her lack of communication with her brother—her only living relative—be considered an equally grievous sin? Perhaps so. Especially to people like the McLeods for whom family loyalty was among the highest of virtues.

Mrs. McLeod recovered from her surprise first, and Anne was relieved to see the clear look in the older woman's eyes. She was curious, but she wasn't going to pass judgment.

Connor seemed to feel no such reservations. His eyes lingered on her for a long moment; then, with a cynical twist of his mouth, he went back to his lunch as if to say her actions, or lack of them, were in keeping with his opinion of her.

Matter-of-factly, Mrs. McLeod informed her, "Aaron's engaged to Miss Blaine Thorpe. She owns an estate on Trippe Creek."

"Yes, I remember the family," Anne replied. "But you say she owns Holly Knoll? Did her parents die?"

"Several years ago, in a boating accident. Being an only child, she inherited everything." Sighing a little, Mrs. McLeod added, "In any event, with the manor in such a state, I suppose it's fortunate Aaron already stays at Holly Knoll more than he does at home. We rarely see him, even when he's in town. And he does travel frequently."

Anne hesitated. "Is he...working?"

Connor's derisive snort bought him a sharp look from his mother, to which he merely said, "Anne knows what Aaron's like. He hasn't changed since the days when he was getting kicked out of every boarding school in the country. If he has a function in life, it's getting drunk and raising hell."

"Connor!"

Ignoring his mother's horrified expression, he added, "Life around here, this past year, has been one big party. I've spent ninety percent of my time fixing things Aaron and his friends have broken. You can almost count on them trashing the place at least once a week."

Anne frowned, casting her gaze between Connor and his mother. It was unthinkable that she would interfere in any situation between Aaron and the McLeods, yet she had a stomach-churning desire to know more about what her brother was doing. Connor, however, gave her no opportunity to ask.

Dropping his napkin next to his plate, he pushed away from the table, announcing, "I've got to get back to work." Rogue hopped up, ready to go, too, but Connor shook his head. "You know how hot it is out there. Do yourself a favor and stay put." When the dog merely barked and wagged his tail, he shrugged. "Suit yourself."

"Will you be here for dinner?" Mrs. McLeod asked.

"No. I want to grab some sleep before I go to Pat's."

"I thought you'd finished with his article."

"I decided it needed more work. I told him I'd go over it with him." Heading out the door, he paused with his hand on the latch to speak over his shoulder. "If the light's on when I get home, I'll stop in to see how you made out this afternoon."

"All right," his mother agreed.

With that, he walked out, Rogue at his side—and Anne left wondering what the brief exchange over an "article" he had to "go over" was about.

Mrs. McLeod's eyes met Anne's across the table. "I'm sorry. I'm afraid he was very rude. I suppose the weather and—"

Anne shook her head. "It's not your fault. And it's not just the heat or the fact that he's tired."

Mrs. McLeod caught her breath and held it for a moment; then, with a heavy sigh, she gave up the pretense.

Anne looked at her hands, still folded on the table, their knuckles white. "It's pretty clear he's not pleased to see me."

"But that isn't—" Mrs. McLeod cut herself off, pressing her lips together against the obvious desire to say more. Finally, she said, "You should talk to him."

Anne studied her, trying to discern if she knew why Connor was being so cold or if she were merely making a sensible suggestion. It was impossible to tell, and Anne drew a shaky breath to probe a little deeper. "I asked him if I'd done something to upset him, and he said I hadn't."

Mrs. McLeod neither confirmed nor refuted her son's claim, but the fleeting frown that touched her brow answered Anne's question. It wasn't true that Connor wasn't upset with her; his show of indifference was an act. And he seemed determined to maintain it.

A lump formed in Anne's throat, and she spoke slowly and distinctly to hide it. "I know we weren't really...well, friends, in the usual sense," she said. "But I always thought he...it always seemed as if..." ...*as if he liked me.* When she couldn't say the words, her hands clenched in frustration. "He used to be so open. So direct."

"Mmm," his mother agreed. "Quick to anger, quick to forgive."

"But now he's..." Anne stared at the door through which Connor had gone. "He didn't used to hide his feelings."

"Well, dear..." Mrs. McLeod rose to clear the table. "Time changes us all."

And not always, Anne added silently, for the better.

Chapter Three

Anne spent the afternoon at Mary McLeod's on the phone. She talked to the fire marshal, who confirmed what Connor and Mrs. McLeod had told her and said his report would be on file for her insurance company's use. Then she tackled the daunting list her housekeeper had compiled.

She spoke with several restorationists who said they'd be delighted to work on such an important example of colonial architecture as Yesterday's Dream and that Anne should call back when the initial cleaning was completed. Sighing, Anne began dialing cleaning services, and for the following two hours she talked to companies that cleaned everything from clothing and oil paintings to wood floors and exterior brick. Salvage work was easier; a single hauling company would take away everything she cared to give them.

Finally she called Howard Stone, the attorney who, for the past twenty-two years, had managed the estate. Having read about the fire in the morning paper, Stone had tried to reach her and, that proving futile, had called the insurance company. When Anne told him she'd like to see him while she was in town, Stone agreed it was time they talked, and they made an appointment to meet at his office in St. Michaels on Friday morning.

By four-thirty, Anne was worn out. The next step was to look over the contents of the manor. But she simply couldn't face it. Tomorrow would be soon enough.

She accepted Mrs. McLeod's invitation to stay for dinner, and she enjoyed listening to the older woman talk about her involvement with the historical society and her bridge club. Yet all the while, in the back of Anne's mind, the thought nagged that Sandcastle awaited her.

Several times she thought about the empty bedrooms on the second floor of the caretaker's house, and she almost asked Mrs. McLeod if she could stay with her. But in spite of the growing warmth between them, she felt awkward about imposing. Besides, Connor had said he'd stop in to see his mother that night. Anne wanted to be gone before he arrived.

At eight o'clock, she said good-night to Mrs. McLeod and began the drive to Sandcastle. Yet when she reached the side road to the cottage, the old, uneasy feeling took hold that compelled her to check out her surroundings before settling in for the night. Thus, she passed the turn and continued toward the river.

Once, in colonial days, Yesterday's Dream had encompassed a thousand acres, an entire peninsula jutting into the Tred Avon out of Maryland's Eastern Shore. But by the time her great-grandfather purchased the estate, it had dwindled to less than a third of its original size, essentially the eastern portion of the peninsula.

It was at the northernmost tip of the property, where the gravel drive ended, that Anne parked and walked out to the small sandy bluff overlooking the river. On her left, to the west, the sun hovered above the river's edge. To the east, the sky was deep purple. No moon tonight. Straight ahead, the river flowed, wide and dark and quiet. In the fading light, the black silhouettes of the trees on the distant northern shore were barely visible.

Turning, she let her gaze follow the shoreline as it curved eastward to the point where Sentinel—Connor's place, now—stood sheltered by a few tall locust trees and loblolly pines. Red zinnias grew alongside the stone cottage and, at the back door, the bright blue-and-white sail of a Windsurfer lay secured from the wind with a bag of sand.

Aptly named, Sentinel guarded the secluded beach beyond.
Past it, the shoreline dipped inward, then out to another point
of land, the arc forming a wide bowl, at the center of which
stood the manor. Sandcastle nestled among the trees on the
opposite point, and beyond that, on the inward curve of a
protected cove, was the boathouse.

Three hundred lovely wooded acres. Nothing as far as the eye
could see but water, cattails, grass, and trees. Nothing to hear
but the gulls' keening screech.

Anne cast a jaded eye over all that beauty and serenity,
thinking she'd have given it away gladly if she could have jus-
tified the act to her conscience. But she couldn't reconcile herself to seeing the property parceled out, plowed up, and built
on. The Chesapeake had enough problems without her upsetting its ecological balance any further. Besides, for some reason she couldn't explain, she felt bound to the place. She hadn't
wanted it, wouldn't have cared—nor been surprised—if her
father had left her none of it. But neither did she seem able to
let it go.

With a quiet sigh, Anne noted the position of the sun, halfway below the water's edge, and turned to leave. Connor's
house was dark; he wouldn't be home until late. She was alone.
The only person on Yesterday's Dream but for Mrs. McLeod.
The smart thing to do would be to go unpack and try to get a
good night's sleep so she could face tomorrow's tasks.

Yet on the return trip through the property, she stopped at
the stables—empty since her mother had been thrown and
killed and her father had gotten rid of the horses. The manor—
dark and sorry-looking, all its broken windows boarded. The
maintenance shed and the garage—both shiny white with new
coats of paint. And, from a cautious distance, the boathouse—doors closed, water lapping gently at the pilings.

No sign of anyone anywhere.

The single-story, gray bungalow called Sandcastle sat in a
clearing ringed by wild dogwood and azaleas about thirty feet
back from the river. It had a small covered porch where one
could sit and watch the fish jump and the ducks glide by. No
flowers had been planted around it, but the holly and rhodo-
dendron were neatly pruned.

Inside, the scent of lemon rose from the newly polished furniture in the sitting room. Lacy blue towels hung on the rods in
the bathroom, and snowy white sheets covered the four-poster

in the bedroom. A tall cut-glass vase of gladiolus and cosmos graced the embroidered scarf covering the bureau. In the kitchen, the cupboards held cereal, several cans of soup, and a variety of other staples, while the refrigerator was stocked with eggs, milk, vegetables, orange juice, and an enormous cantaloupe.

Everything perfect. Every small consideration attended to. All of it designed to make her feel at home.

Anne checked the locks on both doors, shut and locked all the windows, and pulled the shades and curtains closed. Opening her suitcase, she hesitated, then took out only her nightgown, toiletries, and the clothes she'd need for tomorrow before closing the case and setting it behind the bedroom door. Perhaps she'd still get a room at the Inn.

After carrying her shampoo and nightgown to the bathroom, she stood for a long time under a cool shower, until a noise from somewhere in the tiny house made her freeze. Fumbling to turn off the water, she realized it was the teakettle whistling. She'd forgotten she'd put it on to make iced tea.

She hurried to the kitchen with a towel wrapped around her, eyes darting to the shaded windows. She turned off the kettle, abandoning her plans for tea, then rushed back to the bathroom to dry her hair and put on her plain cotton gown. Then she climbed into bed.

She had deliberately left a light burning in the sitting room. But, on second thought, she went to turn it off. It was only a short distance from the cottage to the main drive. A light would be seen. No sense in advertising her presence to anyone who might happen to drive by.

Climbing back into bed, she lay in the dark, stuffy room and stared at the ceiling. Her conscience was unsympathetic company.

Go to sleep.

I can't.

Yes, you can. You drove a long way this morning on very little sleep. You've had a stressful day. You're tired.

But what if—

Forget it. Nothing's going to happen. Go to sleep.

* * *

It was eleven-fifteen when Connor stood at his mother's front door, preparing to leave. He kissed her cheek, saying, "Get some sleep tonight, okay?"

"Con—" Mary McLeod put a hand on her son's arm as he took hold of the screen-door latch. "I want to talk about Anne."

He snorted softly—he'd heard this before—and pushed the door open. "Not tonight. Okay?"

Her fingers tightened on his arm. "You're wrong about her."

"I don't think so."

"She's a lovely young woman."

"Mom, please—" Sighing, he let the screen door bang closed and turned back to face her. "Don't start this again."

Yesterday, he'd have said he rarely thought about Anne anymore, and it would have been true. Today, he'd thought of little but her, which made a joke of his determination not to let her get under his skin again. He hadn't been prepared for the surge of pleasure he'd felt at the sight of her this morning; his first impulse had been to sweep her into a hug. But she'd killed the urge almost as fast as it had hit him.

"You saw how she acted," he said, "sitting there with her neck stretched to keep her nose in the air. If she didn't sound like the lady of the manor talking to the peasants, I don't know what does." Mimicking Anne's precise tone, he repeated her words. "I don't make deals. I offer incentives." With a snarl of disgust, he asked, "How can you listen to that, then tell me what a lovely young woman she is?"

Mrs. McLeod's brow wrinkled. "She is awfully...stiff. I nearly had to beg her to sit down. But, Con, I think she was just uncomfortable."

"You're darned right she was uncomfortable. When was the last time she deigned to sit in your kitchen?"

His mother's frown deepened. "When was the last time I invited her to?"

"Now, don't go feeling guilty for—"

She shook her head. "There's a difference between guilt and regrets. I had you and the twins and plenty of my own problems back then. But Anne had lost her mother—her father, too, for all practical purposes—and I do regret not having had my wits about me enough to realize how lonely she must have been. But you knew, Con. You two were friends, and—"

"Forget about the past," he interrupted. "Let's talk about today. You saw how it is. She bristled like a porcupine the instant I walked in the door."

Mrs. McLeod pressed her lips together. "She thinks you don't like her."

"Well, she's got that right."

"Con, you know that's not true. You—"

"It *is* true." Turning his head to stare out the screen door, he said, "I liked a shy little girl who giggled when I told her jokes and made wishes when she blew the seeds out of milkweed pods. I liked a kid who could talk my ear off one minute, then sit and listen to me for hours and act like everything I said was fascinating. And it never mattered that she was a girl and six years younger than me. I liked her because she was thoughtful and bright and fun to be with."

And maybe, he added silently, he hadn't simply liked her but had loved her, as much as he'd loved his sisters. And maybe he'd felt a kinship with her because she'd lost her mother the same month he'd lost his father. And, too, maybe he'd felt sorry for her because her father was crazy and her brother tormented her whenever he got the chance. Mostly, though, he'd been drawn to Anne for some indefinable reason that he still didn't understand. A sense of rightness and belonging between them, a belief that, in some fundamental way that overshadowed their differences, they understood each other. It had hurt more than he wanted to admit to anyone, including himself, to learn he'd been wrong.

Connor's jaw hardened. "That little girl disappeared somewhere around the time she hit thirteen. And the kid who replaced her didn't give a damn about anybody but herself. She didn't have time for her friends, she could be downright nasty to Nancy and Maureen, and she stopped talking to me altogether by the time she was fourteen. I was the hired help." Looking at his mother, he finished, "She grew up almost as self-centered as her brother. Mom, for God's sake, she didn't even come home for her father's funeral! How much more proof do you need? I don't care what kind of pathetic excuse for a man he was, a child owes a parent at least that much respect!"

Mrs. McLeod held her son's gaze as she murmured, "We don't know what her reasons might have been. You shouldn't judge her without knowing the facts."

He knew all he needed to know, Connor thought. "It's late, and I'm done in. I'm going home to bed." Her look told him she was less than pleased, but she didn't try to stop him when he gave her shoulder an affectionate pat and walked out the door.

At eleven-thirty, Anne heard a car. She got up and went to the sitting-room window to peek around the edge of the curtain. Through the woods, she saw headlight beams bouncing against the trees as a vehicle passed the turnoff to Sandcastle.

Aaron returning early from his trip? Had he somehow gotten word of the fire? Common sense argued that it was only Connor coming home from his meeting. Nothing to be alarmed about.

She went back to bed, but at 1:00 a.m. she was still awake. Likewise, two o'clock came and went....

This is ridiculous. Go to sleep.

I can't. It's too hot. But if I open the windows, I'll lie awake worrying.

You know, you've spent a lot of time and energy fixing this problem. You're supposed to be over it.

Don't forget the money.

Right. You've wasted an enormous amount of money trying to make yourself into a healthy, well-adjusted adult.

It wasn't wasted.

Then why are you still awake?

It wasn't wasted.

Prove it. Go to sleep.

Three o'clock crawled by, then four....

You have to straighten things out with Connor.

He doesn't want to straighten them out.

You have to try. His mother said you should talk to him.

I was horrible with him today. Just like a department store mannequin. It felt exactly like it used to feel when...

You were nervous, being back here, that's all. You know you don't have to be that way. And you know talking to him is the right thing to do.

Yes, but...well, it wasn't just being back here that made me nervous. It was...him.

He's just a man. So he's got a few more muscles than most.

Maybe. I think it's more than that.... I just wish ... But it's silly. It'll never happen. He won't even talk to me. He'd never be interested in ...

Probably not.

I don't even know why I'm thinking about it. A man like him ... well, he's always been so intense and passionate about things. He's bound to be that way when... Well, he'd certainly want a woman who could... And I'd never...

It wouldn't work.

No.

So stop thinking about it and go to sleep.

Yes, but... well, tomorrow I'll talk to him. At least I can do that.

Finally, when a robin chirped in the maple outside the window, announcing the impending dawn, she rolled over among the twisted sheets for the last time and was able to shut her eyes.

Anne awoke to the sound of a chain saw. When putting pillows over her head didn't help, she got up and stumbled to the window to open the curtain and shade. Sunshine poured into the room, and she had to squint to focus. But there was nothing to see. Only the noise.

Letting the curtain fall closed, she hurried to dress. A glance at the bedside clock told her it was 7:00 a.m. People from the hauling company and cleaning services were coming this afternoon to give her estimates. But before she did anything else, she had to talk to Connor.

She didn't know how on earth she would approach him, since he wouldn't admit anything was wrong between them, and since every time she got near him he rattled her so badly she could hardly think. But she was determined to try. Despite her shortcomings, which were very real and, at times, debilitating, she was not, and never had been, an emotional coward.

Throwing on shorts, a sleeveless top, and a pair of tennis shoes, she tied her shoulder-length curls in a scarf and left the cottage through the porch door. She suspected she'd find Connor if she merely walked toward the ear-shattering noise.

The noise took her along the shoreline of the cove. As she drew closer to the boathouse, she veered away from it, up the hill, and soon found the chain saws on the track leading down to the water from the main drive. Two were wielded by men perched in the limbs of a dead oak. More workers stood below, lowering severed limbs out of the tree and turning them into manageable chunks. All of the men were bare-chested, suntanned, and muscular, but Connor wasn't among them. No broken arms or collarbones for him today.

Before Anne could decide where next to look for him, a young red-haired man working on the ground spotted her. Glancing briefly at the operation going on around him, he started toward her, chain saw in hand. Anne stepped forward to meet him, but he motioned for her to stop, shouting, "You shouldn't come any closer! It isn't safe!"

Anne shouted back. "I'm looking for Connor McLeod."

The man gestured toward the boathouse, and Anne's gaze followed. The door midway along the side of the building sat open, and Rogue lay guarding it.

Of all places Connor could have been . . .

Raising a hand in thanks to the man with the saw, Anne drew a deep breath and headed toward the long wooden structure. Rogue greeted her with a couple of lazy flops of his tail that slapped in counterpoint to her footsteps against the boards of the dock. She stepped over him, bending to scratch his ear, then turned toward the open doorway. The interior of the boathouse was quiet but for the peculiar hollow sound water makes slapping gently against wooden hulls. When she saw no one, she hesitated a moment longer, then stepped reluctantly inside, rubbing her arms as she hugged herself against a sudden chill.

This was a mistake. She shouldn't try to have a rational discussion with Connor in here. Not when she could barely think for the memories the place evoked. But what were her choices? She couldn't follow Connor around, waiting for him to be someplace that suited her. She might wait forever.

Connor wasn't in sight, and the twenty-foot fishing boat, moored at the dock in front of her, was empty. There was only one other place he could be.

Anne followed the catwalk to the opposite side of the rough-walled, three-sided structure. There, a fifty-eight-foot motor yacht with the name *Lady Lyn* painted on its stern was tied to the pilings. Built in the late 60's, the yacht had been one of the last to come out of the respected Trumpy boat works in Annapolis before it closed. Luxurious, elegant, the envy of every connoisseur of fine pleasure craft, the *Lady Lyn* was one of her father's larger extravagances. There were no words to describe Anne's revulsion at the sight of it.

Stopping beside the aft deck, she surveyed the white and wood-trimmed yacht: the foredeck where her mother used to sunbathe; the flybridge where her father would sit to drink his brandy; and, behind the flybridge on the top deck, the Boston Whaler, attached to a pair of telescoping davits that would lower the dinghy into the water at the flick of a switch....

Shuddering, Anne tore her eyes away and focused her gaze downward, onto the aft deck, where she saw the engine access hatch sitting open.

"Connor? Are you down there?" She felt foolish calling for him, but nothing on earth could have induced her to climb aboard that yacht. Her skin was crawling simply standing next to the thing.

Connor didn't answer, but Anne heard noises coming through the open hatch—a metallic clanking, followed by footsteps—that told her he was on board. A moment later his head and shoulders appeared through the hatch, and, seeing her, he braced his hands on either side of the opening and hopped out onto the deck. Once again, she noted, he was shirtless, and he had a streak of grease on his left forearm and a smear of it across his stomach.

Gathering her courage, Anne forced a smile. "Good morning."

He inclined his head slightly as he wiped his hands on a rag. "Morning."

"I hope I didn't interrupt anything important."

"Nothing critical." Taking a swipe at the grease on his stomach, then stuffing the rag into his back pocket, he walked slowly over to prop one rubber-soled shoe on the gunwale and look down at her. "Is there something you wanted?"

I want to know why you're so angry with me. Anne tried to say it, but her eyes kept drifting over the yacht, her mind drifting along with them, and she couldn't make the words come.

Gesturing vaguely at the fishing boat behind her, she managed, "Things seem to be in fine shape here."

"If you're looking for a boat to use," Connor returned, "you'll have to settle for the *Spinner*. I just took a carburetor off one of the *Lady Lyn*'s engines. It'll be in the shop a week, and after that, I don't know when I'll have the time to put it—"

"No," Anne cut him off. "Of course, fixing a boat isn't important right now. And that's not why—" She stopped, hesitating. "That isn't what I wanted to discuss with you."

Connor's brows drew together in a wary scowl, and, honestly, she couldn't blame him. She knew how stilted she'd sounded. But seeing him standing there on the deck of the *Lady Lyn,* looking so forbidding, so bare and male, her throat closed up and her stomach knotted so tightly she could hardly breathe. It didn't help when he put a hand on the gunwale and vaulted down to the narrow dock to stand between her and the door, which was several yards behind him. He was only two or three inches taller than she, but when he folded his arms across his chest and planted his feet apart, she felt horribly frail and powerless facing him.

Angry at her own weakness, Anne said the first thing that came to mind simply to keep the conversation going. "The chain saws woke me. I came to see what was happening."

The wariness in Connor's expression hardened. "That tree's hanging over the road, and I want it out of there before storm season. The crew's been scheduled since April to take it down this morning."

Anne spoke through clenched teeth. "I wasn't complaining. I heard the noise and was curious, so—" She drew a shallow breath, gesturing behind him, toward the open door. "Your mother said you'd hired a full-time crew for your business."

"That's right."

"It's certainly nice that you have them available when you need help around here."

Connor's eyes narrowed. "What does that mean?"

What *did* it mean? Lord, she was only trying to talk and had no notion what he might be reading into her words.

"Nothing," she said. "Only that I know taking care of this place is an enormous amount of work." She also knew she was beating the issue into the ground but felt irrationally as if her life depended upon making him understand, so she went on doggedly. "I drove around last night, and I was quite impressed with the way things look. And now I see you've got a convenient way of getting help when you need it. Your mother said you've done very well with your tree service, and I'm glad to see the business has been of use in relieving some of the burdens the estate places on you."

Connor drew back, eyeing her as if he couldn't quite believe she was for real. With her heart racing and her head beginning to spin, she wasn't sure, either. When Connor spoke, Anne nearly screamed in frustration.

"That's my crew out there," he said. "They're on my payroll. But when I hire them for the estate to do a job I can't do alone, they're on their own time. Stone pays them out of the maintenance account, and I don't get any of it. So you don't have to worry that I'm getting paid twice to do my job."

"No, I—" Anne squeezed her eyes closed. "I wasn't accusing you of anything."

His eyebrow arched. "Just filling you in on the facts, Miss Marquel, so there won't be any employer-employee misunderstanding."

She stared at him, her eyes and throat burning. She had to get out of there. She had to leave before—

"Excuse me," she said, her voice cracking on a shrill note as she started forward, trying to brush past him. But he didn't move out of her way fast enough. Her sneakered toe hit the side of his shoe, and she stumbled, teetering on the brink of falling headlong into the water.

"Watch it," Connor said urgently, his arm shooting out to catch her around the waist—an automatic, impersonal gesture, but enough to push the panic button on Anne's raw nerves.

For an instant, reality wavered. All she knew was the angry sound of a male voice. The feel of a man's arm clamped around her. The boat. The water. The threat.

Jerking away, she whirled to face him as he uttered a surprised "Hey, what . . . ?" Dimly, she realized her reaction was totally inappropriate, but the part ruling her missed the baffled expression on Connor's face and saw only that a man was following her as she backed toward the door.

It was some horrible trick of fate that this was happening, the past and present coming together this way. Bringing her back to this place to ruin her life all over again, to prove she hadn't overcome anything. To make her lose. She always lost.

When Connor's hand reached for her, Anne spun and ran. She didn't hear him call her. Freedom and safety lay ahead, in the sunshine, and she ran toward them.

* * *

"Anne! Wait!" Connor jogged along the catwalk to the doorway, grabbing the doorframe to swing outside, onto the dock. There he stopped to watch as Anne ran up the hill and disappeared into the woods, and as he stared after her, his insides churned with indecision.

Tears! She'd had tears in her eyes. She'd stood there getting haughtier by the second, until she'd tried to stalk off and tripped over his foot. But when he'd caught her, she'd jumped as if she'd been burned. Then, out of nowhere...those tears.

Where in God's name had they come from? He hadn't a clue. But, suddenly, an uneasy feeling came over him. Maybe his mother was right. Maybe he'd misjudged Anne badly. He didn't see how he could have. He'd been on the receiving end of her righteous speeches more than once in the past—the last time being the day before she'd left, upon that very spot, beside the *Lady Lyn,* where they'd been standing a minute ago.

But those speeches had never been accompanied by tears. And the possibility that the sensitive girl he'd once known might be hiding somewhere behind all that pretentious garbage was compelling. Compelling enough that his need to know the truth overshadowed his need to protect himself from her.

Connor started up the path after Anne, but he didn't try to catch her. If the tears he'd seen were real, he was fairly sure he knew where she'd be.

Chapter Four

Anne ran blindly, away from the boathouse, away from Connor, toward the only refuge she'd known at Yesterday's Dream. Through the woods and past the stables she ran, then across the meadow where her mother had schooled her precious jumpers. On the other side of the meadow she picked up the course of a stream, following it through the overgrown peach orchard, until she reached another wooded area. There, where the stream widened and pooled, Anne stopped beneath an enormous beech tree that grew, thick and lush and sprawling, on the bank.

Out of breath and sweating, she wiped her eyes, then looked up to find that the old giant had been cabled; lengths of heavy-gauge wire appeared here and there through the summer's growth of leaves, helping to support the largest boughs and, thus, preserve an old friend. Anne ran a hand over the smooth, light-colored bark; then, hoisting herself up, she began to climb.

Connor found her ten minutes later, sitting amid last year's leaves that had collected in drifts inside the railing of the simple wooden deck. Arms wrapped around her shins, forehead resting on her knees, she was lost in her own miserable world and didn't hear him until he swung a leg over the railing and his foot hit the platform. Then she glanced up, startled.

Their eyes met, his a troubled blue, hers liquid pools of green. He paused for an instant, his gaze taking in the tears streaming quietly down her cheeks. When she didn't speak but simply lowered her head to her knees once more, he brought his other leg over the railing, ducked under the overhanging branch, and slowly crossed the platform. Lowering himself cautiously, he sat beside her, facing her, his left leg drawn up to align with her right.

Several minutes passed, and neither of them spoke, Anne not wanting to be the first and, in any case, not having any notion what to say. Connor picked up a fallen leaf and sat twirling it by the stem. When she sniffled, he reached into his back pocket, pulled out a clean handkerchief, and tucked it into her hand without comment. She mumbled a broken "Thank you." And the silence went on.

The silence served a purpose, though. Gradually, Anne stopped worrying about what to say or what Connor was going to say and, instead, began thinking back, reaching across the years to a time when words had come easy between them. A time when they'd known each other's joys and sorrows, and when they'd filled a need in each other's life. He'd made her laugh. She'd listened to him talk about the home he'd lost. He'd shown her what it was like to have a brother who treated her with kindness. She'd shown him what it meant to be respected, no matter what his father had done. He'd made her feel cared for. She'd made him feel important. They'd made each other feel as if there were at least one person to turn to when the adults in their separate lives, caught up in their own sorrows, had no attention for them.

The steamy morning air had mellowed somewhat, grown quieter and less urgent, when Connor finally broke the silence.

"Why didn't you write?"

Anne raised her head and looked at him, but he was staring through the rails he'd hammered into place so long ago.

"I didn't think you'd care," she whispered hoarsely.

His head jerked toward her, his startled gaze met hers, and Anne thought, dear Lord, that's all this was about. No huge and hideous nightmare but something she could face—and overcome.

"Anne, that's crazy," Connor said. "How could you think I wouldn't care? You knew how special you were to me."

Simple words spoken with utter sincerity.

Anne drew a deep, unhurried breath and let it out as the torment of the past twenty-four hours—part of it, at least— seemed to evaporate in the dappled green and golden light. Straightening her back, she lowered her knees to sit cross-legged, slowly uncurling from her tight, protective ball. "Con," she began quietly, "when I met you, I was a child, and—"

"So was I."

She shook her head. "You were never a child. At least, not from the time you came to Yesterday's Dream."

"Neither were you. Not in the sense you're talking about."

"Well, I always felt decades younger than you, and before I left—" she lowered her gaze to her fingers clutching his handkerchief "—especially then, it seemed as if we'd...grown apart."

"Whose fault was that?"

His tone wasn't defensive, but Anne heard the hurt in it. She nearly smiled, not in mockery of his feelings but because he sounded like the Connor McLeod she remembered, the one who wore his heart on his sleeve, where it was forever getting bruised.

"Does it have to be somebody's fault?" she wondered. "You'd become a man, but I was still a girl. You were working night and day, helping to take care of your family. And you were dating and...well, you acted very grown up." Hesitating, she added, "You didn't have to spell it out. I got the message that you were tired of having me follow you around."

"*Tired* of you!" His features twisted in bafflement. "I never got tired of you. Sure, it's true we didn't have much in common by the time I was twenty and you were still in junior high. But let's face it, Anne, we never had much in common to begin with, and that never stopped me from caring about you. It was *you* who started acting as if I weren't good enough to talk to, walking around with your nose in the air, half the time not bothering to say hello if you saw me. God, it got so you were worse than Aaron. At least he *answered* if I spoke to him. But not you. You behaved just like...like..."

"Like all the small-minded people in Boston who treated your family so badly when your father lost McLeod Press?"

Connor lapsed into silence, his face going blank. An instant later, a perplexed frown appeared on his brow.

Anne went on. "Like the ladies who stopped inviting your mother to be on their charity committees? And the kids who stopped being your friend because you'd lost your home and couldn't go to private school anymore?" She paused, then inquired gently, "Is that how it seemed?"

He didn't answer right away, and Anne watched his neck and cheekbones redden—with anger, she thought. Then he spoke and proved her wrong.

"I'm thirty-four years old," Connor growled. "But suddenly I feel like a kid. I can't believe I've been making judgments about you all these years based on nothing more than some rotten things that happened when I was twelve. If you're right—"

"No," she cut him off. "It's not that simple. Your father losing his company, then dying so suddenly, and your mother having to go to work—those things reshaped your life. It would be strange if you *didn't* form opinions based on them.... But...that's not all." She let her gaze slide away from his. "Even if you hadn't been sensitive to condescension, I understand why you thought I'd turned into a...a snob. I mean, it's not as if you were imagining things, because, well, I get like that—stiff and kind of weird—when I'm...nervous or scared."

He was silent so long, she glanced up to find him studying her with a familiar, piercing intensity.

"Nervous or scared," he repeated. "Anne, were things really that bad for you back then?"

The way he asked the question, his deep voice pitched to a tender rumble, almost made her cry again. Instead, she turned her head to gaze through a break in the leaves that gave her a view of the old orchard filled with Queen Anne's lace and black-eyed Susans.

The answer she gave him was part evasion and part truth. "I had some...problems. Problems that made me feel down on myself and on life in general. I— I thought if I could get away from here, things would be better, so I asked my father to send me to boarding school. It took a while to convince him. You know how he was about things remaining exactly as they'd been when my mother was alive. But, finally, he agreed."

Closing her eyes briefly, she thought about the three long years her father had made her wait, refusing even to discuss her leaving. But she pushed the thought away quickly and turned back to face Connor's dark frown.

Giving his head a quick shake, he argued, "But you never even came home for Christmas or vacations. I kept thinking you'd *have* to show up sometime. But, no. Paris, London, Barcelona, Athens—you spent every vacation seeing the world. Which is fine—wonderful, since you could afford it—but, for God's sake, Anne, you were only sixteen! Too damned young to be entirely on your own."

She lifted a shoulder in a small shrug. "I managed. And even if I'd wanted to come home, my father made it nearly impossible. He hadn't wanted me to leave, but once I was gone, he was determined to keep me away."

At Connor's incredulous look, she explained, "He came to see me once during that first year—my junior year in high school. I don't know why he bothered, because all he wanted was to give me a check for a thousand dollars and a round-trip plane ticket to France. He'd made arrangements for me to spend the summer with an old friend of his and my mother's. And every vacation, all during college, I'd get money and another ticket to someplace he had friends—book and art collectors, or horse people who'd known my mother. People willing to entertain me. I wrote to him for a while, but when he never wrote back, I gave up. Except for that one time, I never saw or talked to him again."

Connor's lips parted, his disbelief changing to amazement, then to outrage. "I knew he was unstable—we all did—but... God, I wouldn't have dreamed he'd be that cruel."

Anne lowered her gaze to her lap. "This may seem strange to you, but it didn't feel cruel to me. And after what you and your mother said yesterday, about my looking like my mother, I think it might have been that, the older I got and the more I began to look like her, the more unbearable it was for him to have me around. Or even to acknowledge that I existed."

Pausing to draw a shallow breath, she added, "I could pretend I felt hurt or rejected, but, honestly, I didn't. He'd never been much of a father, anyway, so I didn't feel like I'd lost anything I'd ever had. I certainly never missed him. But, Con—" She met his gaze directly, her eyes imploring him to understand what she couldn't fully explain. "I've always missed *you*. The times we spent together are about the only good memories I have of Yesterday's Dream. And, I promise, if I'd had any notion that you still cared, I'd have stayed in touch."

A light breeze rustled through the leaves as her eyes held his in a long, searching look. Slowly, Connor's expression cleared, the lines of tension around his mouth and brow relaxing, the years of anger and hurt melting away. Still, his eyes held questions, questions Anne hoped he wouldn't ask. And they were very sad as they skimmed her features, reflecting the regret that she, too, felt for the wasted years.

"All this time," he whispered. "And it turns out we both just misunderstood. It's so hard to accept, and yet—" He shook his head. "Anne, I'm sorry. God, am I sorry! I should have known better than to think—"

"No," she put in quickly. "You had no way of knowing I—"

"Dammit, I was old enough to have figured it out."

"No, I—"

"Yes, I was. But I wasn't paying attention to you or anybody else. In those days, I was totally caught up in what was happening for me."

"About college, you mean?"

"And other things." With his elbow resting on his thigh, he leaned to rub his forehead with strong, callused fingers. "I was angry most of the time, I guess. I wanted to... well, I wanted a lot of things I couldn't have. But, Anne, I swear—" He raised his head, tossing the hair out of his eyes to lock his gaze with hers. "I never meant for you to think I was pushing you away."

How different her life might have been, Anne thought, if they'd had this conversation fifteen years ago. But then, she'd been over this ground before and had long since realized that speculation about what she'd have done if she'd been certain of his friendship was pointless. She couldn't turn back the clock. And, truly, there was only one thing to say.

"I'm sorry, too," she told him. "I'm sorry for the time we've lost and for... well, for being such a pain in the neck a little while ago. Lord! Yesterday morning was..." She stopped, her eyes searching Connor's before she spoke again, this time with a hopeful catch in her voice. "Con, please. Do you think we could... start over?"

A sparkle crept into his eyes then, overshadowing the sadness, and, slowly, his lips melted into a smile filled with warmth and affection, a smile that was everything Anne had hoped for yesterday when she first approached him.

"That's the best idea I've heard in a long time," he said. Then, lifting a hand to tug gently at a curl that had escaped her scarf, he added simply, "Welcome home, Sunshine. It's good to see you."

The tears welled up in her eyes, her voice breaking. "Oh, Con, it's good to see you, too." And without stopping to think about what she was doing, she threw her arms around his shoulders and hugged him with all her might.

Catching her to him, he said her name on a low, shuddering sigh. "God, it's been so long."

"Oh, I know!" Anne squeezed her eyes closed. "There've been so many times I've wondered how you were and what you were doing. So many times I just wanted to talk to you."

Connor grunted softly. "You don't know how many times, especially those first few years, I almost got in the car and drove to Baltimore to see you."

"I wish you had...except, I was such a mess then. It's probably better that you didn't." When he shifted her closer, angling her across his chest, she burrowed further into his embrace, saying, "I can't believe we've both been so stupid!"

"Not stupid," he said. "Scared. Scared of having our feelings hurt any worse than they already were."

"You're right," Anne admitted. "But twelve years! It's so much time to lose! So much has happened!" And as she thought of the snatches of news she'd heard from his mother, she added, "I've got at least a million questions to ask you. I want to know everything."

"Ah, Annie...there's not much to tell. Nothing important, anyway." His cheek brushed the hair at her temple. "I'm a little older, but otherwise I haven't changed."

It wasn't true. He had changed. And the very fact that he wasn't eager to share all his news, down to the smallest detail, was proof of that. But they had time. And for the moment she was content simply to rest her head against his shoulder and relish the feel of his heart beating against hers.

"I've missed you," she said. "I've missed you so much!"

"Mmm," Connor murmured. "I wish I'd *known* what I was missing. But, then again...you know, it's almost better this way. I feel like somebody just handed me a present I didn't expect to get." Holding her away a little, he let his eyes caress her features, his voice dropping to its lowest register as he whispered, "Oh, Annie, look at you. You're all grown up...and so beautiful."

His fingertips brushed her cheek. Her lips parted slightly in response. His smile softened. And, suddenly, something was different. All at once, as if a curtain had been lifted from between them and they were looking upon each other for the first time, their eyes met, and within a heartbeat they were bound in a look neither of them seemed able to break. They crossed the line between innocence and awareness before Anne realized what was happening, and by then it was too late to turn back.

With startled wonder, she became conscious that her arms were wound around a man's broad shoulders, that his strong arms were folded across her back. That her breasts grazed his bare chest and that her thigh lay against his as she leaned across his lap. She was close enough to see the dark stubble of beard below the surface of his freshly shaven jaw and to smell the lingering scent of soap on his tanned skin. Close enough to count those long, black lashes that framed his eyes . . .

She could hardly believe she'd put herself in this position, and she was certain that, any second now, she'd pull away. But the seconds ticked by, and she felt no urge to move. For, after all, her heart whispered, this was Connor, and he was no stranger. She'd known him for nearly as long as she could remember. And, though it was true he'd changed, in all ways that mattered, he was the same. The same man she'd looked up to as a child. The only man—the only human being, since her mother died—who'd hugged or touched her with affection.

She trusted him totally, always had. He'd never do anything to hurt her. And, knowing that, Anne felt her body relax, felt the breath leave her lungs in a quiet sigh. Felt the knot in her stomach unravel. And as it did, something quite extraordinary began to happen.

That delicate quivering she'd experienced at the sight of him the day before fluttered to life. Softly at first, then with increasing strength, the fragile stirring trickled through her, seeping into her veins, heating her blood, making her heart beat faster and her breath quicken. She felt warm and kind of all-over trembly. A wonderful, luscious feeling that she recognized purely by instinct, for it was unique in her experience. The word *desire* flashed through her mind, and she thought, So this is what it's like. This is what I'm supposed to feel. And in that instant, her perception of herself and of reality was forever changed.

The summer-scented air seemed to grow heavy, the world blurring out of focus. Anne lost track of time, was aware only of the smooth texture of Connor's skin beneath her hands, the silkiness of the long hair on the back of his neck curling over her fingers. The warmth of his breath on her face...

An endless time ago, in a different life, she'd dreamed of him holding her this way. She'd imagined his eyes looking at her like this, so full of life, so blue and knowing, as if they were sharing some wonderful secret with her, a secret meant only for her: *I see you, I know you, I want to know more of you....* She'd wanted him to want her without understanding what that really meant. She'd wanted him to hold her, to touch her, to sweep her into his arms and kiss her....

She wanted him to kiss her now.

That shocking thought made Anne's gaze fall to Connor's lips. And, in the next instant, her eyes widened when his mouth slanted in a slow, provocative smile and she realized he knew what she'd been thinking. Her eyes flew back up to his, her heart tripping instantly into high gear, for she was sure it would ruin everything if he actually did kiss her.

He didn't. But he couldn't let the moment pass without acknowledging it.

"Well, I'll be damned," he murmured.

And suddenly, inexplicably, Anne felt shy and uncertain, nervous in a way that seemed oddly right. Her gaze darted away from his, her hands sliding from his neck to press lightly against his shoulders.

"Con, please," she said, shocked at the husky quality in her voice.

He loosened his hold, and she sat up straighter; she was unable to look at him, though, and hadn't the foggiest idea what to say. Fortunately, Connor was at no such loss.

"What's this?" He touched the tip of her nose. "Don't tell me a woman who's been around the world can still blush when a man says she's beautiful."

That wasn't why she was blushing, and they both knew it. But she was grateful he was able to treat the moment lightly.

Without lifting her gaze, Anne managed a tiny shrug.

Connor chuckled. "Would it make you feel better if I teased you about this bunch of curls you've acquired? Which I like, by the way. Or, um...how about your bony knees?"

That brought a smile to her lips. "Well..."

"Sorry." He grimaced at that part of her anatomy. "You're out of luck there. Your knees aren't bony anymore. In fact, it looks as if there isn't anything bony about you."

He was flirting with her. It made her incredibly uncomfortable, but Anne couldn't deny that she liked it. Nor could she deny the unprecedented urge she felt to flirt back.

"You aren't exactly all arms and legs anymore, yourself," she mumbled.

"You noticed that, did you?"

"You make it rather hard not to."

She shot a glance at his naked torso, and he laughed. The pleased, earthy sound was entirely male, and it seemed to resonate inside her, as if her body had suddenly been tuned to his special masculine frequency.

But this couldn't go on. Looking at him now, seeing the laughter sparkling in his eyes, it was clear to her that he was a man at ease with his sexuality. Undoubtedly he had women lined up waiting for the chance to stare deeply into those gorgeous blue eyes. And any one of those women would be more able than she to give him what he would require in an intimate relationship. She had Connor's respect and affection. She shouldn't jeopardize their new bond of friendship—which was, after all, what she'd been hoping for in the first place—by expecting anything more.

Needing to bring them back to a level where she could cope, Anne began primly, "Speaking of arms and legs and bony parts, Mr. McLeod, I understand you've been breaking yours with far greater regularity than one might consider prudent."

"Lord 'a mercy!" Connor fell back on an elbow to give her an agonized look. "Do you practice those speeches in the bathroom mirror every morning? You sound like somebody's maiden aunt—or an old-school nun. Where did you ever learn to talk that way?"

"You guessed it," Anne admitted. "From a *very* old-school nun who used to break at least three yardsticks a week on desk tops, making sure we stayed awake in calculus class."

"A nun? Oh, that's right." He shifted to rest on both elbows. "You went to a Catholic girls' boarding school, didn't you. So, where did you end up going to college?"

Trying not to notice the male body stretched out alongside her, Anne replied, "The College of Notre Dame."

"More nuns," he muttered. "And again, all women."

"Yes. But you're changing the subject. I want to know why you're falling out of trees and fixing boat engines instead of ridding the world of injustice in some courtroom."

"Oh, say, that's better. Now you sound like my mother."

"Connor, are you—"

"Uh-uh." He sat up, snatching his handkerchief off the platform where it had fallen, and shoving it into his pocket. "If you want an accounting of the last twelve years, you'll have to wait. Right now, duty calls."

Anne drew a breath to argue, then stopped when their eyes met and he arched a brow in a look of gentle refusal.

"I left a crew of men and a boat engine sitting in pieces to trot over here after you," he said quietly.

It was more than that, she realized. He didn't want to answer her question. She hesitated only a moment though, then released her pent-up breath to give him a smile.

"I'm glad you came," she said.

He returned her smile. "So am I, Sunshine." Then, with a wink, he added, "Don't worry. I'm curious as hell about how you ended up teaching kindergarten, and if I want answers to my questions, I suppose I'll have to let you drag a few out of me."

Anne hesitated, her voice quavering a little as she said, "Well, sure. Fair's fair." But she was already dreading his interrogation. Secrets were such wicked, insidious things.

They climbed down out of the tree to find Rogue waiting for them, his tail in perpetual motion and a stick clenched between his teeth. Connor threw the stick for him to chase as they walked through the meadow, and Anne laughed when, instead of bringing it back to Connor, Rogue consistently brought the stick to her. Chase-the-stick turned into a game of keep-away-from-Connor, and by the time they reached the main drive, both Connor and Anne were breathless.

"Twenty-four hours!" Connor complained loudly. "One lousy day you've been here, and you've already alienated the affections of my dog."

Stooping to lavish the panting setter with pets, Anne grinned. "Oh, he's a sweetheart."

When Rogue licked her in obvious appreciation, Connor snorted in disgust. "He's a world-class flirt. Gets himself into more trouble that way than any other dog I've owned."

"Really? Well, maybe he's just quicker to pick up on the lessons of his master."

Folding his arms across his chest, Connor tilted his head to give her a narrow-eyed look. "Now, what makes you think he acquired that particular bad habit from me?"

"Oh, Con, really." Anne rolled her eyes. "I may have been young, but I wasn't blind, for heaven's sake. I remember the parade of adoring females who used to hang around here, waiting for you. There was Sharon what's-her-name—"

"Hollister."

"And that Myrtle or Myrna something-or-other."

"Myra."

Myra of the blond hair, blue eyes, and big breasts. Anne remembered her perfectly well. "It seemed, at times, as if you were keeping a harem. And you can't tell me you didn't flirt shamelessly with those . . . those . . ."

"The word you're looking for is *women.*"

Actually, it wasn't, but she let it go at that.

The corners of Connor's mouth twitched with repressed laughter. "You're right. I was pretty shameless. But I gave up the harem about ten years ago and mended my ways."

"Am I allowed to ask why?"

"You can ask, but it's a long story, and—"

"You've got a boat engine to fix."

"Right."

Rising to face him, Anne gave Connor's impressive form a quick once-over. "You're not going to tell me you've been living the life of a saint for the past ten years."

His mouth sloped into a grin. "I didn't say that. But I try to stay out of things that look like they might get too serious."

"That doesn't sound like you," she returned, frowning. "What on earth happened? Did some woman run off with your best friend?"

With a beleaguered sigh, he motioned for her to join him as he started down the drive. "No. But if you're determined to swap sordid tales about our love lives, we can do it while I take care of that engine."

When she didn't follow, Connor hesitated, glancing back over his shoulder.

Anne shook her head. "I think I'll go over to the manor and have a look around."

Turning, he retraced his steps slowly, stopping in front of her to give her a searching look. "Come with me," he said. "I'll help the guys finish up the oak and get them started on the next job. Then I'll go up to the manor with you. I can take care of the yacht later."

Anne shook her head again. "Thanks, but I've got some cleaning companies coming this afternoon, and I ought to look things over before they get here."

"Take Mom with you, then," he urged. "Really, Anne, it's damn depressing inside, and I don't like the idea of your seeing it for the first time alone."

She didn't like it, either, but she was frankly worried about her reaction to being in the manor and didn't want any witnesses should she turn into a stammering idiot—or worse.

"If your mother comes with me," she said, "she'll just get upset, wanting to do things she shouldn't be doing."

"That's true, but..." Connor's look remained concerned. "Are you sure?"

Anne nodded. "It'll be okay."

He held her gaze a moment longer; then he unhooked his keys from his belt loop, saying, "All right. But the power's off, so you're going to need a flashlight. There's one in the shed. And do me a favor—keep Rogue with you. I don't like him hanging around when I'm cutting trees, anyway."

He handed the shed key to her, much as he had the one to Sandcastle yesterday. But this time, when he dropped the key into her hand, his fingers closed around hers, and he gave her hand a gentle squeeze. "Be careful," he said, "and pay attention to the tapes the fire department put up."

Anne smiled. "I will."

Looking down at Rogue, Connor ordered, "You stay with Anne, you hear? Take care of her for me."

The dog barked once and moved to her side, which amazed Anne but didn't seem to surprise Connor in the least.

He looked at her intently for another long moment, his eyes skimming her features. Then, with a rough "I'll see you later," he ducked his head and brushed her lips with his before he turned and started walking down the drive.

Anne's wide, startled gaze followed him, her fingers lifting to touch her lips. As her eyes traveled the length of his broad, muscled back, taking in the easy, fluid way he moved and the way his jeans hugged his narrow hips, she felt the tendrils of arousal curl through her again. And, for an instant, hope flared, bright and shining, in her breast.

If only it were possible to tell Connor the truth. If only she weren't certain it would ruin their friendship—forever. If she honestly believed he felt the same attraction for her that she was discovering she felt for him . . . If the whole thing didn't blow up in her face.

The spark of hope died as quickly as it had been born. She couldn't tell Connor the truth, for the secrets that were part of her past were part of his past, too. He'd been there. And what good could come of telling him now what she hadn't told him then? It would only cause heartache. The secrets that had once driven them apart, in being revealed, would loom forever between them as an unforgettable reality. And she wasn't about to risk their new-found friendship, only to be left with nothing. Nothing but an old photograph to remind her of what might have been. Yesterday's dream, indeed.

Besides, truth and secrets aside, it was absurd to think the solution to her problem might be as simple as finding the right man. She wasn't entirely sure there even was a solution. After all this time, it was very hard to keep believing that she'd ever be normal when all her efforts to be so turned into disasters.

Still, as Anne started up the lane with Rogue ambling beside her, she couldn't help but wonder if, with Connor, things might be different. Maybe he really was the right man. Maybe the *only* man. The only one she'd ever trust to help her heal the scars that kept her from being truly alive.

Walking down the drive toward the boathouse, Connor was more relieved than disappointed that Anne hadn't come with him. He needed a chance to think. Hell, what he needed was a cold shower. If he'd spent the afternoon with her... Well, it was just as well he was walking in one direction while she was walking in the other. And he decided then and there to top the dead sycamore himself that afternoon, instead of sending Tim and Jake up to do it. A few hours of hard labor would be as effective as a cold shower—and a lot more productive.

Drawing a slow breath, he stared down the tree-shaded lane before him, trying to remember the last time he'd felt such a breath-stealing jolt of awareness flash between a woman's eyes and his. He wasn't sure he'd ever felt anything like it. But then, he'd never been in the position of suddenly wanting a woman he'd known for twenty-two years. Familiarity coupled with sexual attraction, he had just discovered, was a devastating combination.

What would have happened, he wondered, if he'd kissed her? She'd wanted him to. He knew she had. But they'd both been caught off guard—an understatement if ever there was one—and . . . well, the timing hadn't seemed right.

No, that wasn't true. It had seemed *too* right. As if kissing Anne were the most natural thing in the world, something he'd expected to do someday, when the truth was, the thought had never once crossed his mind.

It was crazy. They'd been apart for years, and a couple of hours ago they'd hardly been on civil terms. But the instant he'd realized Anne had never stopped caring about him, the years they'd spent apart had ceased to feel like an insurmountable barrier and had become, instead, simply a phase of their relationship during which nothing had happened.

She was curious about him, seemed almost worried about the things in his life that she'd missed. But Connor was more worried about the things to come, the things that might happen in this, the next phase of their relationship. He sensed that, if he weren't careful, the sparks that had flown between them in the tree house would start a fire neither of them would be able to control. He'd already given in to one impulsive "goodbye" kiss—and thank God he'd kept it casual enough to be interpreted as merely friendly. If he hadn't turned away as quickly as he had, if he'd waited for Anne's reaction . . . if she'd given him the slightest encouragement . . .

Connor had a good idea of what would have happened. Not right then, but sooner or later. It was a three-letter word spelled s-e-x, and he had the uneasy feeling that sex with Anne would spell trouble. He figured he'd better cool down and get his hormones under control before he saw her again. Or he might end up in the middle of the very thing he'd spent the last ten years trying to avoid.

Chapter Five

It was worse than she'd expected. Black soot clung to every crevice, coating the walls and ceiling, sifting through her canvas shoes as she stepped cautiously into the entrance hall. With no electricity and most of the windows boarded, the only relief from darkness came through the open front door behind her and the blackened panes of unbroken windows—pale trickles of gray-yellow light cast upon a ghastly scene.

Fighting the urge to turn and run, Anne stepped around a murky puddle of water, then glanced back to see Rogue hovering on the threshold, ears flattened and head hung low.

"Believe me," Anne said, "this is not my idea of a good time. But I've got to do it, and Con says you've got to stay with me. So we're both stuck."

Rogue whined and dipped his nose to sniff at the door sill.

"I know," she commiserated. "This isn't my favorite place, either. But look at it this way—at least you match the decor." She guessed, before long, she would, too.

The setter gave up and stepped delicately into the hallway as Anne turned toward the skeletal remains of the wall to her left. Barred from entering by two yellow tapes strung across the doorway, she viewed what had been the parlor, done in white and rose and filled with crystal and cherry wood; it was now a cavern painted floor to ceiling in unrelieved black. The wall between the parlor and dining room was only a few charred supports, as was the wall separating the main house from the gutted wing. Holes in the floor revealed the gaping darkness of the cellar, while holes in the ceiling yawned into the master bedroom. Of the furnishings, only burned sticks and piles of wet ashes remained, and here and there a solid lump that might have been a chair, a broken pitcher, a lamp.

"Creepy, isn't it?" she whispered.

Rogue, who'd come to stand beside her, nudged her hand with his wet nose, and she patted his head in nervous fashion as her eyes moved over the foyer. The scorched floor was awash from the hoses, and the banister to the winding staircase was a mass of splintered oak. The worst, though, was the three-hundred-year-old tapestry hanging beside the front door. It looked like one of her kindergartner's first attempts with poster paints—a dripping abstract of black splashes and waves.

Anne cringed, thinking about the colonial lady who'd taken such care in sewing the words of the Sanskrit verse from which the estate had gotten its name. Illegible though the words now were, Anne remembered them, and their irony was inescapable.

Yesterday is only a dream
And tomorrow is but a vision
But today well lived
Makes every yesterday
A dream of happiness
And every tomorrow
A vision of hope.

Hope. Not a scrap of it in sight.

Glancing down the darkened hall toward the morning room, then up into the shadows of the broken staircase, Anne was filled with an overwhelming reluctance. The voice of reason told her anyone would have been uneasy. It was the voice of the past, though, that made being there nearly intolerable.

Where are you, little girl? You know you can't hide for long. You'll be sorry you hid. I'll punish you. . . .

With her heart pounding against her ribs, her eyes darted from one doorway to the other. "Silly, isn't it, boy?" She spoke to the setter for the comfort of hearing her own voice. "Whoever heard of being afraid of a house? What is it, anyway? A bunch of wood and plaster and brick."

But her trembling knees mocked her, and she had to resist the urge to look over her shoulder. Foolishness. No one here but her and Rogue. Yet, like a child afraid of the wolves under the bed who seeks shelter beneath the sheets, she back-stepped her way across the hall and slipped into her father's study. Paltry excuse for a sanctuary that it was, the room had a lower ceiling and fewer doors, and, in it, she felt less exposed.

Switching on the flashlight she carried, Anne shone the beam over the walls and furnishings. No piles of ashes here. Everything except the rug seemed to be dry and in its place. But the entire room had been painted the same dismal black.

The beam of light skimmed over the wing chairs in front of the fireplace, then paused on the gilt-framed painting hanging over the mantel. The portrait of her mother, to which her father had been almost maniacally attached and to which Connor and Mrs. McLeod had said she bore a striking resemblance. Her mother's face, her winsome smile and laughing eyes, had always been able to bring her a measure of comfort. But there was little comfort to be had from a canvas washed in soot.

Anne stared at the painting, fighting tears, until a whimpering sound drew her attention—Rogue standing next to her, a pitiful look in his dark eyes.

"You're right," she said to him. "The only thing I'm accomplishing is to make myself upset. So what do you say? Shall we call it quits and go fix ourselves some lunch? You understand *food?*"

Rogue uttered a single bark, his tail swishing, and, whether he understood or not, Anne welcomed his positive response. Casting a last sorrowful glance over the bookshelf that held her father's collection of rare edition classics, she turned to leave, but then paused as something caught her attention.

Crossing the room slowly, her sneakers squishing on the saturated Oriental carpet, she stepped around the end of the big walnut desk to stand in front of the shelf. There, she passed the flashlight beam over the rows of books, the titles illegible beneath their coating of soot. Some were knocked over, as though volumes had been carelessly removed.

Using her fingers to smear the soot off the bindings, Anne read through the titles. Many times in the past, she'd stood before these shelves, like a pilgrim visiting a holy shrine, reverently gazing at the books she hadn't been allowed to touch but had read and loved in less expensive editions. So it didn't take her long to conclude that no new titles had been added to the collection.

Several, however, were missing. An unpublished English copyright edition of Joseph Conrad's *The Nigger of the "Narcissus,"* a first American edition of *Moby Dick,* and a fourth-edition copy of Shakespeare's *Comedies, Histories, and Tragedies.*

"That certainly is odd," she murmured, unable to believe her father would have sold them. "Though, I suppose, wherever they are, they're better off." Arching an eyebrow in Rogue's direction, she added, "They're worth a great deal, you know. And I don't know if what's left here will ever be worth much again."

After a final look at the shelves, she turned away, shaking her head. "At least they didn't get drenched with the hoses. I suppose that's someth— Oh, dear." Her gaze fell upon the upper right-hand corner of the desk, and she stopped again.

The bronze miniatures were gone—the Antoine Louis Barye pieces her father had collected. Tigers eating crocodiles, dogs devouring stags. Exquisitely rendered savagery. As a child, she'd hated the tiny sculptures. As an adult, she'd learned the rule of thumb: the more gruesome, the more expensive. Her father's collection had been very expensive indeed. Moreover, he'd prized the miniatures almost as highly as he had his books.

Had he sold them, too? It seemed impossible.

With a tingle of gooseflesh creeping over her skin, Anne let her eyes wander over the well-appointed room, struggling to recall how it had appeared when last she'd seen it—wondering what else might be missing. She was deep in the past when Rogue let out a volley of barks and bounded toward the hall.

Anne whirled, her heart leaping to her throat.

"Down! Oh, dear heavens, *down,* doggy! Miss Marquel! *Miss Marquel!* Are you there?"

The sound of an unfamiliar—and clearly distressed—male voice left her weak with relief. It also told her how rattled she'd become in the short time she'd been inside the manor. Gathering her wits, she hurried to find a small, bald man cowering

in the doorway while Rogue danced in front of him, his tail
wagging in delight. Anne calmed Rogue, then established that
the frightened little man was Mr. Humphrey, the insurance adjuster. Mr. Humphrey was quick to report that a Mr. McLeod
had yelled to him from the top of a tree at the entrance to the
estate, saying that he'd find her here.

Anne's stomach clenched as she immediately conjured an
image of Connor not *in* the tree but lying on the ground at its
base. Her impulse was to run down the road to watch him—as
if her presence would keep him safe—but Mr. Humphrey required her full attention, and she gritted her teeth to give him
the grand tour.

The adjuster's work took up the remainder of the morning,
and when it was done, Anne had been from the attic to the cellar. With Mr. Humphrey and Rogue along, she managed to
keep her fears at bay, but the effort took its toll. Her mother's
room, arranged precisely as Evelyn had left it the day she died,
made her sad. Her room, where she'd lain awake terrified so
many nights, sent chills up her spine. Everywhere she turned,
some memory lurked, waiting to undermine her self-
confidence.

When Mr. Humphrey left, Anne was more than ready to
abandon the manor. But then, Mr. Reed from the hauling and
salvage company drove up in his battered truck. Following on
Mr. Reed's heels came the antiques restorer, who Anne seri-
ously thought might faint when he saw the blisters covering her
mother's red-lacquered Chinese Chippendale desk. Then Mrs.
Mack appeared to inspect the carpets, and by the time she delivered the news that most of the Orientals were probably beyond hope, Anne was grimy, starving, and exhausted.

She was also thoroughly distraught to have discovered a
number of other items missing from the house: a J.F. Herring
painting—a horse portrait, typical of Herring's best, and most
expensive, work; two antique fabergé cosmetic cases; and a rare
German silver spice tower, a gift from her father to her mother
on their tenth-anniversary trip to Europe. Anne's travels abroad
had taught her nothing if not the value of art; she estimated the
total worth of the missing lot to be a staggering sum. And where
was it all now? She wasn't sure she wanted to know.

At five o'clock, when Mrs. Mack left, Anne realized Rogue's
piteous whining probably meant he was ravenous. He'd stuck
with her faithfully, and his company had helped enormously in

surviving the day. She wondered, as they left the manor together, if he could be persuaded to help her survive the night.

They walked through Connor's well-kept gardens in back of the manor, to the river, but when Anne turned to follow the beach to Sandcastle, Rogue balked, looking toward Sentinel.

"I suppose I ought to let you go," she said. "But I don't know if Connor's finished with that dumb old tree, and if he's not, and you go looking for him, you might get yourself squashed. So I think you'd better come along, don't you?" Fully aware that her motives were not entirely unselfish, she urged, "Come on, boy." As further enticement, she picked up a piece of driftwood and tossed it in the direction she wanted him to go.

Rogue cast one more glance homeward, then took the bait, kicking up sand as he bounded after the stick. He wasn't satisfied simply with retrieving it, however, but proceeded to plunge with it into the river.

Anne chuckled, watching his antics. But her laughter faded as her attention shifted from the dog to the wide river stretching before her. The river of her childhood. Once her favorite playground. Now one more source of anguish. One more thing she'd valued, taken away.

Shuddering, Anne focused her gaze down the beach, away from the water, and started walking once more. She was soon brought to a stop, though, when Rogue came racing after her, dropped the stick, and shook himself like a rag mop all over her.

"Rogue! For heaven's sake!" Anne looked at the streaks of wet soot running down her legs. "I guess it doesn't matter. What we both need is a bath." Eyeing the disheveled animal, she spoke as she began walking again. "So, what do you say? Want to spend the night with me?"

Rogue's response was to fall into step at her side, panting gently as he trotted along.

With a tiny smile, she told him, "I'll let you in on a secret. I've never asked a man to spend the night with me." A few steps farther on, she added, quietly, "I'll tell you another secret. I wish it were Con I was asking to spend the night.... Just to hold me. That's all."

That wasn't all. But she was afraid of what might happen if things went any further. She thought it would be okay, though—yes, she really thought it would be—if he kissed her.

And as she strolled down the secluded beach, with nothing but the sound of marsh grass rustling in the breeze to disturb her thoughts, Anne wondered what it would be like to be kissed by Connor McLeod. Not the way he'd kissed her earlier, when he'd said goodbye, but the way he would kiss her if they were lovers. The kind of kiss that was supposed to make a woman's bones turn to water. The kind that was supposed to make the earth move.

Anne's leisurely pace slowed even more, her gaze losing focus as Connor's darkly handsome visage rose in her mind—the way he'd looked at her that morning in the tree house. The heat in his gaze. His sensual mouth curved in that knowing smile. His lips slightly parted, straight white teeth showing just a little. It took no effort at all to imagine his face drawing closer until his lips touched hers...closer still, until his mouth covered hers. She felt the warmth, the pressure. She felt the melting response her body gave to the imagined caress....

With a quick indrawn breath, Anne suddenly became aware that her pace had slowed nearly to a stop, in contrast to her heart, which was beating much too fast. Yet, although she found it somewhat embarrassing, she had few qualms about wallowing in sensations she suspected might eventually lead to sexual frustration. What was a little frustration to a woman whose understanding of arousal, up until a few hours ago, had been limited to words on the pages of a book or scenes on a movie screen? The reassurance that she was even capable of such a feeling was worth any amount of frustration.

When she thought about the men she'd forced herself to date in her campaign to achieve normalcy, it was almost laughable. All those nice, attractive men. Not one of them had inspired even a thirty-second fantasy. So what did Connor have that those men did not? No magic, surely. Only her heart and her faith, and those he'd had for a very long time.

Staring blindly at the glass-smooth surface of the river, Anne acknowledged the truth. She was falling in love with him. Of course, it was too fast; they'd hardly been on speaking terms when the day started. Then again, she'd always been a little bit in love with Connor, and it seemed natural that it should still be so. Natural that, upon seeing him again, she would discover her girlhood infatuation hadn't disappeared but had simply taken on the colors and shapes and dimensions more suited to a woman's feelings toward a man.

That thought, however, cast a shadow over the pleasure of the moment. Connor was a good man, worthy of any woman's love. And he deserved a woman who didn't have a huge dustbin full of fears and anxieties. A mature woman who was confident of her ability to give the man she loved what he needed... A woman who could convince a man who didn't want to get involved in anything "too serious" to reconsider.

Hopeless to think she could be that woman. Still, she'd have given anything for the chance to try.

Upon their arrival at Sandcastle, Anne examined the disreputable-looking setter and led him directly to the bathroom, where, under his suspicious eye, she filled the tub with water. Clearly, in Rogue's canine mind, all water was not created equal, and water in a bathtub ranked beside rabies boosters among things to be avoided. He succumbed to the inevitable with good grace, however, and Anne soon had him out of the tub, standing on the bath mat as she dried him with her hair dryer. His long coat gleamed like midnight, and when she'd finished drying him, she couldn't resist the urge to tie her yellow scarf around his neck.

"There!" Eyeing her handiwork, she grinned—though Rogue seemed less than impressed. "You look smashing," she assured him. "Wait until Connor sees you. Maybe we can talk him into going out to dinner with us—if he hasn't already eaten." A glance at the bedside clock told her she'd better hurry.

By the time Anne had scoured the tub, taken her shower, and dressed, it was six o'clock, and her head was spinning from lack of food and sleep. If she hadn't been anxious to see Connor, she would have fallen into bed and perhaps even slept. But at the very least she had to check about keeping Rogue. So she grabbed her car keys and shooed Rogue out the front door, carefully locking it behind her.

"All right. Let's go find Con," she said. And that, it seemed, was a mistake.

Rogue barked once, then bolted up the drive at a gallop. Anne stared after him, amazed and even a little hurt, until it hit her that he was probably doing exactly as she'd suggested: going to find Connor.

She attempted to do the same, though she took her car, driving first to Sentinel, where she found no sign of either

Connor or Rogue, then to Mrs. McLeod's. She caught Mrs. McLeod leaving for her Thursday-evening bridge party.

"Con's gone to class," the older woman informed her as they stood together at the bottom of the porch steps. "He worked with his crew up to the time he had to leave, then had to hurry. Is there something you needed?"

Anne struggled to hide her disappointment. "I wanted to return Rogue. He's been with me all day. But when I said we were going to look for Connor, he took off."

Mrs. McLeod dismissed her concern. "Con's out most evenings, so he put in a dog door for Rogue. And he always leaves a bowl of dry food down for him, so Rogue will be fine."

But would she be fine?

Moving with Mrs. McLeod toward their cars, Anne strove to keep her tone casual. "How late will Connor be getting home?"

"A little after eleven, probably." Mrs. McLeod rooted in her purse for her keys, then stopped alongside her car to lift her gaze to Anne's. "Did you two have a chance to talk today?"

Anne smiled. "Yes. This morning." And without going into detail, she answered the obvious curiosity in Mrs. McLeod's eyes. "Things are much better."

Mrs. McLeod's answering smile was both warm and relieved. "I'm glad. He's missed you. More than he realizes, I suspect."

Before Anne could wonder at that remark, Mrs. McLeod reached out to give her hand a motherly squeeze.

"Anne, I know this is coming a little late," she began, "but I want you to know that if you . . . well, if you need anything, or if you just want to talk, I'm here."

The words were so unexpected, the thought behind them so obviously genuine—and the day had been so long and wearing—that Anne was afraid she might cry. "Thank you," she said, fighting to control the urge to ask Mrs. McLeod, please, not to go. Not to leave her alone.

Only it wasn't Mrs. McLeod's company she wanted. It was Connor's. After twelve years of not seeing him at all, she'd become nearly desperate for the sight of him in the course of a single day.

Glancing at her watch, Mrs. McLeod said, "I'd better go. Bernice Weathers is a stickler for starting on time."

Anne stood back as the other woman opened her car door and got inside. Then, on impulse, she asked, "By the way...do you know anything about the Herring painting? I saw it was gone from the master bedroom, but I didn't see it stored in the attic."

Mrs. McLeod frowned. "No, it's been gone for some time."

Anne's better judgment counseled her to drop the subject, but she felt compelled to continue. "I noticed that some of my father's books were gone, too. And a few other odds and ends." Odds and ends worth tens of thousands of dollars.

Mrs. McLeod's frown deepened. "I've noticed things gone from time to time, but I assumed you'd arranged to sell them. I'm afraid it never occurred to me that you wouldn't know what—"

"Listen—" Anne shook her head quickly "—I'm sure it's fine. I probably did agree to have the things sold and simply don't remember. I've had so many conversations with Howard Stone in the last year and signed so many papers, I've lost track of what's been decided." In fact, she'd talked to Stone three times, including yesterday's conversation, and knew quite well she'd never agreed to sell a single item. But the last thing she wanted was to give Mrs. McLeod further cause for distress. Forcing a smile, she finished, "Don't worry about it."

"You have an appointment with Howard tomorrow morning, don't you?" Mrs. McLeod asked.

Anne nodded. "Yes. And I'm sure he'll straighten me out. Now, please, don't let me keep you, or you'll be late."

Anne wished Mrs. McLeod a pleasant evening, then stood with her hands clenched inside the pockets of her linen skirt as she watched the older woman drive away. She continued to stare at the empty dirt road for several minutes. Then, with a ragged sigh, she turned toward Sandcastle to face another night alone. Except tonight she was truly alone. There was no one at Yesterday's Dream but her—and Rogue, who was undoubtedly at home, enjoying his dinner. Which was where he would stay, because she was not going to try to coax him through his doggy door to come keep her company. She did have some dignity left.

Too tired to cook, Anne settled for a bowl of cereal and a slice of cantaloupe, carrying both to the porch, where she sank into the Bermuda chair to eat. The evening was quiet, the river peaceful, and with no distractions at hand, her thoughts turned again to the question of the missing books and artwork.

One answer presented itself immediately, and she clung to it as an easy way out. Possibly, her father had sold the items to bail himself out of a financial crisis. After his death, Howard Stone had explained to her the circumstances under which her father had retained him and given him the power to manage the estate, the arrangement extending even beyond Kenneth's death until such time that the property might be sold. Apparently, it was something Evelyn Marquel had often begged her husband to do, but he'd refused; then, after she died, acting out of grief and, perhaps, guilt, he'd made the most sensible move of his sorry life, relinquishing control of what was left of the Marquel fortune before he'd mismanaged it into nonexistence.

The agreement was ironclad; her father had received a reasonable but modest allowance, and he couldn't have fallen back on estate assets if he'd run into personal financial trouble. So perhaps he *had* sold the artwork and his precious books.

Fortunately, by the time Anne had finished eating, her eyes were closing, and her brain had shut down on further ruminations. Not wanting to fall asleep on the porch, she plodded into the kitchen and dumped her dishes into the sink, then closed and locked the windows she'd opened that morning to air out the stuffy cottage. Beyond that, she was past caring. She crawled onto the bed fully clothed, without turning down the spread, and in less than a heartbeat, she was asleep.

At one o'clock she awoke feeling hot and sweaty and vaguely uneasy. She got up to remove her damp clothing and put on her nightgown, then trudged into the kitchen for a glass of water. There, she found the back door sitting open.

But she'd locked it, hadn't she? When she'd come in from eating dinner on the porch? She thought she had. But then, she'd been half-asleep and couldn't be certain.

No matter. Nothing ghastly had happened. And nothing was going to happen.

With that halfhearted reminder that she was perfectly safe, Anne locked the door and went back to bed.

At one-thirty Connor lay awake, staring at the crescent moon hanging above the tree outside his bedroom window. The night was muggy and still, and, as always on his isolated point of land with nothing but water around him, it was quiet. Quiet enough to hear the soft putter of a boat motor through the open windows and balcony door.

More restless than curious, he got up and padded out onto the balcony in time to see a dimly lit boat pass by the point on its way downriver. Crazy people, he thought, out joyriding in the middle of the night. Though, the truth was, the boat hadn't been speeding or behaving recklessly in any way; he was just looking for excuses for his edgy mood. Not that he needed an excuse. He knew why he couldn't sleep.

Leaning a bare shoulder against the doorframe, Connor let out a tired sigh. The resolution he'd made that morning to forget about Anne had lasted maybe five minutes. Even sixty feet up in a tree with a chain saw in his hand, when he should have been concentrating on protecting his neck, he hadn't been able to stop thinking about her. And his thoughts hadn't been soothing.

He couldn't forget her eyes. The way she'd looked at him that morning in the tree house, as if he were the first man she'd ever seen and she found him completely fascinating. The look haunted him—strangely innocent, unconsciously seductive, achingly beautiful. And as he stood there in the still of the summer's night with that image of Anne's green eyes swimming in his head, the fantasies he'd tried all day to ward off became impossible to resist.

Fantasies of talking with her, laughing with her, being with her... Fantasies of holding her again, as he had that morning, and feeling her, warm and pliant, against him. She made him want to forget his responsibilities and, for once, think only of himself, of the needs and desires he struggled constantly to deny.

In that solitary moment, he denied himself nothing. And as he stared out over the dark expanse of the Tred Avon, his blood heated and began to pound. He thought of going to her, of walking down the beach to Sandcastle, of finding her asleep and waking her. In his mind, he saw her eyes open, startled at first, then melting with acceptance, as though she'd been expecting him, waiting for him. She smiled and reached out to welcome him, her body naked and lovely on the cool, white sheets. He could almost feel his flesh meet hers as he came down to lie with her and took her in his arms. His blood pounded harder as he imagined her breasts crush against his chest, her belly press against his loins, her legs entwine with his. He kissed her, a long, deep, lingering kiss, and he could taste her mouth, hot and sweet. He tasted her breasts, satiny white, silky smooth, the nipples hard inside his mouth. He heard her moan. He felt her thigh glide over his... his fingers slide into her... her hand slip down on him. And then...

Drenched in sweat, his breathing ragged, Connor knew *this* was trouble. He could feel it in every unsatisfied nerve in his body. The desire to make the fantasy come true was frighteningly strong. Frightening because this wasn't merely a fantasy of lust with a beautiful woman. It was a dream of fulfillment with a woman he felt he already knew nearly as well as he knew himself.

Anne. The sensitive child with the big green eyes and pigtails. The lovely little girl whose smile and lighthearted nonsense had been capable of dragging him out of the pits of depression and making him feel as if all were right with the world. There were things about her—the reticence, the nervousness, the shadows in her eyes—things he didn't understand and didn't like and wanted to see gone forever. But he knew now that the icy mask she sometimes wore didn't have to do with him. And it hadn't changed her. Not essentially. She was still Anne. Still his Sunshine.

He'd loved her once. And it wouldn't take much...not much at all...to love her again. But if he allowed himself to grow fond of the feel of her in his arms, if they even got close to making love, he was afraid he wouldn't simply love her. He'd be in love with her. And he absolutely did not want to fall in love with Anne Marquel.

He didn't want to fall in love with any woman, having learned the hard way that being in love was a luxury he couldn't afford. Holding back didn't come naturally to him. No, he'd fallen in love with probably half the girls he'd dated before he was twenty-five. But then, when Lisa Atwood had found out she was pregnant and wanted to get married—an idea that hadn't been unappealing to him at the time—he'd had to face facts.

The facts had been, and still were, that he had all the responsibilities he could handle. He could afford neither the time nor the emotional energy it took to care about someone deeply. Nor could he afford the financial burden of a wife and children, whether he wanted them or not. There was only so much of him to go around, and he had prior commitments that, up until now, and for a while longer, took precedence.

He still thanked God well and often, if a little guiltily, that Lisa had miscarried shortly after they'd learned she was pregnant. They hadn't loved each other enough to make a difficult situation work; by now they'd be divorced or miserable, and he'd be responsible for at least one child and maybe others. Still, his close call with Lisa had taught him an important lesson—aside from making him fanatical about birth control.

It was a matter of survival, his own emotional survival, to maintain distance in a relationship. To keep things light and friendly. Not to care too much. Not to get involved with a woman with whom he even suspected he might be able to fall in love. Which meant he'd be out of his mind to get involved any more than he already was with Anne. It would be so easy…so easy to fall in love with her. The chemistry was right, and there'd always been a basic, almost primal sense of safety and trust between them that he'd never come close to finding with anyone else.

But damned few women either understood or accepted his priorities, and he couldn't see why Anne would be any different. Why *should* she understand his commitment to working six or seven days a week at two jobs he didn't even like? Especially when, if she didn't want to, she didn't have to work at all. More than that, how could he expect Anne to understand why the place that was her home—this unspoiled piece of the Tidewater dream from which she'd essentially been exiled, which she adamantly did not want to sell, and to which she might want someday to return—was his idea of a prison?

God, he'd been trying for twenty-two years to get away from this place. To start his own life. To have the freedom to invest all his time and energy in pursuit of his own goals. And he was close to being able to manage it. Close to the point where the only person for whom he had to be responsible was himself. His sisters were on their own, now, and his mother would be secure as long as he put enough time into the business to keep it running smoothly.

Soon he'd be able to quit his job as caretaker and not have to worry about the loss of income or housing. Soon, for the first time since his father had died, he wouldn't have to worry about taking care of anyone but himself. He didn't mind the idea of a few lean years, as long as he'd be the only one to suf-

fer. It would be worth it. Worth it to be away from this place
and to be doing the thing he most wanted to do...if only
somebody would give him the chance to do it.

Turning from the doorway, Connor wandered over to his
dresser, where, for a moment or two, he looked at the thick
packet of papers he'd left lying there. Then, slowly, he picked
it up and carried it to the bed, sinking down onto the edge of
the mattress to stare at the words on the top page.

He didn't need a light to read them. He knew what they said.
They left him little hope, and he supposed he ought to give up
this crazy idea, admit he was battering his head against a brick
wall. It wasn't as if he had no other choices. There were a lot of
things he might do that would be as satisfying...well, nearly
so, anyway. And wasn't he an expert at being satisfied with less
than what he really wanted?

Yes, and he was damned sick and tired of it. But it looked as
though he were going to have to settle for less than what he
wanted in this, in the same way he would have to settle for less
than what he wanted with Anne.

Giving the papers a frustrated toss onto the bedside table,
Connor leaned to pick up the yellow scarf that floated off the
table to the floor. The scarf he'd untied from Rogue's collar.
Anne's scarf. It smelled like her, felt like her...soft in his hands.
She reminded him of what it was like to be young, to view the
world as a place full of hope and opportunities. She reminded
him of what it was like to dream.

But he wasn't young, his opportunities were limited, and this
wasn't the time to start dreaming again about things he had no
hope of having. Nor was it the time to forget his responsibilities and give in to his desires.

So the question was, could he and Anne be friends without
becoming lovers? He guessed it ought to be possible. But if the
stirrings in his body—and in his heart—were anything to go by,
Connor knew he'd be a fool to believe it was going to be easy.

Chapter Six

Friday morning, Anne left for her appointment with Howard Stone feeling half-rested. Her discovery of the open back door had kept her awake for some time, trying to convince herself she'd simply forgotten to lock it. Then she'd slept only lightly, and her sleep had been haunted by dreams of the sort she hadn't had in years—nightmares of being paralyzed while faceless monsters touched her with cold, steel-fingered hands. She'd awakened, screaming, at 6:00 a.m. At ten, she still felt queasy and disoriented, and the feeling persisted as she drove into St. Michaels.

Still, it helped to be away from Yesterday's Dream. After she'd parked her car in a lot near the waterfront, she walked the four short blocks to the attorney's office, focusing on the sights as a means of clearing her thoughts. St. Michaels was a small tourist town whose chief attractions were the Chesapeake Bay Maritime Museum, several outstanding seafood restaurants, and a number of Victorian bed-and-breakfasts. In summer, people came to stroll the brick sidewalks of Talbot Street, browse through the antique and craft shops, and eat at the quaint cafés.

They also came to buy real estate. For even more numerous than the shops and cafés were the real estate offices. Most had windows filled with photographs of available waterfront property. Everything from fishing shacks to thirty-room mansions could be had if one were willing to pay the considerable price. Harder to find, and even more dear, were the colonial estates like Yesterday's Dream. They existed, tucked away on the creeks that veined the Tred Avon and its neighbors, the Miles and Choptank rivers. But what few remained with their acreage intact—or mostly so—weren't often offered for sale.

Passing the windows, seeing the many pictures of newly built homes or two-acre undeveloped lots, Anne wondered which colonial land grant she was seeing meted out piecemeal. And it strengthened her resolve never to allow Yesterday's Dream to be strewn from one end of this street to the other on three-by-four-inch photographs, puzzle pieces that would never again fit together in any meaningful way.

When she arrived at her destination, she was thinking about the nature of human greed, and somehow that gave her the courage to tackle the list of questions she'd compiled for Howard Stone. She'd never met the elderly, semi-retired attorney in person, but through their phone conversations she'd come to trust him. Stone did not disappoint her. He approached her questions in a warm yet professional manner, and by the time their interview was over, Anne was much enlightened about many things related to her inheritance that she had previously chosen to ignore.

She was also horribly upset. Howard Stone claimed no knowledge of her father's having sold any of his books. Moreover, he specifically recalled their being there when he'd inventoried the contents of the manor after Kenneth Marquel's death. Surely, Stone said, Anne must remember getting a copy of the inventory.

Anne refrained from saying that she hadn't looked at it. Nor did she mention that, besides the books, a variety of other things were missing. She didn't want to raise Howard Stone's suspicions until she'd had a chance to think. She mumbled something about the fire department moving things around and said she'd look again. But she knew she could look from now until doomsday and would never find the books or the Herring painting or any of the other items. They were gone. And she knew where.

Anne managed to hide her inner turmoil until she left Stone's office and made her way to the grocery store. But as she wandered up and down the aisles, picking up things she needed at the cottage, she grew more and more unnerved.

What should she do? Go back and tell Howard Stone? What would the consequences be if she tried to recover the loss? The questions lay at the foundation of her deepest fears and worst nightmares, and they battered her like waves beating a ship on a storm-tossed sea.

By the time she left the store with her bag of groceries and headed for the lot where she'd parked, spots blurred her vision and her white heels tottered precariously on the brick sidewalk under her shaky steps. She didn't notice the sound of someone calling her name, and only when a male form appeared in front of her, blocking her way, did she rally enough to take a sideways step to avoid him.

"Anne?"

The man's fingers caught her wrist, and she jerked to a stop, her gaze flashing up to meet Connor's intent regard.

"Con! I didn't see you."

"I called from across the street."

"I'm sorry, I guess I'm . . . not exactly—"

"Anne, are you okay?"

"Certainly. I'm—" She pressed a hand to her forehead, briefly closing her eyes. "No, I-I've just come from Howard Stone's, and he— he said—" She broke off when the knot in her stomach tightened painfully, making it impossible to continue.

Transferring the bag of groceries smoothly from her arm to his, Connor said, "Come on. Let's go sit down and get you something cold to drink, and you can tell me about it."

"No, wait—" She held back. "I can't do this to you two days in a row. You must be here for a reason, and I doubt that I'm it."

He gave her a lopsided grin. "No, you're the pleasant surprise. I came to leave the carburetor off the *Lady Lyn* at the repair shop and my pickup at the garage. I'm waiting for Tim Hutchins, one of my crew, to give me a lift home. But he's tied up for at least another hour—plenty of time for us to go have some lunch and talk."

Anne wavered for another second or two, and the voice of her conscience prodded her unmercifully. *What's the matter*

with you? It's only artwork and books. Not the skeleton in the
family closet. Go with him. Tell him.

The half-hopeful, half-fearful look she gave Connor reflected her ambivalence. "I could take you home," she said.
"And we could pick up something to eat and take it to the
meadow—or to the tree house."

He seemed to hesitate, and Anne felt her cheeks flush at
having made what suddenly felt like a very forward suggestion. But then, as she started to say that perhaps it would be
better if she took herself home and got on with her work at the
manor, Connor smiled in a way that made her think she must
have imagined his hesitation.

Both his voice and his look were intimate as he said, "Walk
with me over to the shop, so I can let Tim know I found a pret-
tier chauffeur."

Anne managed a shy answering smile as he placed his free
hand at the small of her back and guided her across Talbot
Street and down one of the narrow side roads, away from the
center of town. She thought he was leading her to the repair
shop where he'd left the carburetor, but, instead, they came to
a small white building inside a high chain-link fence, the sign
on the door of which read MCLEOD TREE SERVICE, INC.

Anne gave Connor a surprised look, but his only explanation as he opened the door for her was, "Had to have someplace to put the equipment."

In addition to the equipment, Anne learned, his business also
had a secretary who kept track of everybody's schedule and did
the bookkeeping. Connor introduced her to Florence Carter,
then to Tim Hutchins, who turned out to be the redhead with
the chain saw with whom she'd exchanged shouts the previous
morning. Anne went through the motions of being polite, but
her mind was caught in a struggle between truth and lies, rev-
elations and secrets, which to offer Connor when he wanted to
know why he'd found her wandering down the street in a daze.

He wasted no time in telling Tim his services wouldn't be
needed and steering her back out the door, and as they began
the walk to her car, Anne searched for a topic they could safely
discuss. Connor beat her to it.

Flashing her a quick smile, he said, "So, tell me what made
you decide to teach school."

Anne had been about to ask what, if anything, his computer
course had to do with his business, and it took a moment to

shift gears. Letting out a sigh, she began, "I guess I was pretty heavily influenced, being at a college run by a teaching order of nuns. But the main reason was Clarissa Christiana Davis-DeFoe."

"Good God." Connor's grimace was comical. "Is this lady for real or somebody out of a storybook?"

"Oh, she's for real," Anne replied with a smile. "She's an old friend of my mother's—a horsewoman and a retired educator. A very British, very proper maiden lady. I spent the summer after my sophomore year of college in England with her, and I came to admire her greatly. She more or less *pronounced* that I was to become a teacher—wouldn't hear of me considering anything else. By then, I'd given up the notion of being a nun and—"

"A *nun!*"

"Yes, but my vocation was supplanted by visions of becoming a great poet."

"Oh. Sure. A likely second choice."

"It seemed so at the time. I wrote that entire summer in England. Horrible stuff. Very depressing. Clarissa convinced me I'd never give T.S. Eliot a run for his money, and I couldn't bear the idea of being second-rate—"

"Of course not."

"So, with her lectures about the joys of molding young minds filling my head, I came home thinking I'd give it a try. And she was right. I love it."

They'd come to Talbot Street, and she felt Connor's hand at her elbow, steadying her on the uneven pavement as they crossed. But when they stepped up onto the sidewalk, he let go of her arm only to gather her hand in his. He did it easily, as if holding hands was a natural thing. Yet Anne had never held hands with a man as she walked a public street, and she found it very distracting. She also found it extremely nice.

Hitching the grocery bag a little higher in his other arm, Connor picked up the conversation. "I admit, I had a hard time at first, imagining you in a classroom of undersized desks and art easels. A college classroom, maybe, directing some intensely intellectual literary discussion. But kindergarten? Uh-uh. Then I remembered the afternoon you spent teaching Nancy and Maureen vowels and consonant blends."

"Oh, glory," Anne groaned. "You remember that?"

"Sure," he returned. "They were the only first-graders in their class who knew their vowels. They were very proud of that. You were wonderful with them—patient and excited about learning, the way a person ought to be to work with children." He gave her one of those smiles that made her feel warm and fluttery inside as he added, "So, I have to agree with the good Miss Davis-Defoe—you've probably found your true calling. The finger-painting set is lucky to have you."

Anne felt herself blushing, and as she lowered her gaze she cast a covert glance at her small, manicured hand tucked inside his much larger, callused one. "Funny, but I feel lucky to have them. They're so young and . . . oh, I don't know. Fresh, I suppose. They make me feel . . . hopeful."

She didn't add that they also made her feel needed. They filled up a huge part of the empty space inside her and lent purpose and meaning to her life. Once, she'd thought her career would be all she'd ever need to feel fulfilled. Only in the past few years had she come to see that wasn't so. She didn't want to end up like Clarissa—alone at eighty, wise about the ways of the world but ignorant of the ways of love between a man and a woman. Yet when the closest thing to success she'd achieved for all her efforts at intimacy was holding hands with Connor—and, indeed, she looked upon it as a stunning triumph—she had to wonder if she'd ever know what it meant to be fulfilled as a woman.

They'd reached the parking lot where Anne's red Volvo sat basking in the sun, and Connor gave her hand a squeeze, then let go to transfer her groceries to his other arm. "I've wondered about what you were doing," he said. "Since you decided you wanted to work, I'm glad you found something you enjoy."

Anne laughed. "Thanks, but it was hardly a matter of *deciding* to work. I didn't have a lot of choice if I wanted to be able to pay my bills."

Connor's pace slowed, and when she glanced up to find him looking at her in obvious confusion, it hit her that he honestly didn't know. And why should he? Neither he nor his mother had ever been privy to their employer's circumstances. He'd simply made assumptions. Reasonable, but completely inaccurate ones.

With a growing sense of alarm, Anne began to realize that his misimpressions of her must have colored their relationship from its very beginning, without her even knowing it. She'd grown up absorbing Connor's stories about his well-to-do lifestyle in Boston, before his family's financial demise, he'd always talked as if he'd expected to have that "better" life back again—as soon as he was old enough to fight the powers that had snatched it away. In his mind, he hadn't been the son of a housekeeper, but heir to an old and successful publishing firm. And that was the way she'd thought of him; it had never occurred to her to consider Connor "lower class." Yet, it suddenly dawned that he must look upon her—must *always* have looked upon her—as someone who lived in that world to which he no longer belonged.

When they reached her car, she paused to study him over the roof. "Con, I hate to disillusion you, but the Marquels are not rolling in money. My father spent it all. Or most of it, anyway."

He cocked an eyebrow. " 'Rolling' is a relative term."

"Maybe," she conceded. "But I mean it. I'm not wealthy or even what you'd call well-off."

He gave her another dubious look as he opened the rear door to set the groceries on the seat beside the large net bag of volleyballs she kept there for days she helped at her school's recreation center.

Waiting until his eyes met hers again, she continued, "I want you to understand before you go building walls between us that aren't there. Yesterday's Dream is worth a fortune, but you know as well as I do that it also costs a fortune to keep. The property tax alone is astronomical. Howard Stone has worked some sort of investment magic with the little money my father didn't spend, so all the expenses are paid from interest earnings. But beyond that...well, once a year I get a modest check that constitutes the sum total of benefits to which I'm entitled."

Connor studied her, his eyes narrowed against the sunlight, and at first it seemed as if he didn't believe her. But then, she realized, it was bound to be difficult to let go of a belief he'd harbored for twenty-two years.

"Modest?" he repeated.

"*Very* modest."

Drawing back, he let his gaze travel over her Volvo.

"It's five years old," Anne said. "I bought it last January, with seventy thousand miles on it. And it took every cent of last year's check from the estate to pay for it."

Connor looked from the car to her. Then his mouth twitched. "Seventy thousand, huh? I *hope* that check was 'very modest,' because otherwise you got taken."

Her chin lifted a notch. "I bought it from a friend."

"Oh, God," he groaned. "Annie, don't you know better—"

"And as long as we're on the subject," she continued, "I live on the third floor of an old house that one might politely call 'charming.' It's big, but it's not air-conditioned, there's no dishwasher, and in winter the storm windows leak. I admit to having some expensive clothes, but I bought them years ago in Europe with money my father gave me to keep me from coming home. Everything I buy now comes from local department stores, not designer boutiques. So, you see, I work not out of some sense of noblesse oblige but because I'd starve if I didn't. And if you want the *whole* truth, you make more than I do."

"Okay," Connor laughed. "I'm convinced. I'll put you on the list of charities I send money to at Christmastime." And as they got into their respective sides of the steamy-hot car, he leaned back against the door to look at her. "I guess I have to apologize again for jumping to conclusions. But, Anne, you realize the only information I've ever had about your family is what I see. And what I see is Yesterday's Dream. As you said, the place is worth a fortune. Smoke and soot notwithstanding, the manor is a damned museum."

Pausing briefly, he added, "I'm sorry. I didn't know your father left Aaron a bigger chunk of the pie than he left you."

Anne's lips thinned as she turned the key in the ignition. "He didn't. We each got half."

Connor didn't respond immediately, but she felt him watching her as she backed out of the parking space and headed across the bumpy dirt lot toward the exit.

"That's very interesting," he murmured finally. "You each got half. And you still have to earn a living . . . So how do you think Aaron manages to afford a new Jaguar every year when he's never worked a day in his life?"

Anne clutched the steering wheel, oblivious to its searing heat. They were approaching the end of the line of cars where she had to turn right to head out the exit. Straight ahead was a quay that served as a dock for large boats, and she stared at the sun sparkling on the water as she moved her foot to the brake and drew a painful breath. Then, before she could change her mind, she started to say, "Con, I'm not sure about this, but I think Aaron's been—"

"Hey—" Connor straightened abruptly. "Anne, slow down!"

The brake pedal slapped to the floor beneath Anne's foot without a scrap of resistance, and it didn't come back up.

"I can't stop!" she cried.

"Pump it!" he ordered.

"I'm *trying!*"

And that was all either of them had time to say. She'd reached for the emergency brake, her hand just gripping the handle, when the car bounced over the edge of the quay, sailed out into midair between two white sailboats, then dove, nose first, into twelve feet of water.

Chapter Seven

"Get out before it sinks!" Connor unsnapped his seat belt as water poured in through the car's open windows. "Forget the door. Just swim out the window."

Anne heard the words, but she couldn't move. Her heart was racing, light and fast, and her entire body was trembling. It should have been easy. No reason to panic. But in those few heart-stopping seconds that the car had been in midair, she'd traveled through a time warp. Suddenly, she was thirteen again. The hot, sunny day was a chilly spring night. Her white dress was a nightgown. And the water rising past her legs, her waist, her chest, was the cold, deep water of the Chesapeake Bay.

Only instinct made her take a breath before the water covered her head. The car began its downward journey through the murky darkness, and, for a second or two, Anne's rational mind tried to do battle with her subconscious. She felt Connor's hand on her arm, urging her to hurry, and she actually reached for the window frame to pull herself out. But the seat belt and harness held her fast. Then, from above, the net bag containing the volleyballs, now plastered to the car roof, floated down over her shoulders and head, and, in that instant, she lost all touch with reality. The knot of anxiety inside her stretched past the breaking point and burst, its poison spreading rapidly throughout her body. The poison had a name—terror—and it drove her as no other emotion ever had or ever would.

Her hands tore at the net, her arms flailing as she tried to get free. Her eyes were open wide, but she couldn't see. Couldn't hear. Couldn't breathe. She knew only the water, the net, the burning in her lungs. The fear. The specter of death looming as a certainty before her. Her punishment for disobedience. For daring to speak the truth.

The car bounced onto the muddy river bottom. Twelve feet to the surface, but it could have been a hundred. She wouldn't have known the difference. Her mind dimmed, her thoughts reduced to a litany that consisted of one word: *Help!*

But when help came, in her panicked state she identified it as further peril. The hands untangling her from the net were tying her up in it. And they were trying to strangle her when they pulled her forcefully away from the window—the only escape she knew. She fought the arms that clamped around her ribs and chest, clawed and scratched and beat at them. And when those steel hands dragged her backward and locked her against a body she instinctively recognized as male, she resisted with the mindless strength of a madwoman.

Kicking and shoving, her white dress floating up around her, her body twisting in a frenzied effort to free itself from the loathsome embrace, she had no awareness of being hauled out the passenger's door and upward, toward the surface. The water temperature rose, the pressure dropped, the gloom lightened, and still she fought. Nor did she stop after she broke through into the sunshine. Coughing and choking, she tried to fight. And the instant she was able to gulp a lungful of air, she screamed.

It came out in a hoarse choke. To her, though, the sound was deafening, and she went on making it, over and over again. She didn't hear the man holding her gasp her name.

"Anne! Anne...stop! Let me— Ouch!"

Nor did she hear the splashes and shouts of others jumping in to help.

"Hang on to her, Con! We're almost there!"

"Anne, listen! You're okay!"

"She ain't list'nin', buddy. She's out of it.... Damn!"

"Okay. Okay, now, Ed, get 'er arm."

"Careful, she'll...go back down if you...let go."

"Relax, Con, she's not going anywhere. You need help?"

"No. Just . . . get her out."

Then there were many hands dragging her through the water—all drowning her. She was weakening, her struggles growing feeble, but she kept fighting because to give up was to die. Every scrap of strength she possessed was concentrated in her single-minded attempt to thwart the efforts of those trying to save her—to save her from herself.

A siren approached, grew louder, then suddenly stopped. Urgent words were exchanged over her head as she was passed from hand to hand—hands on her everywhere, too many to fight—and in spite of her, they lifted her up the five feet of concrete wall rising above the water, onto the quay.

Being out of the water should have helped, but by then she was too far gone to notice the difference. Her strength was drained, her screams mere whimpers. But still Anne remained caught in the past, her body, her mind, all her senses absorbed in reenacting the most vivid and powerful nightmare of all.

It was a voice that finally broke the spell, although it took a minute for her brain to sort it out from among the other voices around her.

"Anne!"

"What's the matter with her?"

"Is she hurt?"

"Anne, talk to me. Say something."

"Don't seem to be nothin' broken anywhere."

"She's breathing all right. But, damn, she's shaking hard enough to rattle teeth, ain't she?"

"Looks hysterical to me."

"Slap her face a little, Ben. See if you can snap her out of it."

"No! Don't hit her!"

"Relax, Con. You know me better than that. Who is she, anyway? New friend of yours?"

"An old friend. Here—let me have her."

"Crissakes, she just about drowned the both of you, and you want her back again?"

"She's not going to hurt me."

"What about you, Con? You okay?"

"I'm fine. Now, let her go, Ben. I've got her. . . . Annie, look at me."

A man's voice, deep and gentle despite its raw, breathless quality. Her brain registered the familiar sound and all the

pleasant feelings associated with it. And at the instant of rec-
ognition, her breath caught in her throat, choking off another
hoarse scream.

"Easy," he said softly. "Everything's all right now."

She hung for a moment between past and present, holding
her breath, every muscle in her body tense.

"Anne? Listen—it's over. No more water. You're safe."

"C-Connor?" she whispered.

"Open your eyes, Sunshine, and take a look. I'm right here."

She felt a gentle hand pushing the wet hair out of her eyes as
she blinked against the sunlight, and finally she was able to
meet his gaze. His eyes were bloodshot, his face drawn beneath the dripping wet black hair. But he smiled at her, and
suddenly reality clicked back into place.

They were slumped gracelessly on the quay, their sodden
clothing streaked with oil and gasoline from the marina water.
Connor's hands were holding her upper arms, and her fists were
pressed against his chest. There was an angry red scratch on the
right side of his jaw, one on his neck, more on his arms, and his
green T-shirt was ripped along the left shoulder. Taking in his
battered state, her eyes returned to meet the warmth and concern of his steady blue gaze. Then she burst into tears.

"Oh, Lord!" Her hands flew to cover her face. "Oh, Con,
what . . . what have I—"

"Anne, it's okay," he said, wrapping a hand around her neck
to pull her forehead against his shoulder.

"The water, and— and the n-net . . . it must have been
the . . . the b-bag of balls . . ."

"I know."

"I'm s-sorry," she choked out. "I could have drowned us
both, and I—"

"No," he cut her off.

"But you—"

"It's not that deep. There was never any danger that I'd have
let *either* of us drown." Pausing, he growled, "That was the
damnedest thing, though, the brakes going out like that. When
was the last time—"

"Con, I need to know if either of you want an ambulance."

Anne went still at the sound of another man's voice, then her
head came up with a jerk. A tall, middle-aged man in a uni-
form stood looking down at them. And there were others, a
dozen or so strangers, all men, gathered around. She cast a

quick look at the crowd, saw the gaping curiosity, the blatant stares. She'd been quaking inside and out, tears pouring down her cheeks like rain, but in those few seconds the tears dried and her insides tied themselves back up in knots.

"Are you hurt anywhere?"

Connor asked the question quietly, and her gaze flashed to him. He was holding her hand, and, when their eyes met, his fingers squeezed hers. Don't be bothered by the crowd, he was telling her. But it was hopeless.

She pulled away from him, dropping her gaze as she mumbled, "I'm okay."

"You sure?"

"I'm . . . not hurt. Just . . . please. Can we go?"

It wasn't that simple. The policeman, Ben Whitlow, needed information for his accident report. And her car was sitting on the bottom of the marina, where one of the deep-keeled sailboats might run into it.

Connor dealt with the practical matters, and Anne knew he did his best to hurry. But it seemed like forever that she sat, freezing under the blazing sun, on one of the pilings along the top of the quay. With her back to the water, her hands folded in the lap of her ruined white dress, and her bare feet together—Lord knows where her shoes were—she stared at the waves of heat rising from the hood of Ben Whitlow's patrol car and tried to look composed. It had never been a more difficult task.

Eventually, Whitlow, who seemed to be a friend of Connor's, as did most of the people who'd gathered at the scene, offered them a ride home. Helping her into the back seat of the patrol car, then sliding in beside her, Connor asked the policeman for a blanket. She guessed it was to keep the seat from getting wet, but when Whitlow produced a wool Army blanket from the trunk, Connor wrapped it, then his arm, around her shoulders, murmuring, "Your skin's like ice. You sure you don't want Ben to swing by the hospital and have them check you out?"

She shook her head. But as she clutched at the blanket, offering him a whispered "Thank you," she knew he wasn't fooled in the least by her flimsy attempt at self-possession.

"Hey, Ben, do me a favor," Connor said as they drove out of the parking lot. "Go through Easton."

"Sure," the other man agreed. "You want to stop somewhere?"

Connor hesitated. "No."

"Then why go the long way? You got something against the—" The policeman cut himself short, and Anne saw him give her a quick once-over in his rear-view mirror. "Oh, yeah," he murmured. "Guess the ferry might not be a great idea, at that."

Connor didn't reply, but Anne knew what he was thinking. He wasn't bothered by the notion of crossing the Tred Avon on the tiny, seven-car Oxford-Bellevue ferry. But he was guessing that she might be. And he was right.

She'd forgotten what it was like to be the focus of his keen regard, and how fiercely protective he was of those to whom he gave his affection and his unswerving loyalty. She'd also forgotten how, when he was paying attention, he always seemed to have an uncanny sense of what was going on inside her. All of which made her wonder how she was going to explain this to him.

They'd been swimming together hundreds of times in water much deeper than that dredged marina. Would he assume her hysterical behavior was merely a reaction to the accident? Or would he realize how truly phobic she'd become of water? And, if he did, and if he asked her how it had happened, what on earth would she tell him?

Anne rode in silence, listening to the absent replies Connor offered in answer to Ben Whitlow's attempts at conversation. She was aware of his frequent glances, but she kept her eyes glued to the back of the front seat. Gripping the edges of the blanket together over her breasts, she held herself as still as she was able beneath the weight of his arm, which remained steadfastly around her shoulders.

When they arrived at the estate, Connor solved the problem of how she was going to get into Sandcastle without a key before she'd even thought of it. He had Whitlow stop at the caretaker's house, where, although his mother's car was gone, he took an extra key from the housekeeper's set. Anne expected to be dropped off at Sandcastle while Connor went the rest of the way to Sentinel. But when they pulled to a stop at her cottage, he got out with her.

Anne gave him a startled look as he said their goodbyes to Ben Whitlow. Then, when he put a hand under her elbow and guided her to the front door, she said, "You didn't have to come in with me. You must want to go change clothes."

Connor dropped his soggy work boots and socks, which he'd taken off in the car, beside the front door, then stuck the key into the lock and turned it. "I'm not the one who's freezing," he said, ushering her inside. "Being wet when it's ninety-five degrees feels okay to me."

It should have felt okay to her, too, but without the blanket, which she'd left in the car, she was cold again. Anne stepped into the sitting room, then turned to watch Connor close the door. It clicked shut behind him, but he held on to the knob as his eyes met hers.

Now, she thought, he'd start asking questions. And she simply couldn't face it. Not when she could barely keep herself together. She'd end up saying things she didn't want to say, telling him things she intended never to tell him.

When Connor came slowly toward her, Anne took an involuntary step backward. "Con, I— I need to get out of—"

"Now, let's see . . ."

"—this dress and take a shower and—"

"Where were we?"

He pulled her into his arms, and her fists balled against his chest, her body stiffening like a board against his. "Con, I'm— I'm okay. Really. You don't have to—"

"Annie, do you have any idea how scared I was?"

She hesitated in mid-sentence. "Y-you?"

"God, yes," he said, his voice rumbling in her ear. "That water was so filthy black. I couldn't see you. When I found you all tangled up in that damned net, I thought—" He broke off, a shudder running through him. "I thought I was going to lose you, and I couldn't have stood it. Not again. Not that way."

A tiny moan escaped her, but her shoulders stayed hunched, her elbows tight against her sides, and her hands remained clenched between them.

He stroked her hair, which had dried in dull waves. "I'd have drowned before I'd have come up without you."

"No!" The denial burst from her, harsh, emphatic.

"It's true," he insisted quietly. "I told you it couldn't have happened, but down there, I thought, God, what if I can't get her out? What if she's too tied up in the net? What if the seat belt won't open? And I know, no matter what happened, I couldn't have left you."

His hands moved up and down her back, finding the knots of tension, massaging them gently. "Anne . . . tell me it's over, and that I don't have to worry. Hold on to me, Sunshine. Put your arms around me and tell me you're safe."

Her muscles twitched. A shiver raced up her spine. "C-Connor . . . ?"

"I'm right here. And I'm not going anywhere."

"It's . . . hard to . . ."

"It's just you and me. Nobody you have to pretend with."

Her breath caught, seeped out, then caught again.

"Let it go, Annie," he urged. "Don't keep all that bad stuff bottled up inside you."

She couldn't have if her life had depended on it. "Con—" Her hands unclenched, and her fingers gripped his shirt. "Oh, Con . . ." And as the tension inside her unraveled, she let out an agonized groan and collapsed against him.

It was like watching a sheet of glass shatter. Or an iceberg crack apart and melt in a warm ocean. Connor caught Anne in his arms, knowing if he hadn't she'd have been doubled up on the floor. All at once she was shaking so hard her legs wouldn't support her, and her body was wracked with the most heart-wrenching sobs he'd ever heard. And he thought that, whatever he'd expected to find beneath the brittle facade she'd tried so hard to maintain, this wasn't it.

This was something much greater, something far more deeply rooted, than anything the morning's experience could have produced. Her terror was a tangible thing that washed over him, chilling his blood as though it were hers. For a brief instant he wondered what in God's name he thought he was doing, deliberately taking her meager defenses away from her. Was it really for her sake that he'd set out to break them down? Or was he simply unable to bear the idea of her shutting him out?

He remembered the moment below the water's surface, when he'd realized she was panicked and that, if he couldn't drag her from the car, she'd be lost to him. At that instant, the notion of being separated from her, physically, emotionally, or any other way, had become intolerable. So, yes, he guessed it could have been his own need that had driven him to do this to her.

But not entirely. Instinctively, he knew she needed this the way she needed air to breathe. This sobbing, nearly hysterical woman was so much better than the rigid stranger who'd appeared back on the quay and who'd ridden beside him all the way home. She felt real and alive. She felt like the Anne he'd known almost all his life, the woman he'd have died trying to save that morning. With her delicate, small-boned form trembling in his arms, her face buried against his neck, and her fingers digging holes in his back, she felt like the woman who'd haunted his dreams last night—a hope and a promise of something wonderful he wanted badly to have and didn't dare touch.

But he was touching her now. And the longer he stood there, holding her, the harder it became to remember why it had seemed so important that he not let this happen. That he not care about her this much or get this close. That he keep things light and friendly between them. Light and friendly was a joke. Reality was the terror wracking Anne's slender body. She needed to be held. She needed someone to hold on to. Clearly, she'd needed it for years. And if he hadn't been aware enough in the past to give her what she needed, he was now.

Eventually, after an eon or two had passed, words began to form out of the chaos of her emotions.

"Cold," she rasped. "So...cold. Couldn't...breathe. I thought you were...trying to drown me, but it wasn't you, it was— Oh, Lord! Oh, Con, I was...so upset and I was going to tell you, and then we just f-flew into the water, and it was almost like...like I *had* told you and... But that can't be! It just can't!"

For a while she babbled semi-coherent phrases, things about nets and her hands being tied, something about letting her die. He didn't try to sort it out but simply held her. And long after her shaking had subsided and her crying had calmed to an occasional hiccough, he went on stroking her back, murmuring reassuring words, and pressing brief, tender kisses in her hair and on her forehead.

His actions were spontaneous, completely unguarded. He'd stopped planning his tactics some time ago. So he didn't know how it happened that, one minute he was kissing her temple— or maybe it was her cheek—and the next thing he knew, her lips were trembling against his. Had he made the move, or had she? He didn't know, but she wasn't pulling away. Her lips were soft and warm and moist. Salty-sweet from her tears. He touched them again. And again. And each time his mouth lingered against hers a little longer.

He'd seen this coming. He'd told himself to avoid it. But the morning had left him nearly as vulnerable as she, and he simply didn't have it in him to resist. To hell with common sense. To hell with worrying about tomorrow. For once, he was going to take something he wanted when it was being offered, something he felt deep inside was rightfully his.

When he brought his mouth together with hers for the fourth time, it was a deliberate act. His lips opened over hers, then slowly closed, tugging persuasively at her upper lip, then her lower one. She made a throaty little sound, a combination of surprise and arousal, then her lips parted beneath his, moving in a hesitant, almost innocent caress that sent shards of desire slicing through him.

"Anne..." Connor sucked in a quick breath. "Ah, Annie, where have you been?" He'd been waiting so long, it seemed. Waiting for her. He didn't understand it. Wouldn't ever have thought of it that way. But having her in his arms, kissing her like this, it flashed through his mind that he'd needed her to come home so *he* could come home. *Home,* that place of warmth and safety. That special place where dreams came true and the world was his for the taking—or the asking. And, inexplicably, Anne made that place possible. She made it real.

He had one exquisite moment of being there, of seeing it, touching it, feeling it embrace him. Then, suddenly, something went wrong. Anne was pushing him away, resisting the pressure of his fingers threaded through her hair. He stopped to look at her, but she turned her head aside and lowered her gaze.

Had he imagined her response? Could it have been wishful thinking? Last night's fantasy overshadowing reality? He hadn't thought so. But her entire body was tense against his, her lips pressed tightly together in refusal, and he thought, yes, maybe he'd conjured her arousal out of his own. As for the rest, all those wonderful feelings of homecoming...well, now sure as hell wasn't the time to wonder where they'd come from.

"Anne...?"

She stepped back immediately, wrapping her arms protectively around her middle. "I— I'm not very...I shouldn't have—"

She broke off, and for several painful moments silence hung between them.

Connor drew a ragged breath. "I'm sorry."

She shook her head. "I'm ... well, I'm pretty worn out and ... and—" She broke off, and silence descended once more.

"I should go," he said, wanting her to contradict him, wanting her to reassure him that he hadn't made a mistake. But she only cast her gaze around the room and made an ambiguous, fluttering gesture with one hand that told him nothing.

Half-turning away from her, he spoke in a voice that was tightly controlled. "Are you going to be okay?"

Her reply was barely audible. "I'll be fine."

"Sure?"

"Yes." She nodded. Then she spoke with a little more warmth and conviction. "I'm sure. You— You go ahead."

His eyes raked over her once, quickly, then he walked toward the door. "I told Mel, the guy from the garage, to call me about your car when he's had a chance to look at it."

"Oh, you shouldn't have to be bothered with—"

"It's not a bother." Taking hold of the doorknob, he turned back to her. "Besides, there's no phone here."

"Oh. Well, yes ..." She frowned. "There is that."

"You're going to need transportation," he continued. "The garage is bringing my truck out late this afternoon. I'll be leaving for class at five, and tomorrow morning I've got some things to do. But I can take you into Easton in the afternoon, if you want to rent a car."

"If it's no trouble."

"I'll pick you up around one." Pulling the door open, he started to leave, but she stopped him.

"Connor?"

He glanced over his shoulder, not quite meeting her gaze.

"Thank you for ... for everything," she said. And her voice seemed to reach for him, across the room, sending him some message that went beyond the words she spoke.

He didn't try to interpret the message but tossed her a brief, forced smile and said, "What are friends for?" Then, feeling more of a fool than he'd felt in years, he walked out, closing the door behind him.

Anne listened to the door click shut and thought she'd never heard a more desolate sound. A minute ago her body had been melting with arousal. Real, take-your-breath-away arousal. Now it was numb. Numb and cold.

She stared at the door, tears trickling down her cheeks, wishing Connor would come back, wishing he would kiss her again. Wishing he would make her *feel* again. It was a mistake, she wanted to tell him. I didn't really want you to stop.

But she had wanted him to. Then. And she had little, if any, hope that a repeat performance wouldn't end the same way.

Why would he want to kiss her again, anyway? What man would want to face rejection a second time? She'd seen the confusion, the hurt and disappointment, in his eyes. And she realized she'd seen that same look before, all those times in the past he'd approached her in friendship and she, in her desperate efforts to keep her shameful secrets, had frozen him out. She hadn't known she was hurting him then. But she knew now, and it filled her with despair to think it might always be this way. Always.

He'd given her so much. Lord, he'd just given her what she'd never had from another living soul: a shoulder to cry on, a pair of strong arms to keep her safe, an open heart filled with warmth and tenderness from which she could draw strength. And what had she given him in return? Pain.

She didn't want to hurt him. She wanted to love him. She wanted to share herself with him the way he shared himself with her. She wanted to give him pleasure. She wanted to give him . . . everything.

She wanted him to give her another chance.

Chapter Eight

Anne spent a long time in the shower washing the oil and gasoline from her skin, but she couldn't wash away the sick feeling of dread that clutched at her stomach. After getting dressed, she spent an hour wandering around the silent cottage. Sitting on the couch, staring at the wilted flowers on the coffee table. Lying on the bed, staring at the ceiling. Standing in front of the refrigerator, staring at food she couldn't possibly eat. She straightened the bedroom, putting her things into her suitcase, then setting the case back behind the door, where it had been since she'd arrived. All the while, she was waiting.

Something terrible was going to happen. She felt it. She felt *him*. He wasn't gone. He was close—and getting closer.

When she couldn't stand listening to her mind's irrational machinations anymore, Anne walked over to the caretaker's house, looking for company. But Mrs. McLeod still wasn't home, and after she'd fought off her disappointment, she decided it was just as well. If she told Mrs. McLeod about the accident, the older woman would shower her with sympathy, which would make her cry again, and she couldn't burden Connor's mother.

What she really needed, Anne decided, was a phone....

Hesitating, her common sense saying Mrs. McLeod wouldn't mind, she ran her fingers around the rim of the porch lamp in search of the key once kept there for emergencies. Amazingly, it was still in its place, but when she went to use it, she found the door unlocked. As careful as she was about locking doors, it threw her to recall that, in this out-of-the-way place, people were more relaxed about security.

Replacing the key, Anne stepped inside, her sandals slapping softly on the dark pine floor as she walked through the hallway into the kitchen. The phone hung on the wall by the back door, but as she reached for the receiver, a note pinned to the bulletin board beside the phone caught her eye: *Con: As planned, am picking up Nancy this a.m. and going into D.C. to have lunch with Maureen and shop for the baby. Have decided to stay the weekend at Nancy's. If Anne needs me, have her call.*

No doubt Connor would be pleased to have his mother's attention focused on something more positive than a fire-riddled house, and Anne had to agree, it was for the best. Still, as selfish as it might be, she wished Mrs. McLeod were coming home.

Picking up the receiver, Anne dialed the phone, waiting through four rings until a woman's voice answered.

"Dr. Abrams' answering service."

Her breath escaped in a quiet groan. "The doctor isn't in?"

"She's on vacation this week," the operator replied.

Anne realized her mistake even as the woman spoke. Miriam Abrams had told her that she'd be away, but since her visits had been cut to every other week and she hadn't been scheduled for this week, the information hadn't registered. It seemed more than ironic that the one time in six years she had an emergency, Dr. Abrams wasn't available.

The answering service operator went on to explain, "Dr. West is taking Dr. Abrams' calls, if you'd like to leave a message."

Anne thought about it. Then, drawing a ragged breath, she said, "No. I'll wait and talk to Dr. Abrams when she gets back."

Hanging up the phone, her hand clung to the receiver as she squeezed her eyes closed. She couldn't wait until Monday. She couldn't wait until tomorrow. She needed to hear Miriam Abrams' voice, the calm voice of reason. Needed to hear *someone* tell her that the world was still turning and that she was perfectly fine.

"So, Anne," she could hear Dr. Abrams saying, "it sounds as if you're having some anxiety."

"Yes."

"Is it as bad as it used to be?"

"Close. I knew being back at Yesterday's Dream would be hard, but..."

"You got more than you bargained for?"

"Much more. It started off so badly with Connor. Then I discovered the missing books and art, and I didn't know whether to tell Howard Stone or Con... whether to risk telling anybody. But I think I'd have done the right thing if my car hadn't gone into the water."

"Ah. The threat."

"Yes. I'd have drowned if Con hadn't been there. But then he kissed me, and now—"

"Connor kissed you?"

"Yes. But I ruined it, and now things are all unsettled between us again. And it just seems like... Well, I know it sounds paranoid, but it *feels* like everything's conspiring against me. Like...like the house or the place or *something* is trying to scare me off. It's ridiculous, but it feels like he's here somewhere. He can't be. I mean, he *isn't*. But, well, that's how it feels. And I'm afraid if I have to spend the night alone in that cottage again, with no phone and no car, I'll be a basket case by morning."

"So...what would you like to do?"

"Run away...well...no. That's not true. I don't want to leave Connor."

"I see."

"And I don't want to give up, either. I know I never wanted to come back here, and I'm never going to want to live here again, but it's my home! It *belongs* to me! I hate it that it feels like I'm forbidden to be here."

"So you'll force yourself to stay there alone? With no car and no phone?"

"I can't. I just can't."

"What are your alternatives?"

Anne's eyes blinked open, the question hanging in her mind. What *were* her alternatives? With Mrs. McLeod away, the caretaker's house was as empty, and therefore as vulnerable, as Sandcastle. And she couldn't...no, she couldn't ask Connor if she could stay at Sentinel with him, though the idea was enormously appealing.

But where else could she go, and how would she get there? She couldn't even pay for a cab. She thought of Howard Stone and started to dial his number, then hung up when she remembered he'd said he was leaving at noon to go...where?...for the weekend. She couldn't remember. She'd been too upset when she left his office to remember much of anything.

More than a little desperate, Anne leaned against the wall, wrapped her arms around her waist, and ordered herself not to panic. The word *trapped* flashed through her mind, and she quickly pushed it away. She wasn't trapped. She was temporarily stranded, which didn't mean she had to be isolated.

She did her best to hold that positive thought as she picked up the receiver and punched out another number. Yet again her efforts were thwarted. Her closest friend, Diane Hitzrow, was out with her husband for the day, according to the babysitter. Janet Stilts didn't answer. Sister Bernadette at St. Catherine's School was away on summer retreat.

By the time Anne had made her seventh call, she'd run out of numbers to dial; everybody was either at work or away on vacation or out for the day, and with every failed attempt to make contact with a familiar, sympathetic voice, her resolve not to panic weakened. She ceased to care that she was behaving like a paranoid, crazy woman. Her entire purpose in life had been reduced to one thing: to get through the night without coming completely unglued.

"What are your options?" she imagined Dr. Abrams asking.

"I don't have any more."

"Oh? I thought you mentioned one other."

"All right. Yes. But it's four-thirty already. He'll be leaving soon."

"And you can't go with him?"

"He won't even want to see me, much less take me with him."

"Because of the way you reacted when he kissed you?"

"It was awful. He didn't know I was afraid. He thought I was rejecting him, and...he was hurt. I have to apologize, but...well, that's not enough. Not for Con. He'll want to know why I froze up...why I got scared."

"Yes...so...?"

So, she couldn't explain. No, it was impossible. After all the years of keeping the secret, the idea of telling it felt nearly sacrilegious, like robbing a grave. But, sooner or later, she had to tell Connor *something*—unless she was planning simply to run away and never see him again. A notion more impossible than the first.

There had to be a way. And in her desperation to find one, at last it occurred to Anne that, although she couldn't tell Connor the entire story, she might tell him part of it. The general facts...without the details. Enough so that he'd understand her fear and wouldn't think it was *him* she was rejecting. She could manage that, couldn't she? He'd be horrified and, no doubt, enraged. But he wouldn't be destroyed—and neither would her fragile hopes for the future.

Quickly, Anne scribbled a note to Mrs. McLeod and pinned it to the bulletin board. Then she left the house and started up the driveway to Sentinel. Her floppy sandals slowed her pace, and she told herself there was no need to hurry; Connor couldn't leave without passing her. But she was beyond the point where common sense and self-administered pep talks made any difference.

Her eyes darted nervously to the woods on either side of the sun-dappled lane. Every ten steps she glanced over her shoulder. And every time she did, her pace increased. She felt exposed, vulnerable, easy prey.

By the time she reached Sentinel, she was running, stumbling when her sandals caught on bumps in the road. When she saw that Connor's truck wasn't there, her heart sank, and she collapsed against one of the pines along the drive to the cottage. Then she remembered he didn't have his truck, that someone from the garage was bringing it to him. The possibility that the truck hadn't yet arrived and that Connor was still home pushed her away from the tree and toward the back door.

She knocked twice, then she banged, peering around the curtains that partially covered the windowpanes. But finally she had to accept that she'd missed him. Now she was truly alone. Not another soul anywhere to talk to...or run to.

Groaning, Anne sagged against the door. Her fears were foolish, entirely unfounded. Somewhere in her head she knew that. But standing outside Connor's empty cottage at the end of that silent, lonely point of land, with the sun headed toward the western horizon, she felt eyes on her back. And the feeling wouldn't go away.

He was here, somewhere. Waiting for dark. Waiting to catch her. And there would be no one to stop him. There never was.

With that hopeless thought, Anne rolled her head to the side and opened her eyes. Then, seeing the furry black form streaking up the beach toward the cottage, she instantly straightened. With a little sob, she skipped down the steps and hurried to the front of the cottage, where she posted herself by the screened porch to prevent her potential companion from disappearing through his doggy door and being lost to her.

Rogue had no intentions of disappearing without greeting her. He barreled toward her, slowing only fractionally as he approached. Anne dropped to her knees, and he ran straight into her arms, nearly knocking her over.

"Oh, you wonderful animal!" she exclaimed, wrapping both arms around his neck. "You don't know how glad I am to see you!"

Rogue covered her with licks as she petted and hugged him, but after several moments of unbridled affection, he broke away.

"Rogue! Wait!" Jumping to her feet, she followed him onto the porch, and she was ashamed to hear the quaver in her voice as she pleaded, "Stop! Oh, please, don't go."

He crossed the porch, then halted in front of the door to wait for her. It took Anne a few moments to interpret his stance—tail swishing as he panted, his eyes glued to the door. Finally he gave her a couple of barks, and she realized he expected her to open it. When she made no move to do so, he crouched to slither through his private entrance.

Eyeing the hinged metal plate in the bottom panel, Anne weighed her level of desperation. The upper half of the door consisted of uncurtained panes of glass, and she watched as Rogue stood up, turned, and looked at her. His deep bark was only slightly muted, and its meaning was obvious.

"I can't!" she called to him. "It's locked. See?" Taking hold of the knob, she went to rattle it, wanting to show him that at least she'd tried. But the knob didn't rattle. In fact, it turned quite easily, and Anne let out a startled sound when the door swung open, affording her entry into Connor's living room.

Rogue sat down, cocked his head, and lifted his ears as if to say, "Well?"

Anne stared at him for an instant. Then suddenly she grinned, stepping inside to quickly close the door behind her.

It felt nearly as good as stepping into Connor's arms. The old stone cottage embraced her, and the knots in her stomach immediately began to relax. He wouldn't come here. He'd always avoided Connor, or tried to. But all that was foolishness, anyway. He wasn't here. He was gone. She'd never have set foot back on Yesterday's Dream if she hadn't been assured of that.

As the churning inside her slowly dissipated, she began to take in her surroundings. Connor's home. The place bore no resemblance to the cottage she remembered. The brocade chairs and Queen Anne tea table had been replaced with a rattan couch piled with pillows, a bentwood rocker, and a drop-leaf table along the back of the couch. The mantel above the stone fireplace, a single rough-hewn beam, was no longer graced with Delft china but a large piece of driftwood and an earthenware vase filled with scarlet zinnias. Instead of plush drapes, a profusion of hanging and potted plants decorated the two large windows, filtering the late-afternoon sun and bathing the room in mellow gold. The overall effect was bright and comfortable, and Anne loved it.

What she loved most, though, were the books that lined every inch of wall space. Moving slowly around the room, she took inventory. Sections of classics and recent popular titles. Then, three sections of volumes with the words McLeod Press printed on their spines—literary works published by Connor's father and grandfather, many of them winners of prestigious awards. It seemed to her a crime that there would be no others. A worse crime than the one Connor's grandfather had committed that ultimately cost Connor's father, Ian McLeod, the company.

With a wave of anger, Anne recalled the story she'd heard so many times. Connor had been eleven when the government had filed suit against McLeod Press for repeated dumping of printer's ink into a tributary of Massachusetts Bay. The violation had occurred thirty years earlier, before the environmental protection laws were passed, but the laws were retroactive. The government won the multimillion-dollar suit, and because McLeod Press was a family-owned business and Ian McLeod himself had guaranteed the company's debts, the McLeods lost not only the business but all personal assets, as well.

The tragedy hadn't stopped there, however. The stress of prosecution, of personal and corporate bankruptcy, and of laying off people who'd been with McLeod Press all their lives had been more than Ian McLeod could bear. He'd died of a heart attack, leaving his wife no recourse but to find a job to support herself and her children. Through mutual acquaintances, Mary McLeod had secured the position at Yesterday's Dream, and she'd made the best of an awful situation. But her son had been one of the most bitter, angry people Anne had ever known when he came to live on the Tred Avon.

How many hours had she listened to Connor's talk of getting back at "The Enemy"? The Enemy meaning the government, the Justice Department attorney who'd prosecuted his father, environmentalists—anyone who might have been remotely responsible for the demise of McLeod Press and his father's death.

It seemed that now, at thirty-four, with his own business prospering, Connor's attitude might have softened. Yet as Anne continued to scan the shelves of books, she wondered. Textbooks, journals, volumes on subjects ranging from marine biology and forestry to business administration and environmental law. Texts on marketing, communications, and engineering. Here was the long-term result of the downfall of McLeod Press. Here she was seeing Connor's self-designed college education. The education he'd missed because he'd been too responsible, too loyal—too good a person—to leave his mother to bear the burden of raising his sisters alone.

Looking at Connor's library, Anne had to wonder if perhaps he still hoped for a future that didn't include chopping trees and fixing boat engines. Given the long hours he worked, she couldn't imagine when he'd have a minute left even to think, much less orchestrate a new future. Yet, when she peeked through the doorway to the tiny downstairs bedroom, she realized instantly that he was certainly orchestrating something of a grand nature.

The room had been transformed into an office, complete with filing cabinets, an L-shaped desk, and computer. Stacks of paper covered every available surface, and she glanced at the stack on the shelf beside the door to read the blue type filling the masthead of a newsletter. *Chesapeake News*, a Bi-Monthly Publication of The Bay Action Group. Not at all the sort of literature she'd have expected Connor to collect.

Picking up the newsletter, she read the lead article about a planned reenactment of the voyage of Captain John Smith, who had first explored the Chesapeake. A modern-day "Captain Smith" was going to retrace the voyage, stopping at ports to talk to citizens in an effort to raise consciousness about the Bay's ecological problems and to outline what must be done to save it.

Impressed, Anne read two other articles, then glanced at the organization's "statement of purpose," which said The Bay Action Group was a nonprofit organization whose goal was "to support and encourage the intelligent management of the Chesapeake Bay." Below was a list of the organization's officers . . . and the name of the editor of *Chesapeake News*. Connor McLeod.

Stunned, Anne looked again at the stack of newsletters, the office, the elaborate computer setup, and quickly realized Connor was both editing and publishing this newsletter. Which explained the computer course he was taking and the books on marine biology, environmental law, and all the rest. What it didn't explain was how he'd come to join forces with The Enemy. Another question to add to her growing list.

Returning to the living room, Anne found Rogue lounging at the foot of the stairs, blocking her path to the bathroom. "Excuse me," she said, stepping over him. "No, don't bother getting up. I'll be back in a minute."

She made her way up the stairs, where a narrow hall divided the cottage into front and back halves, the back half being storage space, and the front a large bedroom. Pointedly ignoring the open bedroom door, she walked to the bathroom tucked between the sloping sides of the roof. But a few minutes later, when she passed the bedroom on her way back downstairs, something bright caught her eye and she forgot not to peek. She looked without thinking, and what she saw brought her to a halt: her yellow scarf, the one she'd tied around Rogue's collar the day before, lying on the table beside Connor's bed.

Hesitating, biting her lower lip, she stepped through the doorway—quietly, as if someone might hear—and crossed the room, stopping beside the brass bed. She looked at the scarf for a moment, then, with her hand trembling, she reached to pick it up.

The scarf might have been anywhere—in the living room, the kitchen—but, no, it was here, by Connor's bed. Which didn't necessarily mean a thing. Maybe this was simply where he'd untied it from Rogue's collar. Then again . . . he *had* kissed her this morning. . . .

Anne tried without success not to let her fantasies run away with her. Her eyes fell to the unmade bed, her expression softening as she unconsciously fingered the silky yellow fabric. Had Connor lain here last night thinking about her? Did having her scarf—looking at it, touching it—make him feel the way she felt looking at the place he slept? The pillow still had a dip where his head had lain, and when she reached hesitantly to touch it, a melting sensation wafted through her.

Could she? Could she ever . . . ? Their kiss this morning, before she'd gotten scared, had promised wonderful things. Tenderness and the sort of fervent, honest passion she would have expected from Connor. He'd wanted her. She knew he had. But would he still?

The scarf gave her hope.

Replacing the scarf exactly as she'd found it, Anne went downstairs to find Rogue lying where she'd left him.

"How about it?" she said, pausing to scratch his ears. "Was dinner good? You know, I'm starting to feel hungry myself. Good sign, huh? What's Con got in the way of people food, I wonder."

Anne found a bag of huge, ripe peaches in the refrigerator, and she picked one out, deciding it would do for now. Then, pulling out a chair at the table, which was cluttered with mail and the day's newspaper, she sat down to eat her peach. But when she tried to gather the spread-out pages of the paper to read them, a stack of opened mail fell to the floor.

With a sigh, Anne moved to collect the scattered sheets, stooping to pick up several letters. Then, at the top of one, she recognized the distinctive logo of one of the country's largest grant foundations. The next letter she plucked off the floor was also from a grant foundation, and, to her increasing puzzlement, so were the others. Not today's mail, she realized, but a stack of letters received over the course of months.

Anne started to set the letters aside, but her eyes slid over the words . . . *we regret to inform you* . . . And once she'd read that much, it was impossible not to read the sentence that began, *Dear Mr. McLeod: We read your proposal with interest, but we regret to inform you that we are unable to make a commitment at this time to a project of this nature.*

A project of *what* nature? What were these foundations rejecting? A glance told her all the letters said the same thing: no.

The floor was still littered with pages filled with paragraphs of text. Not letters, but the mysterious proposal. The bold-faced heading on the top of the first page made her eyes widen in astonishment, and it would have taken an act of God for her to be able to resist reading the rest.

Settling cross-legged on the floor, Anne read each page, and as she finished the last one, there were tears in her eyes. She had her answers now. The answers to all the questions she'd wanted to ask Connor about the past twelve years. She knew the extent to which the angry youth she'd known had come to grips with fate, the extent to which he'd turned his passion and energy to positive use. The extent to which he'd grown into a man. She realized, too, how great his frustration must be over his current life—though he no longer allowed it to show.

How long, she wondered, would he avoid telling her about his dreams? A long time, she thought, if she didn't press. If she hadn't stumbled upon these pages, she might never have known. It was hard to talk about important things, especially when it seemed they might never happen. Safer to keep them secret.

Anne stacked the proposal and the letters neatly on the table, then wandered out onto the screened porch, where Rogue was curled up on the glider, asleep. Sinking onto the canvas hammock that hung between two overhead beams, she lay back to watch the sun drop toward the horizon.

She wouldn't tell Connor she knew his secret. She didn't believe he'd be angry at her for the manner in which she'd found out—he'd never had her ultra-developed sense of privacy—but she wanted to give him the chance to tell her himself. If he would. If he'd trust her not to call it grandiose and foolish. Not to think of him as a hopeless dreamer. As if she ever would.

She was aware she was asking for more than she was prepared to give. She wanted him to tell her everything when she planned only to tell him what he absolutely needed to know. The bare essentials, carefully censored to protect the innocent—the innocent being him. Even then, she worried that he'd decide her problems were more of a burden than she was worth.

Closing her eyes, Anne let out a drowsy sigh. Regardless of the outcome, she'd have to tell Connor something when he came home. For even she was aware enough to know that, when a woman rejected a man's kisses, then showed up at his door asking to spend the night, she darned well owed him an explanation.

Chapter Nine

At ten forty-five, fifteen minutes earlier than he'd ever made it home from class, Connor drove between the entrance posts to Yesterday's Dream. He wouldn't have gone at all, but tonight's class had been the last, and he'd had to take the final. Though he might as well not have bothered; his concentration had been torpedoed by worried thoughts about Anne.

He never should have left her this morning. She'd been horribly upset by the accident, and despite her claim that she was fine, he knew damned well she hadn't been. But he'd been too busy hurrying off to nurse his wounded ego to pay attention to what she might be feeling. As the day had worn on, though, he'd begun to feel guilty as sin.

He shouldn't have kissed her. His timing couldn't have been worse if he'd planned it. He'd had no right to use the emotional intimacy between them as sexual leverage. The line between emotional and physical closeness hadn't been all that clear to him. Kissing Anne had felt right. But obviously it hadn't felt right to her. And he hadn't bothered to ask first.

Hell, for all he knew, she could be involved with someone, and her rejection could have been her way of saying she was otherwise committed. And how would he feel about that?

He couldn't answer the question. Not without putting a label on his feelings for her, which he wasn't willing to do.

Connor passed the caretaker's house without slowing down, having seen his mother's note about her plans to stay at Nancy's. But when he came to the turnoff to Sandcastle, he brought the pickup to a stop and leaned across the seat to look toward the cottage.

The light was on in the bedroom. Anne was still awake.

The pickup's engine rumbled quietly while he chewed his bottom lip and stared at the soft lamplight flickering through the leaves. He wanted to see her. He doubted that she wanted to see him, but his need to know that things were okay between them made him turn onto the track leading to her cottage. He knew he was acting like an adolescent, but the truth was, he *felt* a little like an adolescent when it came to Anne. Kind of breathless and slightly desperate, as if he were caught in something beyond his control.

His insides were quivering as he parked and walked toward the cottage, and, distracted by his anxious thoughts, it took a second before he registered that the door was slightly ajar. Taking hold of the knob with one hand, he rapped lightly. When he got no response, he knocked again.

"Anne? It's Con. Can I come in?"

The door opened into a dark room, and Connor stepped inside, grimacing at the hot, stuffy air. Calling again, he waited but, again, got no answer, and as the light beneath the bedroom door drew his gaze, he crossed the room.

"Anne?" He knocked on the door, calling loudly. "Annie, are you awake?"

Had she fallen asleep with the light on and the front door sitting open? Odd, that door open when every window in the place was closed. Maybe she was asleep, he thought, and, then again, maybe she just didn't want to talk to him. On the other hand, maybe her dunk in the marina had made her ill. Her icy skin, a symptom of shock, perhaps, could have been a prelude to something worse.

Cautiously, Connor opened the door to Anne's bedroom, hoping to see her comfortably asleep, not ill—or sitting there waiting for him to go away. But she wasn't in the room. His eyes drifted from the poster bed, which showed no sign of having been slept in, to the bureau drawer sitting open—and empty.

His gaze snapped to the closet door, and in three strides he crossed the room and yanked it wide to find that the closet, too, was empty. Whirling to face the room again, he searched for some trace of Anne's presence but found only the lit bedside lamp and the open window. Somehow the window had lost its screen, and the breeze had pulled the frilly white curtains over the sill to hang outside. The cottage was closed up but for one forgotten window and the front door sitting open—as if it had been pulled shut in a hurry and hadn't caught.

Anne was gone. But where? And how? Connor didn't yet dare ask himself why.

He slammed the window closed and locked it, flicked off the bedroom light as he passed, and strode out of the cottage, the front door banging shut behind him only seconds before the pickup's engine roared to life. The wide tires spewed gravel as he tore down the drive, pulling to a stop at his mother's side door. Maybe, he thought, Anne had moved over here. Though he didn't know why she would have.

The house was dark. Connor flipped light switches on and off as he went through, checking rooms. He checked them all, but Anne wasn't there. He was starting to panic about where she could possibly be with no car and no money, no means to leave on her own. Then he found her note, pinned beside his mother's, on the bulletin board in the kitchen.

Dear Mrs. McLeod: Forgive me for intruding, but I needed to use the phone and didn't think you'd mind. The following are the long-distance calls I made. Please let me know how much I owe you when you get your bill.

Connor looked over the list of phone numbers and immediately drew a conclusion: Anne had called friends until she'd found one who would come get her.

But why? Because he'd kissed her? Even as the thought occurred to him, he realized how ridiculous it was. She might have been angry or embarrassed; she might have felt awkward, not knowing what to say to him. But a grown woman didn't run away from a man she'd known all her life only because he'd kissed her.

Yet the fact remained: She was gone.

Swearing, Connor stormed out to his truck and raced up the drive at a speed he'd have judged unconscionable had he been thinking clearly. At Sentinel, he parked, walked the thirty feet to the back door, strode through the kitchen and up to his bedroom without turning on a light or even acknowledging Rogue, who'd come to greet him. Tearing off his clothes, tossing them every which way, he fell onto the bed and immediately rolled to his side, drawing a pillow down beside him to hug as he closed his eyes and consciously willed the world to go away.

Rogue's cold nose on his back was an unwelcome intrusion. Connor tried to ignore it, but Rogue persisted, and finally he twisted around to ward him off.

"Cool it," he said, giving the animal half a pet before pushing him gently away. "Go on, go to bed."

Rogue whimpered, nudging Connor's shoulder with his nose, then lifting one paw onto the edge of the mattress.

"Aw, for Pete's sake! What's your problem, huh?" Connor twisted toward him, and as he did, he caught sight of the yellow scarf on the night table.

With a wrenching curse, he snatched it up, wadded it in his fist, and flung it as hard as he could. Then he flopped back onto the bed and lay staring at the ceiling, the rasp of his breathing the only sound in the room.

A minute passed; then something tickled his arm, hanging over the edge of the bed. He turned his head on the pillow, and there was Rogue, giving him a soulful look. And there was the damned scarf, lying across his wrist, where Rogue had draped it.

Connor gave up. Heaving a sigh, he rolled to his side and reached out to scratch Rogue's ears. "It's no good, buddy," he murmured. "She's done it again." And he wished he could say it didn't matter, convince himself that he didn't care that she'd gone without even saying goodbye. But it wasn't going to work this time. He did care. He cared too damned much.

Eventually, Rogue ambled out of the room, his claws clicking on the bare pine boards, and Connor rolled to his back, shutting his eyes as he fought to bring his hurt and anger under control. What good would it do? What good had it *ever* done him to seethe and agonize over things he couldn't change? Raw emotions only clouded his brain.

He knew all that. Still, it was a long while before his heart stopped pounding and his taut muscles began to relax. Finally, taking a deep, slow breath, he opened his eyes and, turning his head, looked out the window at the stars flickering through the leaves of the locust tree.

It was true. Anne had done it to him again. Left with no explanation and without saying goodbye. And, yes, he was hurt and angry. God knows, he was confused. But he couldn't write her off as a snob or a spoiled bitch the way he had in the past. She was neither. She was an extremely thoughtful person who rarely did anything without care and deliberation. Beyond that, she was—and always had been, even when he hadn't known it—his friend. If she'd run away, which it surely looked as if she had, she had a reason. And the reason wasn't him. His worst sins had been bad timing and poor judgment, and he figured he was probably getting what he deserved for kissing a woman when she was still crying and shaking from having nearly drowned.

For that matter, she hadn't been in such terrific shape even before that. With a sound of self-disgust, Connor recalled the agitated state in which he'd found Anne walking down the street in St. Michaels. What had she said? That she'd been to see Howard Stone... but she'd never gotten the chance to tell him what had happened with the attorney to upset her.

Was the estate in trouble? If Aaron's behavior was any indication, the answer had to be no. But then, he'd realized this afternoon, when Anne had enlightened him about the mythical Marquel fortune, that Aaron's lifestyle didn't fit the real picture. He'd asked her how she thought Aaron managed a new Jaguar every year, and she'd started to answer... but, again, she'd never gotten the chance.

Connor frowned. Was Aaron spending Blaine Thorpe's money? From what he'd heard, there was enough of it. But on second thought... the white Jag sitting in the garage was the fifth Aaron had bought in as many years, and he'd only been engaged to Blaine Thorpe for two. Where had all those new cars come from?

That question led to others, and suddenly Connor's thoughts began to churn. He thought about Aaron Marquel's lifestyle—the new cars, the expensive clothes, the frequent trips abroad. He'd always lived like there was no tomorrow, but it had gotten worse this past year, since Kenneth Marquel's death. That's when the parties had started. The parties that he and his mother had been told always to be prepared for and that lasted days, during which the champagne never stopped flowing. He'd often wondered what other substances might be flowing along with the champagne but had decided, as long as it didn't hurt his mother or him, he didn't give a damn.

It wasn't his business what Aaron Marquel did with his life. And the truth was, when he put aside his dislike of the man he'd watched grow from a hostile, selfish youth into a callous, arrogant adult, Connor had to admit that Aaron's spending habits weren't necessarily out of the ordinary for the wealthy.

Except for one salient fact: Aaron wasn't wealthy. He didn't work. And he got only enough money in one year from the estate to buy the equivalent of a five-year-old Volvo with seventy thousand miles on it.

On the other hand, he owned half of a three-hundred-year-old house that appeared on the historic register and that was filled with millions of dollars in art, antiques, and books... a house that, three days ago, had nearly burned to the ground. A house that sat on an extremely valuable piece of property. A piece of property Aaron wanted to sell...but that Anne wanted to keep.

Connor's heart thudded in his chest as the bits of seemingly unrelated information slowly began coming together in his head. He thought about the parade of land developers Aaron had brought to look at Yesterday's Dream. He thought about Aaron announcing that he'd be selling the estate. He thought about Anne stating firmly that she *wasn't* going to sell it. He thought about heater cords and fires. And when his brain was full to bursting with suspicion, his thoughts returned to Anne.

Should he try to get in touch with her and tell her what he was thinking? Quickly he decided it would be better to call Howard Stone. No point in upsetting Anne when he had no proof. And if there was one thing he'd learned in the three days she'd been at Yesterday's Dream, it was how easily she became upset.

It was strange, Connor thought. Anne had always been sensitive, impressionable, but he'd never seen her hysterical. In truth, of the two of them, she'd been the steady one. The one who'd maintained an even keel, while his moods had swung from one extreme to the other.

The longer Connor lay there, listening to the night sounds, feeling the river breeze temper the heat of the day, the stranger Anne's behavior began to seem. And the more concerned he became about her sudden departure. It was just plain too extreme.

While the moon arced across the night sky, he tried to make the things he knew about Anne fit together in a way he could understand. But one mismatched piece led to another, until he was left with a picture of two entirely different women. The one reticent, nervous, easily frightened. The other bright, quick-witted, and thoroughly seductive in her delicate, almost ethereal sensuality.

He'd met the former Anne the morning she'd arrived at Yesterday's Dream. He'd met the latter the following morning in the tree house. And Connor had a feeling that somewhere in the middle of their ill-fated kiss, the two Annes had changed places. He'd started off kissing one and ended up kissing the other. And he wanted to know what the hell had gone on during that kiss to make the switch take place.

Maybe, in a few days, when he could think about her without wanting her, he'd call. Out of friendship, he told himself. Out of concern. Not out of this gut-wrenching, hopeless longing.

Anne awoke when the sun was only a quarter of the way above the eastern horizon. Disoriented, vaguely aware of having heard a noise, she tried to sit up, only to have the bed sway beneath her. When she realized where she was and what time of day it was, she uttered a quiet groan.

A couple of seconds later, she rolled forward to sit and swing her feet to the floor. A movement brought her gaze up in time to see Connor walking past the porch, headed toward the beach with a towel slung over his shoulder and Rogue trotting beside him. Anne opened her mouth to call to him, then shut it, deciding to wait until he came back to explain her presence. By then, maybe, she'd be more awake and less fuzzy-headed.

Her eyes were only half-open as she watched Connor jump down the bluff to the beach, pick up a stick, and toss it into the water for Rogue. But she was jolted into full awareness when he dropped his towel onto the sand and stepped out of his cut-offs.

He had nothing on. Nothing at all. And every stunningly bare inch of him was tanned the same coffee-and-cream brown. His back was to her, and he was thirty yards away, but she saw enough to make her blush to the soles of her feet. Still, despite her embarrassment and the uncomfortable sense that she was spying, Anne couldn't tear her eyes away.

She watched, entranced, as Connor ran into the water, then dove under. Surfacing farther out, he stood up facing the shore, the water lapping around his hips close to the line of decency. Rogue brought him the stick, and he threw it again, then both swam after the floating driftwood for all they were worth.

The game went on for the longest time, and Anne began to feel she was watching some lush travelogue. The sunrise, the water, the pink-golden tones serving as backdrop for the man and his beast. It was the man, though, whose exuberance made the scene come alive, who made her pulse race and her breathing grow shallow. No camera ever could have captured the energy, the sheer passion for life, displayed in every movement of Connor's bare masculine form. He was beautiful. And the sight of him made her wish she could join him, wish she could walk straight into the water, dropping her clothes along the way, and become a part of that alluring scene.

Anne lost track of how long she sat there, watching Connor play with carefree abandon. Finally, as he threw the stick onto the beach and took off in a steady crawl, paralleling the shore toward Sandcastle, it hit her that, when he came back, he'd probably get out. Which meant she had to leave, for she absolutely couldn't cope with the embarrassment of his knowing she'd been a spectator to his private morning ritual.

Anne left Sentinel the way she'd arrived, through the screened porch door. But as she walked down the lane to Sandcastle, her mind was conjuring images not of danger lurking in the trees but of a man diving, naked, through sun-kissed waves.

Connor's usual practice was to swim as far as Sandcastle and back again. He did it twice that morning. Then, walking out onto his own stretch of beach, where Rogue lay waiting for him, he snatched up the towel to wrap around his waist, saying, "What do you say we take the day off? The guys can handle the Layton job without me, and I could stand a break."

Rogue panted as he looked up at him.

"Let's get some breakfast, then walk over to the manor and make sure it got locked up yesterday. Then let's just take it easy, huh? Maybe give Sandy Burns a call.'' Whatever it took, he thought, to get his mind off Anne.

He followed Rogue onto the screened porch and sank down onto the hammock. In a while, he'd take a shower and get dressed. But he didn't often allow himself a day off, and he might as well enjoy it. Lying back to watch the sun rise, he drew a deep breath, his nose twitching in response to a whiff of something sweet and citrusy mingled with the salty air.

The scent was familiar yet out of place, and Connor frowned as he tried to identify it. Turning, he rolled onto his shoulder, following his nose to the source of the pleasant fragrance.

Odd, he thought. The hammock smelled light and sweet and lemony. Like the lemon thyme his mother grew in her herb garden. Like Anne's yellow scarf...

Like Anne.

Chapter Ten

She'd survived the night. Indeed, a good night's sleep had gone a long way toward restoring Anne's sense of balance, and by the time she'd showered and eaten, she was ready to strike a blow for her personal liberation. Connor had said he would pick her up at one o'clock to go to Easton; she would have fifteen miles to make things right between them. But before then, she had things to do.

She was determined never to spend another day like yesterday, sick with fear. She was also determined not to run away. She'd done that. For twelve years, she'd been recovering from having grown up in a hopelessly dysfunctional household, the past six working with Miriam Abrams. Yet, one dunk in the river, and she was back to where she'd begun—or nearly so.

No, running away was not the answer. And neither was running to Connor. It would be easy to fall into the trap of depending upon him—everyone did, didn't they?—but she didn't want to be one of his many burdens. She wanted to be able to depend upon herself. She needed to know that she alone was capable of facing—and defeating—the demons of her past. And the way to banish specters of all kinds, she decided, was to throw them out, literally.

Anne knew exactly where she was going to start. Dressed in her oldest cutoffs and work shirt, armed with boxes of trash bags and a flashlight, she walked up the beach to the manor. Her determination carried her to the front door, at which point she realized she didn't have her keys. She faltered only briefly, though, before recalling she'd left the door unlocked for the antiques restorer, who'd said he'd be coming back. Then, with a last breath of fresh air, she opened the door and stepped inside.

Once again, Anne's senses were assailed by the devastation. The place was such a mess, so godforsaken and forlorn, she couldn't help but feel a pang of regret for all the hateful, bitter thoughts she'd ever had about it. Indeed, seeing it in this sorry state filled her with something approaching compassion. Yesterday's Dream hadn't been the cause of her problems, only the place where they'd begun. In a way, the house had been as much a victim as she, and she shouldn't hold a grudge against it.

Crossing the hall, she started up the damaged stairs. But as she put her foot on the second step, the sound of a door squeaking behind her made her whirl around. The broken banister cracked off in her hand, and she plunked down hard on the third step, flashlight and bags flying as her eyes darted to the open door of the study.

Hadn't it been closed when she'd passed it?

Before she could decide, a movement drew her gaze to the open front door, and, an instant later, she groaned, seeing Connor walk across the porch. The last thing she wanted was for him to find her in the same rattled state in which he'd last seen her—all because she'd heard the front steps squeak under his feet. She was sure that was all it had been.

Standing quickly, arranging herself at the bottom of the stairs, she tried to appear composed. But when Connor reached the doorway, stopping short at the sight of her, one look at his broad-shouldered form ruined her attempt at composure and brought a blush to her cheeks. He was dressed in cutoffs and Docksiders, but the image that sprang vividly to mind was of him swimming naked at dawn.

"Anne?" The light behind him cast his face into shadow, but his deep voice registered shock.

The greeting she returned was breathless. "Hi."

Taking a couple of steps into the hallway, he asked, "What are you doing here? I stopped at Sandcastle last night, on my way home from class. But the place looked empty, and..." He took another step toward her. "Where were you?"

Anne's gaze fell to her fingers, laced together at her waist, as she managed, "I was ... asleep in your hammock."

"In my..."

His words trailed into silence, and she glanced up to find his lips parted and his eyes wide with astonishment.

"Well, at least I wasn't hallucinating," he muttered. At her puzzled expression, he gave his head a quick shake. "Never mind. But why? Was something wrong at Sandcastle?"

"No, I..." She drew a steadying breath and forced the words past the tightness in her chest. "I was scared. Your mother was gone, and I got nervous, thinking about ... well, being alone. I tried to catch you, to see if I could ride along with you to class, but you'd already gone."

"Mel finished the truck early," he said.

"Rogue was there, and your door was unlocked, so I let myself in, and..." Her hand fluttered. "I went out onto the porch to wait for you, but I— I fell asleep." Pausing, she finished on a tentative note. "I hope you don't mind my letting myself in like that."

"Of course not." He moved a step closer. "I'm sorry you missed me."

Anne hesitated, then, before she could change her mind, spoke in a shaky whisper. "I wasn't sure you'd want me with you after ... well, the way I acted yesterday morning when you ... well ... I handled it very badly."

"Ah, Annie, no..." Connor spoke on a sigh as he came to a halt not a foot away from her.

She tried to meet his gaze, but her eyes kept getting caught between the broad expanse of his bare chest and his beard-shadowed jaw, along the right side of which she saw the mark her fingernail had made the day before.

"If either of us handled anything badly," he murmured, "it was me. You'd been scared half to death, and I only wanted to hold you and make it better. I didn't plan on turning it into something else, but ... I got carried away. I'm sorry."

Anne wasn't sorry he'd gotten carried away, but before she could say so, he added, "I saw the note and list of phone calls

you left at Mom's. I thought you must have found someone to
come take you home."

At that, her gaze flew up to meet his. "To Baltimore?"

Connor lifted one bare shoulder in a vague gesture that told
her a great deal about how uncertain he truly was of her and
how much her rejection had affected him. It suddenly became
more important than ever to tell him why his kiss had frightened her. But not here. No, this house was not the place to have
that discussion. Not if she had any hopes of getting through it.

Clearly, quietly, she told him, "I wouldn't have left like that,
Con. Not without saying goodbye."

His eyes searched hers for a moment. "Anne, I'm not ready
to say goodbye."

She held his gaze, thinking she'd never be ready, as she
whispered, "Neither am I."

He looked at her a second or two longer, then his mouth
curved slowly into a smile. "Now that we've got that straight,
why don't you come spend the day with me. I'm taking the day
off, and we could rent you a car, then maybe go for a drive or
to a movie or . . . well, whatever sounds like fun."

It was a straightforward offer, with no trace of innuendo. Yet
the intent, heated look in his eyes made Anne's stomach flut-
ter with that familiar mixture of eagerness and apprehension.
She started to accept the invitation, but as she did, she glanced
at the flashlight and plastic bags scattered across the floor.

Connor followed her gaze with his own. "What's all this?"

"I dropped them," she explained. "I heard you coming up
the steps, and . . . well, the noise startled me."

"What were you on your way to do?"

Anne laughed. "A little ghostbusting, actually."

"Oh?" His eyebrow arched in speculation. "Which—or,
rather, whose—ghost did you have in mind?"

"My mother's—for starters. She's been dead twenty-two
years, and I decided it was time someone gave her a decent
burial. Her room is a shrine, with all her things sitting around
exactly the way she left them."

Connor snorted. "Tell me about it. It's driven Mom crazy for
years to have to send maids in to dust for a dead woman."

"Well, she'll never have to do it again after I'm through."

"Want some help?"

Anne shook her head. "I won't let you spend your day off working. Besides, I can do this tomorrow." But as she said it, she glanced guiltily at the plastic bags.

"Come on." Connor bent to snatch up the flashlight and bags. "Our mothers have both waited long enough for somebody to do the right thing. We can play later."

Anne didn't argue but let him take her hand and lead the way up the stairs.

Twenty minutes later, Connor was taking down drapes and rolling rugs, and Anne was stuffing plastic bags with soot-permeated clothing, all to be sent out and cleaned. They'd opened the four windows to clear the smoky air, and sunlight flooded the large, high-ceilinged room.

Sitting cross-legged on the floor in front of her mother's dresser, Anne sighed as she opened a drawer. "I never realized what a clotheshorse my mother was."

Connor grunted a response as he lifted an upholstered chair off the rug in front of the fireplace. "From the looks of the racks in the dressing room, she never wore anything more than once. Have you decided what you're going to do with this stuff?"

Anne shot him a look over her shoulder. "Have you ever heard of the Goodwill?"

"*All* of it?"

She started to say yes, but then she found a blue angora sweater that brought back memories of her mother's soft, perfumed hugs. With a faint smile, Anne set the sweater aside, saying, "Well, maybe I'll keep a few things."

Opening the lingerie drawer to a raft of negligees—as if the two dozen she'd taken out of the armoire weren't enough—she immediately began stuffing them into a bag. Then, near the bottom of the drawer, where the soot was negligible, she found one that made her pause. Her head tilted as she took a closer look, and finally she lifted the gown from the drawer and let it unfold.

It was winter white and high waisted, with narrow straps and a plunging bodice made of rose-patterned lace. The skirt consisted of V-shaped panels of lace and silk that would cling to the body, then flare dramatically from the hips into a floor-length, sweeping cloud. It was beautiful. A provocative, sensual creation that conjured images of candlelight and tulips of Château d'Yquem and the soft murmur of a man and woman whispering words of love. Things Anne knew nothing of but could imagine her mother and father having shared. They'd been devoted to each other to the point of obsession.

Lost in her thoughts, Anne stared at the creamy white negligee, thinking it curious and, at the same time, terribly disheartening that she could look so much like her mother yet be so unlike her. If circumstances were different, she wondered, if her mother hadn't died, would she have grown up to be more like her? A free-spirited, sensual creature who expressed her thoughts and feelings easily, without fear or reserve? The kind of woman who would wear a gown such as this one to greet her lover at night? Perhaps, she thought. For she hadn't always been the way she was now—so fearful, so inhibited, so reluctant to express her feelings—and maybe the child she'd been wasn't entirely lost.

Anne's fingers clutched at the silk, as if she might draw upon the spirit of the woman who'd worn it. Could wearing a gown such as this make her feel passionate, sensual, aroused? Could it make her feel the things a woman was *supposed* to feel . . . ?

With one hand holding the straps above her breasts, she smoothed the skirt down across her lap and tried to imagine her body clothed in it. The lace was so sheer, so revealing. The roses in the bodice would cover her nipples but wouldn't conceal their darker color. And the silk was nearly transparent, a bare glimmer of fabric, like a coating of frost on a pane of glass. . . .

"I'm putting all the rugs for the cleaners in the morning room."

Connor's announcement brought Anne's gaze up to collide with her own image reflected in the oak-framed standing mirror five feet away—and behind her, Connor's image as he walked into the room. She hadn't even been aware that he'd left.

Quickly she began stuffing the gown into the plastic bag beside her. But she wasn't quick enough.

"Find something you wanted?" he asked, coming up behind her.

"Oh, no, it's just old stuff." She had the gown halfway into the bag when he stooped down next to her, his hand capturing her wrist.

"Wait," he said, his tone curious. "Let's see."

She gave up trying to hide the gown and let it fall across her lap. "It's just a nightgown," she said. "Nothing special."

"Mmm..." Connor reached as if to touch the gown, then hesitated, frowning at his sooty hand. He didn't pull back, though. Not right away.

It was only a couple of seconds, but to Anne it seemed an eternity that his hand hovered over the roses in the bodice. And as he paused, his fingers moved ever so slightly, as though he were smoothing out a tiny wrinkle...or caressing the breasts the roses were designed to adorn. With her eyes fixed on his hand, she felt her heart miss a beat. Her breasts began to tingle, the nipples tightening until they ached. When his fingers curled inward a bit, then spread open, his strong, work-roughened hand easily encompassing the rose pattern that would cover a single breast, the breath trickled out of her lungs, and she had to bite her lip to keep from moaning.

She wanted his hand on her, wanted it as she'd never wanted anything in her life. He was so close; his thigh, thick with muscle and dusted with black hair below the edge of his cutoffs, brushed her arm. If she raised her head, his face would be only inches away. What would she see in his eyes? Did he know what he was doing to her? She wanted badly to know but didn't have the nerve to find out. Yet when he pulled his hand away and spoke, the husky note in his voice struck a corresponding chord in that place inside her that felt warm and liquid and empty.

"Keep it," he said.

Anne caught her breath. "Oh, I don't...I'd never—"

"Keep it," he said again.

Her eyes flickered upward, saw he was looking at her, then darted away. "I don't know if the cleaners can save it."

"Show it to my mother. She'll know what to do with it without ruining it."

"Well, I suppose I could...."

"Don't give it to the Goodwill, Anne."

The quiet insistence in his voice brought her gaze back to his. A moment of silence passed between them. Then he said it for the third time.

"Keep it."

Anne's reply came out in a thready whisper. "All right."

Connor's blue gaze held hers for an instant or two, then he stood up and started to move away.

Anne drew a shaky breath, and, in a sudden flurry of nervous activity, she set the gown aside and reached for the next one. But when she snatched it up, dozens of pieces of paper flew out of the drawer along with it. She let out a startled cry, bringing Connor back to her side at the same instant she realized the papers were green bank notes. Money.

"Oh!" Anne stared at the bills lying all around her. None of them had fewer than two zeros tacked after the initial digit. "Oh, my heavens... Con, look!"

Dropping to his knees beside her, he picked up a handful of hundred-dollar bills and snorted in derision. "So, Aaron's been using this dresser as a bank, huh?"

"No. No, this is..." Anne trailed off, her head suddenly spinning with bits of the past and the chill of gooseflesh raising the hairs on her arms and scalp. "This isn't Aaron's money. It's my mother's."

Connor's eyebrow arched in skepticism. "That would mean—"

"Yes, I know. It's been here more than twenty-two years. But I remember... Lord, am I dreaming this, or did it really happen?" She closed her eyes, her mind wavering on the border of past and present. Then, with a quick shake of her head, she dismissed the notion. "My memories of my mother are so hazy. It could be something I'm making up."

Settling back on his heels, Connor picked up another handful of bills and held them in front of her. "Anne, this isn't something you made up. Tell me what you're thinking."

"Well..." Anne watched him gathering the scattered notes as she began. "I remember running into the parlor, looking for my mother... I don't remember why. She was kneeling by the fireplace, and... I know this sounds crazy—more like a dream than a memory—but she was putting money into a hole behind the panel down the left side, under the mantel."

As she said the words aloud, Anne heard the clear, unaffected voice of a child asking, *"Mother, is that real money?"* Then, suddenly, the pieces came together, the image crystallizing in her mind, and what came to her was a memory of her mother more vivid and precise than any she'd ever had before.

"Oh! Anne, you startled me!"

"I'm sorry, but... Mother, why are you putting money in the fireplace?"

"Well, it's not actually the fireplace. It's... a safe. A secret safe—like a hiding place for very important things."

"Like the box where I keep my jewel rocks?"

"Exactly. Now, darling, you understand about secrets, don't you? They're things you never tell anyone."

"Like Christmas presents."

"Yes, but this secret is even bigger than Christmas. I hadn't planned to share it with you yet. But...well, perhaps it's time. One never knows what will happen. You might need to know someday. But, Anne, you must promise never to tell."

"Not even Father?"

"No, especially not your father. This is . . . well, it's a ladies' secret. My secret hiding places are only for the ladies of the house. Now, promise me, Anne. . . ."

And so she had promised. Dimly, Anne remembered the strange trip through the manor her mother and she had made that afternoon, with Evelyn showing her the places she'd hidden bundles of money, repeating continuously that it was a secret, a ladies' secret. And wasn't it nice that the two of them had this special knowledge that the men of the house didn't share?

Blinking to clear her head of the memory, Anne murmured, "She was hiding it from my father."

Connor's brow furrowed. "She told you that?"

"No, but given what Howard Stone has said about how she tried to persuade my father to be more responsible, it makes sense." Frowning, she added, "She was probably afraid he'd bankrupt them—which he nearly did—so she hid cash all over the house, figuring even if he found some, he'd never find it all."

"Anne—" Connor glanced around the room "—are you saying there's more?"

"There was, but...well, it can't still be here. My father would have taken it after she died."

"But she died instantly, of a broken neck," he reminded her. "So unless she told him where to look before she died—"

"No, she was adamant. She'd never have told him."

"Do you think she left the information in her will, or in a note to your father?"

"I don't know. . . ."

Connor paused in the act of counting the money to look at her. "Anne, there's got to be over ten thousand dollars here."

For a long moment their eyes exchanged silent messages.

"Con, do you suppose . . . ?"

"This money was still here, wasn't it? Why not the rest?"

"Some of it would be in ashes," she said. "Like the roll be-hind the fireplace. There was another place in the parlor, too...I think. It *seems* as if there were dozens of places, but maybe it only seems that way because I was so young!" Anne's voice rose on a panicked note. "Oh, Con, what if I can't re-member them all? She only showed me one time, and I couldn't have been more than four or five!"

"Take it easy," he said. "If you've remembered this much, you'll remember the rest. Just relax and try to think."

She closed her eyes and tried to do as he'd suggested. But it was hopeless. Too many things had been at work on her nerves that morning. She couldn't concentrate, and finally she let out her pent-up breath and opened her eyes.

"It's no use," she said. "The minute I *try* to remember, my mind goes blank."

"What if we walked through the other rooms?" he offered. "Maybe you'd see something that reminded you."

"Well...maybe." Anne caught her lower lip between her teeth as she let her gaze travel over the bedroom. She didn't want to wander through the manor. She felt enormously pleased to have been in the place as long as she had without wanting to race outside. But if she had to go upstairs to her old room, or to the attic, or...

"Anne, stop. That's enough."

Connor's gentle order brought her troubled gaze to his.

"You don't have to torture yourself over this," he said. "The money's not going anywhere." As his eyes searched her tense features, he added, "I'd say it's time for a break."

"But if I don't try now," she began, "maybe I won't ever—"

"Uh-uh." Dropping the thick packet of money into her lap, he placed his hands on top of his thighs and gave her a look that didn't allow for argument. "You're starting to look like the ghosts you're supposed to be busting—white as a sheet. A lit-tle fresh air is definitely in order."

Anne stared at the money for a moment, then offered Con-nor a shaky smile. "All right. Get me out of here. I think my brain is starting to clog with soot—like the rest of me."

Chuckling, he pushed to his feet, taking her hand to pull her up with him. "Why don't we both go get clean? Then, if you want, we can drive into Easton."

Anne hesitated. "I'm not in a hurry about the car. I could...well, maybe just come up to Sentinel after I change. Unless you really want to go someplace on your day off."

"No," he replied, looking slightly bemused. "I almost never spend a day at home, so that suits me fine."

Smiling, she suggested, "We could take lunch down to the beach. And you can tell me how you ever got to be the editor of a newsletter for a conservation organization."

"You saw it?"

"Uh-huh."

"It's a long story."

"My favorite kind."

"Yeah—" his mouth sloped into a grin "—I seem to remember telling you one or two of those."

"You can call this one a sequel," she put in brightly, stooping to shove the money into the pockets of her shorts. But as she gathered up the clothes she was keeping, a movement caught her eye. She glanced toward the sitting-room door and saw that it was closed, as it had been all morning. But a second ago, she could have sworn she'd seen it move.

Right. Just as she'd heard the study door creak earlier, when it had only been Connor crossing the porch.

Rattled, angry at herself for being so, Anne clamped down on the urge to run and straightened slowly, her gaze sliding to Connor's in search of reassurance. But she found his eyes directed at the garments in her arms. Her gaze fell to the folded pieces, saw the negligee on top, then snapped upward to collide with his.

The look in his eyes was explicit. He was thinking about kissing her. She knew it. She also knew that, at that moment, it would be a dreadful mistake.

"Con, let's leave," she whispered hoarsely.

He nodded slowly, motioning her to precede him, and they left the room. They walked in silence down the stairs and out, through the garden entrance, following the flower-bordered walk to the beach, where they paused before going their separate ways.

"I won't be long," she said.

"No rush," he returned. "That's what days off are for."

She flashed him a shy smile, then turned and started quickly down the beach toward Sandcastle.

Connor watched Anne go, his thoughts, as they had been for days, in turmoil—troubled one instant as he tried to fathom the anxious, fearful side of her, elated and aroused the next as he imagined her sleeping in his hammock, pictured her wearing that lacy nightgown, saw her lips part and her eyes go soft and hazy, as they had when she'd looked at him a minute ago. She was halfway down the beach when she glanced behind her, caught him watching, and flung him a wave before hurrying on.

If he got through the day without exploding from pure sexual frustration, Connor figured, it would be a miracle. Then again, maybe by the time the day ended, he'd have found the satisfaction his body craved. The look in Anne's eyes had been very promising. And if he could only believe that losing himself in her body wouldn't mean losing his heart and all prospects of freedom, as well . . . if he could manage to think of making love with her as nothing more momentous than sharing a little pleasurable sex with a friend . . . well, then, maybe he'd be able to let go and actually enjoy life. For a while, anyway.

Chapter Eleven

She was being pursued. She was certain of it now. Pursued in the nicest way. The thought occurred to Anne when she saw Connor waiting for her, hands in his back pockets, bare feet planted wide in the sand, at the same spot on the beach where they'd parted. Drawing closer, seeing the unguarded approval in his eyes as they traveled over her unremarkable white peasant blouse and lime-green shorts, she felt a flush of warmth rising in her cheeks. She'd never in her life tried to impress a man, had never wanted to before, and it was nice to know she'd succeeded with so little effort. But then, Connor had made no more effort than she—a shower, a shave, and a less-worn pair of cutoffs—and she couldn't have been more impressed. Except perhaps by his tanned, muscle-sculpted body in its unadorned state.

Stopping a yard or so away, Anne offered him an uncommonly flirtatious smile. "You know, if we go on meeting like this, the fish will start to talk."

Amusement sparkled in Connor's eyes as he replied, "I don't have a problem with that. Do you?"

She shook her head. "Not a one."

His gaze held hers, his expression slowly changing, the light in his eyes growing warmer, his smile growing softer, amusement giving way to intimacy. Irresistibly, she felt herself smiling in return, as if answering a question that hadn't yet been asked. Without another word, Connor turned and began strolling up the beach, and Anne fell into step at his side, her heart racing.

They hadn't gone far when he bent to snatch a smooth, flat stone and wing it across the water. He watched it skip four times, then sink, as he asked, "Did you stash that money someplace safe?"

Anne patted her pocket. "Right here."

His head snapped toward her, his look horrified. "You've got it with you?"

"All eleven thousand three hundred dollars of it," she returned lightly. "I couldn't find a place to put it that I wouldn't have worried about it. Weird, isn't it? It's been perfectly safe for over twenty years wrapped in a nightgown, but the minute it's unearthed, no place seems safe."

"I don't like you carrying all that money around."

"Well . . . okay." Pulling out the thick wad, Anne divided it at random and shoved a handful toward him. "Here."

Connor glanced from her to the money, then laughed. "Oh, that's a *whole* lot better."

"You want all of it?"

"Anne!"

"Go on," she insisted, poking the entire pack of hundred, five hundred, and thousand-dollar bills into his ribs. "Take it. It's kind of fun, really, holding this much cash at once."

With a derisive snort, he took the notes and proceeded to divide them among his pockets. "If it's yours, it's fun—maybe. If it's somebody else's, it's pure headache."

"Ah, but that's the beauty of this little gold mine. It doesn't belong to *anybody.* It isn't on Howard Stone's inventory of the manor, so, technically, it doesn't exist."

Connor grinned. "Finders keepers, huh?"

"Why not?" With a breezy wave she added, "We could take your day off and, oh, let's say, fly to Paris for dinner. Or, no, let's go to San Francisco for lunch."

"Now, why didn't I think of that?"

"Because you're too busy thinking of all the boring, *responsible* things you could do with it."

"I've got a feeling one of us better."

"Trust me. You can pay your bills later. You *need* to go to San Francisco."

"And spend eleven grand on lunch? What? Do they lace the champagne with gold dust?"

"Oh, but lunch is only for *starters*. If we're on the west coast, we *have* to take a trip to…well, Hawaii or Tahiti or…I know! Let's go to Alaska."

"Say, now, there's an idea."

"Forget the day off. We'll make it a month, because if we're going to be in Alaska, we really should go on to Moscow. And on the way home, we'll stop in Rome."

"Since when is Rome 'on the way' from Moscow?"

"*Then* we'll go to Paris."

"Not unless we're flying baggage."

"I *beg* your pardon."

"Sorry, but it's my boringly responsible guess that you've overshot the budget."

"All right. We'll leave out Rome. It's too hot this time of year, anyway."

Connor's grin became a chuckle. "I'm a fool to ask this, but what *are* you going to do with it? For real, that is."

Anne's lips thinned, her playful attitude giving way to the underlying anger. "I've half a mind to do exactly what I said. Spend it and deduct it from what Aaron owes me."

She'd spoken without thinking, and a quick glance told her that Connor found her remark of great interest. She considered telling him about the missing books and art but hesitated. The theft was, after all, a *fait accompli*. He could do nothing about it—except add it to his lifetime list of wrongs he had no power to right. Searching for a distraction, she was saved by Connor's sudden warning.

"Uh-oh. Here comes trouble."

Anne's gaze snapped upward, and she immediately identified the "trouble" as one Gordon Setter bearing down on them at lightning speed through the tall grass along the bluff. It looked as if he were going to launch himself at them until Connor's arm shot out and he uttered a single command.

"Stop!"

Rogue skidded down the bluff, his paws digging into the sand as he came to a halt alongside Anne.

Connor waved him off. "Now, go on. Go chase squirrels."

"Oh, don't send him away!" Anne pleaded.

Connor arched an eyebrow in a skeptical look. "He gets wild as a March hare around the water. You sure he won't bother you?"

She looked down at Rogue, his feathery tail sweeping the sand and his ears cocked as he waited for the verdict.

Smiling, she said, "Look at that face, will you? Is that the face of a wild animal?"

"Oh, for crying out loud..."

"Of course he can stay. What on earth can he do to me?"

What he could do was get her soaking wet. Connor found a piece of driftwood, and soon the three of them were engaged in a raucous game of keep-away. Anne, standing ankle deep in the small waves washing ashore, guarded the beach, while Connor claimed the territory thirty feet out, where the water hovered at the bottom edges of his cutoffs. Rogue swam and jumped between them, taking every opportunity to slip past their guards, running up the beach, in which case Anne chased him or swimming in circles around Connor, forcing Connor to charge after him.

As the game progressed, growing ever louder and wetter, Anne failed to notice that the water lapping around her ankles soon began lapping around her knees, or that some of the gentle swells rose up her thighs to the edge of her shorts. Nor was she aware that, the farther from shore she unknowingly progressed, the closer toward her Connor moved. She had no idea he was watching her so carefully until she took a step to grab the stick, which was floating in front of her, and suddenly the bottom shelved off. The water rose to her armpits at the same instant Connor's arms came around her waist to haul her back.

"Whoa," he said. "I don't think you want to take that next step."

Anne drew a startled breath, but before she had time to panic, he swept her out of the water and into his arms.

"You okay?" he asked, a frown creasing his dark brow.

Thoroughly disoriented, Anne tried to gather her wits to answer. She didn't know whether her heart was racing because she'd nearly gone under or because of the unexpected contact with Connor's body. Lord, he was strong. She could actually feel the cords of muscle in his arms around her back and thighs, while ridges of it in his neck and shoulders bulged beneath her hands. Her ribs, plastered to his midsection, might as well have been against a brick wall—except that walls weren't warm and resilient and embellished with silky black hair.

Swallowing, Anne gave him what she hoped was a reassuring smile. "I'm fine. But thanks."

He studied her closely, then asked, "Are you going to tell me what's made you afraid of the water?"

She drew a quick breath. "I'd...rather not. Talking about it makes me...relive it." Which, under the circumstances, would be disastrous. "It's okay, usually, if I can see my feet."

He looked at her a moment longer; then, with a smile tugging at his lips, he said, "I don't know whether I should mention it, but you passed that point a long time ago."

Startled, Anne twisted to peek around his arm, and it stunned her to discover that she was a good forty feet from the beach. If she'd been standing, the water would have covered her to the hips. She was in deeper water than she'd been in—voluntarily, anyway—for fifteen years. Deeper than she'd expected ever to be in again. And until the bottom had disappeared, she hadn't even noticed.

Suddenly, Anne grinned, and as if he'd read her thoughts, Connor bent his head to murmur in her ear.

"Feels good, doesn't it?"

Twisting back around, she beamed up at him. "Will you take me windsurfing next week?"

At that, he threw back his head and laughed. "Sunshine, I'll take you anyplace you think you want to go."

Watching the way the sun danced in his eyes, glistening off the water clinging to his lashes, Anne knew one place she wanted him to take her. And thoughts of the brass bed on the second floor of his cottage produced an immediate physical response from those places in her body she was rapidly discovering were not nearly as dysfunctional as she'd once thought. She cautioned herself not to let this small triumph go to her head. But, suspended over the water, with Connor holding her so tightly and no sign of panic in sight, it was easy to believe it could work. Easy to believe it could be wonderful. Easy to believe all things were possible...

Reaching up, Anne ran a fingertip along the fading scratch on the right side of his jaw. "I don't know why you'd want to be within a hundred miles of me in the water," she said quietly.

The laughter faded abruptly from Connor's expression, his eyes darkening to a deep, fathomless blue. "Haven't you figured it out yet?"

"Figured what out?" she wondered.

A moment passed during which the only sound was the raucous cry of a gull soaring above them.

Then, very softly, he said, "Anne, I've about reached the stage where I'd do almost anything to be near you."

For the space of several heartbeats, blue eyes held green ones in a searching look. Then, because he deserved this much from her and because she simply couldn't wait any longer, Anne hooked a hand behind Connor's neck, leaned upward, and pressed her lips to his in a sweet, fervent kiss.

Connor's reaction was immediate. His arms tightened around her, his chest rumbling with a sound that seemed caught between agony and delight. His head tipped, his mouth seeking firmer contact with hers, but before he found it, she pulled back.

Their eyes met again, his reflecting surprise and obvious desire, hers filled with equal measures of hope and longing.

He spoke in a hoarse whisper. "Anne, yesterday it seemed like—"

"Don't." She put a finger to his lips. "Don't make me talk about yesterday. Not now. Just kiss me before—" ... *before I remember I'm terrified of this,* she started to say. But her words were lost beneath the crush of his lips.

He kissed her hard, with all the ardor of a man to whom passion has been too long denied, and within moments, she was drowning. Not in water but in sensation. Thought fled. Her world was reduced to the feel of his mouth, the smell of salt water, the taste of man. He kissed her thoroughly, his lips rocking over hers with a confidence and surety that made her weak, his tongue painting her lips open, then sweeping inside to teach her things that made her yearn. He kissed her with a majesty that shattered every imagined notion she'd ever had about desire and carnal need. And when he tore his mouth away from hers, her only thought was that she wanted more.

"Anne, I have to know," he rasped. "Is there anyone else? Anyone who you—"

"No." Breathless, she tried to answer. "There's...no one." *No one but you. Always you...*

The words ran through her mind as he took her mouth again. And again her senses were flooded, entirely focused on tastes and textures, scents and sounds. The luxurious length and thickness of his hair twined around her fingers. The warmth of his body through her wet clothing. The slight roughness of his jaw, the firm pressure of his lips, the slick heat of his tongue swirling around hers. And the sounds, those impossibly deep, rumbling sounds he made, hungry, needful sounds that turned the warmth curling through her into a hot, pulsing ache.

Somewhere in the blessedly mindless world to which she'd been transported, Anne felt herself being lifted and turned, Connor's arms wrapping her closer until her breasts were molded against his chest. Then, with his mouth still joined to hers, he carried her toward shore.

He got as far as the water's edge, then dropped to his knees, tearing his lips away from hers to tell a disgruntled and curious Rogue, "Take a hike, buddy. Games are over."

Anne didn't argue but simply clung to him, clung to the moment, clung to the swelling hope that this time it would be different. This time it would be all right. This time the fire he'd kindled inside her couldn't be quenched—except by him.

With his face hovering inches above hers, Connor breathed her name. Then, without letting go of her for even an instant, he lowered them both to lie on the sand with his arm beneath her head for a pillow and the foamy surf rippling over their feet. His eyes were so blue, so full of heat, gazing down at her; they made the sky above him seem pale and tepid. Her fingers trembled against his cheek, the line of his brow, stroking a lock of wet hair away from his eyes. His eyelids drifted closed at her touch, his lashes lying in black crescents against his dark skin. Without opening them, he leaned down to kiss her once more, his lips tugging lightly at hers as he spoke.

"I wasn't sure," he whispered. "I was afraid I was wrong about you wanting this."

"No," she whispered back. "You're not wrong. It seems as if I've been waiting all my life for you to kiss me."

He said something she didn't catch, something dark and heartfelt, as he buried his face against her neck. "God, Annie, you don't know . . . I feel like I've been blind. Or asleep—like Adam must have felt when he found Eve in the Garden. I woke up, and there you were, waiting for me."

"Oh, Con..." Tears stung her eyes, hot and sweet, like the string of kisses he trailed down her neck and across her shoulder. Moist, sucking kisses that sent goose bumps racing down her arms and across her breasts. Then his lips came back to settle over hers, and for a very long time they remained there.

The sand was firm and wet beneath her. The sun was hot and sultry beating down from above. Connor's mouth was all those things and more as he tutored her in the ways of intimacy and pleasure. Anne followed his lead instinctively, eagerly, realizing he was taking her deeper and deeper into something she knew nothing about. Desire. Need. The two became the same. She learned the meaning of both at the same time she learned the meaning of the word *more*. She wanted more. More of him. More of what he was giving her.

When he wrenched his mouth away from hers to gasp for breath, her mouth felt open, sensitive, vulnerable, and, without his joined to it, utterly bereft.

"God, look at you...."

Connor's breathless words brought her eyes open far enough to see him leaning on an elbow, his gaze transfixed by the sight of her top clinging wetly to her breasts. The gauzy white fabric had become nearly transparent, as had the wisp of lace she wore beneath it, and, through them both, her nipples were blatantly revealed.

Caught between acute shyness and wanton pleasure, she turned her face into his shoulder, but she made no move to cover herself—or to stop him when his hand glided upward over her blouse, stopping with his thumb and fingers spread to frame her right breast.

"That nightgown..." he began, and those two words alone forced a moan from her lips and made her thighs press together in an unconscious effort to ease the throbbing ache.

"You knew, didn't you?" he asked. "You knew what I was thinking...what I wanted to do."

Her body answered the question for her, her breath catching, her back arching sharply as his hand slid slowly upward, lifting the soft mound into higher relief.

"Yes," he whispered when the nipple strained against the cloth. "Oh, yes," he said again when his thumb rubbed across it and it swelled and hardened.

"Oh... Oh, Con..." Anne's breath poured out in a groan, and he captured the sound inside his mouth at the same time his fingers sank gently into her supple, responsive flesh.

His mouth was hot and passionate. His touch, sure and knowing. Between the two, Anne was lost, totally, in a world she'd never dreamed existed. It was a world of no thought, only feeling. A world of no memories, no ghosts, no demons. It was a world where only she and Connor dwelled, one of their making. A world from which she never wanted to return. She clung to it fiercely, rejecting all reminders that any other world existed.

But then, she didn't count on the very thing she craved becoming the greatest reminder of all.

"Anne... Anne... Oh, God, I want you." Connor's voice was raw, his lips moving feverishly across the skin above the loose neckline of her top. "I want you now, in my bed... with both of us naked.... I want to touch you and kiss you everywhere, and I want to lie on top of you and feel you wrap your legs around me. I want to be inside you. Deep inside..." And in a surge of passion that drew every muscle in his back taut beneath her hands, he slid an arm under her hips, his leg across her thighs, and pulled her belly tight against his loins.

With that, the bubble burst. Her dream-world shattered, and reality hit with brutal force. Male flesh, hard and formidable, ground into her. Arms like steel bands and thighs like rocks trapped her. A crushing weight pressed her into the sand—demanding, smothering. And, suddenly, before she could stop it, before she had any idea it was about to happen, the nightmare clicked into action.

Anne screamed, mindlessly, without restraint, and instead of clinging, she shoved with all her might to rid herself of the suddenly terrifying embrace. Connor jerked away as if he'd been scalded, and she scrambled out from under him, crawling perhaps five feet to sit huddled in a ball with her knees drawn up to her chest and her breath coming in ragged whimpers.

It was over in seconds. Anne realized almost immediately what she'd done. But almost was too late. She opened her eyes to find Connor on his feet, staring down at her, his face contorted with shock and confusion and a horrible, wrenching pain. She couldn't bear it, couldn't bear the sight of the devastation she'd wrought. With an agonized moan, she buried her face in her hands and burst into tears.

The tears were the final straw. Connor took one look at them and pivoted away, swearing. He knew he had to find out what in God's name had gone wrong. Knew he had to do *something*. But he didn't trust himself to say or do anything at that moment. Was afraid he would simply blow up if he didn't cool off first.

Rubbing a hand across his face, he muttered another explicit oath, then strode several yards down the beach to stand with his arms wrapped tightly around his ribs and his feet buried in the surf as he stared at the gray clouds gathering on the horizon. For a moment or two he was aware only of the blood pounding in his head, pounding in his chest...pounding hard and fast and painfully in his loins. But the sound of Anne's tears drew him like a magnet. He couldn't ignore them. Couldn't turn his back on them. Not for long. Not nearly long enough...

Whirling to face her, he spoke roughly. "I'm not leaving this time, Anne. I'm not going anywhere until I know what the devil is going on." When she didn't answer, didn't even raise her head to look at him, his frustration got the better of him, and he stomped back toward her, exclaiming, "Anne, for God's sake! If you wanted to stop, why didn't you just say so? What did you think I was going to do? Rape you?"

Her reaction was instant. Her head jerked up, and she cowered, her body curling in on itself and her bare feet digging furrows in the sand. But it was her stricken expression, her face pinched in agony, that brought Connor to a halt. At first he simply stared in bafflement. Then, all at once, his eyes widened, and the breath left his body in a broken rush.

"Oh, God...Oh, God, no..."

His hoarse denial trailed into silence. And for one chilling moment, time stopped. The sun beat down. The waves lapped at the shore. In the distance, a boat horn sounded.

Then, as Anne raised her tortured, tear-streaked countenance to his and he saw her lips trying to form his name, the scene zoomed into focus before Connor's horrified gaze. The blood drained out of his face, all the roiling emotions and sexual frustration solidified in the pit of his belly, and for an instant he was sure he was going to be violently sick. But it wasn't sickness that brought him to his knees. It was seeing Anne huddled in that dreadful ball, her shoulders quaking with silent sobs and her eyes huge and scared and begging for help.

"Oh, dear God... Oh, Anne..." He dropped to the sand a few feet away from her, his heart shattering when she cringed from him again. "Annie, please... please, let me..." He had no idea what he was doing, knew only that the gap between them was intolerable. Sliding on his knees and shins, he began inching toward her, his words coming in thick, broken phrases. "Anne, look at me. I'm not going to hurt you. I swear to God, I won't. Just... just look at me. Please..."

She met his gaze, her knuckles pressed to her mouth, her slender shoulders jerking with sobs.

"It's okay. It's okay..." he said, stretching a hand toward her, inching closer, all the while repeating every soothing word he'd ever learned, reassuring her constantly that she had nothing to fear, that he wasn't going to hurt her and that everything was all right now. Though he didn't see how anything could ever be right again.

Her eyes remained wide and frightened, and she flinched when he touched her shoulder. But she didn't pull away. And, finally, he skated up close, tucking her between his thighs. Her skin was icy cold, and she was shaking violently, but when he slid an arm around her shoulders she went rigid, and he was sure she was going to yank away. Then one of her fists opened, her hand fluttering in a small, searching gesture. He lifted his free hand, palm up, beneath hers, and she instantly grabbed on.

"C-Con..." she sobbed, her fingers squeezing his with a strength that shocked him. Struggling, she managed a few incoherent words. But finally she simply turned her face into his shoulder and cried.

"Shh," he breathed. "It's all right now." For a minute he only held her, his cheek against her hair, his body rocking back and forth, soothing them both. But as her shaking began to subside and the sound of her crying lost some of its terror-stricken, hysterical edge, he drew a ragged breath and spoke.

"It's true, isn't it? Some stinking bastard raped you."

Her head jerked in a nod, killing any hope he might have had that he'd been wrong.

"I-I'm s-sorry," she croaked. "I'm s-so sorry, I—"

"Hush." His arms tightened around her. "You've got nothing to be sorry for. You understand?"

She shook her head almost violently. "But I didn't m-mean to...again. I th-thought it would be okay, but...I sh-should have told you f-first." Her hand crept around his neck, and she spoke with her forehead leaning against his shoulder. "I knew I had to tell you after yes...terday. I knew you were hurt, and I f-felt awful, but I couldn't ex...plain then. I just couldn't. And last n-night I fell asleep b-before you...got home, and this aftern-noon we..."

"We got sidetracked."

She nodded. "I thought—I thought it would be different. Everyth-thing *seemed* so different. The w-water...I p-*played* in the water and it was okay, and I thought it would be okay to— to k-kiss you, but...but... Oh, dear Lord..."

Her half-formed sentences gave way to another bout of tears, and Connor murmured reassurances as he tried to make sense of what she'd told him. The only thing he really understood, with ruthless clarity, was that she'd been violently abused, and that her mixed messages to him were signs of the conflict raging inside her. She wanted him every bit as much as he wanted her. But the fear wouldn't let her have what she wanted, and the explosion that had just occurred was the result of her desperate attempt to do something that, in fact, scared her half to death.

He didn't blame her for not telling him sooner, for grabbing the moment, as he had yesterday morning. He just wished she could have given him some warning, wished he could have saved her the agony of reliving that terror. Wished he could have saved them both this pain. Filled with regret, Connor watched the clouds roll across the sun as he listened to the words Anne whispered against his neck.

"I wanted to...to kiss you so much," she said. "I didn't know...I n-never dreamed anything like this would happen."

A frown appeared on his brow. "Are you saying this hasn't happened before?"

"No. I've never...well, I haven't tried to...to..." She made an exasperated sound, straightening her back and squaring her jaw as she rushed to say, "Con, I've never even l-let another man *kiss* me, m-much less..."

"Anything else."

Her head bobbed once, and Connor sighed, thinking it a dubious sort of pleasure to know he'd tempted her beyond the limits of her endurance. "So, I'm the only man who's kissed you since it happened," he concluded.

Raising her tear-filled gaze to his, Anne spoke solemnly. "You're the only man who's k-kissed me *ever*."

Stunned, Connor sank back onto his heels and stared at her as she continued.

"There hasn't been anyone I've w-wanted to kiss since . . ."

"Since this animal raped you. But, Anne—" He shook his head to clear it. "Are you telling me there wasn't anyone before? How long ago—"

"A long time," she interrupted, her words scarcely audible. And, as her gaze fell to her lap, she added, "Th-there's never been . . . anyone."

"A long time." What the hell did that mean? How young had she been for there not to have been anyone before? She'd gone to women's schools—convent-run schools—where she probably hadn't started dating until later than she might have otherwise. So it made some sense that she'd remained unkissed longer than most young women might today. But she'd been all over the world—alone. A chilling thought. God, it could have happened anywhere. Anytime.

Suddenly Connor's head was bursting with questions, but before he could ask any of them, Anne struggled to continue.

"I've t-tried dating men I f-felt c-com . . . com . . ."

"Men you felt comfortable with?"

"Yes. But it never works. I u-usually freeze up, like I did with you y-yesterday, if a man even tries to h-hold my hand. I— I don't like to be . . . to be touched." She shuddered once, then added, "At least, I've n-never liked it b-before."

Drawing a raspy breath, she raised imploring eyes to his. "When you touch me, some . . . times there's an instant when I'm startled, like there is with other m-men. But then it registers somewhere in my head that . . . that it's you. And somehow that makes it different. It makes it s-seem . . . right. And then I don't feel cold and scared, I feel . . . Oh, Con, when you touch me, I feel shivery and warm and . . . and wonderful inside."

The way you make me *feel, hearing you say that.* Her admission humbled him, filled him with a rare and awesome pleasure. And he knew he was very close to saying he wanted to go on making her feel wonderful forever. He'd do whatever he had to do, give her anything she needed. Whatever it took to wipe this vile terror out of her mind and let those shivery, warm feelings reach their natural conclusion. He wanted her to be happy again. He wanted her to be his. And at that moment, he didn't give a damn what it might cost him to have what he wanted.

Fighting to contain an onslaught of emotions more demanding and intense than any he'd felt in years, Connor hugged Anne to him fiercely. Her arms slipped around him, and for several minutes they simply held each other. He watched the clouds darken, felt the wind pick up out of the northwest and start to rustle the cattails on the bank behind them. All the while he was aware of the warmth returning to Anne's icy skin and the gradual lessening of tension in her body.

Her voice was almost normal when she spoke. "It's so hard to talk about this. I've never told anyone except..."

"Except?" Connor prompted.

"My psychiatrist."

That surprised him for all of two seconds. "You went into counseling?"

"Finally." Anne drew away, sighing. "It took me a long time to admit my problems weren't just going to disappear. I had horrible nightmares. And I wanted to go to graduate school, but I'd never been in a classroom with men, and I couldn't cope with it. I needed help. And therapy *has* helped. A lot. Except when it comes to...to sex." Lifting a hand to wipe her eyes, she mumbled, "But you must think I'm a total wreck."

"What I think is that you've been terrorized," he corrected, his voice edged with a mere trace of the fury he felt. "And I'm beginning to realize that things around here haven't been helping a damned bit. Being back home after all this time, having to cope with the fire—and with me being such a bastard when you got here. Then that damned accident yesterday. And on top of everything, finding out we turn each other on like wildfire. It's no wonder you've been a bundle of nerves. The past four days must have been hell on you."

She shot him a dubious look. "What about you?"

He gave her a dry smile. "There've been some interesting moments. Right now, I'd guess we're both feeling pretty raw. But I tell you what—" he cast a look at the sky "—if we sit here much longer, we'll be adding 'drenched' to our complaints."

Anne glanced upward, clearly surprised to see the change in the weather. As they watched, a speedboat passed the point, racing home to beat the storm.

When it disappeared, she looked down at their fingers laced together on her knees. Then, in that soft, whispery tone she used when she was feeling shy, she told him, "I *am* sorry, you know—sorry I ruined it. I wanted . . . more."

She raised her eyes to his, and the unconscious sensuality of her look made Connor burn all over again. Lifting his hand, he brushed the backs of his fingers against her flushed cheek. "Annie, you don't know how many hours of the past four days and nights I've spent thinking about us making love. Believe me when I say you didn't ruin anything. Kissing you was wonderful. Your getting scared doesn't make the good part bad."

Blinking back sudden tears, she whispered a little desperately, "Con, what are we going to do?"

He hadn't the vaguest idea. He was no expert on rape, but common sense told him that, for Anne, half measures would never do. His earlier thought of enjoying a little pleasurable sex with a friend had become an extremely unfunny joke. What Anne needed was endless patience and a wholehearted commitment from a man who loved her deeply and without reservation. A man whose ego could tolerate rejection—repeatedly, indefinitely. A man who was in it with her for the long haul. And as much as he wanted to be that man, Connor was acutely aware of the enormity of the choices he'd first have to make.

Sighing, he admitted, "I don't know what we're going to do. But I *do* know sex and worry don't mix. If you worry that it isn't going to work, you can bet it won't."

"You sound like a book," Anne told him, and when he drew back, amused skepticism lifting his brow, she rolled her eyes. "Believe me, I've read every book written about sex from the *Kama Sutra* to Masters and Johnson, and they *all* say not to worry."

Connor tried to hide the grin that twitched at the corners of his mouth. "Sounds good in theory, huh?"

"It's the curse of being such a cerebral person. I'm always better at theory than practice."

"Mmm, I don't know, Sunshine. . . ." He gave her a slow, easy smile. "You keep practicing the way you were a little while ago, and I think you'll be writing your own book before long."

Her blush was lovely, and she'd have looked away if he hadn't put a finger under her chin and tilted her face up to his. "Take it from the only man who's ever kissed you," he said. "You're beautiful and passionate and sexy as hell. And you aren't going to be able to keep it locked inside forever."

Anne's eyes held his for a moment or two, and, slowly, she smiled. His mouth sloped into an answering grin. But then a distant roll of thunder made them both glance at the sky.

"That does it." Giving her a wink, Connor said, "Time for a change of scene and topic. And I vote for lunch. I don't know about you, but all this thwarted passion has made me hungry."

Anne's look became pained. "You actually want to eat?"

"Take my word for it. It's a great idea. I've got a couple of perch and a half-dozen ears of corn in the fridge. I'll cook, if you keep me company."

She glanced down, taking in her disheveled state. "Okay. But I'm full of sand, and I need dry clothes. Let me run down to Sandcastle and change. It'll only take a few minutes."

"Fair enough." Rocking back on his heels, he pushed to his feet and held a hand out to her. "I'll bring the truck down to get you."

Anne took his hand and let him pull her up, dusting off the sand stuck to her legs as she said, "You don't need to do that. I can walk back."

"Not with your suitcase, you can't. You do have one, don't you? I didn't see it last night."

Straightening, she gave him a look that Connor realized was an eloquent summary of the past hour of her life. Half-wanting. Half-afraid. But he also realized she didn't understand.

"Yes, I have one. It's behind the bedroom door. But I wouldn't think you'd want me to—"

"Do you *want* to stay at Sandcastle, alone?" he asked.

Her expression changed instantly. "No."

"So...?"

She stared at him. "You mean I'd...sleep with you?"

"You can sleep wherever you're comfortable. But I'd like it to be with me." Her eyes widened, and he added softly, "No sex. It would feel good just to have you close. But it's up to you."

When Anne went on looking at him with a sort of helpless wonder, Connor drew a shallow breath, stuck his hands in his back pockets, and motioned her with a nod. "Go on. Get out of here before I kiss you again, when I'm trying so hard not to."

Her lips curved in a smile, and she started to scurry off. But as he turned to go in the other direction, she stopped him.

"Connor, wait."

He turned back a fraction of a second before she threw her arms around his neck and kissed him. Startled, he reached automatically to hold her, but she drew away quickly, leaning back in his arms to meet his gaze. And while his lips still felt the heat of hers upon them, she looked at him with her green gaze warm and glowing and said, "I love you, you know."

Then she was running down the beach, snatching up her sandals as she passed them, tossing him a wave over her shoulder...and he was left staring after her, knowing in his heart that he was well and truly lost.

Chapter Twelve

Anne approached Sandcastle, her head filled with thoughts of Connor—the look in his eyes when she'd told him she loved him, the alluring prospect of sleeping beside him that night. Wanting to be showered and dressed when he arrived, she hurried to unlock the cottage door. But she'd no sooner stepped inside than she stopped, numb with shock.

Couch cushions ripped open, drawers dumped, lamps shattered, bedclothes and the contents of her suitcase scattered in a trail leading into the bedroom. The place was in shambles, and the sight of it sent adrenaline shooting through her veins. She didn't pause to question who or when or why. Instinct took over, and she spun and ran out the door.

Three feet from the cottage she was grabbed from behind. Two hands dug into her shoulders, and the alarm blared in her head. *It's him! Dear Lord, it's him!* Couldn't see him. Didn't need to. She knew those hands. No time to wonder where he'd come from. Time only to register the feel of his hands on her flesh. Then she was screaming and fighting for her life.

He wasn't strong, but he was stronger than she, and he didn't care if, in restraining her, he hurt her. He wrenched her arm high behind her back, and her scream of terror became a scream of pain. But the sound was cut short when his arm locked around her neck, cutting off her air. Gasping, she clawed at his arm and kicked at his shins. But the only pain she inflicted was to herself as he hauled her backward into the cottage and sent the door banging shut with a shove of his foot.

The sound reverberated through every cell in Anne's body. Trapped. No way to escape. Unable to breathe. Too painful to struggle against the force that wrestled her across the floor toward the bedroom. On the verge of passing out from lack of oxygen, she scarcely noticed where they were going. Then, suddenly, the pressure on her throat was released, and she was shoved, facedown, onto the mattress, beside a pile of clothing.

No! Memories of agony merged in a flash with the present. *No! Not again!* The words roared inside her head, though all that escaped was a hoarse, incoherent cry. Wild with panic, she swatted backward with her free hand at the hands that sought to control her. But she didn't connect even once with anything solid, and the battle was lost when her attacker put a knee low on her back and gave her twisted arm a vicious jerk.

Searing pain flooded her senses, and the sound of her own scream filled her ears. Out of the corner of her eye, she saw him snatch a pair of pantyhose from the pile of clothing and knew immediately what he planned to do. She made a last desperate effort to break free but was unable to prevent him from hauling her hands to the small of her back and tying her wrists together.

Sheer nylon, tough and unforgiving, cinched Anne's flesh, and within moments her hands tingled with the onset of numbness. Squeezing her eyes closed, she lay panting, sweating, drained of strength. Expecting the worst. Wondering how much she would be forced to endure...

"Now, where is it?"

She barely registered the sound of a raspy voice, and when she didn't answer, he smacked her across the side of the head. She winced but didn't cry out, and he repeated his demand.

"Let's have it! Now!"

"Wh-what? I d-don't know—"

"The money. What did you do with it?"

Money? What was he talking about? Her money was in her purse, in the car. In the water. But he must know...

"I d-don't have any—" she began in a whisper.

"Don't give me that crap. I saw you find it, and I saw you leave the manor with it."

Slowly, it sank in that he meant the money from her mother's bureau—that he'd been there, listening, while she and Connor worked that morning.

Connor. He'd be here soon. Soon... Please, Lord, soon.

"I've been through this place twice," he snapped as his hand slid under her hips to dig through her empty pockets. "Where the hell have you hidden it?"

Oh, please, Con, hurry...hurry....

"Now!" he shouted, his knee grinding into her back.

"I don't have it!" she gasped. What to tell him. What to do. If she told him Connor had it, he might...

"What have you done with it?"

"I— I took it...to the bank, and—" She choked back a cry as his knee jabbed her again.

"You lie, bitch! Where is it?"

"Howard Stone! He's taking it for me to—"

"Lies! You and your muscle-bound boyfriend spent the afternoon on the beach. And you didn't go anywhere else, because I'd have heard—" He stopped short, then, an instant later, spat out a curse and flung himself off the bed.

Anne drew a couple of ragged breaths, massaging her bruised back with her tied hands, then rolled to her side, struggling to an upright position. But when she raised her head and got her first look at her attacker, her eyes widened in shock.

It wasn't him.

At least it didn't *look* like him. Anne strained to see through the distorting layer of nylon covering her assailant's face. Another pair of pantyhose, with one leg pulled over his head. How crazy, she thought. Why would he disguise himself? Didn't he realize she'd know who he was? But then...maybe it *wasn't* him. The stocking flattened his features, making it impossible to tell.

Her gaze skimmed over the man furiously pacing the floor in front of her, muttering obscenities. Medium height and build, yes, but far too thin. And his hair, beneath the stocking, looked gray, not brown. His clothing told her nothing— dark shirt and slacks and boat shoes...shoes black with soot.

Her eyes snapped upward, trying in vain to see through the film of nylon. It *had* to be him, didn't it? For who else would be here? Who else would attack her? Who else...

Who else, indeed.

Swinging to a stop a few feet away from her, he balled his fist, shaking it as he spoke. "You gave it to him, didn't you?"

Too harsh. Too old. Now that she was truly listening, she realized his voice wasn't right, either. Yet she'd been sure—gut-level sure—when he'd touched her... Regardless, it registered in Anne's terror-stricken mind that it would be wise not to voice her doubts about his identity. He wanted money. And maybe if she kept her wits about her and didn't do anything to make him any angrier, she'd be all right until Connor arrived. He'd be there any second now, any second, and this creature wouldn't stand a chance of overpowering him.

"You took the money with you when you left here," her assailant ranted. "You gave it to that bastard!"

Her expression remained rigidly impassive, but it didn't matter. He knew. Cursing violently, the would-be thief strode to the bed and began pawing through the clothing beside her. On top of the pile lay a pair of leather driving gloves—gloves that weren't hers. Had he worn them to search the cottage? When he pulled her last pair of pantyhose and a scarf from the pile, Anne's eyes darted warily from his masked face to the garments.

"What are you—"

"Shut up."

He shoved her back onto the mattress, and her knees came up reflexively to ward him off. Unwittingly, her maneuver aided his cause. Grabbing her right foot, he held her leg under his arm and rapidly tied the top of the pantyhose around her ankle.

"Wait!" she cried, kicking. "Don't! Oh, don't tie—"

"You kick me again and I'll break a toe."

Her foot stilled, yet she continued to plead. "I'm not going to run away. I swear. You don't have to—"

"Damned right you won't. Now shut up."

Squeezing her eyes closed, Anne stifled a moan. No point in begging; he'd do as he pleased. And she was too exhausted to offer even token resistance when he shoved the scarf into her mouth and tied the ends tightly at the back of her neck.

Straining to hear Connor's pickup, she uttered a muffled cry of surprise when her assailant yanked her to her feet. Looking down, she saw that her ankles weren't tied together but hobbled. She couldn't kick or run, but she could walk, a fact soon proven when he took hold of her arm and led her, stumbling,

toward the front door. Short of falling and refusing to move—
an act certain to incur his wrath—she was helpless to resist.

She was also helpless against the panic that threatened to
overwhelm her when he opened the door and shoved her outside. Where was he taking her? She couldn't imagine. But the
question kept Anne quaking for many painful, barefoot steps
as her attacker pushed her ahead of him, across the cottage
clearing, and onto the path leading north, through the woods.

Minutes after Anne had left him on the beach, Connor
stepped out of his third shower of the day. Drying off on his
way to the bedroom, he tossed the towel over the back of a
chair, snatched a pair of jeans out of the closet, and pulled
them on, zipping them as he walked to the window. A quick
look told him that the river had turned to a mass of whitecaps
and that the sky had gone from gray to black.

Hurrying, he shut the windows, then started for the door,
combing his fingers through his damp hair and sliding his feet
into his Docksiders on the way past. On second thought, he
back-stepped to the bureau, grabbed a dark blue T-shirt from
the top drawer, and stretched it over his head as he headed
down the stairs. Bare chests, it had occurred to him, were male,
and, though he'd like to think Anne found *his* chest pleasing,
rather than intimidating, Connor figured either possibility
could land them in trouble.

His keys lay on the kitchen counter, next to the phone, and
he reached for them at the same instant the phone rang. Hesitating, he picked up the receiver, hoping to God, as he always
did when his crew was working a big job without him, that he
wasn't about to hear one of them had broken his neck.

The voice of Mel Beatty, the garage mechanic, came as a relief—but it also made him wish he'd let the phone ring.

"Con! Well, now. Been trying to get you all day."

"Sorry, Mel. I've had my answering machine off."

"That's okay. Figured you must be working."

"No, but I've been outside. What can I do for—"

"Truck running all right?"

"Just fine." Tucking the receiver under his chin, Connor
picked up the phone and carried it with him to shut the window above the sink. "I appreciated your getting it back to me
early. I know you were busy."

"No problem," Mel said. "Knew you needed it. Listen, though, I wanted to tell you—that bug spray you made up for me? That organic stuff?"

"Right . . ."

"Works like a charm. Stop by the house Monday or Tuesday, and Ethel'll have a mess of tomatoes and squash for you."

"That would be great." Looking out the window at the three-foot breakers battering the shoreline down to the opposite point, Connor added, "I tell you what—I'll leave the recipe for the spray with Ethel, so you can make it yourself the next time. But is there something you wanted to—"

"I'd be much obliged," Mel replied, then proceeded to go on, in detail, about the mysterious disease that seemed to be afflicting his peach trees.

Connor half listened, waiting for a place to jump in and say he had to leave. But he stopped listening altogether, his gaze shooting to the kitchen doorway when Rogue came running down the stairs from the bedroom, barking to beat the band. Bounding across the living room, the dog wiggled out through his door, and Connor whirled back to the window in time to watch him race up the lane and disappear into the woods along the main drive.

Frowning, Connor stared at the empty drive. Rogue heard everything that went on in three counties, and he barked at most of it. But he hated storms. So what was he doing tearing off into the woods when all hell was about to break loose? In the next moment, when a jagged streak of lightning lit the sky, Connor half wondered if he ought to be looking for smoke.

"Mel, listen—" he began, his voice urgent. "I'll have a look at those trees for you next week, but I think I'd better—"

"I'd appreciate that, Con. I surely would. Now, before I forget, let me tell you about that Volvo we hauled in yesterday."

Connor stopped in mid-sentence, hesitating, an inner voice urging him to hurry—hurry to find Rogue, hurry to get Anne. Hurry somewhere for some reason he couldn't explain. But another voice compelled him to listen to what Mel had to say.

"I didn't think you'd get to it before Monday," he said.

"Made time this morning," Mel replied. "Knew you were anxious about it. Ben, too. Needed the information for his accident report. How's your lady friend, by the way? Heard she was right upset, taking a dunk in Louie's boat slip."

"She's okay. What did you find?"

"Well, her pocketbook for one thing. Miss Marquel, right?"

"Hmm." Connor leaned over the sink to glance upward, through the window, at the wind-twisted trees.

"Thought so," Mel said. "Anyway, things got kind of scattered out of this bag of hers when they hauled the car out of the drink. Can't promise some of it ain't still down there."

"I'm sure she'll understand."

"Want me to send it around? Toby's here, and—"

"Don't bother with it tonight. Tell me about the brakes. Were they shot?"

"Nope. She'll need new pads on the front in another ten thousand or so, but there's plenty on 'em now."

Of all the things Connor had expected, that wasn't one of them. He was about to say so when a crack of thunder rattled the windowpanes of the stone cottage and his eyes were drawn once more to the dramatic show nature was putting on outside. Distracted by the menacing sky and the feeling it stirred in him that something—something big—was about to happen and that he wanted Anne here, safe with him, he focused on the far end of the beach, on the grove of trees that hid Sandcastle from his view.

"Mel, that doesn't make sense. I was in that car when—"

"Damnedest thing," the older man cut in. "You know the clip that holds the brake pedal to the linkage? Some people might call it a pin, I guess. Ain't got a name that I know of, but you know what I'm talking about, don't you?"

"Yes. What about it?"

"It's gone."

"You mean it wore out?"

"I mean it ain't there. Probably happened before she started up. Then, driving across the lot, she must've hit a bump— wouldn't take much of one, just a big rock or a hole, and you and I know that lot's full of both."

"Yeah, so..."

"Well, when she hit this bump, the linkage and the pedal disconnected and, presto, no brakes."

"Presto, no brakes." It took about two seconds for the words to sink in. Then Connor felt the hairs rise on the back of his neck and a chill run up his spine. Suddenly, Mel had his full attention.

Carefully, he asked, "Are you saying somebody removed that clip?"

"Not necessarily," the mechanic returned. "Could be. Wouldn't take a minute. But it could've fallen out, too. Odd if it did, but wouldn't be impossible."

"If you had to guess . . ."

The mechanic drew a breath and let it hiss out between his teeth. "Con, I don't know. That's a hard one."

"It's just me you're talking to, Mel, not Ben Whitlow. This isn't for any accident report."

The mechanic sighed again. "I'll tell you this. I've only seen that clip fall out on its own maybe a half-dozen times in thirty years. And it was on cars that nobody'd taken care of. Not like this Volvo, here . . . if you understand my meaning."

Yes, Connor understood. And it made his blood run cold.

He told himself to take it easy. Reminded himself he'd been jumping to a lot of conclusions lately, none of which had any basis in fact. But his intuition wasn't listening to reason. He was thinking, again, about fires and heater cords. He was remembering Sandcastle's door sitting ajar last night and the screen missing from the window. He was imagining Anne waiting for him at Sandcastle . . . alone.

Or *was* she alone?

All at once, as he imagined what might be going on to send Rogue tearing off into a storm, the vague agitation inside him crystallized into a knot of cold, shaking dread.

Striding to the utility room, Connor snatched a gray rain poncho off the door. "Mel, thanks, but listen—"

"No problem. Tell Miss Marquel her car'll take a couple of days to dry—"

"Mel, I hate to cut you off, but I've got to run. Say hi to Ethel for me."

Connor threw the receiver onto the hook, the phone onto the table, and ran for the back door.

"All right," Anne's assailant growled. "You said there's more cash hidden in this place. Now, find it."

Anne sagged onto the bottom step of the broken staircase in Yesterday's Dream, her feet too sore to hold her any longer. The walk through the woods had been hellish, with the wind howling and lightning slanting across the sky above the trees.

Inside the manor, the only relief from blackness came from the
beam of a pocket flashlight her attacker had produced, and that
piercing light was now directed at her face. When he reached
over to yank the scarf out of her mouth to hang around her
neck, she turned her head and tried to work moisture into her
mouth to speak.

"I . . . can't."

"You'd better," he returned sharply.

"You heard me say I didn't know where the rest of the money
was."

"Yeah, it was real sweet the way lover boy didn't want you
getting all worked up over your memory problems. But I don't
give a damn how upset it makes you. I want that money, and
if you want to walk out of here, you'll remember where it is."

"If you kill me, you'll never get it," Anne reasoned.

His form was only a silhouette beyond the beam of light, but
she heard the evil amusement in his tone as he replied, "Did I
say I was going to kill you?"

No, he'd said if she didn't find the money, she wouldn't walk
out of here. If she'd known where it was, she'd have turned it
over instantly. But she hadn't a clue. And the chances of her
remembering were growing dimmer by the second. Her head
was spinning, and her chest felt so tight she could barely
breathe.

How much time did she have? How long could she stall?
And, oh, dear Lord in heaven, where was Connor? Surely he'd
gotten to Sandcastle by now and knew she was in trouble. But
her hopes wavered as she wondered how he'd know where to
find her.

"Come on! Get started!"

Anne jumped at the harsh order. "I'm . . . thinking."

"Well, think fast."

Shutting her eyes, she tried to do exactly that. If she could
remember where to find even one more bundle . . . "I— I don't
know . . ." she began.

The floorboards creaked and the flashlight beam moved as
he took a step toward her.

"Wait!" She flattened herself against the stairs. "You heard
me say there was money behind a panel in the parlor fireplace.
There was another panel like that one in . . . the upstairs sitting
room." She was guessing. She had no idea if other false panels

existed like the one in the parlor. But it seemed a logical idea. And any idea was better than none.

Wasting no more time, he grabbed her arm, hauled her to her feet, and pushed her recklessly up the broken stairs. At the top landing, he turned right, propelling her past the open doorway to her mother's bedroom and on into the sitting room.

Funny how he knew exactly where it was. But then, she thought, he'd already said he'd been in the manor. And more than likely, he'd been hiding in this very room, listening through the door—the door she'd thought she'd seen move—while she and Connor talked in the adjoining bedroom.

"Sit," he ordered, pushing her to the floor against the wall by the fireplace.

Anne clenched her teeth against a moan. Her wrists hurt abominably, her feet felt like pincushions, and the smell of her own fear filled her senses. But while he poked and prodded the painted wood surrounding the brick fireplace, she tried to ignore the pain and, instead, focus all her thoughts on willing Connor to come for her. Here. Now. Before it was too late...

Minutes ticked by. Outside, thunder crashed, and flashes of lightning streaked across the sky, slashing into the gloom inside the ravaged house through the unboarded windows. Brief illuminations cast from heaven into hell.

Anne's hopes of rescue faded, and rather than praying for deliverance, she began looking for places her mother might have hidden money. The drawer of her secretary? The ginger jar on the mantel? Everyplace her eyes came to rest seemed likely. No place sparked even the vaguest memory.

"These panels are solid." He turned the light toward her.

Anne shook her head. "I don't know. I thought—"

"You're playing games with me."

"No, I—"

"I think you are."

"No! Wait! I thought one of the boards came off. I swear. Maybe... maybe it was a different fireplace. I-I told you... or you heard me say I wasn't sure where—"

He was on his feet, pulling her up with him, before she could finish the sentence. "We're going to have a look at the fireplace in the parlor."

"But we can't go in there," she cried, resisting as he pushed her out of the room. "The floor is—"

"Shut up," he ordered.

"But the fire will have—"

"*Shut up!* Or maybe you'd like a trip into the cellar—a trip through the floor. That ought to cure your amnesia."

Hands. Those agonizingly familiar hands. They were the only thing that kept Anne from falling as he pushed her ahead of him, down the stairs. All thoughts of stalling him with another false lead vanished. Her life depended upon her ability to remember her mother's hiding places, and to remember them correctly. But the only memories Anne could recall were of being dragged through this same house, much in this same way, wondering how—and if—she would survive *this* time.

Without hesitation, the demon of the present, living nightmare shoved her past the yellow ropes into the ruins of the parlor. It was the way he followed her, though, completely oblivious to the danger, that, at last, made her see the truth. He wasn't only criminal, nor was he simply cruel. He was crazed. Obsessed with a goal he was pursuing with single-minded disregard even for his own safety. His identity remained couched in ambiguity, but she knew then that she didn't know this man. Regardless of who he was, his mind, his reasoning, was a mystery to her, a realization that heightened her fear a thousand-fold.

Rain pounded against the boarded windows, drowning out the sound of the floor cracking under Anne's raw feet. The flashlight beam cut only a short path into the inky blackness. But when she tried to step cautiously, her assailant propelled her forward, and she came within a hairsbreadth of tripping directly into a gaping hole. The board at the edge of the hole broke off and fell into the cellar, and she would have fallen, too, had the fingers digging into her upper arms not been quick to yank her back.

Anne never knew how they managed to cross from one side of the room to the other, but when he shoved her to the floor, she drew her knees up and huddled in as small a space as she could manage, not daring to move, hardly daring to breathe, praying that the trembling of her body wouldn't be more than the splintery boards beneath her could withstand.

It took only seconds for her attacker to scan the wall beside the chimney with his flashlight and see that it was little more than cinders. He poked the panel behind which Anne had seen her mother stash her money, only to have it crumble away. Behind it, there was nothing, Nothing but the outer brick wall.

"Too bad," he muttered. "Too bad."

"But you knew it couldn't still be there!" Anne protested, realizing she was trying to reason with a madman. She didn't want to move, but as the light approached her, she began desperately, "Let me go up to the bedroom, where I found the money this morning. Maybe it'll help. Maybe if I—"

"You're doing this deliberately."

She shook her head. "I swear I'm not. I really don't remember, but if you—"

"I say you *do* remember."

"No, I—"

"I say you're lying. And little girls who lie need to be punished."

Anne sucked in a breath, her heart leaping to her throat. Suddenly her whole awareness focused on the piercing white eye directly above her and the words that seemed to come drifting out of the darkest recesses of her mind.

"I'm going to punish you," he said. "And when I'm finished, you'll do as I say. You need a lesson in obedience, little girl. And I'm going to give it to you."

She knew then. Beyond a shadow of a doubt. And when he reached for her, the scream torn from her lungs was that of a woman being kidnapped into hell by Satan himself.

The sheet of rain, traveling across the water, hit land as Connor pulled his truck to a stop at Sandcastle. The front door sitting open served to justify his fears, and in the next instant, when Rogue bounded out of the cottage and raced off into the woods, barking, Connor bolted from the pickup and all but flew across the clearing toward the gaping doorway. He didn't pause until he was through it and halfway across the sitting room. Then, the sight of the ransacked room brought him staggering to a halt.

The scene didn't hold him for long, though, before terror drove him into action.

"Anne!" Racing toward the bedroom, kicking drawers and pillows and lamps aside, Connor shouted, "Anne! Where are you?"

Not in the bedroom, or the bathroom, or the kitchen. It took less than a minute to search the cottage, a minute filled with bloodcurdling images of what he might find. But he found nothing. Only Anne's sandals, dropped amid the wreckage in the sitting room.

With a hoarse cry, he flung the sandals aside and ran outside, into the pouring rain. "Anne! For God's sake, answer me!" He was drenched to the skin within seconds, and his shouts were lost in the storm. But he kept calling as he searched. He covered every inch of ground surrounding the cottage, even checking the shoreline, where breakers washed over the edge of the bank to soak his feet. All the while, the litany pounded in his head: *Don't let it be too late, oh, Jesus, please, don't let it be too late.*

He'd scoured the bushes beside the front door of the cottage three times and was on his way back inside to search again when it hit him that he was running in circles. He made himself stop. Made himself stand still. Forced himself to acknowledge the fact: She was gone.

Standing in the center of the clearing, with the rain beating down upon him, Connor pressed his hands to his head and tried to keep the panic rising like a volcano inside him from erupting. He had to *do* something. Go back to Sentinel, call the police. But by then, Anne could be . . .

No. Don't think it. Think about where she could be. *Think.* Somewhere on the property? Or had he taken her away? Dear God, would he actually kill her? Or would he be satisfied with scaring her into giving him what he wanted?

Feeling more helpless than he'd ever felt in his life, Connor was about to go call the police. But as he started for the truck, Rogue ran into the clearing from the woods. His head jerked toward the dog, and he said the first thing that came to mind.

"Rogue! Find Anne."

He knew, even as he said it, that it was hopeless. The setter had a better sense for trouble than any dog he'd ever owned, and he sure as hell was trying to tell him *something,* barking and dancing around in front of him. But he wasn't trained to hunt. Besides, the rain had washed away whatever tracks there might have been. And he'd only known Anne four days. He probably wouldn't recognize her name.

"Find *Anne,*" Connor tried again. "You understand? Find . . ." He trailed off, struck by the sudden thought that he was going about this all wrong.

"Rogue! Come here!" he ordered. And when the setter responded instantly, racing over to him, he stooped down to take the sleek wet head between his hands and force the dog to meet his gaze.

"Find *Aaron*," he said.

The setter barked once and squirmed to get away.

Connor's hands tightened on the black fur. "Find Aaron, Rogue. Find *Aaron*."

The instant he let go of him, Rogue turned and ran for the path leading into the woods, his black form disappearing quickly among the blowing trees and undergrowth. Rising to stand, Connor tossed the wet hair out of his eyes, then squinted at the path through the wind and rain that whipped at his face. He knew where the trail ended, and he guessed Rogue was heading for the manor because he knew Aaron lived there. But it was as good a place as any to look. And as Connor jumped into his truck and tore off along the mud-washed track, it occurred to him that, in its current state, the manor was a fitting setting for someone with murder on his mind.

She was alone. Alone with the demon. Again. Still. Would it never end? Was she to relive the past over and over with no more power to change the course of events than she'd ever had?

With her tied hands grinding into the burnt floor beneath her, Anne let her eyes drift closed and consciously willed her mind away from her body. Willed herself not to hear the harsh breathing. The ripping cloth. Not to feel the hands. Not to whimper or flinch. Not to notice the satisfied grunt when her efforts failed.

No! Don't let him! Fight!

How? With what?

You've still got your voice! Scream!

So far away. Storm's so loud. Who would hear? He'd hit me, gag me. Better to ignore him. Better to lie still and quiet. Better to act like nothing matters. He hates that. Think of something else. Think of anything...books...a story...Connor... Oh, Lord. Oh, Con...

No! Don't think about Connor. You'll cry. Think of...home. Friends. School.

School. Yes. School will be starting soon. Have to get ready. So many things to do. Need to find out if those new books came. See if they— Oh! Oh, Lord, no. *No*...

An involuntary cry. A laugh. Wicked sound in the darkness.

Don't listen. Don't feel.

Oh, mercy, oh, dear Lord, no, please, no, I can't live through this, I can't . . .

You will! You must!

I'll never survive it again. I'll—I'll—

Suddenly, a split second short of hysteria, Anne's eyes flew open, and she caught her breath. At the same time the man above her went completely still. And in the dark, ensuing silence, there came a sound that was, to Anne's ears, the herald of salvation: the familiar bark of a large dog.

In the next instant she was screaming at the top of her lungs, and her attacker was scrambling away, muttering curses about the interfering bastard who'd ruined his plans too many times. Struggling to sit up, Anne saw him crawling, fumbling with his clothes as he tried to flee, and something inside her snapped. With a savage growl, a primitive sound that contained all the rage of a lifetime, she drew her knees up and shoved with both feet, shoved with all her might, and sent him sprawling, face-down, on the undermined floor.

The floor cracked. The boards beneath him broke. And before he could roll to safety, he plunged, cursing her to hell, into the cellar below.

The cellar floor was dirt, awash from the fire hoses. He landed with a sharp cry, followed by a long, loud groan. Then she heard some sloshing sounds, more groans, the rasp of metal sliding against metal, the rusty squeak of the little-used door that led from the cellar into the garden.

He was getting away, but she didn't care. It only mattered that he was gone. And a second later, her head jerked around when the front door crashed open and Connor ran into the hall.

Chapter Thirteen

"Miss Marquel, I'm sorry. I have just a couple more questions, if you—"

"Come on, Ben. That's enough."

"Con, I've gotta find out—"

"Go catch Aaron, and let *him* answer the damned questions."

"Well, maybe if I knew for certain—"

"Connor, it's all right." Anne murmured the reassurance without a scrap of conviction. It had been, perhaps, a half hour since Connor had rescued her, but her head still felt as though it were shrouded in fog. She barely remembered how he'd gotten her out of the manor, recalled only that he'd yanked the wood off the window from the outside, climbed up, then somehow leaned in to untie and lift her before lowering her to the tailgate of his truck, parked below. After that, her only memory was of being in his arms, of him holding her, saying her name, calling her his love, his darling Anne, as they'd huddled together in the rain.

She would always remember the rain. Cold, clean torrents of it pouring down upon them. She'd have stood there with him indefinitely. But Connor had bundled her into the truck, hastily pulling his rain poncho over her head, growling something about calling the police. And so, here she was—when the only place she wanted to be was in a steaming-hot bath.

Tucked in a corner of the couch, her fingers curled around a mug of peppermint tea, Anne caught a glimpse of Connor as his restless pacing brought him across the stone hearth in front of her and around Ben Whitlow, seated in the rocker to her left. He thought Whitlow should be out catching Aaron. She, too, wished the policeman would leave. She felt dirty, inside and out, and, as courteous as Whitlow had been, she hated having his curious brown eyes peer at her from beneath their bushy brows.

Was he remembering how she'd looked the previous morning, when he'd helped to haul her, screaming, out of the water? No doubt he was. No doubt his first, unfortunate impression of her was being well reinforced and she imagined that, in Ben Whitlow's eyes, her credibility was rather low.

"Listen, Con," Whitlow said, a trace of impatience coloring his Eastern Shore drawl. "If it's going to be necessary, I can take Miss Marquel down to the station, and you can stay—"

"No!" Halfway back across the hearth, Connor pivoted to face the older man. "She's not going anywhere."

"It wouldn't be my choice," Whitlow returned, the inference being that Connor's behavior would determine the issue.

"Con, please." Anne raised her eyes to find his blue gaze upon her. "I'm all right."

His mouth twitched downward, and it was clear he knew she was lying. But he didn't argue. His eyes swept over her once more, ferociously protective; then, with a muttered oath, he stalked away.

Whitlow shot him a wary glance before focusing his attention on the clipboard resting on his thigh. "Now, let's see.... You say your assailant was masked."

"Yes," Anne replied.

"And he wore gloves to search your cottage?"

"I think so. They were there, and they weren't mine."

"And you didn't recognize his voice or anything else."

"His general size was right. But he was thinner."

"How long has it been since you've seen your brother?"

"Twelve years."

Whitlow gave her a startled glance. Then, frowning, he studied his notes, his pencil tapping his clipboard. Finally, he shook his head. "Miss Marquel, I guess I don't understand how come you're so sure this man who attacked you was your brother."

"Dammit, Ben, what are you trying to do?"

Connor's rough comment drew a sigh from Whitlow and brought Anne's anxious gaze flashing toward him.

Standing sideways in the doorway to the porch, his arms folded across his chest, he stared at the river, now flowing quietly under a lavender sunset, as he said, "We both know Aaron's turned into a scarecrow and that his hair's gone mostly gray. I haven't noticed that his voice has changed, but I hear it all the time. Seems as if it's *always* sounded like a radio speaker with holes punched in it. Anne's description matches any I'd give of him."

"That's not the point. I want to know—"

"It *is* the point!"

"It isn't, unless *you* can tell me why Aaron Marquel might be running around with a stocking over his head, beating up his sister, after he got into his girlfriend's car and left, saying he'd be in Europe for a month!" Holding up a hand to stop Connor's protest, Whitlow continued more sympathetically. "Look, I know your lady friend's been through the wringer. But I've got a job to do. So will you please just relax and let me get it over with?" Without waiting for a response, Whitlow shifted his attention back to Anne. "Now, Miss Marquel—"

"Wait."

"Aw, for Pete's sake, Con, why don't you go—"

"Aaron's here because he wants Yesterday's Dream."

Connor's statement brought a puzzled frown to Anne's brow. But while she could only look at Connor in hazy bewilderment, Whitlow asked, "What the devil are you talking about?"

Raking a hand through his damp hair, as if debating how to continue, Connor swung around to face them and announced, "I think it was Aaron who started the fire Tuesday night."

The rocker creaked as Whitlow straightened, his expression becoming thoroughly skeptical. "You're not going to tell me you think he was trying to cheat the insurance company, are you? Because the fire marshal's report—"

Connor gave his head a shake. "This isn't about insurance—at least, not anymore." With a harsh laugh, he added, "Though I'm sure Aaron's looking forward to collecting his half, and maybe, at first, that's all he wanted. God knows, he seems desperate enough to try anything to get his hands on some fast cash.''

Anne didn't understand why Connor thought Aaron would destroy what he wanted to sell. But while she tried to force her brain to reason it through, Whitlow chose the direct approach.

"Explain," he said.

Connor did so in blunt terms. "Aaron's made Anne several offers to buy her half of the estate, but she won't sell it to him. He's had developers looking over the place, and I think it's *that* money he's really after. He doesn't give a damn about the manor. It's only worth a fraction of what he'd get for the property. And I'm guessing that, since Anne won't sell, he's decided to get it away from her some other way."

"*What* other way?" Whitlow asked, clearly baffled. "How does burning the place down—"

Connor waved him off. "I told you, I don't know what his original plan was. Maybe he thought Anne wouldn't care about the property if the manor was gone, so he torched it. *I* think he did it to lure her home, knowing she'd be called to handle things after the fire. But it doesn't matter. One way or the other, she's here, and—" Halting in front of the fireplace, Connor let out a shuddering breath. "Ben, I think he wants to kill her."

In the silence that followed, Anne felt the shock roll through her. Yet she didn't doubt Connor's thinking. She only wondered why she hadn't seen it herself. She should have known when she refused Aaron's offers that he wouldn't take no for an answer. When had he ever?

Whitlow, however, wasn't convinced. "Con, do you know what you're saying?" he asked slowly.

"Yes, I know, dammit!" Connor's hand slashed the air in a silencing gesture. "And before you ask, I'll tell you, I don't have any proof. I just started putting it together last night. I was going to call Howard Stone and ask him what he thought I ought to do. But I was only thinking about the fire—how Aaron might be trying to manipulate Anne into selling. It didn't cross my mind that he might actually go as far as murder—not until this afternoon." Pausing to give Anne a worried glance, Connor told Whitlow, "I was on my way out the door to get Anne when Mel Beatty called about the brakes on her car."

Whitlow's brow furrowed. "You talking about that missing clip? You think Marquel did it?"

Connor nodded.

Anne didn't know anything about a "missing clip," but, again, she was certain Connor was right. It was too perfect to be coincidence. Aaron knew better than anyone what throwing her into the water would accomplish—and that's where her car was almost guaranteed to land when she headed for the lot exit.

A shiver raced up her spine, and, although she wasn't aware of it, she realized she must have made some sound of distress, for the next instant, Connor was sitting on the edge of the couch beside her, setting her tea mug on the table behind them, then wrapping her hands in his.

His eyes were dark, his tone anguished. "Annie, I'm sorry. I wish you didn't have to hear it this way. And I wish to God I'd let the damned phone ring, so I'd have gotten there sooner. But if I hadn't answered it, I wouldn't know about the brakes, and—"

"No," she interrupted him in a whisper. "You got there in time, and that's all that matters."

"It's *not* all that matters," he growled, a look of raw fury passing across his features as his eyes skimmed over the faint bruise on her cheek, then fell to her hands, lying in his. His thumb brushed gently across the red mark around one wrist as he muttered, "He's crazy if he thinks I'll let him get away with this. If I'd gotten there and found you... If I'd been too late... God help me, I think I'd kill him."

Anne started to protest, then hesitated. And in the next instant her blood ran cold, imagining Connor's reaction if he learned how close Aaron had come, not that day but long ago, to accomplishing the deed.

He's going to find out.

No!

Yes, he is. You're going to tell him.

No! No, I don't want him to hear it!

You're going to tell him and this policeman what they need to know, because if you don't, Aaron will kill you.

Seized by a rush of panic, Anne felt her entire body tense. When Whitlow cleared his throat, reminding her of his presence, she withdrew her hands from Connor's and lowered her gaze.

"Look here, Con," the policeman began, "this business about the brakes seems pretty farfetched when you consider—"

"Have you asked?" Connor demanded. "Have you asked *specifically* if anyone saw Aaron Marquel—or anybody else—near that car before the accident?"

"No," Whitlow drawled. "But Mel didn't say anything to me about the brakes being tampered with."

"But they *could* have been."

"Maybe. Most likely not. I'll ask around some more. But unless somebody turns up who saw Marquel, I can't arrest him for attempted murder with nothing to go on but your guesswork."

"Nothing to go on!" Connor's eyes blazed in outrage. "What about Anne? Doesn't looking at her tell you anything?"

Whitlow's kind but skeptical gaze slid toward her, and Anne shrank into the cushions, wrapping her arms about her waist, feeling the policeman's eyes upon her . . . feeling the thin, rubberized fabric of the rain slicker sticking uncomfortably to her skin through the tears in her clothing.

You can't keep it a secret anymore.

Yes, I can. It's over. Part of the past.

The past is here, you fool. It's happening now. You can't hide or run from it. You have to say it. Now!

Shaking his head, Whitlow concluded, "The way she looks doesn't tell me anybody was trying to murder her. And neither does anything she's said. Hell, this character didn't even have a weapon. It sounds to me like he was more interested in scaring her than anything else."

With a growl of supreme frustration, Connor surged to his feet, his angry strides taking him behind the couch, out of Anne's line of vision.

"Con, be reasonable," Whitlow said. "You know I can't go stirring up a hornet's nest at the station without having some sort of evidence that these ideas of yours might be right."

Connor's response was a brief, uncommonly vulgar oath that expressed his opinion of the need for more evidence.

Whitlow sighed and rolled his eyes.

Anne sat in stony silence.

"Come on, Con," Whitlow urged. "What have you given me? A *guess* that a man *you* saw leave for Europe started a fire the fire marshal says started with a space heater. There's not a word in that report about arson. Now, I know it's gotta be hard, having the finger pointed at your mother, but—"

"Is that what you think I'm trying to do? Get my mother off the hook?"

"What I'm *starting* to see," Whitlow replied carefully, "is that you've got a lot of personal reasons for being upset, and that you're blowing this thing all out of proportion by—"

"Oh, right! I find Anne tied, hand and foot, in a fire-gutted room, looking like she's been dragged along the river bottom, but *I'm* way out of line!"

He's fighting for you. For your honor. For your life. Help him....

Anne's eyes drifted closed, her arms creeping further around her waist, her fingers digging into her ribs, squeezing tightly...tightly....

"I'm not making light of what happened," Whitlow argued. "I'm only saying you can't go turning a brother-sister squabble over the sale of some property into a motive for murder!"

"God Almighty, the property's worth a good seven million!"

"Okay, but, dammit, that doesn't make Aaron Marquel an arsonist and a murderer! Con, be realistic! They're having a fight. Brothers and sisters fight all the time. It's *normal.*"

"It's *not* normal how Aaron has always treated Anne. But I'll be damned if I'm going to stand here arguing about it. If you won't go after him, I will."

"Now, hold on there just a minute!"

Anne's eyes flew open, and she looked to see Connor moving rapidly toward the porch, and Whitlow, out of his chair, striding after him, insisting, "You're not going anywhere," and Connor shouting back, "The hell I'm not!"—at which point she slammed her eyes closed and pressed her hands to her ears. But she couldn't shut out the sound of angry male voices.

"Con, have you lost your mind? If you think I'll let you go off half-cocked like this—"

"Ben, I *know* Aaron Marquel. I've known him for twenty-two years! He's a mean, vindictive sonofabitch, and I'm telling you, if he wants something and Anne won't give it to him, he'll take it any way he can get it!"

"But we don't even know for sure it was Marquel!"

"Dammit, we do know! Anne saw him!"

"She saw a man she didn't recognize, who tried to rob—"

"God, even my dog knew it was Aaron! And he's going to kill her if—"

"A minute ago you were talking about killing *him!* And I'll be damned if I'll let you go ruin your life just because some jackass was beating up on your—"

"Stop! Stop, I can't stand it! It *was* Aaron, I know it was, and he wasn't beating me, he was trying to rape me, and I can't prove it, but it's true, I swear, it's all true!"

The shrill outburst shocked Anne so deeply that she scarcely realized it had been she who'd spoken. Her eyes opened in both alarm and bewilderment at the sudden and complete silence that had fallen. When it hit her that it had been her voice, her words, blackness threatened to overwhelm her, and she felt weak all over.

Horror overcame the weakness. Horror over what she'd done. Her breath caught, and her head jerked around, her gaze shooting across the room to find both men looking at her, their faces frozen in shock. For one awful moment they stared at each other as people might who'd seen a freak tornado whirl past or a sea monster rise from the ocean. It couldn't have happened. It wasn't real. Then, slowly, his appalled gaze never leaving her face, Connor crossed to stand in front of the fireplace. And, from across the room, Whitlow voiced a single wary question.

"Pardon me, Miss Marquel . . . what did you say?"

A whimper escaped her, and Anne's hands flew to cover her face. He'd heard her. Just as Connor had heard her. No chance that they hadn't or that she could take it back. She'd have to go on. She'd have to speak the words. Forbidden words. And, in her heart, Anne knew it was time . . . far past time. . . .

With her voice muffled against her hands, she said, "Aaron wasn't beating me. He never beat me. Not after Con caught him trying, once, and made him stop. Usually, he . . . he broke my things and did things to make my father mad, then made it look as if I'd done them. But after he left boarding school and . . . and came home to stay . . ." She sucked in a quick breath and squeezed her eyes closed. "He started molesting me. He did . . . sexual things to me, and he made me do them to him. And this afternoon, he . . . he would have raped me. And it wouldn't have been the first time he'd done that, either."

Silence. It hung, quivering, in the air. A light wind blew, sending a shower of raindrops from the leaves of the locust beside the cottage splattering across the porch roof. The floor creaked beneath Ben Whitlow's footsteps as he came to stand at the foot of the couch. Then, suddenly, the silence exploded in a burst of shattering glass.

Anne's head snapped up, her hands falling from her face, her startled gaze focusing instantly on the mass of scarlet zinnias and chunks of brown earthenware lying scattered across the stones of the hearth. Half-dazed, she stared at the wreckage, watching water spread and darken the slate-gray stones, seeping through the cracks in the mortar, until a thin trickle reached Connor's right foot.

His feet were bare and appeared horribly vulnerable beside the broken pottery, and it seemed quite logical to her, at that moment, that she should do something to prevent him from being cut.

"Oh. Oh, no, let me get—"

"Here, now, Miss Marquel, wait—"

She was halfway off the couch when Whitlow stepped in front of her, his hand outstretched to stop her. But when he took hold of her elbow, she gasped and jerked away.

Her action startled them both, but the policeman was quick to understand.

"Here, now," he said again, his hand hovering but not touching as he urged her back onto the couch. "You don't need to be cleaning up messes just this minute, do you? Con'll take care of it later. You just sit and relax . . . that's right. . . ."

Flustered, embarrassed, Anne perched on the edge of the cushion, her gaze skidding across the floor, darting from the flowers and the broken vase . . . to Connor's feet, which hadn't moved . . . then, finally, upward, seeking Connor's.

But he was standing with his back to her, his hands clutching the mantel—his left hand wrapped over the edge of the beam where, moments before, the vase of zinnias had been. She watched his knuckles whiten, saw his shoulders heave in a ragged gasp for breath, while words like *Please, I'm sorry, it wasn't supposed to happen this way,* ran through her mind. The sheer inadequacy of them sickened her.

"Con . . ." she began, but the whispered plea was soundless, and he didn't give her a chance to repeat it.

Suddenly, with a low, strangled cry, he flung himself across the room, heading toward the porch. She thought he was going to leave, and she started after him. But he came to a halt in the doorway, his hands gripping the frame on either side, and she stopped, too, her hand outstretched toward him, imploring.

He didn't want to look at her, it was clear. And the truth was, she understood. She could hardly stand it herself.

Sagging back onto the couch, Anne let her arm drop to her side and her gaze fall to the floor, to the ruined vase and the bright red flowers. Her lower lip trembled.

She was barely aware of Ben Whitlow, pulling his rocker closer to her and lowering himself into it. Leaning forward, forearms resting on his thighs, he started to speak, hesitated, then began again in subdued tones.

"I, um, take it that Con didn't know about...this."

A few seconds passed before Anne shook her head.

Whitlow let out a labored sigh and ran a hand across his jaw. "Did you tell *anybody?*"

Again, she shook her head. And because she knew that if any purpose was to be served by this torture, she had to convince Whitlow that her life was in danger, she forced herself to add, "I tried to tell my father once. It was a mistake. I think I was trying to make him behave the way a father should... to prove he loved me, when it had always been clear he didn't. It had been a month, maybe a little longer, since the...first time Aaron...did it. But Aaron heard me talking and came into the study before I'd said anything... anything too damning."

Anne paused, staring at her fingers twisting the folds of the gray slicker. "My father was drunk. It passed over his head that anything was really wrong. He sent us both away and told us not to bother him. That night Aaron broke into my room. I'd been locking it, but he always found a way in. He tied me up, and he took me to the boathouse, onto my father's motor yacht. Then he took us out into the Bay. It was late, and I couldn't see land, and there weren't any other boats around. He took the Boston Whaler off its davits, and I...I thought he was going to set me adrift in it, but he... hung a big fishnet from the eyehook between the davits, and he...put me in it."

A noise from the other side of the room, a choked-off sound of distress, made Anne shut her eyes. If she looked at Connor, she'd never finish.

"I was still tied," she went on, "so when he lowered the net, I couldn't keep my head out of the water. It was spring, mid-May, and the water was cold. It made it harder for me to hold my breath for very long. I thought that was what he wanted, that he wanted to drown me. But he hauled me up and waited until I was breathing all right, then he dunked me again."

Struggling to overcome the nausea rising in her throat, Anne drew a slow breath. "I don't know how many times he did it. But every time he hauled me up, he said he was punishing me. That when he was through, I'd do exactly what he told me to do. And that if I ever again tried to tell anyone what he was doing to me...he'd kill me." Taking another controlled, steadying breath, she finished. "I believed him. I still do."

When Anne shifted her gaze to Whitlow, she was certain she knew what she'd find. After all, she'd spent years imagining how people would look at her if they knew. And, indeed, the policeman's expression reflected horror. But his brown gaze held compassion, too, and, most important, it was clear that he believed her. Which should give her some sense of relief or satisfaction...shouldn't it?

"Miss Marquel—" Whitlow broke off, his gaze sliding from hers. "I'm sorry, I don't have much experience with...this sort of thing, but...why in God's name is your brother so...so *hostile* toward you?"

Anne had spent years asking the same question, too many of them blaming herself, feeling like a terrible person, abandoned by her will-o'-the-wisp mother, unworthy of her father's most casual regard, and, therefore, deserving of the punishment Aaron meted out. Only in working with Miriam Abrams had she realized the truth. At the moment, though, the only way she could talk about it without coming unraveled was in cold, clinical terms.

"Aaron is sick," she said. "Mentally ill. Sociopathic, if you need a label. He can be charming. The perfect host for the kind of parties I understand he throws. But he'll do anything to get what he wants. He has no conscience, no mercy or compassion. He doesn't understand right and wrong." Pausing, she added, "And he hates me."

"But do you know *why?*" Whitlow prodded.

"For being born," Anne replied tonelessly. "I think he believes I stole our parents' attention, when there wasn't any to steal. That I'm the reason he got sent to boarding school at six, when the truth is my father sent him because he was jealous of my mother's attention for either Aaron or me. He would have sent me, too, but my mother died, and after that...well, he didn't care. Mostly, my parents ignored me. But Aaron believes I got what he didn't, and so he begrudges me everything—everything I own...every breath I take."

Carefully, she reasoned, "I'm sure, in his mind, I owe him Yesterday's Dream. If he has to kill me to get it...well, it would give him an excuse to do what he's wanted to do for years."

A minute passed before Whitlow voiced his troubled thoughts. "Well, *I'm* ready to pick him up. But I know damned well what's going to happen if I bring him in without any evidence against him. He'll get off without our being able to charge him with anything. I just wish there was something—something concrete—like if you could give us a positive ID or—"

"It was his hands."

He frowned at Anne's quiet interruption. "His hands? The way they looked, you mean?"

"No. The way they felt." She pressed her lips together, her voice cracking. "Officer Whitlow, I spent three years of my life enduring Aaron's sexual abuse, from the time I was thirteen until I finally left home to get away from him. I swear to you, I could be blindfolded and I'd be able to pick him out of a thousand men, just by the feel of his hands on me. If I live to be a hundred, I'll never...*never* forget what it's like to be touched by him."

Whitlow studied her for a moment, then, dropping his gaze, he murmured, "No, I don't suppose you will."

They sat for several moments in silence. Anne stared at a single red zinnia lying amidst the wreckage on the floor, its petals crumpled, its stem broken.

Finally, Whitlow stuck his pencil into his shirt pocket, tucked his clipboard under his arm, and rose. "I'd better get into the station," he said. "Soon as I report this, we'll start looking for your brother. Bring him in for questioning. If he's hurt, like you said, he'll have some explaining to do."

"Try Holly Knoll. The Thorpe place."

Connor's rasping comment made Anne's heart leap painfully. She took a quick look, saw he'd turned to face the room, then dropped her gaze.

He spoke directly to Whitlow. "Blaine Thorpe's got a runabout that Aaron uses to go back and forth to her place."

"You think he came in by boat?" Whitlow asked.

"It's a guess. A boat would be easier to hide than a car."

"That's where we'll start, then." Somewhat awkwardly, the policeman added, "Miss Marquel, I'm . . . sorry. That's a helluva thing to say, I know, but . . ."

"Thank you, Officer." Anne spoke without lifting her gaze. "You've been very kind."

He hesitated. "You know, it might be good if you went home. Might be best if you could stay with a friend. Somebody your brother doesn't know. As long as we know where to find you." Turning to Connor, he started to add, "In the meantime—"

"She won't be out of my sight," Connor cut him off.

Whitlow nodded as if satisfied and, saying good-night to her, motioned for Connor to see him out.

Ironically, Anne half wished he'd take her with him. But with that route of escape closed, she sought another. Unable to face her shattered hopes, she rose from the couch and crept up the stairs, intent upon being in the tub before Connor returned.

Chapter Fourteen

Connor returned to the living room, found Anne gone, and immediately went into panic mode. Starting for the porch, he called her name, but when a board creaked overhead, he tossed a glance at the ceiling, then headed up the stairs two at a time. He arrived at the top as the bathroom door at the other end of the hallway clicked shut. A second later he heard the metallic clank of the tub drain, then a loud rush of water.

Staring down the length of the dark corridor, he wondered if she had everything she needed—towels, soap, shampoo. But then, even if she didn't, he didn't know what he'd have done. He was no more ready to face her than he had been twenty minutes ago.

He didn't know if he'd ever be ready.

He didn't know how he was going to go on.

He didn't know what power was keeping him on his feet, moving, breathing, thinking about things like towels and shampoo.

Turning abruptly, Connor ran back down the stairs. Afraid to stop, afraid to think, afraid of what would happen if he let go for even a second, he willed his body to physical activity and his mind to anything but Anne.

The dead zinnias and the broken vase hit the trash with a thought about Leila Hornsby, who'd given him the vase three ... no, four years ago. Leila had hated dogs. The mug Anne had used got washed and put away with a reminder to himself that he was low on peppermint tea. He liked it cold with lemon. He checked the porch to see if Rogue had come home, then he made himself a peanut butter and jelly sandwich. He should be hungry. He hadn't eaten since breakfast. But the first bite he took turned his stomach, and he threw the rest away.

Connor was relieved when Rogue trotted in as he was straightening the couch. He'd been worried. The setter appeared his usual cocky self, but he was wet and matted with burrs and twigs. Grooming him took fifteen minutes, and every second that passed Connor expected to hear the water draining through the pipes from the bathtub, telling him that his time had run out. But he heard nothing, and when Rogue was back to normal, he locked the windows and doors on the first floor of the cottage, then went upstairs to find Anne some clothes.

He wasn't about to go to Sandcastle to get her things, so he rooted through his closet for something she could put on. Jeans and an oxford-cloth shirt would do, he decided, and he was laying them across the back of a chair when an image flashed through his mind of Anne's own clothes as they'd appeared when he'd lifted her through the parlor window. Signs of struggle, he'd thought, without it occurring to him what the nature of that struggle had been. Her blouse ripped, bra straps broken and her breasts exposed, shorts bunched oddly around her hips as if they'd been shoved down and she'd wiggled them on with her hands tied—as if she'd been trying to hide the truth, as if she hadn't wanted him to know ... as if she thought she could keep it from him ...

Suddenly, Connor couldn't go on. Couldn't keep moving. Couldn't pretend he was handling this when he knew he wasn't.

A surge of grief and fury rose from deep inside him and burst out in an anguished sob. And it kept coming. All at once, he couldn't see for the tears streaming down his face, and he was doubled over, hugging his ribs against the pain tearing at his gut. But as another cry escaped, he made his way out onto the balcony, where he clutched the wrought-iron railing and tried for all he was worth to stay on his feet.

He *couldn't* fall apart. He would *not* let Anne hear this. It was his problem, not hers, and he wouldn't burden her with it. She'd suffered enough. God, what she'd suffered...

Oh, God, make it a lie.

The night was dark. No lights of civilization to disrupt the velvet cloak, save the stars dotting the sky, and a quarter moon rising in the east. The air was clean from the rain, and warm, and it smelled of salt and summer.

Leaning heavily on the railing, Connor sucked in huge draughts of it as he struggled to keep from getting sick. It had been bad enough this afternoon, picturing Anne being raped by some anonymous villain. It had been worse searching for her during the storm, imagining Aaron murdering her. Now he knew there were things worse than murder—or as bad—and it required no effort at all to imagine what Anne had been made to endure.

The scenes hung there, painted in hideous detail against the black expanse of the river before him. Sexual acts. Things meant to be shared in love, perverted and defiled by the use of force and the repulsive notion that it had been her brother forcing them upon her. He saw it happening in the boathouse, in the empty stables, in Anne's room at night when her father was insensible with drink and wouldn't have heard a thing. He saw it happening everywhere, at every time of the day and night. And emblazoned across all these sadistic scenes, he saw her dangling in a net above ninety feet of cold, black water, gasping for breath and certain she was about to die.

It was real. Not a fantasy. And, God help him, he'd been there. *Here,* in this miserable prison of a place somebody'd had the appallingly bad judgment to have named Yesterday's Dream. *Three years,* Anne had said it had gone on. And he hadn't had a clue. Maybe someone trained to know the signs might have guessed that her sudden withdrawal was an indication of abuse, but it certainly had never occurred to him.

So, here he was, fifteen years after the fact, finding out that Anne, his friend since childhood, once the keeper of his most private confidences, now the woman he loved, had been brutalized by a depraved maniac. Her brother. And he could do nothing—*nothing*—about it. It was too late. The damage was done. And he was left to "handle it."

Nothing new. Yet even as Connor recognized that he'd been here before, he knew this was worse. His life was replete with circumstances and events he'd had no power to change, a long string of them beginning with his father's death. But this wasn't a sudden tragedy for which no one was to blame. Someone was to blame, all right. Someone for whom he'd never felt anything but intense dislike.

Hate, real hate, was an awful thing, and it took root with terrifying speed, growing, spreading, filling him with a poisonous, obsessive need to hurt, to do harm. He saw Aaron's face, dissipated and indifferent, and he wanted him dead. Smashed. Pounded to hell, where he belonged. The bastard. The malignant, evil-minded bastard.

He'd known it, too. He'd *known* Aaron Marquel was no good. Since the week after he'd come to live at Yesterday's Dream, when he'd followed a little girl's cries into the woods and had caught Aaron beating Anne with a switch made of sticks. He'd looked at Anne, who'd been six, and at her scrawny nine-year-old brother, and he'd spent about two seconds considering the ill effect his actions might have on his mother's new job. Then he'd made Anne leave, and he'd beaten the daylights out of that wretched little jerk. And he'd told him if he ever laid a hand on Anne again, he'd break his arms.

He wished he'd done more than that. He wished he'd killed him. What did they do to a twelve-year-old who'd beaten another kid to death? Whatever it was, it couldn't be any worse than the punishment Aaron had inflicted upon Anne for having done nothing but exist. And, at that moment, it seemed as if any penance he himself might have paid would have been worth it, not to be standing here, all these years later, sickened with the knowledge of how little heed Aaron had paid to his warning—or, God help him, that the warning might even have made matters worse.

How was he ever going to live with this? He didn't think he'd ever be able to look at Anne again without wanting to break down and cry. To cry for her pain and her loneliness, for the dreams and the innocence laid waste. To cry for his own dreams, because he didn't know how, given a lifetime to try, he'd ever batter down the wall of fear that had been built with such thoroughness around her.

How could *he* hope to accomplish what professional help and her own courageous efforts had not? Was he really so arrogant as to think that his love—oh, yes, that sacred, long-hoarded gift he'd been considering he *might* decide to bestow upon her—

would ever be enough? He'd be a fool to believe it. A simple-minded, heartsick fool. And after today's refresher course in terror, which had undoubtedly reinforced the lessons that touching meant pain and that men were animals, he'd be lucky if she'd even look at him....

Anne's bare feet made no sound on the bedroom floor as she padded cautiously toward the balcony. The bath had done lit-tle to soothe her ravaged nerves, and as she stopped a couple of steps from the open doorway to fix her anxious gaze on Con-nor, standing at the railing with his back to her, common sense argued that she should probably just swallow a tranquillizer and go to sleep. But she didn't have a tranquillizer, and she wouldn't have taken it if she had. For now that she felt clean again—outside, anyway—she was obsessed with the need to face what she'd hidden in the bathtub to avoid.

Watching Connor's shoulders rise and fall in a heavy sigh, she felt the knot in her stomach tighten, and her hands moved up and down her arms, covered in Connor's dark blue robe. The summer-weight flannel seemed a thin shield against na-kedness. But it was soft, and it smelled like Connor, and she hugged it to her as she moved a step closer to the balcony doorway.

Anne wasn't conscious of having made a noise, but she knew the instant Connor became aware of her presence. His body stiffened and his head snapped to the side—not enough to see her but enough to notice her out of the corner of his eye. He straightened, letting go of the railing, but he didn't turn.

"Con..."

"Yeah." Showing her the back of his head once more, he rubbed a hand across his jaw and cleared his throat. "Are you all right?"

His voice startled her. It was little more than a raspy whis-per, nothing like his usual smooth rumble. Taking another step, into the doorway, she replied. "Better, thanks. I used up the hot water, though."

He didn't bother to acknowledge her concern but threw an-other glance over his shoulder that didn't quite reach her, then moved a few steps to the right, making room for her at the railing. Anne accepted the invitation with the same hesitant ambivalence with which it had been delivered.

The balcony was tiny, about three feet wide and five long. But it was blessedly dark, illuminated only by moonlight and the muted glow from the lamp beside Connor's bed. She moved to the left, into the shadows, while Connor shifted a couple more inches to the right, putting an empty stretch of railing between them.

He was silent, his gaze seemingly fixed on the river. Once, he passed a hand across his face in a quick, almost furtive gesture, and she wondered briefly if he could be crying. But it seemed far more likely that he simply didn't know what to say and was feeling the strain of her presence. When he spoke, the controlled, careful tone in his voice made her want to shrink into a tiny ball and disappear.

"How are your feet?"

"Much better."

"I'd have carried you upstairs."

"No, they're fine. The hot water helped a lot."

He made another swipe at his face. Anne shifted nervously, the warm breeze, blowing under the robe along her bare legs, making her feel terribly exposed.

"I guessed you wouldn't mind my using your robe," she said. He cleared his throat again. "Of course not."

She hesitated briefly, then asked, "Has Rogue come back?"

"A little while ago."

"Is he ... all right?"

"Fine."

"Good. I was ... worried."

A minute passed. Neither of them spoke. Anne's jaw began to ache from being clenched. The breeze stirred, lifting the curls drying around her face and sending a scattering of frondlike locust leaves, torn loose in the storm, blowing across the deck. Just as Anne was about to turn and run—to where, she neither knew nor cared—Connor spoke in a thick whisper.

"Annie, why didn't you come to me?"

The question brought her head jerking toward him, but before she caught a glimpse of his face, he turned away, swearing.

"I wasn't going to ask," he rasped. "I know I should leave it alone, but ... God, I just can't. I have to know. Were you really so convinced I didn't care about you anymore that you thought I wouldn't help you?"

Anne bit her lower lip, fighting to control a sudden rush of tears. Was that what all this awkwardness was about—or part of it, anyway? Misplaced guilt over his part in the nightmare? She'd always known he'd take it this way, but knowing didn't lessen the pain of seeing her fears realized.

"That wasn't it at all," she whispered. "I never doubted for a second that you'd have tried to help, if I'd told you."

"Then, why—"

"Con, I was ashamed." *Ashamed like I am now, seeing you standing there with your back to me.* Struggling for words, struggling against the humiliation of talking to a man who wouldn't look her in the eye, she said, "The things Aaron made me do...it wasn't only that I knew they were wrong because he was my brother. I didn't know *anybody* did those things. It all seemed unnatural and...vile. And a part of me believed it must be my fault. That there was something wrong with *me* that made him want to... to do it. I know I shouldn't have felt that way—*now*, I know. But then the idea of telling anyone was—" She shuddered. "I just couldn't."

Standing with his hands deep in his pockets and his head bowed, Connor remained silent. The moon had risen above the trees, and its pale white light turned silver where it touched his black hair, then trickled downward to outline his darkly clothed, broad-shouldered form.

Finally, when he didn't speak, Anne lifted her gaze to the stars and continued. "After that night on the *Lady Lyn,* I was afraid to see or talk to you. I was afraid if Aaron saw me with you—or anybody else—he might think I was talking about him. He'd never have believed me if I said I wasn't, and then he would have... Con, he was telling the truth. He'd have killed me."

"But I'd have stopped him!" Without warning, Connor's fist slammed into the stone wall beside him, and Anne flinched, her startled gaze traveling quickly from his fist upward over the thick muscles in his arm and shoulder.

"How would you have stopped him?" she whispered. "By killing him?"

"No!"

"You didn't sound so sure a little while ago."

"I was—" He broke off, shaking his head. "I was angry."

She pressed her lips together. He wasn't any more certain than she what he'd have done. Starkly, she told him, "I thought of killing him myself. But I was too scared to try, and I couldn't think of a way to do it."

"Oh, God..." Groaning, Connor dropped his forehead onto his arm, resting bent against the stone.

Anne went on. "And I thought of going to a teacher, or to your mother. But eventually I'd have had to tell the police. And you know they'd have wanted *evidence,* and I didn't have any. He was very careful about that—not marking me or, let's say, leaving anything behind that could be proven to be his. So it would have been my word against his. And if anybody had tried to stop him in the meantime, he'd have taken his revenge on me—and on whoever else had made him angry."

"If I'd known," Connor muttered, "he'd have played hell getting near you, and I sure as the devil wouldn't have been worried about his doing me any damage."

"He wouldn't have had to touch you. I doubt he'd even have tried." Pausing, she added, "But think about what he might have done to Nancy or Maureen."

Connor buried his face against his arm, his head moving back and forth as he groaned in denial.

Anne would have liked to deny it, too. But she'd denied it for years, letting the wounds fester inside her, poisoning her and every aspect of her existence until she'd been literally unable to function. She'd kept the secret. And for what? To lead them, blindly and unprepared, into this—this night, this pain, this hideous scene that they were both bound to live out.

Steeling herself to go on, she told him, "He would have done it, Con. I thought about it. I spent *most* of my time thinking about ways to escape or make him stop, without me or somebody I cared about getting hurt. I'd never have been able to live with myself if you or any of your family had been hurt because of me. Maybe there might have been a way, but I couldn't see it."

Connor didn't answer. He was still making low, pained noises, and Anne doubted he was even aware of it. Her heart urged her to go to him, and she even reached toward him. But the wall of icy fear rose to stop her, and her arm fell to her side. She wasn't afraid of him. Truly, she wasn't. But it was impossible at that moment to convince her body of that.

And what would she do if he cringed from her touch? Die. A thousand times over. She'd simply crumple up and die.

Squeezing her eyes closed, she breathed, "Oh, Con, I've been trying so hard not to tell you. I knew you'd tear yourself apart, wondering if, somehow, you could have kept it from happening. Just, please, remember that, for whatever reasons, I didn't want you to know. I *made sure* you wouldn't know. So, *please,* don't ever think any of it was your fault. It wasn't, any more than it was mine."

He was silent for a long time, leaning against the wall, letting the stones support his weight. Finally, he said, "I'm not blaming you—or myself, really. I'll just never be able to believe there wouldn't have been something...*something* I could have done to prevent it."

Drawing a deep breath, Anne held it for a moment, debating the line between truth and cruelty. Not that she was any judge. But it didn't seem as if she could possibly make matters worse.

Letting her breath out slowly, she turned to face the river. "Maybe instead of torturing yourself over the things you didn't prevent, you should think about the things you did."

Connor snorted softly, his voice muffled against his arm. "I hope you're not handing out medals for either yesterday morning or today. Because I'd find it a little hard, right now, to bask in the glory of being a hero fifteen years too late."

"No, that's not what I mean." Anne hesitated, chipping nervously at a loose piece of paint on the railing. "You did something before...something you don't know about."

She threw a quick glance over her shoulder to see that he'd turned his head to listen. Then, in a brittle voice, she said, "He only actually raped me once. Probably because of his fanaticism about not giving me a way to prove anything against him. Besides, I think he got more pleasure out of *not* doing it. Sex was a weapon he used to frighten and humiliate me. And rape was the ultimate threat. He held it over me constantly, telling me he was going to, then not—until the day before I left. Then he decided to punish me for leaving by making the threat good."

"Anne, wait. You don't have to—"

"I'd gone looking for you to say goodbye."

Connor cut himself short, and a moment later whispered, "You'd what?"

Anne kept her gaze directed at the paint she was methodically picking off the wrought iron. "I was leaving the next day, and I wanted to tell you goodbye. But he ambushed me and took me to the boathouse—onto the *Lady Lyn.* He knew I was terrified of it and the water. And, actually, once he got me on board, I was terrified enough that I was hardly aware of what he was doing. But I wasn't so out of it that I didn't realize he didn't get to...finish." Swallowing the lump that kept rising in her throat, she said, "You came."

"God Almighty..." Connor straightened and took a step away from the wall, toward her. "I was looking for you. I hadn't seen or talked to you in weeks, and I knew you were leaving the next day, because Mom had told me. I didn't want to believe you'd go without saying goodbye, but..."

"But I did," she finished for him. "Aaron heard you calling me, and it made him stop. He was furious. Told me to hurry up and put my clothes on, so I could go see what you wanted. I was supposed to get rid of you."

"But you hardly spoke." Connor's shadow fell across her right arm as he moved a step closer. "You just stood on the dock and stared out the door and—"

"And when you said you'd heard I was leaving the next day, I said, yes, and that I had to go pack. And I left you standing on the dock while I ran out the door and got away from him. I went to the tree house and stayed there until the next morning. Until it was time to leave."

"And I thought..." Trailing off, Connor turned away, propping an elbow on the arm he wrapped around his ribs and dropping his head forward to rest on his hand.

Flaking the paint, oblivious to the damage she was inflicting on her fingernail, Anne continued with quiet insistence. "If you hadn't interrupted him, exactly when you did, I might have ended up pregnant."

"God, don't even *think*—"

"But I *did* think about it. I thought about it every time he threatened to rape me." Unable to control her shaking, Anne stopped chipping paint to grip the railing and put all her efforts into forming words. "My will to live was strong, Con. Strong enough to hold on for three years, until my father finally let me leave, then to survive some pretty miserable years afterward, until I got myself the help I needed." *Strong enough to stand here, saying these things to you, when it feels like I'm dying inside.* "But I'm not sure I'd have been strong enough to survive being sixteen and pregnant with my brother's child. I don't know what I'd have done. But you saved me from having to worry about it.''

Pausing, she lifted her gaze to the river, and, as a sense of fatalism stole through her, the familiar, moonlit scene blurred before her eyes. She thought of kinder days, days of tree houses and swimming races and childhood laughter, as she said, softly, ''I survived, Con. And all things considered, I'm doing well. I like my friends and my career—and I like myself. In most ways, I'm happy with my life. And I'd say you have a lot to do with that, too. If it weren't for you, for the years we were close, I wouldn't have had any idea what it felt like to be truly cared about or to care for another person. So, no matter what... happens... well, I just wanted you to know that.''

Falling silent, Anne drew a ragged breath, then turned toward Connor. He hadn't moved, was still standing with his shoulders hunched, his eyes closed, and his head resting on his fist. He looked so tired, she thought. So utterly weary. Nothing like the man she'd watched carousing in the river at dawn. The energy, the passion for life—the joy—was gone.

Because of her. Because she'd tried to build a future with him on secrets and lies when it was no more possible than it would be to build one on the truth. Looking at him now, she realized what a fool she'd been to believe they could ever have something good and untainted by the ugliness of the past, something that was just *theirs*. For, hidden or revealed, the past would always be there, between them. And, like today, it could rise at any moment to consume the present... and to destroy...

''I should go.'' Anne moved away from the railing, toward the door. ''Ben Whitlow was probably right. It would be better if I left.''

Connor raised his head, and there was a new note of tension in his voice. ''You don't think you're as safe here as you'd be anyplace else?''

''I'm sure I am, but—'' Hovering in the doorway, she twisted the belt to Connor's bathrobe around her fingers. ''If Aaron wants to find me, he will, regardless. I just don't like the idea that... well, that you or your mother could be in danger because of me.''

''It's not our deaths he's after.'' Swinging around to face her, Connor argued, ''Besides, once he gets wind that the police are looking for him, he'll know the game's up. He'd be a fool to try anything else, and we both know he's not."

"No. But he's different. Sicker. You said it yourself. He seems desperate enough to try anything." The twisted belt bit into her fingers, and she dropped it to wrap her arms around her waist. "I already feel bad enough that you've been dragged into this nightmare and forced to deal with it. You shouldn't have to . . . well, I just think I ought to leave."

"I'm not the one who's been dragged and forced," he returned. "And now that I know what's going on, I'm not about to let you try to handle it on your own. If you think you'd feel safer, tomorrow I'll take you anywhere you want to go. But I'm staying with you."

"But you shouldn't . . . I don't want . . ." Her voice fell to a whisper. "I just don't want to be a . . . a burden."

Moments passed in utter silence. Even the breeze died, disclosing the muggy night heat it had cloaked. Anne stood hugging her waist, staring blindly across the bedroom into the dark hallway beyond.

Then, in carefully measured tones, Connor said, "Anne, you couldn't be a burden to me if you tried. I'm in love with you."

And, for an instant, Anne's heart stopped beating. Her head snapped toward him, her eyes collided with his, and, suddenly, the knots inside her began to unravel. His features were plainly visible in the moonlight, his face lined with strain and deeply tormented. But his eyes held no hint of pity or revulsion, none of the things she'd most feared. Instead, they were red-rimmed and glistening with unshed tears.

Her heart pounded, and she watched, entranced, as he hauled in a ragged gulp of air.

"It's like I told you this afternoon, on the beach," he said. "As crazy as it sounds, I feel like I've been waiting for you without knowing it. All it took was seeing you again and setting things straight between us, and everything we ever had that was good just . . . grew up." His shoulders heaved in another uneven breath, his hands clenching at his sides. "Anne, I— I ache so bad inside over what happened to you, I . . . I can't describe it. But it hurts *because* I love you. It doesn't make me love you less, and it's . . . God, it's killing me standing here, talking about it when—" He stopped, looking away, looking everywhere but at her as the words poured out of him. "I'm trying not to make things harder for you, trying not to get...upset or...anything...but, God, all I want to do is hold you, and I'm trying not to do that, either, because I don't want to frighten you or make you feel threatened or—''

There was less than three feet between them, and it was gone in the space of a heartbeat as Anne flung herself into his arms.

Connor's speech ended in a hoarse cry of surprise. He saw Anne launch herself at him, and he reacted instinctively, his body bracing and his arms coming up to catch her. For an instant, he held his breath, and his arms hovered, trembling with uncertainty. Then she said his name, her arms tightening around his ribs and her face burrowing against his neck as she whispered, ''Hold me. Please, Con, just...hold me.'' And the battle was lost.

Suddenly he was crying and shaking and crushing her so hard he thought he had to be hurting her, but she just kept saying, ''Yes, hold me, hold me tight, don't ever let me go. I love you, Con, I love you so much.'' And all he could manage was, ''Oh, God, oh, God...'' all the while he was thinking this couldn't be happening, she couldn't be here, in his arms. But she was, and it seemed like a miracle. A miracle that she'd let him hold her, that her body was pressed against his, so warm and soft and fragile...so trusting. And he thought he must have been out of his mind to have imagined he could resist this. He couldn't begin to fathom why he'd even tried. What on earth had he thought he stood to gain in the sacrifice?

Dreams. Things that might happen—and then again, might not. Nothing that would make him happier than he was at this moment. And Anne was here, *now,* and he would never let her go, and he would never let anyone hurt her again. God, no.

''I thought you wouldn't...'' she was saying amidst her own tears. ''When you wouldn't look at me, when you walked away...I was afraid you'd never want to look at me again, that you were so...revolted, you'd never want to see me or—''

''No, love, no...'' Connor tightened his arms around her. ''I am revolted. But not by you. Never you.''

''You're...sure?''

The mingled hesitancy and longing in her voice was devastating, and it took him several moments before he could gather himself to respond. Drawing back far enough to meet her gaze, he took her face between his hands. Her green eyes were dark and filled with tears that sparkled in the moonlight, moonlight that turned her white skin to porcelain and her hair to a burnished chestnut cloud of curls. She'd never looked more beautiful, and Connor thought he'd reassure her forever if that was how long it took.

"I'm very sure," he said, "that I've never known a woman as strong and good and completely desirable as you."

Anne's eyes closed, and she brought her forehead to rest against his chin. "I love you so much. But I won't be able to stand it if being . . . mixed up with me is going to keep causing you such . . . such grief."

Connor's lips curved in a trace of a smile. "Funny. It feels to me like being mixed up with you is the best thing that's ever happened, and all it's causing me is joy."

With a brief pause, she returned, "I guess I just don't see how that could be true. All I've done since I got here is disrupt your life."

"Mmm. Thank God."

She pulled back to give him a bewildered look, and Connor drew a steadying breath. Then, wiping his face with the back of his hand and shoving the hair out of his eyes, he looked for a way to explain. "Anne, I've been living in a box," he said. "I put myself there deliberately, and for the past ten years, every decision I've made has been to stay there. All I've done is work and try to stay out of trouble and make sure I don't get too attached to anybody or anything."

Her gaze fell to her hand, resting against his chest, and she hesitated before asking, "Are you ever going to tell me what happened that made you do this to yourself?"

"I got a girl pregnant."

Her eyes flew back to his, wide and questioning, but he shook his head. "It's another long story, and I don't have the energy for it right now. Besides—" he lifted a curl that had stuck to her cheek and tucked it behind her ear "—it isn't important anymore. She lost the baby, and that was the end of it. Someday, when we've got nothing better to do, I'll bore you with the details—about it and anything else you want to know."

Anne studied him for a moment, her expression solemn. Then, with a soft sigh of acceptance, she slid her arms around his waist and laid her head against his shoulder once more.

God, he'd never get used to it. Her trust, her willingness to touch him and to let him touch her, was a gift and a privilege he'd never take for granted. Closing his eyes, Connor raised his face to the night sky, remembering how she'd said that, if it weren't for him, she wouldn't know what it meant to love or to be loved. As sad as it made him, he knew it was so. She'd had no one else. Still, it humbled him to his soul to think that, in those fleeting years of childhood, he'd unknowingly been sowing seeds that, all these years and heartbreaks later, would reap such rich rewards.

"I don't even think I knew," he whispered, "how lonely I've been. I've been living for tomorrow, for the things I might get if I just worked a little harder and a little longer. Then, the other day, you came along. And for the first time since I can remember, I'm not worrying about what's going to happen ten years from now. I'm happy just being with you. I can't explain it or define it, but you touch something inside me nobody else has ever been able to touch." Sighing, he buried his lips in her hair. "I need you, Sunshine. I need you in my life. You make me feel like myself again, when I'd forgotten how."

"Oh, Con…" Anne's fingers slid over his back and his shoulders, caressing, filling a need at the same time they evoked a nearly painful longing. "Being with you makes me feel *whole* again. I just wish…" She caught her breath. "Oh, Lord, I wish it were true."

Connor felt the pain slice through her and into him, and a fresh surge of rage rose in him at the animal who'd stolen her confidence. His hand lifted to hold her head against his shoulder in a protective gesture as he insisted, "It *is* true."

She squirmed a little, her head moving beneath his hand in denial, and Connor had to clench his jaw to prevent himself from arguing further. Telling her seemed so pointless, so hopeless. Even more hopeless to try to show her. She'd seen their encounter this afternoon as a disaster, absolute proof that she was a failure as a woman. It frightened him to wonder how many such "failures" she could survive. It frightened him more to think that it might never end differently.

Overwhelmed with frustration at his own powerlessness, he breathed, "Annie, I'd give anything to be able to make you see that you're fine and beautiful *and* whole. Nothing he did to you has changed that. You're still the same person you always were, and there's nothing—nothing *real*—standing in your way of doing or having anything you want."

"What I want is you," she murmured. "And it's very hard for me to believe that what happened today on the beach wasn't real."

"What happened," Connor returned quickly, "was that we kissed and touched and loved each other, and it was wonderful—more wonderful than anything I've ever felt in my life. *That* was real, Anne, and, God, I wish—" He sucked in a quick breath, squeezing his eyes closed. "I wish I could make you see it the way I do. I wish I could take this image, this *feeling*, I have of the way it would be for us and somehow give it to you. Use it to wipe out all the ugliness and the fear...wipe it out of your mind and make you forget it ever happened. Then we could make love, and it would be like it was today on the beach, only..." His voice dropped low. "Only it wouldn't end. It would go on and on, and it would only get better. And you'd know...God, yes, you'd know...that your body was made to be loved and to feel pleasure."

And if it took him a lifetime, Connor thought, he was going to make it happen. Somehow. He just hoped to God it *didn't* take a lifetime, because he wanted her so badly, he didn't know how he was going to wait another day.

With Anne snuggled in his arms, he'd been trying not to think about how much he wanted her. Trying not to notice the silkiness of her hair against his face, the softness of her breasts pressed to his chest, the comfortable way her hips and thighs aligned with his. But it was becoming increasingly difficult to ignore what he so wanted to have, and the little things she was doing on the back of his neck, winding his hair around her fingers, weren't helping.

Connor was loath to move, but he'd reached his limit on being able to control the inevitable reaction, and he started to say that maybe they ought to get some sleep. But then Anne spoke, hesitantly, her breath warming the skin below his ear.

"You can't change what happened," she whispered. "And you can't make me forget. But you can make it so it doesn't matter anymore." Leaning back to look at him, she continued urgently, "Con, I want you so much. Just standing here, I— Lord, I *ache* from wanting. Please...make love to me."

Connor's first thought was that she couldn't possibly mean it. Yet, as his gaze took in her flushed cheeks and the melting warmth in her eyes, he saw that, clearly, she did mean it, and he quickly sought to avoid what he was certain would be a horrible end to an ungodly day.

"Anne, nothing would make me happier, but it would be—" He stopped short of saying it would be a mistake and, instead, offered gently, "We've got time. All the time it takes. And it seems to me almost any time would be better than tonight, after . . . what you've been through."

"But that's why it *has* to be tonight," she came back. "If I wait, I know the things he did to me today will turn into another layer on top of this— this ice block inside me. I'm good at that, Con. I had to be. I take all my feelings and freeze them solid until I don't feel *anything*, good *or* bad." Her fingers clenched on the front of his T-shirt. "Don't let me do that. Don't let me freeze up again."

Connor shook his head. "I don't think there's a chance. If it relieves your mind to hear it, I promise I won't let you. But, Anne, I'm not going to put you through another scene like we had on the beach. If you got scared—"

"I don't care if I get scared!" she exclaimed. "I've been scared for years, and I'm sick to death of it! And I'm not scared of *you*. I want you to make love to me. And I don't want you to stop, no matter what."

Connor stared at her, incredulous. "You can't be serious. You want me to force you?"

"I'm asking you to *help* me!"

"By making you a victim? My victim this time?" He scowled. "I couldn't do it. I *won't* do it!" And as she groaned in frustration, he tried, somewhat desperately, to appease her. "Anne, don't you see it would never work? That it would only make things worse?"

"*Worse?*" With a harsh laugh, she stepped back, flinging an arm wide as she railed, "I'm twenty-eight years old. I've got a master's degree, a job I love, good friends who think I'm, oh, so smart and accomplished. I speak three languages fluently. I've been all over the world. Oh, and, by the way, I know all there is to know about sex. Violent, disgusting, coercive sex, or clinical sex written in the pages of a book. But I've never once made love! I don't have any idea what it means to touch a man because I *want* to touch him, or to give myself to a man I *chose*." Standing in the light of the doorway, she shot him a piercing look. "Now, you tell me. How can it possibly get any worse?"

He couldn't. And seeing her standing there, in all her righteous fury, more beautiful than anything he'd ever seen in his life, Connor felt his good intentions and his common sense slam straight into a brick wall. Anne had never asked him for anything, never demanded anything—not once, in all their lives. Which was what made loving her so easy. Like breathing, it was irresistible. Something he had no will or desire to refuse...

His gaze remained locked on hers and she pressed her hands to the spot where his robe lapped across her chest, saying, "Con, I feel like I've been fighting a war for control of my own body. And so far, Aaron's won every battle. Every time I've backed out of a date, every time I've pulled away when a man's tried to hold my hand, the other morning when you tried to kiss me... and this afternoon, Lord help me, when I exploded like a time bomb set to go off! Every one of those times was a victory for him!"

"It's a long way from backing out of a date to what we were doing this afternoon," he murmured.

"I don't care!" she cried. "This war's been going on for fifteen years, and I want it over! I want my body—my *life*—back again! But I won't have either until I refuse to let him control me when he's not even anywhere in sight!"

Connor looked at her for a long, silent moment. Then, quietly, he said, "So don't let him. He's not here now. If you want to make love with me, go ahead. I promise, I won't stop you."

Chapter Fifteen

Anne stared at Connor in speechless confusion long enough to realize that he was serious. He was inviting her to make love to him. Then, she blurted out the first words that came to mind.

"But I don't know how."

The instant the words left her mouth, she was struck by their absurdity, and a hand flew to cover her face.

Connor's voice was gentle. "There aren't any rules, love. You can't make a mistake. And you can't possibly displease or disappoint me."

Lifting her hand slightly, keeping her eyes shaded, she gave him a dubious glance. "What about torturing you? It seems to me that's what you're asking for."

"Uh-uh." He shook his head slowly. "The torture was a little while ago, when I thought you might never let me near you again." Her hand fell away from her face, her eyes widening in dismay, and Connor sighed. "Sunshine, I'm still trying to wrap my head around the notion that I fit into a category of one—the only man you feel able to trust. So, you see—" he shrugged a little "—it already seems like a tremendous gift that you're willing to hold my hand."

Anne's eyes stung with fresh tears as she looked at his shadowed features. He was offering her the sun, the moon, and the earth. He was offering her himself, without reservation. He was offering her the chance to make her dreams come true, and at that moment, she knew it hardly mattered what happened. If she refused his offer, if she didn't at least try to do this impossible thing, it would break both their hearts.

With her eyes holding his, she moved toward him, stopping a few inches away to take his hands in hers. Then, lifting his hands between them, she let her eyes fall to study what she held.

Strong hands, broad and sinewed, with rounded fingers and a sprinkle of fine hair on the backs. A working man's hands, callused and tough, with tiny cuts here and there and a few white scars from injuries his work gloves hadn't prevented. Hands that, once upon a time, had picked daisies to make chains for her hair, and that, twice now, had saved her life. Hands that would, if she would only let them, touch her body in the most intimate ways and teach her what it meant to be loved.

With a blush coloring her cheeks, Anne brought Connor's hands to her lips and kissed them—each one, slowly, letting her lips linger on the backs of his fingers. They trembled at her touch, and their trembling increased when she turned them over to kiss both palms. For an instant she relished the sensation of his rough skin against her face, then, with her fingers laced through his, she lowered their arms and lifted her gaze to watch him take a shallow breath through parted lips.

Leaning toward him, the color in her cheeks deepening under his sensual regard, she brought her lips to his, whispering, "Kiss me." He said her name, their eyes drifted closed, and their lips rocked together, tender and warm and sweet. She tasted tears. She smelled the river and the rain on his skin. She felt the warmth of his breath brushing her cheek, and she thought about how easy this was. How right and good and clean. But she'd been lulled once today into believing it would all be this way, that the rightness and goodness of this moment would stretch to the next, and the next, and she couldn't allow herself to believe it a second time. No. No more disasters today.

Their lips parted, then met again. And again. Soft kisses that stirred the fires quietly, creating a slow, spreading warmth. As the heat began to build, her mouth opened over his in obvious invitation. His response was a sound of surprise that slid into a groan as he accepted her invitation and she proceeded to show him how well she'd learned the things he'd taught her.

Tongues met, warm and wet and seeking. Breaths mingled, sliding back and forth from one to the other until there was nothing left and they had to part to drag in air before their lips came together once more. They kissed again and again beneath the hot August moon, each kiss growing deeper, longer, more explicitly carnal, and accompanying each one were those masculine growls and rumbles that for some reason seemed to turn her body to liquid. Hot liquid.

Swaying slightly, Anne went searching for an anchor, letting go of Connor's hands to reach for the security of his shoulders. But when he didn't follow suit, she cast a heavy-lidded glance to see that his hands had fallen to his sides.

Sensing her confusion, he muttered, "It's up to you, love. I won't touch you unless you tell me to."

With a frustrated whimper, she wondered if he expected her to direct his every move as well as her own. The idea was overwhelming. But she wanted his arms around her, so she managed to find the breath to say, "Hold me. Close."

His arms encircled her before she'd finished speaking, his hands sweeping her back, pulling her into him until her breasts were pillowed against his chest. Her breasts felt swollen, achy, and she wished he would touch them the way he had that afternoon, wondered if she actually could bring herself to ask. But then, as she pressed against him, trying to ease the ache, her body came into full contact with his. And, all at once, passion ground to a halt.

Tearing her mouth from Connor's, Anne gasped, her hands flying from his shoulders to his chest. But she didn't push him away. No. Not this time. She wouldn't.

"Anne . . . ?"

She was keenly aware that his arms dropped immediately to his sides. Their bodies no longer touched, except where her fists remained balled against his chest. She was free to move, to run, if she chose. . . .

"It scares you to feel me hard, doesn't it?"

Breathing raggedly, she responded with a nod. She wasn't only scared, though. She was repulsed. And she had the mortifying feeling he knew that, too. How could he not?

"We can stop right now," he said.

A few seconds passed before Anne managed, "I don't want to stop."

A ridiculous statement. Of course she wanted to stop.

But then, she didn't.

"Well," Connor began in measured tones, "I guess you have a couple of choices."

Impossible. There were no choices in this quagmire. "Like...wh-what?" she rasped.

"Like, we could make love without having intercourse and just...avoid the issue."

And would that accomplish her purpose? To be rid of this all-consuming fear? To be the one in control of her body?

Anne shook her head.

Connor sighed. "So, I could think about something unpleasant, or maybe do multiplication tables in my head, while I'm kissing you. It might go away. Maybe."

The sheer absurdity of the suggestion, made lightly but with all apparent seriousness, took a small chunk out of the icy wall around her. "That's a terrible idea," she whispered.

"It wouldn't be my first choice, either."

"What...would be?"

His reply was immediate and clear. "For you to try to understand what I mean when I say 'I want you.'"

It seemed all too obvious what he meant, and she frowned in confusion, though her eyes remained closed.

Connor went on, the calmness of his voice belied by a trace of urgency. "Anne, I've never been interested in meaningless sex with any woman, and it sure as hell isn't just sex I want with you. I want to make love with you, to share myself with you. I want to *know* you, and I want—" He caught his breath for an instant, then finished on a hushed, raw note. "I want you to know me. More than you already do, which is more than any other woman ever has, or ever could."

Pausing, giving his words time to melt through the wall, he added, "'I want you' means you excite me in all possible ways. And while you're thinking about that, you might consider how you'd feel if we'd been kissing the way we were and it *hadn't* turned me on."

Disappointed...embarrassed...relieved. An assortment of contradictory emotions crowded Anne's thoughts in response to the possibility Connor posed. Gradually, though, one quiet thought grew to overshadow any other. He excited her, too—in all possible ways. None of it was frightening or repugnant. It was good. And, logically, she knew that, if her body's expressions of excitement were good, so should his be.

Yet logic had little to do with her ability to force her body to relax. Anne opened her eyes, her gaze focusing on her fists, still bunched against Connor's chest, and she willed her fingers open. They shook visibly as she slid them upward, an inch at a time. When they reached his shoulders, they dug in. Raising her eyes, she found Connor regarding her with quiet intensity, and she held his gaze as she slowly leaned forward until her breasts rested once again against the wall of his chest. He didn't move a muscle. His arms remained at his sides, and, indeed, his only reaction to her quaking efforts to get close to him was a low, throaty sound that he tried to swallow.

She didn't like that swallow.

She wanted to give him pleasure. She wanted to make him feel good. And she didn't want him to feel he had to hide it from her when she succeeded. Which meant she had to show him that his pleasure was something she welcomed.

Anne's eyes remained glued to Connor's as she took a slow, deep breath. Then, in small, incremental steps, she brought her hips and thighs to rest against his. He was still hard. And the instant the rigid flesh beneath his jeans nestled into the softness of her belly, it gave a small, involuntary leap. Her body's response was equally uncontrollable. She shuddered, then immediately felt compelled to say, "I'm sor—"

"Uh-uh," Connor cut her off. "No apologies. Not for anything."

With her crimson face buried against his shoulder, she grumbled, "If I can't apologize, then you have to promise to tell me to stop whenever you're ready to end this...torture."

It amazed her to hear his quietly amused chuckle. "Don't count on that happening anytime soon. Not as long as I think there's a chance I'll get to kiss you again."

Without lifting her head from his shoulder, she tilted her face upward. Connor turned his head to look down at her, and she whispered, "Kissing is easy. It...belongs to you."

The light in his eyes smoldered as his mouth curved into a slow half-smile. "So...you want to do some more of it?"

Anne's gaze fell to his lips, contemplating them at the same time she continued to contemplate his erection pressing into her. She was tolerating it. But appreciation was a long way off. At the moment her goal was simply to stop viewing it as a weapon. Still, as the chill of fear faded, as she looked at his full, expressive mouth and thought of kissing him again, the banked fires of passion began to stir.

"I might," she said, and as the idea grew in appeal, she added, "Hold me. Put your arms around me, like they were before."

She waited until he'd obeyed her request, putting an arm around her shoulders and a hand on the small of her back. Then, lifting a hand to stroke the hair off his forehead, she spoke softly. "I love you, Connor McLeod. And I'm not apologizing, but I want you to know, those medals you didn't want for saving my life don't begin to compare to what I'd like to give you right now just for being who you are. You've been my hero since I was six years old, and I've never wanted or needed another."

His chest rose against hers as he hauled in a breath. But when he started to speak, she stopped him, saying, "Now, kiss me. Kiss me like you did on the beach. Like you don't think you can possibly get enough."

He hesitated all of two seconds, his eyes skimming her features. Then, with a muttered "God, I love you," his head dipped and his mouth slanted across hers in full possession.

He gave her exactly what she'd asked for, exactly what she wanted. He made her feel as if she were a deep well of some magic liquid and all he wanted to do was drink and drink from her, forever and into eternity. And as he kissed her, his arms tightening around her, a piece of her consciousness remained aware of his hardened flesh, smothered between them. But it was only that—an awareness, slightly uneasy, not unmanageable. And it didn't begin to have the power to distract her from the unique experience of her body being pressed full-length against his.

Lord, to be this close to another human being. To be kissed as if she were his best and last reason for living. To feel her breasts swell and her blood pound in her head and her heart and in that hot, moist place between her thighs. To feel this *alive*. This gloriously alive. Nothing . . . *nothing* could be better than this.

"Oh, mercy . . ." Gulping for breath, Anne dragged her mouth away from Connor's. "The problem with kissing is . . . it makes me feel so . . . weak."

Trailing kisses over her arched neck, Connor suggested, "The usual solution to that dilemma . . . is to lie down."

"Oh, what a lovely idea . . . On a bed, you mean."

"It tends to be more rewarding . . . than most other places."

"And you have that nice bed, sitting in there . . . empty. Except it's so . . . far away."

His mouth curved against hers in a smile. "Is that a backward way of asking me to carry you?"

"I hate to ask. I mean, you must be tired."

"I'm asleep on my feet. Can't you tell?"

"Well, I'd offer to carry you, but . . ."

"Now, there's a romantic idea. Especially the part where we fall over the railing."

"I knew you'd see it my way."

Chuckling, he swept her into his arms and carried her into the bedroom.

The small lamp beside the bed cast an unobtrusive light that left most of the room in shadow. Only the bed was clearly illuminated, its white cotton spread slightly wrinkled and its old polished brass glowing warmly in the soft golden light. A comfortable spot, unpretentious and welcoming.

Connor lowered her to stand beside it, and Anne blinked a little as her eyes adjusted to the light. Then she looked up to see him clearly for the first time in what seemed a very long time, indeed. He was unshaven, his hair was rumpled from her fingers, and, regardless of what he'd said, he looked tired. But his blue gaze was clear and untroubled and warm with intimacy as it caressed her features.

"Do you want the light off?" he asked, his hands moving lightly up and down her arms.

Anne shook her head. "Let's leave it on." It made her blush to say it, and she knew she'd be blushing a lot more if, by some rare chance, things proceeded much further. But blushes were better than screams, and darkness was not her friend.

The blush that stained her cheeks was as red as they came when Connor twisted to reach behind him, pulled open the drawer of the nightstand, and took out a small, square, plastic packet. Anne's eyes remained glued to it as he set it atop the table and closed the drawer.

When he turned back to see her staring, he paused, then, in a matter-of-fact tone, said, "Do you need to ask what that is?"

She shook her head.

He paused again. "Does it bother you?"

Anne had to swallow before she could reply. "I guess it makes me think of all the stories you hear about . . . well, the back seats of cars and . . . one-night stands." It also made her think about what a man did with it. Nothing subtle about that little plastic packet. What shocked her, though, was that Connor thought they might actually need it. Clearly, his faith in her was greater than hers in herself.

"I hope to God I've made it clear I don't think of you as a one-night stand."

His growled statement brought Anne's gaze flashing to his, and at the look on his face she rushed to say, "Oh, Con, of course I know that. I didn't mean...it's just..." She trailed off, her eyes sliding away and the heat creeping back into her cheeks.

She felt his eyes on her as he said, "It has its pros and cons, like any form of birth control. But you aren't prepared for this, and I am." With a long, very silent pause, he came back in an oddly strained tone. "Do you want to get pregnant?"

Anne looked at him quickly, a perplexed frown flickering across her brow. Was he giving her the choice? Surely not. And yet...

With a small, flustered gesture, she murmured, "I don't suppose this is the time to be making decisions like that...is it?"

He didn't answer, and she couldn't tell by the look on his face if he were relieved or disappointed or what.

Afraid that she might have ruined everything yet again, making an issue out of something that should have been simple, she slid her arms around his waist and hugged him. "Con, please, don't pay too much attention to every worried thought that flits through my mind. You'll make yourself crazy, trying to reassure me every time I think of a new one."

Connor's hands came up to tilt her face to his. "You let me worry about what makes me crazy."

"Well, all right, but..." She let out a soft sigh. "While you're worrying, would you please kiss me?"

He did. Then, as she began to sag in his arms, he murmured against her lips, "The bed...?"

"Hmm." She felt him bend a little to reach, one-handed, to yank down the bedspread. But when he put a knee on the mattress, she said, "Wait."

He opened his eyes to meet hers.

"Your shirt," she whispered. "Take it off."

It was a bold request—for her, anyway—and his eyes darkened in pleasure as he complied—arms crossing, hands gathering cloth to pull it over his head, muscles rippling with every movement he made. Anne watched, something terribly excit-

ing skittering through her as he bared the upper half of his body
expressly because she'd wished it so. And her excitement increased as she took in what was revealed. A woman would have
to be made of stone not to be moved by the sight of him.

She wasn't only moved, though. She was scared. Nearly as
much because she didn't know what she was doing as by anything else. So much for myths about lovemaking—that amor-
phous experience wherein two lovers were mysteriously swept
along on an ever-growing tide of passion toward an equally
mysterious and purportedly earth-shaking conclusion. Reality
consisted of a brass bed, her trembling knees, and a shattering
desire to love the man dropping his shirt on the floor and tossing the hair out of his eyes to meet her gaze.

He kept his eyes on her as he stretched out in the middle of
the bed with one knee bent and one arm behind his head, leaving ample space for her to join him. Then, with a crook of one
dark eyebrow, he offered her a hand in invitation.

The glittering blue light in his eyes was a beacon in the fog,
and Anne held on to it as she took his hand and let him pull her
down beside him. Leaning on an elbow, she cast a furtive glance
to see that she was decently covered by the folds of his robe,
then looked back to find him waiting patiently for her to make
the next move.

Anne sucked on her bottom lip, her eyes drifting downward
over the broad expanse of his chest. "You look so different,"
she said. "Different than when I left, I mean."

"You may have noticed I was a little...shocked myself." His
breath hitched up a notch as she drew a tentative line with her
fingertip across a ridge of muscle covering one rib.

Keeping her eyes averted from both his face and anything
below the top of his jeans, she continued tracing his ribs, wondering which ones had been broken. "I know men aren't supposed to be called beautiful, so I hope you don't mind. But I
think you're the most beautiful man I've ever seen."

His reply was a little hoarse. "I don't care what word you
use. I'm just glad you think so."

"I do," she whispered. "And I hate thinking about you
falling out of trees and getting hurt and...breaking things. I
know why you do it, but...well..." Leaning over, she allowed her lips to follow the path of her fingers across his collarbone. "I wish you didn't."

"No fair," he whispered.

"What?"

"You're trying to seduce me out of my job."

"No. I wasn't, but..." Her lips nuzzled through the silky hair on his chest to find the warm, smooth skin beneath. "Could I?"

"Unlikely." He drew a quick breath. "But, God, I wouldn't swear to it . . . Ah, Annie . . . that feels good."

"Does it?"

"Mmm."

"The books say . . . well, they say some men are more . . . sensitive in . . . certain places. And I . . . I wondered if . . . well, if you like it when you're touched . . ."

"Love, right now I'd like it if you touched my toenails. Do anything you want. Just— Ahh..." His breath left his body in a sigh as she took him at his word.

The flat, brown nipple beaded at the touch of her lips, and as she brushed across it, he let out a quiet groan. Encouraged, she touched it again, with the tip of her tongue. But then, in a rush of shyness, she buried her face against his chest, saying, "Con, I don't know how to do this."

"Oh, yes . . . you do." His hand came up to stroke the hair away from her face. "Forget the books, love. Just do whatever makes you feel good."

Whatever made *her* feel good? It seemed an odd way to put it. Yet, as she placed another experimental, open-mouthed kiss on the spot she'd previously abandoned and felt it pucker against her tongue, Anne began to understand. Her own nipples hardened and tingled, and his sigh of pleasure was echoed by her own. Nowhere had she read that to arouse was to be aroused. But she was fast learning that it was so.

And the lesson had scarcely begun.

His skin was warm, nearly hot in the closeness of the summer night, tasting of salt and something else she decided was simply him. Sun-darkened in startling contrast to her own, it was smooth and supple, the scattering of black hair adding texture in only a few places. His shoulders were impossibly broad, his upper arms too large for her hands to span. His stomach was a hard, flat plane, and the line of hair that bisected it was especially soft, almost baby-fine. His neck, on the other hand, was a strange assortment of textures—rough below his jaw from his beard, tender and clearly sensitive, like hers, below his ear and toward his nape, where his hair grew so long and thick and shiny. Oh, she did love his hair. She loved all of him. Every strong, healthy, beautiful inch . . . except . . .

Except a few.

Her fingers had been trailing almost idly up and down the arrow of hair on his stomach as her mouth explored a spot where his neck met his shoulder that produced an especially gratifying amount of uneven breathing. But as curiosity and passion began to do serious battle with fear, her fingers paused at the break in the line, above his navel. Her lips, opened against his shoulder, also paused. Then, before her courage could abandon her, she dipped one fingertip in and out of his navel, picked up the downward trail for another couple of inches, then stopped at the waistband of his jeans.

Anne's heart was lodged in her throat, and her breath was coming in shallow pants as her fingers hovered above the snap that held the denim closed. She had no awareness that Connor had ceased to breathe altogether until she heard his hoarse whisper.

"Anne, you'd better know, there's nothing under these jeans but me."

She considered his warning. Then she brought her shaking fingers down to curl under the snap and pull. It gave easily, and the tab of the zipper was just as easily found. She lowered it slowly, with two fingers, the rest of her hand held well above the parting cloth.

But this was agony. Agony to stretch it out this way. Agony to have to endure this horrible, stomach-churning dread over something that any normal woman would welcome. Indeed, by this time, any normal woman would probably be out of her mind with frustration. She *was* out of her mind with it.

Suddenly impatient with herself—and in a hurry to get "the worst" over with—Anne moved quickly, sitting up, grabbing the top of Connor's jeans and pulling downward. She didn't look. Kept her eyes on his knees, his feet, not even noticing that he did his best to aid her nearly frenzied efforts, lifting and, finally, kicking the jeans over the edge of the bed.

Breathing hard, her eyes tightly closed, Anne sat back on her heels, praying as she'd never prayed in her life that the coiled knot in her stomach wouldn't cause her to do something thoroughly humiliating. Then, drawing a long, uneven breath, she opened her eyes.

Seconds passed in silence. A minute slipped by. If anything moved or made a sound, it went unnoticed. The only thing Anne heard was the blood pounding in her head. She had no idea how long she sat there, scarcely breathing, before Connor interrupted the silence.

"I, uh...think one of us could use a little reassurance here."

Her gaze flew to his, her wide green eyes clashing briefly with his all-too-knowing blue ones. Then, her face burning, her eyes darted back down the length of his body, drawn like a magnet to that part of him that, earlier, had both terrified and repulsed her.

She wasn't terrified or repulsed. She wasn't sure what she felt. She only knew she couldn't stop staring. As mortifying as it was, she was mesmerized—fascinated, as one might be, given the opportunity to examine an implement of torture without the threat of being its victim.

"Anne...?"

She spoke in a whisper. "I... have a confession."

When Connor didn't respond, she looked to find him watching her with a hint of wariness flickering in his eyes. And well he might be wary. What must it be costing him to lie here like this? No doubt he was expecting to hear, "I've changed my mind. I don't want to make love with you, now or ever," as she ran, screaming, from the room.

Holding his gaze, Anne took a deep breath. "This morning, when I woke up in the hammock, I...saw you swimming."

His eyebrows quirked upward, amused curiosity replacing the wariness in his expression. "Is that so?" he said softly.

"Yes."

"I guess that explains why you didn't stay for breakfast."

"I was..." Her hands fluttered in her lap. "Embarrassed. I felt like I was...spying on you."

"Were you?"

"I guess. A little."

"And were you horrified?"

Her gaze fell to watch her fingers toy with the edge of his robe. "No. I...enjoyed watching you. You looked like you were having a wonderful time, playing with Rogue. I kept wishing I had the nerve to join you." Pausing, casting a covert glance along the length of him, she added, "But you looked... different, then."

Connor sighed. "Nothing like a little cold water to minimize the effect."

No cold water around at the moment. Not a drop of it.

Anne was staring again as she began, "You're so..."

"Male?"

"Big."

A moment of silence passed before Connor muttered, "I suppose all those helpful books gave you a pretty clear idea of what to expect."

Anne met his gaze. "If you mean, can you convince me I'm wrong, no, you can't."

He studied her for a second or two. Then, suddenly, his face scrunched in a grimace that might have been comical had she been in the mood to laugh. "Well, but you know..." He squirmed against the mattress, bending one leg and letting it flop to the side in a shockingly casual pose. "Big is such a relative term, don't you think? I mean, something can be big as compared to average and still be, uh... *moderate* in the overall picture of *normal.*"

Impossibly, Anne felt the glimmer of a smile tug at her lips. "You're not average."

"But I'm *normal.*"

"And that's supposed to reassure me?"

"Maybe it's time I resorted to multiplication tables. See if I can bring this problem down into the, uh, average range."

The smile refused to be contained.

"I'd go for *below* average, but..."

A giggle escaped, and Anne gave up, saying, "You really are ridiculous, you know."

Connor's smile was tender, and the look in his eyes quite serious, as he replied. "Sunshine, I'll do or say whatever it takes to help you get over being afraid of me."

She lowered her gaze, ashamed to admit but unable to deny that, after all, she was afraid of him. Yes, she trusted him as she'd never trusted any man. But he *was* a man. Indeed.

"Anne, look at me." Connor waited until she raised her eyes to his. "There are two important things to remember. The first is that I love you. The second is that no part of my body is separate from *me.* It doesn't have a will of its own. It can only do what I make it do. And all I want to do is love you."

"You make it sound so simple," she whispered.

"It is simple," he returned. "It gives me pleasure to give you pleasure. It wouldn't give me any pleasure at all to hurt you. It would be like hurting myself."

She held his gaze for a moment, then let her eyes drift slowly downward. "That's how it feels to me. That I'd never want to do anything to... to hurt you." And, without thinking—or, rather, thinking only about how she'd feel if she ever did hurt him—she placed a hand on his thigh.

Instantly, she drew back. Not from fear or revulsion but from nerves and shyness. But he'd given her the right to touch him in any way she wanted. And, oh, she did want. Despite all embarrassment and nerves. Like a blind person compelled to touch in order to know, or like a child drawn to feel things that were fascinating and new and beautiful, she wanted to touch, to feel, to know the body of this man who would be her lover, if only...if only...if only...

It became a litany, a prayer that kept fear at bay and moved her onward, toward her heart's desire. It was desire that lifted her hand out of her lap and carried it to a spot halfway along the top of his thigh. There it rested for a moment, trembling slightly, feeling the strength, the sheer power of him...and the warmth. Then, with her gaze fixed on her hand, she traced an upward path—only with her fingertips—hesitant, featherlike strokes across his hip, his ribs, and his belly, where the muscles contracted in reaction to her touch. Traveling back down his thigh, she began the journey again, repeating the process several times, with variations, before she gathered the courage to touch that which she had managed so far to avoid.

His aroused sex rose in formidable proportions from a thick gathering of black hair at the juncture of his thighs, and she was utterly unable either to ignore or to deny the truth: It was just as magnificent as the rest of him. It *belonged* there, exactly as it was, somehow seeming to serve not only as a declaration of gender but as the locus of the strength and vitality that emanated outward, throughout the whole of his body.

And she was afraid of it?

She didn't want it?

Was she truly out of her mind?

No, but she still shook as she reached to touch it, and when it jumped beneath her fingertips at the same instant Connor drew a sharp breath, she jerked her hand back and pressed it to her waist.

Her gaze shot to his. "Did I...hurt you?"

"No." His lips formed the word as he moved his head back and forth on the pillow. Then, in only slightly more audible tones, he said, "Go ahead. Anything you want. Just please..." He shut his eyes and clenched his jaw.

He wouldn't ask. But the plea was evident in the white-knuckled grip he had on the sheets on either side of him.

She touched him lightly, and this time, when the rigid shaft gave that involuntary little jerk, she didn't pull away. Instead, very slowly, she trailed her fingertips down the length of him, listening as his breath poured out in an almost agonized groan. The sound, different from any he'd yet made, was enough to make her wonder again if she was hurting him. But she knew she couldn't be. And as she continued to explore the shape and texture of the hot, silky flesh beneath her hand, the rapidly changing expressions on his face spoke of something far different from pain.

Anne watched and listened in growing wonder. Was he really so very sensitive? Could he actually feel every little movement of her fingers? It seemed so, for he couldn't possibly be pretending. Nor would he. But where was the silence, the grim drive toward a single-minded goal? The flat, unemotional expression? How odd this seemed. How different . . .

How completely unprepared she was for the stunning realization that her hand, her touch, was capable of imparting such obvious and acute pleasure. Did she really have the power to do this? Could she really affect *anyone* this strongly, through *anything* she might do or say? It seemed so, for her increasingly confident attentions were the indisputable cause of this ever more astonishing display of male arousal.

She didn't understand such arousal—pleasure that seemed almost unbearable—hadn't any notion what it would be like. But she understood something more important. *This* was how it should be. This aching striving to get closer, these hoarse groans and sighs, most of which began and ended with her name. This was good and clean and right. And how incredibly right it seemed that she should want to love him, and that, through her touch, she could.

So simple. So blessedly simple.

She'd told Connor that he couldn't make her forget the past, but watching him now, she thought this one moment alone had replaced a legion of memories. And as she looked down at her hand encircling him, gliding over his extravagantly aroused flesh, she became absorbed by the notion of replacing other memories, as well—ones of the act that constituted the most humiliating portion of what she'd endured. By doing something in love, she could erase the ugliness and the horror. She could take all those horrible memories and strip away their power, vanquish them with a *new* memory, a new way of thinking and feeling, and she was suddenly filled with the desire—truly, the need—to do so.

Connor said her name in question as she bent over him. And in the next moment, when her lips touched him, he swore, calling upon God to help him, as he threw his head back against the pillow and gripped the sheets.

She was intent. Careful. Slow. Her attention focused on his reaction to the intimate caress. He couldn't possibly understand what it meant to her to hear him gasping, "Oh, God, Anne, yes...God, yes," in raw, nearly incoherent tones. He couldn't have begun to imagine what it meant to her to feel his powerful body shaking, or to feel his heart pound and the skin across his chest and stomach grow slick beneath her hand.

Nor did she think he knew what it did to her to realize he was struggling against his body's natural responses, no doubt in fear of scaring her off if he truly let go. His hips wanted to move; she could feel them trying in the fine quivering of the muscles in his thigh, beneath her arm. But he kept them plastered to the bed, with one knee bent and his foot flat on the mattress as a brace, and she thought, no, no, that wasn't what she wanted at all. She *wanted* to feel him move. She wanted to feel and hear and know everything there was to know about him.

Without pausing in her ministrations, Anne reached for Connor's hand, beside her thigh, and tugged it away from the sheets to guide it around her back. His other hand she placed on her shoulder, the thought flickering briefly through her mind that, now, he could ruin it. Now he could force her to do it his way. But he banished the fear before it had even a second's chance to take hold.

"Ah, God, Annie..." Rolling forward, his knee falling to the side, he curled his body over hers, his arm cradling her body against his. And as he murmured words that told her how beautiful she was and how much he loved her and how good what she was doing felt to him, his other hand stroked her hair, her cheek, the line of her brow. But when his fingers trailed downward to trace her lips, trembling as they followed the line she formed around him, she couldn't bear it, couldn't go on.

The intimacy, the tenderness, the honest expression of feeling. She was shattered. Undone by the realization that this was love shared, as it was meant to be, and that she was making love truly for the first time. No longer with any sense of deliberation or idea of undoing the past but with a passion that lived and breathed in the moment. And the moment was theirs—hers and Connor's.

The full heat of desire rocked through her with a sudden and stunning force. All at once, she came to understand need. Not want or desire but *need*. Need that filled her body and consumed her mind. Need that drove her to fulfill her heart's yearnings and to discover an end to this longing that made her throb and ache and burn.

With a helpless moan, she raised her head to bury her face against his belly, her hands clutching at his arms, groping for his shoulders, her lips moving against his heated skin to form a single word. "Con..."

It was all she could manage, and he didn't wait for her to say more. His hands slid to her waist, and he lifted her against him, helping her crawl her way up his body. And when their faces were level, he didn't make her ask but covered her mouth with his, somehow seeming to know how vulnerable she was, how needy her mouth was, how horribly empty she felt, and he took her mouth in a way that both filled the need and made it greater.

When she had to wrench her lips from his to gasp for air, he rained kisses all over her face, growling, "Don't ever let me hear you say again that you don't know how to make love. Nobody's ever loved me like that, so I felt like I was the only thing that mattered in the world."

"You are," she breathed. "I love you so much, and I... Oh, Lord, I want... Oh, Con..."

"Tell me. Tell me what you want."

"You. I want... I need..." Shifting restlessly, needing desperately to be closer, her legs straddled one of his thighs as she knelt, pressing against him, rubbing, mindlessly seeking.... "Oh, Lord, I need *something*, and I don't know how or— Oh!" Her words ended in a gasp as his hands glided upward from her waist to cover her breasts.

"This?"

Anne's reply was a groan, her body arching as he stroked and kneaded the small, firm mounds, his fingers rolling the swollen tips that strained against the fabric of his robe. "Yes," she told him. "Oh, yes...but..." But it wasn't enough. Not nearly enough.

Her hands shook, and her fingers were clumsy as they tugged at the knot of the belt around her waist. She'd tied it so tightly, hadn't wanted to chance its coming undone. When it wouldn't yield to her increasingly frantic efforts, she whimpered and sank back onto his thigh, the robe tucked beneath her robbing her of contact between his skin and the part of her that ached most. An instant later, when Connor's hands joined hers, she simply held on to his arms while he loosened the knot and let the belt fall away. But when he slid his hands under the lapped edges of the robe to push them open, her fingers tightened on his arms, and her face grew warm.

He paused, his eyes coming up to meet hers. "Do you want me to stop?"

Her eyes drifted closed. "No. I'm just..."

"I know," Connor murmured in a low, gentling tone. "My Sunshine's shy. Shy and sweet, and I've always loved her for it." And as his hands slowly slid beneath the robe, he continued softly, "And she's always been pretty...pretty, like an old-fashioned picture postcard. But she's grown up to be... Oh, God... Oh, sweet heaven..."

Her breath caught, hitched up a little, then caught again, as the robe parted and his fingertips feathered downward, along the sides of her breasts.

"Anne, you're perfect," he breathed. "Completely, God's honest perfect." And he touched her as if he believed it was so, with wonder and devotion, his fingers trailing down her sides, over the gentle swell of her hips, then up again, creating rivers of gooseflesh that danced across her skin.

He made the trip several times; then, as her hands glided up his arms to cling to his shoulders, his fingers began drawing slow circles around each uptilted breast. Smaller and smaller the circles grew, drawing closer to her nipples, making them darken, harden, tighten in anticipation of his touch. The first teasing brush made her whimper. Then, as he caught the hardened peaks between his fingertips, her breath left her in a groan, her hips rocking unconsciously against his thigh.

It made no sense. No sense at all that his fingers, rolling and gently tugging on her nipples, should create such a hot, aching heaviness in her womb. But she'd abandoned sense some time ago. Somehow, there was a path inside her body between the two places, and he knew it. Oh, yes, he knew it.

With her eyes still closed and breaths coming in uneven gulps, she felt his lips nudge at hers. He knew that, too. Knew she needed to be kissed. And as her lips sought his, she hoped he'd simply go on knowing, for asking had become impossible.

He kissed her with tenderness, then he kissed her with passion. Then he let his lips trail down her neck, pausing at the base of her throat while his hands slid to her waist. He lifted her to her knees, and, as she rose against him, his mouth kissed a path down her chest and across her breast. No teasing in this. Not a bit of it. His mouth opened over her nipple and drew it inside.

He groaned. She sobbed. Her fingers burrowed through his hair to hold his head against her. His hand came up to cover her other breast, and she covered it with one of hers. His mouth sucked. His hand stroked. And she melted. Trembled. Needed. And the need consumed her. Managed her. Took over her mind and controlled her body until she knew desperation in a way she'd never known it in her life.

Her hands told him of her desperation, fingers clutching at his hair, running over his back and shoulders, urging him, telling him, *More, more, please, more*... Her legs were quivering, threatening to give out, by the time he put a hand on the mattress behind him and began lowering them to the bed. His mouth left her breast, climbed its way up her chest and her throat, his lips finding hers at the instant she dropped the robe from her shoulders and her body slid downward to meet his fully, unhindered by either cloth or fear, for the first time.

"Ohhh . . ." She gasped. "Oh, Con . . ."

"Yes," he said, sinking onto the bed, his hands gliding down her back, over the curve of her bottom, brushing the robe aside. "Feel it, love. Feel how good it is for us."

Had he known this, too? Had he known how this would be? Wonderful to feel his heated skin against hers. Wonderful to feel the soft curves of her body molding to all the planes and muscled contours of his. Glorious and exciting . . . yes, dangerously, breathlessly exciting . . . to feel the hard, hot length of his sex crushed into the damp curls between her thighs.

Her mouth found his again as she moved against him, sinuously, like molten lava flowing over a rock, like wax dripping down a candle. Like a woman melting with need for the man she loved. The need grew with each stroke of his hands over her hips, each mating of his mouth with hers, each shockingly intimate caress of his rigid flesh against that soft, pliant place that seemed, of its own will, to keep rubbing against him.

Her legs glided along his, up and down, twining one way, then the other, restless, so restless . . . so easy to let them slide apart. So easy simply to let it happen. To end this terrible ache.

To fill this awful need. Just a little more. It would be so easy. And it wouldn't hurt. No, not at all ...

"Anne ..."

But it did.

"Wait."

It did hurt.

"Don't."

But it *shouldn't*.

"Anne, stop." His hands tightened on her hips, restraining her movements. "I won't let you hurt yourself."

Balanced on her arms above him, Anne threw her head back and let out an agonized groan. "So empty ... I feel so *empty*, and I ... ache! Oh, Con, please ... help ..."

Her breath caught on a sob, and his arms encircled her, pulling her down to him, saying, "Ah, love, come here. Let me hold you." He brought her down beside him, rolling to face her, his arm beneath her holding her to him as his other hand stroked and soothed. "Shh, now, it's all right," he said, planting soft, gentle kisses, one after the other, on her lips.

"But I want you," she kept saying, frantic at the thought that, after all this—*after all this*—she might have to give up.

But he just kept telling her, "I know, love, I know." And finally, as his hand slipped down the back of her thigh, he said, "Will you let me touch you?"

She knew where he meant, and her answer was an emphatic, indeed, nearly hysterical "Yes! Oh, please ..."

"Shh." His lips plucked at hers as he drew her leg over his hip, draping it across his waist. Then, with his hand gliding up and down the back of her thigh, slowly, almost absently, straying closer and closer to the goal, he added, "I'm telling you it's going to be all right. Trust me. This is where you've got to relax and not worry."

Impossible. She couldn't do it. But, somehow, he coaxed her into it, anyway. Between all the kisses and the words and the mesmerizing caress of his hand, she felt the brittle edge of frustration evaporate—though it didn't take one drop of aching arousal with it.

"Just breathe once in a while," he urged her with a nudge of his mouth on her chin. "And don't bite those beautiful lips ... no, you don't want to do that when you can kiss me instead... That's it. Kiss me while I touch you. Just with my hand now. Nothing else. Just like ... like this."

Her breath spilled out in a sudden rush as his fingers found and parted her tender folds, then took their first gentle glide through the slick heat.

"Oh, Annie, love..." His hand covered her, fingers moving with increasing boldness. "God, it's true—you are perfect."

Panting, she managed, "Then why couldn't I—"

"Shh," he said. "It's okay. You're still just a little scared, I think."

Anne squeezed her eyes closed. "But I don't *feel* scared. I feel... Oh, mercy, I can't... describe it."

"I know. But that feeling's not going to go away. And even if it does, it'll come back. Just let me—"

"Oh! Oh, Con..."

"You like that?"

"Yes, it's... Oh... Oh, *Con*..."

"Do that again." His lips tugged at hers. "Say my name."

An easy request to fulfill, and as she did so, he kissed her—a gentle brush of her lower lip.

"Again," he ordered softly.

"Con," she breathed, though she didn't understand why. And again, he teased her with another small kiss.

"Keep saying it for me, love. Don't stop."

With her attention totally absorbed in the knowing touch of his fingers and the magic they were working on her wildly sensitive flesh, she didn't question him. She simply complied. "Con." She said his name. Then she said it again. She couldn't say it without her mouth being wholly open, and it soon became clear that his intention was to keep it so. For as her lips continued to form the soft sound of the word, "Con," he began tracing a path around them with the tip of his tongue, coaxing them apart, teasing them open—at the same time and in the same way his finger traced the entrance of her feminine passage, coaxing, teasing, encouraging her to unfold for him.

"Con..." His tongue tasted the inside of her lips at the moment his finger dipped almost imperceptibly inside of her. His tongue grazed past her teeth to briefly touch hers, and so his finger followed the pattern. Closer, deeper, a little deeper each time. And soon she was saying his name, not because he'd asked but because she couldn't help herself. She had to say it, compulsively, breathlessly, until, finally, as he covered her mouth with his and kissed her deeply, fully, his finger slipped inside her and stayed, lingering to stroke, to caress, to charm her body into making him welcome.

Pleasure. Pleasure so intense it was almost pain. He was making her insane with it. She arched against his hand, gasping, "Con... Oh, Lord, I— I—" Then, suddenly, a series of tiny electric charges rippled through her, and, for an instant, she lost control of her body. It ceased even to feel like *her* body but became, for that instant, a mass of raw, exquisite sensation.

Her eyes flew open to find Connor's steady blue gaze upon her. He was watching her closely at a distance of mere inches, and as she stared at him in astonishment, he spoke softly.

"There's more."

Anne swallowed, trying to speak. "More?"

"Where that came from."

Her eyes widened further and a blush rose to her cheeks, though she didn't know how anything could still, and under their present circumstances, embarrass her. Yet she had to ask, "You could... tell?"

"Mmm."

"What did it... feel like to you?"

"Waves. Little ones. But I think you could catch a bigger one if you don't try to stop it. If you just... just let it..." Connor trailed off, an odd frown twitching at his brow. An instant later he withdrew his finger, then, carefully, slid back inside with more than one. This time, though, as his fingers moved deeply within her, she caught her breath.

His frown deepened. "That hurt?"

She nodded. "A little. Wh-what's wrong?" She expected him to confirm her deep-seated fear that she was somehow damaged and wasn't at all prepared for what he finally said.

"Nothing's wrong." His eyes closed for an instant, then opened to meet hers in a fiercely tender look. "God knows how, but, for once, something's right. Anne, you're a virgin."

She stared at him in utter lack of comprehension. "That's not... I mean, I can't be."

"But you are," he insisted.

"Maybe... maybe something *is* wrong. Maybe I'm—"

He cut her off with a kiss. Then, with his lips brushing back and forth over hers, he whispered, "There's not a blessed thing wrong with you. You're soft and wet and... Love, I swear to you, you're perfect. And you're a virgin."

"But how can I be when—" ... *when he raped me?* She refused to say it, refused to defile the moment with thoughts of the other. Still, it was impossible to accept that what she'd believed to be true for so long wasn't true at all. "But, Con," she insisted, "it ... it *hurt* when ..."

His eyes darkened as she trailed off. "Like it hurt a few minutes ago, when you were on top of me?"

"Yes," she replied. "But... worse." Much worse. Like it would have hurt if Connor had been battering at her, trying to get inside, when her body wouldn't admit him. And, suddenly, without his having to explain, she understood.

She'd read all those books; she knew the names of every sexual dysfunction known to womankind, including one often produced by the kind of terror she'd experienced that caused a certain muscle to clamp shut, making penetration impossible. Nor could a woman will the muscle to relax, no matter how aroused she might be. If her subconscious refused to cooperate, her desire would be for naught—as hers would have been a few minutes ago if Connor hadn't been able, literally, to seduce her subconscious into surrendering its vigil. So it could be true. And it certainly also could have been true that she'd been too crazed with terror—and too naive at sixteen—to have realized that what she'd thought had happened hadn't. She'd only known it hurt.

So much for the power of threats. They'd kept her a virgin. Connor said she was. Never mind how he could speak with such confidence; she didn't care how he'd acquired such thorough knowledge of a woman's body. The only thing that mattered was that, when he'd walked into the boathouse all those years ago, he'd saved her from more than even she herself had known. Her virginity might be little more than a technicality, but it was here. Hers to give, still and in spite of everything.

And she wanted to give it to him. He'd be the first. The first and the only. And he knew it. His eyes blazed with the knowledge as she moved against him in an invitation that was impossible to misunderstand.

"Con, please," she whispered.

His eyes never left hers as, very slowly, he withdrew his fingers from her and reached across her for the plastic packet he'd left on the nightstand.

She had no idea what he must have seen on her face, but, as he was tearing the packet open behind her back, he stopped, his look questioning, as if he might be worried this detail was going to ruin things yet.

"I wish..." she began, then hesitated.

"You wish what?" he asked.

She wet her lips with the tip of her tongue. "I wish you wouldn't."

He paused, his eyes searching hers. Then, carefully, he posed the question for the second time. "Do you want to get pregnant?"

It wasn't that, precisely. It was more that she didn't want to prevent it. She wanted him, and only him, inside her, and she would welcome whatever came of their union. Maybe it wasn't rational—no, it certainly was not the sensible time to be making such fearfully serious decisions. But she didn't care. It was a statement of hope about the future that she'd never imagined making. And she wanted to make it with him.

Nothing would have made her happier than to have his baby. Still, what she said was, "Not if it would make you unhappy."

"No." His lips formed the word soundlessly. Then, in slightly broken tones, he said, "No, it wouldn't make me unhappy at all."

The packet hit the floor behind her. Then he was shifting her, tucking her leg more securely around him, and his fingers were touching her again, easing her apart. His arm beneath her tightened its hold, his hand splayed against her bottom drawing her hips into close alignment with his. And, suddenly, it wasn't his fingers anymore that were parting, caressing, gently probing...

"Oh!" It was almost too much. Too new, too completely shocking to feel the heaviness and the heat and the hardness of him, poised there, at the entrance he'd so deliberately opened. "Oh, Con..." Her eyes squeezed closed, her leg clamping around him, her fingers gripping his back.

Connor spoke in an urgent whisper. "Anne, look at me. Open your eyes and look at me."

Her eyes flew open at the command, passion-drugged and a little frightened, holding his as he told her, "Now, watch me. Stay right here with me when I—" He broke off, drawing a quick breath. "I love you, Anne. I love you with all my heart. I'll always love you... always..." And as he said it, his hands tightened their hold on her hips, the muscles along his thigh flexed, and slowly...so slowly she thought she'd die...he sank his body into hers.

She clung to him, trembling, her eyes bound with his. She saw the sweat form and run down his face. She heard "I love you" become a breathless rasp. She felt her heart swell to bursting, along with her body, at the care—the *love*—with which he took her. Love. The word had power. It opened her, transfigured her. Expanded her mind, her body, her soul. There was pressure. So much pressure. Then a single stab of deep, burning pain.

She cried out. He swore. She gasped, her fingers digging into his back. He kissed and held her, saying, "I love you... God, how I love you..." And, gradually, intrusion became melding. Invasion became joining. Pressure became the most amazing feeling of being filled. And pain slowly gave way to pleasure. Compelling, tantalizing pleasure that lured her with the promise of more.

Groaning, she moved, easing him deeper inside her, her body stretching and molding to the shape of him, testing the limits until she couldn't have taken any more, and there was no more to take. "Oh... Oh, *Con*..."

"That's it," he urged her. "Make it yours. Show me how you want me to love you."

She didn't have to. Her body did it for her. Without any conscious effort or thought, her body found the notes and the rhythm and set about making a symphony inside her. A symphony with him as the conductor, his body providing both the music and the means to play it. No instrument of torture, this, but a source of the most heavenly sensations, stroking her, filling her, inspiring her, until her entire body was singing, striking chords that carried her upward until she hovered, dancing on a peak, sure she couldn't climb any higher. Then he proved her wrong. His hand joined the orchestra, caressing her, working its special magic again, all of it building, building inside her, until, suddenly, she was flying, flying on waves of the sweetest, most beautiful music she'd ever heard.

It captured her heart. It thrilled her soul. It surprised her utterly. Never could she have imagined it. Never had she dreamed such pleasure existed, and as she rode the vibrant strains, it seemed certain no innocent ever could have felt such wonder, such awe. Or such gratitude. That she'd been given this. That it could be hers. That after such a long, barren time she might know the full wealth of her body's treasures. In those few exalted moments, everything that had been taken away from her was returned, and, although she'd never have wished for what had come before—the pain, the ugliness—she wondered if, without it, this pleasure could have been as rich and full and complete.

She would never know. And she would never care. Never again. But it seemed to her, then, that it had to be true: Heaven must be greater for having known hell.

The music faded slowly, the notes growing fainter until, finally, they were lost in the sound of her quiet sobs. Anne's eyes fluttered open to the feel of Connor kissing tears from her cheeks, tears she hadn't known were there, and he was saying her name again and again.

But his voice had a note of tension in it. And she knew why. This man who would die for her or kill for her would also sacrifice his own needs and desires for her. He'd been keeping them under nearly brutal control, she realized, for the longest time. And she had no doubt he'd give them up entirely if she only asked. A request she had no intention of making. She loved him more than life itself, and it was time...yes, for once, exactly the right time...that she let him know.

"Con..." Her hand slid over his back, her leg tightening around him, trying to pull him toward her.

But he resisted. "Anne, I—"

"Yes...yes, on top of me."

"Oh, God, love, I don't think—" He shut his eyes, his hips moving, his hard flesh pulsing. "I don't want to—"

He never finished the sentence, but she understood. And she was having none of it. She wanted to feel the weight of him, wanted him to know it was all right, wanted it exactly as he'd described it that afternoon—lying on top of her with her legs wrapped around him, his body deep inside of hers.

"Con—" Her hands tugged, her leg gliding up and down the back of his thigh. "I'm yours. Just yours. For always. I'll never leave you. And I'll never be afraid of you." And as she rolled slowly to her back, he came with her, covering her as she whispered, "Please. Show me how it is for you. Show me...."

And he did. Groaning, giving in to her and to passion, he buried his flesh in hers, full and deep, his hands lifting her to make it deeper. Holding it there as he breathed her name. Touching her soul.

Then, gasping, sucking in air, he levered his body above hers, let his eyes rake over her, looked down to watch his flesh sink into hers. Thrusting slowly, his thighs pushing hers wide, his hand stroked across her belly, downward over her hip, reached to touch the place they joined and the blood smearing her thighs.

"Oh, God... Oh, Anne..." His arm slid beneath her, arching her back, his mouth moving feverishly over her throat, her shoulders, her breasts. "Mine...my Annie...my love..." he whispered. Then his mouth was on hers, and he was gathering her to him, holding her, cherishing her, all the while he was molding her pliant, willing body to his desire.

And as she felt him moving inside her, felt the weight and the heat and the strength of him, she thought this was how she'd known he'd be, this was the man she'd known all her life. The man she'd always loved. All this sweat-slicked skin and these quivering muscles and the soul-deep groans torn from him with every long, slow, gliding journey his body made into hers. This was the man she'd seen greet the dawn—with fire and passion and joy. She'd become the river, and he was reveling in her, with her, through her.

The climax that wracked his body drove him deep, crushing her into the mattress, and she savored each moment of it, wrapping her legs and her arms around him and holding him. Tightly. So tightly. And when it was over, and he lay in her arms with his face buried against her neck and her fingers stroking, gently stroking, the hair lying across his forehead, she listened to the quiet and breathed deeply of the salty breeze blowing in from the river. And she knew peace.

How good. How right. How perfect it seemed.

Her head turned on the pillow, her eyes met his, and, slowly, a smile formed on her lips.

He smiled in return and murmured, "Welcome home, Sunshine."

Her smile broadened into a grin. So did his, and, a moment later, a chuckle began rumbling in his chest.

Then, all at once, they were laughing, wrapped in each other's arms, rolling on the bed like children playing, like comrades reveling—like lovers rejoicing in the moment that courage and hope and love had made theirs.

Chapter Sixteen

Anne wanted to hang the bloodstained sheet from the balcony railing. But then, she considered all the people who might see it besides the one in whose face she wanted to wave it—people, for instance, such as Connor's mother. She blushed at the thought, then blushed some more under Connor's frankly possessive glances as they changed the sheets together. She blushed furiously when he led her into the shower. But no amount of shyness could have lowered her high spirits, nor did it lessen her pleasure in sharing each new intimacy with him.

They fixed supper. Corn-on-the-cob in bed, with butter drizzling over hands and chests and various other parts. Anne would have opted for another shower á deux, but Connor proposed a different solution to the butter problem that eventually led to making love again—after she convinced him that she wasn't sore and would be most disappointed if she couldn't enjoy her newly deflowered state at least once more that night. They both enjoyed it quite a lot.

And they talked. For endless hours, they lolled across the bed, and each other, and rambled on about her teaching, about his involvement with The Bay Action Group, about people they knew in common and what they were doing now. Several times, when the conversation strayed to his business or to plans for the future, he started to say something, then didn't. Nor did he mention anything about a certain grant proposal. Anne didn't press; she wasn't ready to talk about the future or grant proposals, either. Not until she'd had a chance to do a little planning of her own.

The moon was sinking low when they decided they ought to go to sleep. They even turned out the light. But saying goodnight began with a kiss that didn't want to end. Before long, the fires were burning with a tender, unhurried passion. This time, though, he didn't wait for her arguments about how fine she was and how he wouldn't hurt her. Rather, he covered her body with kisses, overriding blushes wasted in the darkness to kiss one particular place long and well, loving her as she had loved him earlier—and did again, then.

Finally, about an hour before dawn, as they lay exhausted and content in each other's arms, they slept.

Anne was awakened twice before the sun rose, the first time because she was being licked in the face. Swatting vaguely at the amorous attack, she dragged her eyes open to find Rogue's nose an inch from hers, his black form barely distinguishable in the darkness. In no mood for canine games, she turned over to face Connor, who was sprawled on his stomach, asleep.

Rogue whined. She ignored him. He barked, and she quickly rolled to sit on the edge of the bed, whispering that he should lie down and be quiet. He ran to the door and back again, and when he'd done it for the third time, she guessed he needed to go out but that Connor had locked his dog door.

Sighing, Anne searched in the dark for Connor's bathrobe, which she couldn't find, and instead, came across a long-sleeved shirt draped over the back of the chair by the closet. It covered her to mid-thigh, and she buttoned it as she made her way down the stairs with Rogue on her heels.

The setter was through the dog door the instant she unlocked it, and Anne started to turn away. Then she hesitated, staring at the hinged panel. Locks were worthless, she knew, but she carefully relocked the panel, anyway, before trudging back up the stairs. Climbing into bed without bothering to remove the shirt, she took a moment to draw the sheet up to cover herself and her sleeping lover. Then, planting a soft kiss on his shoulder, she lay back on the pillow and, immediately, fell asleep.

The second time Anne awoke, it was light enough to see. What she saw was a gun. It was pointed at Connor's head, and Aaron was standing next to her, holding it. His other hand was over her mouth, or she would have screamed.

She came fully awake in an instant, her heart pounding and sweat breaking out on her brow as she stared at her brother's undisguised face above her. Wasted. Hollow. Aged beyond his years. No longer boyishly appealing by anyone's standards. Her father's face, except that the bloodshot, brown eyes weren't sad but cold. So cold. They chilled her to the marrow.

He grinned down at her. She didn't move. He glanced at the gun, made sure it was aimed directly at Connor's head, then looked back at her with one eyebrow arched. She got the message. She didn't make a sound when he removed his hand from her mouth. And when he stepped back, motioning her to get up, she did so carefully, despite her trembling, not letting the mattress bounce or the bedsprings squeak.

He was going to kill her. No question about that. But if Connor awakened, Aaron would kill him, too. No question about that, either. Or about her choices. There weren't any.

Standing, shoving the hair out of her eyes with a hand that shook visibly, Anne tugged at the bottom of Connor's shirt, cringing as Aaron's gaze swept over her bare legs. He wasn't grinning anymore. He kept the gun trained on Connor as he took another step back, then, with a nod, gestured for her to walk toward the door.

Anne cast a single glance at Connor—his skin so dark against the white sheet, his hair so black on the pillow, his lashes lying so softly against his cheek in the vulnerable soundness of exhausted sleep. Her lower lip trembled, and she quickly turned away. Then, with a swift look at Aaron—or rather, at the gun—she crept out of the room.

Aaron waited until she reached the doorway, then followed, urging her down the stairs, through the kitchen, and out the back door. It was already open, the glass from two broken panes lying scattered on the floor. No point in locks without an alarm to back them up, and she'd de-activated the "alarm" when she'd let Rogue leave the house. He'd have heard Aaron and barked in plenty of time for her and Connor to take some kind of action.

And how many times a fool did that make her?

One too many.

Aaron pushed her down the back steps and directed her to the left with a sharp "This way."

Casting glances over her shoulder, Anne winced as she banged into the end of Connor's Windsurfer. "Where are we going?"

"Shut up."

"But can't you—"

"I said shut up. And be careful where you're going, unless you want to wake up McLeod and watch him get blown away."

It was true, Sentinel's second-floor windows were open, and, with the breeze blowing in from the river, any noise would carry into the bedroom as they passed the front of the house. Anne tried to get a look at the windows while Aaron kept her moving toward the beach, but she saw little through the trees in the dim light. The urge to scream was overwhelming, but the thought of Connor waking up and running out to be shot kept her silent.

She didn't think Aaron would shoot her. He needed to get rid of her so that no one could prove he'd done it. Without noise. Without mess. Without a body left lying in plain view. But with the gun jabbing her in the ribs at every step, she was too petrified to test the theory.

High tide left only a four-foot strip of beach that shrank to three with every sluggish little wave that lapped onto shore. There wasn't a trace of breeze to relieve the already oppressive warmth, but the beads of sweat on Anne's forehead were clammy cold. Keeping a firm hold on the bottom edges of Connor's shirt, she waited until they were off the point, away from Sentinel, then spoke in shaky, breathless tones.

"You're going to kill me, aren't you?"

Aaron didn't reply.

"Over the property," she continued. "Because I wouldn't sell it to you."

Silence.

"Aaron, for Lord's sake, if you want it that badly, take it! I'll sign it over to you. Today. Or tomorrow, if we can't find Howard Stone on a Sunday."

He didn't answer, just kept urging her with the gun to keep walking. Walking toward her death.

"Listen," she said. "I don't care about this place. I really don't. You can have it. And every blessed thing that's left in the manor, too."

"Shut up," he muttered, and that was all he would say.

Anne bit her lip and kept walking, taking care not to fall over the driftwood that had washed in during the storm as she continued to toss glances over her shoulder at her brother. She'd been right: He was different. Much different. As sick as Aaron had always been, he'd retained his hold on reality. But the twitching muscles in his face and the fine tremor in the hand wielding the gun made her think that hold had grown very tenuous.

Was all of this even real to him? Did he actually have a reason for killing her? Or was he merely acting out a long-harbored fantasy?

Never mind terror. Never mind fury. She couldn't afford them. She was dealing with a madman. And as she noted the glazed look in his eyes, his flushed skin, and his rapid, uneven breathing, it became more and more obvious that he was ready to snap. Which meant she'd better keep her wits about her, if she had any hope whatsoever of getting out of this alive.

And she did have hope. Oh, yes. With thoughts of Connor and the previous night filling her mind—proof positive that the impossible could happen and that she was capable of controlling her own destiny—she wasn't giving up. Not yet. Not as long as she was still breathing.

They'd passed the manor and were on the outward curve of the point leading to Sandcastle. Anne had a terrible feeling she knew where they were going and for what purpose, and her voice had a desperate quality to it as she continued. "Aaron, killing me is not going to get you what you want. The police know it was you who attacked me last night."

No reply.

"The police know everything, Aaron. *Everything*. They were here last night, and I told them. They know you set the fire Tuesday night, too, and that you sabotaged the brakes on my car. They're looking for you right now."

It startled her when he spoke in that gravelly, hard-edged voice she didn't recognize. "They've got a witness who saw me mess with your car?"

"Yes," she replied without hesitation.

He snorted. "You lie, little girl. You always lie."

Did he actually know that? Or was he merely assuming it, as he always did? Either way, this wasn't the time to argue. "I'm not lying that the police are looking for you," she said.

"It doesn't matter."

"It does matter!" Panic clutched at Anne's stomach as they rounded the point and the boathouse loomed before her. The beach gave out a few yards farther on, and when Aaron shoved her up the muddy bank onto the narrow path that ran along its ridge, she rushed to say, "Right now, even if the police catch you, they—"

"Too late," he muttered. "Too late."

"It's *not* too late! But it will be if you kill me!" Fighting to control her voice, to keep it calm and reasonable, she said, "Put the gun away, Aaron, and let me go. We'll find Howard Stone, and we'll get the money you need. For heaven's sake, think! There's *got* to be a better way to get out of whatever trouble you're in than murder."

"Too late," he said again.

And she began to believe he was right. The shrub-lined path ended, and they came to a grassy stretch of open space. The boathouse sat twenty yards straight ahead. Anne came to a stop, turning abruptly to face him as she began to speak, began one more time to try to reason with him. But he raised the gun and leveled it at her head, and she knew then, absolutely, that he'd use it, regardless of the inconvenience it might cause him.

The vacant eyes and blank expression told the story. She knew, as she had always known, that there was neither reason nor feeling nor any scrap of humanity in him. At least, none that could be reached by her—or, she thought, by him. He was lost. Gone. Living in hell without having to die to get there. And he intended to take her down with him.

Backing away, she turned and continued onward, tripping when he pushed her onto the dock that ran along the outside of the boathouse. She clung to the side of the wooden building for support, flattening her back against it, scuttling sideways as her eyes darted between the gun and the water. When she reached the open doorway, she fell through it, then caught herself on a piling to keep from going over the edge of the narrow dock.

A small, fast runabout was moored next to her, behind the *Spinner*. The boat Connor had mentioned to Ben Whitlow the previous night. As surely as she knew her own name, she knew Aaron was going to put her in it, take her out, and drown her.

If she let him.

Lifting her gaze, she looked at him standing in the doorway, his face fully lit now by the newly risen sun. Her brother, the demon. And, suddenly, something inside her snapped. She didn't care about the gun. Didn't care about dying or anything else. She was through with this. Through with being terrorized. She'd had enough. *Enough.*

When Aaron came to a halt beside her, Anne hung on to the piling for all she was worth. "That's it," she said. "You can stick that gun in my face all you want, but I'm not moving."

She did move, though, when his foot came out and swept her legs from under her, knocking her off the edge of the dock, at the same time he gave her hands clutching the piling a whack with the butt of his gun. She cried as she fell, but the sound was cut short by the shock of landing, not in the water, but in his runabout.

Anne wasted about two seconds in getting her breath. Then, hauling herself up on the back of the captain's seat, she reached for the keys hanging in the ignition, snatched them out, and threw them overboard. They hit the water at the same instant Aaron landed beside her, the small boat rocking violently beneath his weight.

"Bitch!"

His hand connected with her face and snapped her head sideways. But she didn't scream, and her gaze met his with defiance as she said, "You can hit me and swear at me all you want. But if you want to kill me, you're going to have to do it here. I'm not going anywhere with you."

He swore violently and hit her again. Then, before she'd had a chance to recover, he grabbed her and all but threw her out of the boat, onto the dock. Pain shot through her, along with shock. He shouldn't be strong enough to throw her. He was too thin, too wasted. But with madness driving him, he seemed to have the strength of ten men as he jumped onto the dock, dug his fingers into her upper arm, and lifted her.

Panting, stretching, she went for the gun, but he held it out of her reach as he dragged her, like a rag doll, around the catwalk to the opposite side of the boathouse. He was headed for the *Lady Lyn*, and Anne was about to tell him that the yacht wouldn't run, either, because one of the engines was missing a carburetor. Then, suddenly, just as he reached the aft deck and was about to toss her over the gunwale, he let out a curse and dropped her as he whirled back toward the open doorway.

Sprawled facedown on the dock, Anne heard it, too. Rogue's enthusiastic bark. But it only meant the setter had happened upon them in his morning travels—not that Connor was on his way to save her. Not this time. Connor was safely asleep, not getting shot. She was going to have to save herself.

Now. Or never.

Anne looked at the three feet of space between the edge of the dock and the side of the *Lady Lyn*. She thought about Connor and about doing things that had seemed impossible. She thought about dying. She drew a deep breath. And when Rogue bounded through the doorway, barking a blue streak, she threw herself over the edge of the dock—at the same instant she heard the crack of the gun and Rogue's anguished yelp.

The phone rang in Connor's dream. He answered it, and it was Owen Thackery, his family doctor, calling to say that Anne had delivered twins, and he could come and get them. But he couldn't, because he didn't have a place to live, and he didn't have any money, and he had to hurry up and cut down Forest Sloane's old black walnut to get money to buy a house so he could bring Anne and their babies home. But the chain saw kept stopping. Starting, then stopping . . . But, no it wasn't the chain saw. It was the phone again.

It rang eight times on the table beside Connor's head before the dream gave way to reality and he grabbed the cordless receiver to drag it off its cradle. Hauling it across the pillow toward him, he muttered something that was better for being incomprehensible.

A male voice responded to his dubious greeting in urgent tones. "Con, it's Ben. Drag your eyes open and listen, will you? I've got some news."

Ben Whitlow's words penetrated the fog surrounding Connor's brain, and he replied groggily, "I'm here."

"Doesn't sound like it, but try to pay attention, because a swarm of federal drug agents are on their way over to your neck of the woods to search for Aaron Marquel."

With his eyes still closed, Connor frowned. "Drug agents?"

"You heard it. I went from your place to Blaine Thorpe's last night, and it didn't take much to get her to crack. Marquel's been financing small drug deals by selling art from his house. But recently, he *borrowed* some huge amount of money to bring in a big shipment of cocaine. The feds found the stuff, though, strapped to the bottom of a cargo ship—saw an article in the paper about it three or four weeks ago—so Marquel's got nothing to sell. Which means he can't pay back the loan, and, according to Miss Thorpe, the character he borrowed the money from is going to waste him if he doesn't come up with it by the end of next week."

"God..." Connor levered himself onto his elbows, rubbing the sleep out of his eyes as he tried to take in the barrage of information. Not wanting to disturb Anne, he kept his voice low as he began, "And Blaine Thorpe just told you all this without..." But the words trailed off, alarm sizzling through his veins, as he opened his eyes and looked to see that Anne wasn't beside him.

But where else could she be? It hadn't been but a little over an hour since they'd gone to sleep.

Throwing off the sheet, telling himself not to panic, Connor got up to go look for her as Whitlow continued.

"Miss Thorpe's been here at the station all night, crying and babbling all over the place. The lady's a wreck, but she's being real cooperative. Seems Marquel's spent all her money, and she's not too happy about that."

Connor glanced toward the open bathroom doorway, saw in the thin gray light seeping through the window that the room was empty, then headed for the stairs as he asked, "Did she tell you Aaron's trying to kill Anne?"

"Yeah, she signed a statement," Whitlow replied. "Says all Marquel can talk about is how everything bad under the sun is his sister's fault—the mess over the drugs, his never having any money. It's like Miss Marquel said—he blames her for everything, and none of it makes sense. This lady we've got down here is scared to death. Says losing the drugs has sent him into a real tailspin. And to make it worse, he's got a drug habit himself that he's been indulging nonstop for the past two weeks."

"Good God," Connor muttered.

"Yeah, I know. And I want to come get you and your lady friend out of there. You weren't exaggerating, Con. This guy sounds like the meanest, craziest bastard I've come across in twenty years, and until the feds pick him up, I don't want you—"

"Ben, he's got her!" Standing in the kitchen doorway, Connor took one look at the open back door and the broken glass, then whirled to race up the stairs. "The door's busted open, and she's gone! I'm going to—"

"Con, you stay there! Don't you—"

"Just get out here, Ben! Fast!"

The phone bounced onto the bed as Connor flung it aside and snatched his jeans off the floor, dragging them on as he strode onto the balcony to scan the beach. Daylight, barely, the sun's first pale rays stretching across the river to lighten the deserted strip of sand. Connor's panicked gaze swept over the peaceful scene once, then he turned to run for his truck.

He didn't get past the doorway. A noise—the distant but unmistakable crack of a gun—spun him around, his gaze riveting to the spot where Sandcastle sat hidden among the trees.

"Oh, no... Oh, Jesus, please... *No!*"

He didn't stop to think. His mind made the leap to the other end of the half-mile stretch of beach, and, as if he could will himself there, his body followed the shortest distance between the two points. His hands grabbed the wrought-iron railing, and, with a flex of his knees, he vaulted over it, dropping easily to the porch roof, then to the ground. Then he was running, flat out, flying across the point and down the beach, his bare feet kicking out sand behind him.

Heading in a straight line for Sandcastle, he reached the far end of the beach, leaped up the bank, and tore through the woods, oblivious to the damage being done to his feet and bare skin by the brambles and sticks. But then, as he approached the cottage, another gunshot split the air, confusing him. It hadn't come from Sandcastle but farther on, toward the boathouse. And as he adjusted his course and raced onward, a jolt of some bizarre kind of hope slashed through him.

It only took one bullet to kill. Unless the bullet missed.

The third shot shocked the morning silence at the same instant Connor hit the path around the cove, where he got a clear view of the boathouse—and of Aaron, pacing back and forth along the bank, holding a gun, looking at the water, clearly searching for something... searching for...

Anne. Her head popped out of the water some fifty feet from shore. Aaron halted, raised the gun, and fired off the fourth shot—at the same instant Connor let out a thunderous *"No!"* and came bolting along the bank, either jumping over or crashing through every log or bush that stood in his path.

He didn't look to see if the shot had hit its target. Nor did he stop when Aaron whirled at the sound of his voice and began firing at him. Pure, mindless rage turned his vision to a blood-red mass of flashing lights and filled his head with a deafening roar that blocked out even the spit of the bullets flying past him. The bullets kept missing, and he flew out of the relative safety of the trees and shrubs onto the clear stretch of loamy turf. Then there was nothing between him and his startled, snarling target but twenty yards of open space.

Twenty became fifteen, then ten, then five. Then his feet left the ground and he launched himself across the remaining distance, arms outstretched, hands going for the neck, brain registering dimly the fiery pain of a bullet slamming into his side as he landed, plowing a knee into the groin of the cursing, flailing animal who'd tried to kill his woman and his dreams, thinking he'd live to tell of it.

Below the water's surface, she was safe. Above it, she'd die. Anne focused all her attention on that ultimate irony to prevent the fear from overwhelming her. The water wouldn't hurt her. The seaweed slithering along her arms and legs wouldn't hurt her. Nothing in the water would hurt her. It was protecting her. Hiding her. Keeping her alive. And she would stay alive as long as she could hold her breath.

Twice, she'd had to surface for air. Twice, Aaron had shot at her and missed. She willed herself not to think about Connor's dog as she counted the shot that hadn't missed, the one that had given her the chance to escape. She wondered how many bullets the gun held. A few more, at least. But when they were gone, what could he do to her? Nothing, as long as she stayed in the water. If only she could avoid the bullets, not let her shivering terror of the dark, weed-ridden sanctuary send her clawing for the surface, she might just make it. She might.

The awful moment came again. The one when Anne couldn't hold her breath any longer, and she had to give in to her body's instinctive urge to breathe. Her feet stopped kicking and reached for the bottom, her toes sinking into mud as she pushed off, swimming for the surface, only eight feet above, where the shimmer of sunshine beckoned.

Anne broke the surface with her eyes open, ready to gulp another lungful of air and dive under again. She expected to hear the gun go off, and it did. But at the same instant, over the single blast of gunfire, she heard an enraged male voice, a familiar voice, yelling, "No!" And her startled, water-blurred gaze whipped to the right to see Connor hurtling along the bank.

Another shot rang out, and she looked to see that Aaron had whirled and was firing, not at her, but at Connor. Then she was the one crying, "No!" But Aaron went on shooting and Connor went on running, the space between them disappearing in seconds, until, all at once, Connor flung himself at Aaron, literally roaring. She saw Aaron fly backward as Connor's body struck him. She saw the gun sail through the air as Aaron hit the ground with Connor on top of him. She saw a splash of water as the gun landed in the cove and sank.

She saw blood running in a thin stream down Connor's side.

"Oh, dear Lord . . . Oh, no . . ." Anne forgot the water. Forgot she was afraid of it. Forgot nearly everything in her panicked rush to get to shore.

She had not forgotten how to swim. With a sharp kick, she threw both arms forward, ducked her head, and started toward the bank at a fast crawl. The movements were automatic, nearly instinctive, and she covered the distance quickly. The muddy slope rose in front of her, a nearly vertical five-foot drop. She clawed her way up it, clutching handfuls of marsh grass and exposed tree roots, her efforts becoming more and more desperate as she listened to the sounds of struggle above her. Horrible sounds. Growls and snarls cut short by strangled curses.

Her hands and feet slipped in the mud, and she slid back into the water several times. Sheer terror that Connor was shot and might be dying drove her to keep trying, until, finally, she got a hold of a scrawny mulberry sapling growing at the top of the bank and was able to pull herself up over the edge.

The men were fighting less than ten feet away, and her first view of the scene sent shock waves rocketing through her. Blood everywhere, oozing from the hole in Connor's chest, dripping from the scrapes and gouges Aaron's fingernails were tearing in his arms, running down his hands, locked around Aaron's neck.

"Con . . . wait! Stop!" On hands and knees, Anne crawled toward them, throwing herself on Connor, tugging uselessly at his arms, trying to break his stranglehold on Aaron's throat. "Don't! Don't kill him! Please! Oh, don't . . ."

It didn't seem Connor heard or even knew she was there. His eyes were squeezed closed, his teeth bared in a snarl, every muscle in his body bulging with the tension of a single-minded purpose: to grind Aaron into the ground as he strangled him to death. But she couldn't let him do it. She had to stop him. For as wicked as her brother was and as many times as she herself had wished him dead, she didn't want his murder on Connor's soul. No. Not that, too. Not another atrocity for them to have to overcome—if they ever could.

"Con...Con, listen to me... Oh, please, listen!" Appalled at the sight of blood covering her own hands and at the slow but steady stream of it coming from the bullet hole in the lower left side of Connor's chest, she threw her arms around his neck, sobbing, "Con, I don't want you to do this. Please...please, stop..."

And, finally, his breath caught in his throat, and his body went rigid and still.

"Please," she whispered, her eyes wide with fright as she glanced at Aaron's straining form and the now-feeble attempts his fingers made to loosen Connor's hands from his neck.

Connor's eyes opened to stare at Aaron. Then he jerked his gaze toward her, and Anne shivered at the blind fury that burned in his eyes. Then, as he focused on her, really *saw* her, kneeling there beside him, crying, she saw the fury dissipate and reason return. He looked back down at Aaron, saw his hands gripping the other man's neck, saw the blood...suddenly seemed to realize that it was his own blood, that he was shot.

"Oh, God..." With an anguished groan, his hands loosened their hold, his eyes dark with pain, now, as they met hers. "Anne..." His arms came around her, and he crawled off Aaron to crush her to him. "Oh, God... Are you all right?"

"Yes. Yes, I'm fine," she sobbed. "But you—"

"I heard the shot. I thought he'd—"

"It wasn't me, it was—" She cut herself off, unable to tell him that Aaron had shot Rogue. If she thought about it, grief over the dog would finish her, and it might set Connor back on Aaron with renewed fury. And the only thing that mattered was getting Connor to the hospital before he bled to death in front of her eyes. "Con, we've got to—"

"You were in the water."

"Yes. It was the only place I could—"

"And you didn't panic."

"I couldn't. I had to—"

"And you're really all right? He didn't touch you or—"

"No, I'm fine, but, Con, you're bleeding, and—"

"I'm okay."

It was a ludicrous statement. He was weakening even as he knelt there, trying to hold her. She felt the quivering in his arms and the swaying of his body against hers.

"Let me go call—" she started to say, but again he interrupted her.

"The phone woke me up. Ben called to say... to say that... But I saw you were gone, and I...I...God...'" Suddenly he slumped back onto his heels, shaking his head, blinking, lifting a hand to rub his face.

"Con!" Anne's voice cracked as fear shivered through her. "I'm going to call an ambulance. Please, don't try to move or do anything. Just stay here and let me—"

"I'm all right. Just a little dizzy, and— Hey! Damn, he's— Anne, let go, I've got to—"

"No!" Anne held on to him, her gaze darting once to Aaron, who was crawling away, staggering to his feet as he headed toward the boathouse. Uncaring where he went or what he did, as long as it didn't have to do with her or Connor, she said, "He isn't going anywhere. But we have to get you to—"

"I've got to stop him." Unable to throw her off, which, in itself, alarmed her, Connor grabbed her shoulder, using her as a brace as he struggled to stand. He didn't make it. His knees buckled, and he sank back to the ground, groaning, his arm hugging his waist as he doubled over in pain.

He was fading fast, and Anne hurried to reassure him so he wouldn't try to move while she was gone. "Con, it's okay. He can't leave. I threw the keys to his boat overboard, and it's docked behind the *Spinner*, so he can't use that, either. And the *Lady Lyn* won't run. The police can worry about him when they get here. Now, I'm going to your mom's house to call—"

She broke off when Connor's head snapped up, his eyes wide with alarm as they met hers.

"Oh, God," he muttered. Then his head jerked toward the boathouse, and, suddenly, in a burst of energy that came from Lord knows where, he managed to push to his feet, holding his side as he stumbled toward the boathouse, shouting, "No! No, Aaron, wait!"

"Con, let him go!" Anne cried, tripping after him, pulling on his hand in an effort to stop him.

"No, you don't understand. If he tries to use the *Lady Lyn*, he'll—Aaron, don't! Don't start the yacht, it'll—"

A sudden, horrific roar swallowed the rest of his words. Anne cried out, appalled, her eyes wide at the sight of the boathouse shaking on its pilings. Tongues of orange flame licked through the cracks in the rough-walled structure, setting it ablaze, and, as the gasoline spread, fire raced across the water, roaring briefly, then, as quickly, dying. But while she stood there, immobilized by shock, Connor grabbed her arm, yanking her backward, yelling, "Run! Get out of here! When the propane goes, the place'll blow sky high!"

"But—"

"It's too late! He's gone! Now, run!"

But it was too late for them, too. She hadn't taken three steps when a second explosion rocked the air, shattering the boathouse into a million pieces and shooting it skyward on a sheet of flames. A searing blast of heat hit them, and Anne screamed, her arms flying to cover her face.

She never knew whether she fell or Connor threw her to the ground, but suddenly she was lying facedown, and he was lying full-length on top of her, his body pressing hers into the tough, bristly grass as his hands covered her head, protecting her from the sparks and burning shards of wood that rained down upon them. It seemed an eternity that she lay there, unable to move, too terrified even to scream. The heat was terrible, sucking the oxygen out of the air, making it impossible to breathe, and several times she was dimly aware that moments passed when she lost her grasp on consciousness. Once, Connor swore, his body jerking atop hers as he batted at something behind him.

Then, suddenly, as quickly as it had happened, it was over. Everything was utterly still and silent. Not a sound anywhere as the roar of the fire became nothing more than the hazy golden heat of daybreak.

Anne tried to move, but Connor's body was dead weight. She said his name in question, and, when he didn't answer, she said it again. Again, he didn't respond, and Anne panicked.

She called to him sharply, trying not to hurt him as she struggled to get up, though he made no sound to indicate he was even aware of her. He was a good sixty pounds heavier than she, and it seemed every pound of it was in his shoulders and chest, lying on her back. Finally she got a hand braced on the ground, then, panting, slid the rest of her body free. Connor rolled the other way, onto his back, his body limp, his eyes closed.

"Con!" Scrambling on her knees, Anne knelt by his side, her hands fluttering over his unconscious form. Blood everywhere, all over both of them. "Con! Answer me!" Sobbing, pressing white knuckles to her mouth, she cast her gaze around for help—over the quiet waters of the cove, the silent woods, the place fifty feet away where two pilings jutted out of the water, marking the spot where the boathouse... wasn't.

Gone. All of it. All the stuff of her nightmares, including the demon... vanished, as if it had never existed. And she was alive. Alive and unharmed. Because of the man lying so still and silent beside her.

"Oh, Lord, please..." Dripping wet and half-hysterical, Anne looked at Connor's pale, unresponsive face, knowing she had to go for help, fearing he'd die while she was gone. Fearing he was going to die, anyway, and it all would have been for nothing. Fearing she had won the battle but lost the war. Lost. Again. Still. This time, forever. And as she sat there, crying, covered only by Connor's shirt and his blood, faintly, in the distance, a siren wailed.

Chapter Seventeen

"*Here, now, Miss Marquel, don't you cry. You heard what the doctor said. Con's going to be all right. I know it sounds bad hearing they took out his spleen, but lots of people—plenty of football players—lose their spleens, and it doesn't stop 'em. You watch—in a week or so, he'll be good as new. And that dog of his, too. The federal agent who found him swore he was only winged, and he couldn't have been too bad or he wouldn't have been able to crawl to the road. So don't you cry anymore. And don't you worry over this other nasty business, either. The way I see it, your brother solved the problem himself, and . . . well, you know . . . maybe it's better this way. The things you told me last night aren't on any report, and I don't see any reason they ever have to be. Can't think of a soul who needs to know—including Con's mom, when she gets here. Far as I'm concerned, your brother went crazy on drugs, and that's the end of it. We're just going to let the past stay where it belongs—buried along with the dead—so the living can get on with their lives. . . .*"*

Sound advice, indeed.

Driving up the gravel road toward Sentinel, Anne recalled the words of comfort Ben Whitlow had offered in the hospital emergency room as she waited to see Connor. In retrospect, she was able to appreciate the policeman's wisdom as well as his kindness. Yes, it was time, not to forget or to hide the past but to let it go, and she'd spent a good part of the week doing precisely that.

A week. A week ago today. It could have been a decade for all the changes it had seen. It was as if she were seeing the world clearly for the first time. Never had she felt so entirely free. Never had she experienced such a strong sense of purpose. Nor could she have imagined what it would be like to know deep in her soul that her life was finally on the right track.

Her most fervent desire, was to help someone else whose life had been wrenched off course find *his* path to happiness, as well.

Glancing at the envelope on the seat beside her, Howard Stone's return address engraved in the upper left, Anne felt a ripple of excitement. Tomorrow was Monday. Tomorrow Connor was coming home, and, at last, she'd get to talk to him alone. With his roommate and an endless stream of visitors acting as constant chaperones, they hadn't had a minute of private conversation. But tomorrow... She could wait that long, couldn't she?

Humming tunelessly, Anne parked beside Connor's pickup at Sentinel and hopped out, slipping the all-important envelope into the pocket of her yellow sundress before gathering her purse and the two bags of groceries off the seat. It was close to seven. She'd have to hurry or she'd miss evening visiting hours.

The back door of the cottage was open, and as she juggled the grocery bags to reach for the screen door handle, she assumed Mrs. McLeod had stopped by with the day's mail. She wondered why Rogue hadn't limped into the kitchen to greet her, as he'd been doing since she brought him home. Then, as she dumped the grocery bags on the table, she saw the mail, scattered and open, on the counter beside the phone.

Puzzled, Anne frowned. Mrs. McLeod wouldn't open her son's mail... nor was it likely she'd wear her son's Docksiders. When Anne saw the shoes she'd taken to the hospital for Connor kicked under the bookshelf by the stairway, her frown evaporated, and she went running to find him.

His white shirt, draped over the cattails edging the bluff, acted like a signpost. He was on the beach, bare-chested, slacks rolled up above the ankles, idly skipping stones over the river's glassy surface.

Anne spotted him from the screened porch, where Rogue lay at the door, whining unhappily that Connor was where he couldn't go; with the wound in his hip still healing, he wasn't yet up to negotiating the sandy embankment to the beach. Anne paused to give the setter a quick pat; then, as she skipped down the porch steps, he issued a soulful bark at being abandoned.

The announcement made Connor turn, and when he saw her, his face split into a grin. He moved to wait for her at the foot of the bluff, and she kicked off her sandals and ran lightly down to him, saying, "I thought I was picking you up tomor—" And that was as far as she got before he caught her and pulled her into his arms.

Suddenly, then, tomorrow became today. It might have been a year ago, or forever, since they'd last met for all the unleashed longing in their intimate greeting. Kisses followed one after the other, tender and warm, laced with lingering touches and long, heated glances.

"God, Annie, it's been so long."

"Oh, I know.... But when did you get here?"

"About twenty minutes ago. Nancy brought me. The doctor came in while she was there and said I could go."

"What did he say? Shouldn't you be rest—"

"He said eat, sleep, make love three times a day, and I'd live to be a hundred and ten."

"Con, please, don't tease—"

"I'm not teasing you, Sunshine. He said I can do anything I want. To use my own judgment. Now, for God's sake, hug me."

"I don't want to hurt—"

"You won't. Just hold me.... God, yes, hold me.... It's been so long...."

She complied willingly, unable to argue that he looked anything but healthy and strong. With the red-orange rays of the evening sun bronzing his skin and deepening his eyes to a shade close to midnight, she found no sign of pain or discomfort in him. Indeed, the only visible reminder of his ordeal was the four-inch square bandage on the lower left side of his chest. She'd seen the incision yesterday and knew it was healed. Still, she was careful as she slid her arms around him and snuggled her body close to his.

"Mmm, that's better," he murmured, pulling her even closer, his hands confident and possessive as they roamed over her.

Her lips brushed his neck, planting kisses between whispered phrases. "I'm so glad you're here...so glad I don't have to leave again . . . when visiting hours are over."

"God, yes. I've been going crazy lying there, wishing I was with you, needing to hold you . . . needing just to talk to you." Pulling away a little, Connor held her face in his hands as his eyes skimmed her features. "I've got to know. You've looked so happy and full of energy all week. Was it real, or an act to keep me from worrying?"

She turned her lips into his palm. "Yes, it's real. Do you honestly believe I could have fooled you?"

"I didn't think so, but . . ." A frown touched his brow. "Anne, you know damned well I'm not sorry Aaron's dead, but that was a godawful thing to witness. You've been alone here, every night, and—" He broke off, his eyes searching hers. "You're really all right? No bad moments?"

Anne's expression softened. "Not one. You're right, it was horrible. And I don't guess I'd be human if I didn't feel . . . *something*. Regret, I suppose, for a wasted life. But for me, it's...well, it's almost like a miracle." She shook her head. "I can't explain what it's like to realize I'm not looking over my shoulder anymore. But I can't feel sorry about it."

"I don't know anybody who'd expect you to," Connor growled.

She lifted a hand to brush the hair away from his eyes. "Con, it's over. Let's not talk about it anymore."

"No," he agreed. "Let's not. Let's talk about other things.... God, Annie—" he sucked in a quick breath "—let's not talk at all." And his head dipped, his mouth covering hers for another deep, increasingly passionate joining.

Caressing her through the thin fabric of her dress, Connor muttered, "You feel so good . . . so good...."

Pressed full-length against him, she knew exactly how good she felt to him, and his arousal fueled her own. As his hand found her breast, she dearly hoped the doctor's orders to "use his own judgment" allowed for intimate activities, because her will to say no was nonexistent. Indeed, having lain in his bed every night that week fantasizing about making love with him, she was embarrassingly ready to pick up where they'd left off in the predawn hours of last Sunday morning.

Connor began toying with the buttons down the front of her dress, and she wondered if he even intended to wait long enough to walk to the cottage. Then his hands glided down her thighs, bunching cloth and the envelope in her pocket along with it, and she felt him smile against her throat.

"Since when do you crinkle?"

"I don't. That's your welcome-home present."

"Mmm, can't be. The welcome home I want doesn't crinkle. It sounds wet and soft and—"

"Oh, Lord...Con, are you sure you ought to be doing this? Because if you—"

"It'll be all right, love, if you do most of the work."

"Okay, but..."

"But what?"

"Well...do you think you could wait a minute or so?" Anne gave him a hesitant smile, letting go of his shoulder to dip into her pocket for the envelope. Showing it to him, she said, "I've been practically bursting all week, wanting to tell you what I've been doing." She was also a little nervous about the things the envelope contained—after all, they would change his life forever—and she didn't want her nerves in the way of their lovemaking.

Connor's mouth sloped into a grin. "Yeah, I noticed a couple of times you were biting your tongue awfully hard. And we can't have that, can we?" Taking her hand, he tugged her away from the bluff. "So, come on. Walk with me while we talk."

The tide was at a low ebb, and he strolled at the water's edge, letting it wash over his feet. Anne ambled along on his right, enjoying the damp coolness of the sand squishing between her toes. Overhead, the gulls were searching out their dinner, circling and diving through the twilight sky.

"Okay." Connor tossed her a smile. "What's in your mysterious envelope?"

"I told you—welcome-home presents." Sorting through the items, Anne pulled out one and handed it to him.

He took it, looked at it, then came to a dead stop. "What the devil is this?"

"Your severance check."

His astonished gaze flashed to hers. "You're joking."

She beamed at him.

"You're *not* joking." Glancing once more at the check, he uttered a laugh. "I'll be damned. I was planning to quit, anyway, the first of the year. But I didn't expect to get fired first. What's the story?''

Anne began walking again as she spoke. ''As of today, I don't own Yesterday's Dream anymore.''

''You don't . . . *what?*'' Striding after her, Connor guessed, ''You sold it?''

''No, I gave it to the nuns who run St. Catherine's—my old boarding school. They're going to use it for a retreat.''

Again he came to a halt, his face a study in baffled disbelief. ''But I thought—'' He stopped short as understanding flooded his features. ''No, of course you're never going to want to live here, are you?''

The question didn't require an answer. Anne lifted one shoulder in a shrug. ''The only reason I didn't want to sell it before was because I didn't want the property developed. This is the perfect solution. The Sisters are thrilled to get it, I'm thrilled to get rid of it, and it'll never be sold off in two-acre lots.''

Connor looked at her for another long moment, then, folding his check, he slid his hands deep into his pockets and began walking again. He kept his eyes on the sand, and Anne trailed beside him, her sidelong glances taking in the frown creasing his brow.

''What about Mom?'' he asked, his too-casual tone a dead giveaway to his thoughts.

''Oh, she knows,'' Anne replied. ''I haven't told her *why* I wouldn't live here if it were the last place on earth, but—''

''No, there's no point in it,'' Connor put in. ''She'd be as upset as I was, finding out why you really left home.''

''I agree. And she seems perfectly willing to accept the idea that I'm donating the estate to St. Catherine's out of the goodness of my philanthropic heart. In fact, she seems delighted.''

Connor snorted softly. ''She won't be any sorrier than you or I will be to leave Yesterday's Dream. But I have to say—'' he shook his head ''—as outrageous as the idea of giving it away is, I'm glad it's going to people who'll get some pleasure out of it. It's a beautiful place, Anne. It deserves to be enjoyed.''

His words mirrored her own thoughts exactly, and she smiled her agreement. Then, her smile broadening, she said, ''To answer your question, your mother is going to be fine. In fact, she's going to be better off than she's been for the past twenty-two years—without your having to support her.'' At Connor's curious—and somewhat skeptical—look, she explained,

"Howard Stone is setting up a pension for her from those magical investments that have been paying the bills around here. She won't have to worry about a thing. I told her I'd make it a condition of granting the estate that she could stay in the caretaker's house, but she doesn't want it. She says she wants to move to Easton to be close to her first grandchild. And she's talking about how much more time she'll have for her historical society work. But I got the impression there might be a gentleman in the picture, too."

Connor grinned. "Fred Maxwell, her bridge partner. Moved out here from Washington last year, after his wife died. He's got a place on the Wye River outside of Easton."

"Oh?" Anne arched an eyebrow. "Do you think her moving to Easton is a signal to Fred that she'd like the partnership to progress beyond the bridge table?"

"I wouldn't be surprised. But then . . . God, I don't think anything would surprise me anymore." Connor heaved an exaggerated sigh. "Mom's moving to Easton, I'm out of a job—*and* a house—and you just gave away half a billion dollars in real estate to the nuns. I don't know, Sunshine. This new impulsive streak of yours has me a little worried."

Anne flicked an empty sand-crab shell with her toe. "I haven't done anything impulsive. I'm just . . . fixing a few things. Things that should have been fixed years ago."

"I see. Amazing how many things you've fixed in a week."

"Isn't it?"

"Mmm."

"And there's more."

"Oh, God. Maybe I'd better get my two cents in here, before you tell me you've decided to move to Alaska."

Connor reached to take her hand, and Anne looked to find him watching her with an intensity that belied the lightness of their banter.

"I don't have any immediate plans," she said slowly.

"Then how about making some. With me."

Pulling her to a stop, Connor swung around in front of her. His gaze never left hers as he produced an item from one of his pockets that made Anne's heart skip a beat, then begin to pound. She watched, her lip caught between her teeth, as he slipped the diamond onto the proper finger of her left hand, the round-cut solitaire sparkling like a kaleidoscope through the rush of tears that blurred her vision.

Here it was. The dream as she'd always imagined it. And it was happening exactly as she'd wished it would all those years ago when she'd believed in fairy-tale endings. She'd grown up, Connor had fallen in love with her, and they were going to live happily ever after. Oh, yes, of that she hadn't a single doubt.

Filled with the sense that she was living out some preordained plan, Anne raised her eyes to Connor's and saw in the depths of his blue gaze that he felt it, too. No great surprise that it should come to this. Only a sense of fulfillment. As if this moment were a gathering of all their yesterdays and their tomorrows, melded into something new, something bright and filled with promise. Something that was entirely *theirs*. A warm and vibrant flame brought to life from the embers of a love that would sustain and nurture them into eternity.

His eyes locked with hers, Connor lifted her hand to his lips and kissed it, his other hand trembling as he touched her face. His voice was a sonorous rumble in the lavender quiet of twilight. "Annie, love, will you marry me?"

He couldn't have had any doubts about her answer, and it was just as well, for no sound came as her lips formed the words "Oh, Con . . . yes . . ."

She heard him say, "God, I love you." Then she was in his arms and he was kissing her, telling her again and again how much he loved her. And the tears were spilling down her cheeks, and she couldn't stop them, couldn't seem to cope any other way with the joy that filled her.

And somewhere in the midst of all the kisses and tears, Connor said, "I can't count how many times I almost asked you to marry me last Saturday night. After we made love, all night long, it was all I could do not to say it. But with things in such turmoil . . . well, I didn't want either of us to remember it that way."

"No," she said. "I'm glad you waited."

Holding her away a little, he smiled, his thumb brushing her lips. "Besides, I didn't want to ask you without the ring."

"Oh, and it's so beautiful. But when did you—" Anne stopped, her look slightly horrified. "Con, you *didn't* sneak out of the hospital—"

He laughed. "No, there was no sneaking about it. This ring belonged to my father's mother, and it's been mine since I was ten, when she died. Mom's kept it for me. I had Nancy stop at the house on the way in, so I could get it."

Anne looked at her hand, resting on Connor's bare chest, and at the diamond glittering in the waning light. Then, raising her eyes to his, she spoke hesitantly. "So, your mother knows?"

He gave her a tender smile. "I think she knew the minute you showed up here, Wednesday a week ago. Smart woman, my mother."

Yes, Mary McLeod was a smart woman, and a warm, generous one, and the thought of becoming part of the McLeods' loving family circle made Anne's eyes brim with tears once more.

"Oh, Lord, Con, I'm sorry, but I think I'm going to cry again."

"Go ahead," he said, chuckling as he wrapped her close. "Mom cried, and so did Nancy. You might as well, too."

Squeezing her eyes closed, she buried her face against his neck. "I don't know if I can stand being this happy."

"Get used to it. I'm planning to."

"I love you so much."

"I love you, too, Sunshine." Pausing briefly, he continued, an odd note of tension in his voice. "I don't know how we're going to work this out, and we don't have to decide anything yet, but I guess I need to know if you're willing to look for a teaching job down here."

Anne sniffled a little, her eyes blinking open.

"I hate asking you," he added, "but McLeod Tree Service just isn't portable. It would take years to establish the business in a new place."

She started to speak, but Connor went on almost doggedly. "I know you don't like my doing tree work, and, mostly, these days, I only estimate jobs and consult, meaning I walk around people's yards and hand out advice. But I can't promise I won't ever work with the crew. Sometimes I don't have a choice."

"What if you did?"

"Anne, I—"

"What if you could give up chopping trees forever?"

"Believe me, I'd love to, but I can't, and I—"

"You could if you started Bay Press."

Silence fell like a stone and lay, heavy and still, between them. A line of squawking Canada geese passed overhead, gradually disappearing in the darkening purple sky to the east.

Anne leaned back in the circle of Connor's arms, reaching slowly for the envelope in her pocket to withdraw another item.

Holding it out to him, she raised her gaze to his. Then she waited, absolutely certain that she knew what his response was going to be....

For a long moment Connor remained oblivious to the paper in Anne's hand. He stared at her, speechless, couldn't have formed a coherent word if his life had depended upon it. The irony of which was that he'd been sure, by now, he had to be shock-proof. Then he looked at the check she was holding, and as the figures typed boldly across the pale gray bank draft sank in, he found out exactly how far from shock-proof he was.

"Holy Mother of..." He took a step back, his arms falling away from Anne's waist, his eyes darting to her face, then back to the check, as he tried frantically to figure out how she could know. Nobody knew. Nobody but him and the two dozen foundations who'd turned down his requests for funding. God, he'd never even said the words *Bay Press* aloud, and hearing her say them, he felt as if she'd somehow read not only his mind but his soul.

This time, though, he wished she hadn't.

Finally, Anne answered his unspoken question. "Your proposal was on the kitchen table the night I slept in your hammock. I'm afraid it was rather impossible to resist." Her lips were curved in an expectant smile, her voice filled with thinly veiled excitement. "Oh, Con, it's such a wonderful idea. I can just imagine how proud your mother is going to be. And how proud your father would be, if he knew."

After a year's worth of cold, impersonal rejections, her warm and very personal approval caught him totally off guard. Suddenly, Connor's throat burned and his chest felt tight, and he had to look away.

Staring across the river, he wondered if it were true. Would his father be proud? Would it please him to know that his son had spent most of his adult life preparing himself and devising a plan to start a publishing firm committed to the very laws that had brought the prosperous and venerable McLeod Press to its ignoble end? A nonprofit company whose sole purpose was to publish books on conservation. Books about water, forests, and toxic wastes, not award-winning literary fiction. Books to raise the consciousness and educate, not to entertain or thrill the intellect. Books that were, in fact, tools for people engaged in solving the world's environmental problems. Books produced under strict guidelines, using only ecologically sound printing methods.

Would his father have been proud? It was a question Connor had asked himself many times, knowing there could be no answer. Ultimately, though, the answer hadn't mattered. Bay Press had been *his* dream, no one else's. And it had served his purpose. It had been a means out of anger and bitterness. For the past ten years, it had been the thing that had kept him sane—something to look forward to that made the day-to-day drudgery and sacrifices of the present tolerable.

Against all hope, though, the present had become far more than tolerable, and he didn't need Bay Press or any other grand scheme anymore. He'd made the decision to give it up without regret... but he'd never expected to face *this*.

Drawing a ragged breath, Connor shifted his gaze to Anne. The slight frown flickering across her brow spoke of confusion—yes, why wasn't he shouting for joy?—and he wracked his brain for a plausible excuse.

"I don't know what shocks me more," he muttered. "That you know about Bay Press, or the size of this check. God, Anne, what did you do? Rob the manor of every piece of art in it?"

"No," she replied. "Unfortunately, almost everything will get auctioned to pay for the repairs, since the insurance won't cover damages caused by arson. That money came from my father's rare-edition collection."

Connor closed his eyes, feeling the horror wash over him. "You sold his books?"

Looking up to find her nodding and smiling, it appalled him further to realize she was genuinely pleased with herself.

"Yes," she said. "I thought they'd be worthless because of the soot, but I met with a restorer, and he said they could be cleaned. So I called a bibliophile friend of my father's, and he was so thrilled to have them—and so worried I might change my mind—that he wired me the money the same day. He bought the whole collection."

Connor drew a steadying breath. What the hell was he going to say? What the hell would any man say if the woman he loved handed him the world on a silver platter—and he couldn't take it? Couldn't take it because he didn't see any way he could have it and her, too, and he wasn't about to give *her* up. Not for anything that existed—or could exist—between heaven and hell.

Her next words only added to his torment.

"I had wonderful time taking all those books to be cleaned and shipped off," she said. She was looking at her ring, toying with it as she spoke, but she paused to give him a smiling glance from beneath her lowered lashes. "It was even more fun than giving away Yesterday's Dream. I kept thinking about Bay Press being funded by Poe and Sir Arthur Conan Doyle and Shakespeare and . . . well, the idea just makes me very happy."

And he was going to make her unhappy. Lowering his gaze to the check in her hand, Connor murmured, "It's a nice thought . . . a very nice thought."

"Those foundation people are fools," Anne continued softly. "Either that or they're so inundated with restrictions and worries about the bottom line that they can't recognize genius when it hits them over the head."

"I think 'genius' is carrying it a little far."

"I don't."

Connor felt an unfamiliar heat climbing his neck. "I can't say I mind your being biased," he grumbled. "But the people who wrote those rejection letters aren't in love with me. You can't blame them too much for being skeptical about handing money to a man who hasn't got a credential to his name that says he can do anything more than take down trees."

Moving closer, Anne ran a hand up his arm, letting it rest lightly on his shoulders. "I still think they're fools. It's perfectly obvious that the idea of Bay Press is a stroke of visionary genius. And I don't see how anybody could read that proposal and not realize you're fiscally reliable and that you have everything it's going to take to make Bay Press happen—college degrees be damned."

Connor glanced up quickly, startled at hearing Anne swear.

She grinned. "I, on the other hand, don't have a single doubt. I also don't have a fussy board of directors telling me what I can do with my money. All things considered, Bay Press seems to me like a splendid way to invest in the future—on both a global and a very personal scale."

God, he'd be crying in a minute if she kept this up.

Swallowing hard, Connor kept his eyes glued to the check. "Anne, I— I don't know how to say . . ." Trailing off, he raked a hand through his hair. "That proposal was on its way to the trash, and I'm sorry as hell it didn't get there before you found it. It kills me to think you sold those books for nothing, but that's the way it is. Because I'm not going to do it." And turning away, he paced a couple of yards up the beach before stopping to fix his gaze on the sun-dyed orange sail of a boat moving slowly across the point under a drowsy breeze.

Behind him, Anne spoke in shocked tones. "What do you mean, you're.... Con, *why?*"

"Time and money," he said flatly.

"But you don't need those foundation grants anymore. This check is for three times—"

"I know what it's for." Squeezing his eyes closed for an instant, he shuddered, then whirled to face her. "Anne, listen to me—visionary or not, Bay Press is one huge gamble. It would mean years of work without any guarantees it would ever pay off. Even assuming I've judged the market correctly and that, eventually, the company would be able to help support itself, it would be a long time before I'd be drawing anything but a token salary. And it could just as easily go down the tubes. Then I'd be left with nothing—including no business to fall back on, if I do what you're suggesting."

Starting toward him, Anne began, "Con, I know it's a risk, but I—"

"But I don't *want* you taking risks for my sake!" His hand sliced the air in an emphatic gesture, and she came to a stop several feet away, her eyes wide.

Swearing under his breath, he went on in a more controlled tone. "I've spent years saving to do this, and if it were just me I had to worry about, I could handle a financial disaster. But when I think about you..." His eyes raked over her, his head moving slowly back and forth. "God, Annie, all I want to do is keep you safe and... and take care of you."

Her look softened, her breath rushing out in a quiet sigh. "Oh, Con..." Then, holding his gaze, she tucked the check into her pocket and slowly closed the gap between them.

He stiffened at her approach, his heart pounding against his ribs as she placed a hand on his chest and gave him a small, apologetic smile.

"I guess I forgot I was fighting twenty-two years of worry," she said. "I'm sorry for that—for just assuming you'd be overjoyed. But I think you're forgetting something. I've been on my own, managing my life, since I was sixteen, and, darling, honestly, I don't *need* you to take care of me. Not in the way you mean. Now, in other ways..." Lowering her gaze, she watched her hand slide across his chest as she whispered, "In other ways, I think you know I need you quite a lot."

When she looked at him once more, Connor saw the love and hope and promise shining in her clear green eyes. He shook his head. "Anne, I love you more than anything on earth, and it would be easy—too damned easy—to convince myself we could live on love. But I'm not going to start a marriage with you with every other aspect of my life in chaos." He snorted softly. "God, I don't even know where I'm going to be living next month. And you want me to give up a business that's making a healthy profit to start one that will always be dependent on grant money to stay afloat? It'd be just plain crazy."

She sighed, giving him another of those sad little smiles. "I never should have hit you with all of this at once. I know how hard it must be for you to think about things being uncertain when your main goal for years has been to see to it that your family is secure. But, Con, it's going to be all right. I know it is. And besides . . ." Pausing, moving away a couple of steps, she added hesitantly, "We do have a place to live."

His eyebrows came together in a wary frown. "You mean the third-floor disaster you told me about—the one with the leaky storm windows?"

Keeping her gaze averted, she gave him a sketchy nod. "The house isn't a *disaster*. It's just old and run-down—three stories and an attic of Victorian gingerbread, complete with turrets . . . and a roof that's just a little bit leaky, too. But . . . well—" she grimaced "—it's mine."

"Yours?" Connor's frown deepened. "You *own* this nightmare?"

"Uh-huh." With a flustered gesture, Anne hurried to explain. "I'm sure you'll groan when you see it, but it was what I could afford, and, really, it's going to be beautiful when I finish fixing it up and—"

"When *you* finish? *You're* doing the work?"

She nodded. "Room by room." Then, drawing a shallow breath, she rushed on. "I've been renting the bottom two floors to college students. But it occurred to me that we could live on the second and third floor, and you could use the first-floor apartment as office space—at least for a while."

Ending on a breathless note, she looked at him, and Connor knew she was waiting for a response. Scowling, he wondered how long he thought he could hold out against the beguiling, almost childlike expectancy in her eyes. The alarming thing was, he was beginning to wonder why he was even trying.

Clinging desperately to the fraying rope of anxiety that had bound him for so many years, unprepared to let go, uncertain that he even should—or could—he spoke more roughly than he'd intended. "And how do you expect us to eat?"

Anne's chin lifted. "Well, I do have a job. I don't make a lot, but we wouldn't starve."

"It sounds as if you're planning to take care of me."

"I'd hardly say that, when you're probably going to be working even harder than you do now. But even if it came to that—" her shoulders rose and fell "—why shouldn't I take care of you? You've certainly earned it. And unless your ego really can't take—"

"Forget my ego. I'm just plain scared." Connor's scowl remained in place, but as his eyes drifted downward over Anne's slender body, his mind conjuring memories of her lying beneath him, holding him to her, whispering her love as he filled her body with his own, a soft catch crept into his voice. "What if you're pregnant?"

Her gaze slid from his, focusing on her toe tracing patterns in the sand. "I'm not."

"You're certain?"

"Yes." The word was barely audible, and her cheeks had turned a lovely shade of pink.

"Hmm . . . that's too bad."

Her startled gaze flashed to his.

"I dreamed you had twins," he murmured. "Other parts of the dream were a little hassled, but that part was . . . very nice."

"Oh, Con . . ." Stepping toward him, Anne lifted a hand to touch his cheek. "I want children, too. But right now it's more important to me that you're happy."

His hand covered hers. "If you think I wouldn't be happy raising a family with you, you're wrong."

Slowly she said, "Are you sure you wouldn't be happier if you had a chance to do something for yourself for once, without the responsibilities of parenthood hanging over you?" Then, leaning forward, she placed a brief, soft kiss on his lips. "Oh, Con, we're going to have beautiful babies . . . but we can wait, can't we?"

Wait? How long? He'd been waiting years already, and he didn't want to wait any longer. But then . . . why should he? Why should *either* of them wait for *anything?*

Try as he might, the truth was he couldn't think of one good reason.

Connor felt the last tenacious thread of the rope of anxiety snap. His heart skipped, his breath hitched, and all at once he was free-falling through time, with the great expanse of the future stretching before him, waiting for him to fill it. Possibilities. Life was full of them. And it seemed that, for the first time in twenty-two years, he was being given the chance to pick and choose to his heart's content.

A smile twitched at the corners of his mouth, and, slowly, his hands trailing from Anne's shoulders to her wrists and up again, he said, "What if I don't want to wait? What if I told you I'm sick and tired of waiting? What if I want it all—everything at once?"

"Well," she began softly, "I guess you'd have to have it, then. And if I get pregnant and have to stop working...we can live on this—for quite a while, I'd say."

Reaching into her pocket, she took what he saw was the last item out of Howard Stone's business envelope. Not a check this time, but a savings account passbook. There was just enough light left in the sky to read the single entry on the page she showed him.

Connor's eyes grew wide as he read the figure. "You haven't saved all that on a schoolteacher's salary."

"No," Anne replied. "My mother saved it."

"You found the other stashes."

"Most of them, I think. Your mom helped me." Her cheeks coloring, she smiled. "I don't see any reason why my mother's 'rainy day' money can't be our...'happy event' fund."

It was going to take him some time, Connor supposed, but he was ready and willing to begin getting used to the idea that he wasn't alone anymore, that he had a partner, a friend, a mate, whose judgment he trusted and who was as capable as he was of handling the practical details of life—and a good deal more. He didn't even doubt that this house-from-hell she owned would turn out to be pure gold. Anne was too careful to have bought it otherwise. He'd probably love it. In fact, he was certain he was going to love everything about his life—most of all the woman with whom he was sharing it.

God, he loved her. And it was going to be heaven being married to her. He'd never get tired of her shy blushes—or her rapidly blooming passion.

Plucking the bank book from Anne's fingers, Connor dropped it into her dress pocket, then splayed his hands over her hips to tug her close. Blinking lazily, loving the way she snuggled into him, he allowed a slow smile to spread across his face. "Just tell me one thing. Does this monstrosity of yours have a yard big enough for a large, slightly hyperactive dog?"

Anne's lips curved upward. "It's huge. And it's got lots of big old trees."

"Trees, huh?"

"Nice *live* trees that don't need any pruning or cabling."

"Got one that might handle a tree house?"

"Mmm ... I think so." She held his gaze, her eyes and her heart brimming. "You're going ahead with Bay Press?"

Connor laughed. "If I didn't, I don't know which one of us would be more disappointed. And God help me if it doesn't work."

With a happy cry, Anne threw her arms around his neck. "Oh, Con, it's going to work! It's going to be wonderful!"

He crushed her to him, hugging the breath out of both of them, his body shaking with the craziest mixture of passion and excitement and, yes, plain old-fashioned nerves. "You're sure of that, huh?"

"Absolutely."

"Interesting, since you don't know beans about publishing."

"I don't have to," she whispered. "I know you."

Threading his fingers through her hair, he angled his head and covered her mouth with his, kissing her long and well, until she was breathless and clinging. Then, lifting his head an inch or so, far enough to let his gaze sink into hers, he said, "Yes, you know me. And I want you to know me again. Here. Now. Always. Love me, Anne..."

"Oh, Con..." she sighed.

And as the sun's last rays glazed the river gold, she did.

* * * * *

This is the season of giving, and Silhouette proudly offers you its sixth annual Christmas collection.

SILHOUETTE

Christmas Stories

1991

Experience the joys of a holiday romance and treasure these heartwarming stories by four award-winning Silhouette authors:

Phyllis Halldorson—"A Memorable Noel"
Peggy Webb—"I Heard the Rabbits Singing"
Naomi Horton—"Dreaming of Angels"
Heather Graham Pozzessere—"The Christmas Bride"

Discover this yuletide celebration—sit back and enjoy Silhouette's Christmas gift of love.

Silhouette Special Edition®

is pleased to announce

WEDDING DUET
by Patricia McLinn

Wedding fever! There are times when marriage must be catching. One couple decides to tie the knot, and suddenly everyone they know seems headed down the aisle. Patricia McLinn's WEDDING DUET lets you share the excitement of such a time.

December: PRELUDE TO A WEDDING (SE #712) Bette Wharton knew what she wanted—marriage, a home... and Paul Monroe. But was there any chance that a fun-loving free spirit like Paul would share her dreams of meeting at the altar?

January: WEDDING PARTY (SE #718) Paul and Bette's wedding was a terrific chance to renew old friendships. But walking down the aisle had bridesmaid Tris Donlin and best man Michael Dickinson rethinking what friendship really meant....

NORA ROBERTS

Love has a language all its own, and for centuries, flowers have symbolized love's finest expression. Discover the language of flowers—and love—in this romantic collection of 48 favorite books by bestselling author Nora Roberts.

Starting in February 1992, two titles will be available each month at your favorite retail outlet.

In February, look for:

Irish Thoroughbred, Volume #1
The Law Is A Lady, Volume #2

Collect all 48 titles and become fluent in the Language of Love.

LOL 192

THE LANGUAGE of LOVE